The Forever Young Prisoner

Marcus Lessard

Putnam Heights
PUBLISHING

CONTENTS

ADVANCE PRAISE

"The Forever Young Prisoner" is a superbly atypical debut that boasts ample literary strengths. With its sharp social observation and incisive dialogue, the book occasionally brings readers to a gasp-worthy surprise, inevitably leading them to stop and catch their breath before proceeding to the next phase. Intense and affecting hooks, and vividly drawn world-building rove towards a climactic level, while reflections about the meaning of life, human relationships, and amplitude intrigues make for an engrossing and assured read.

— READER VIEWS

Lessard blends otherworldly with human drama in his electric debut.

— THE PRAIRIES BOOK REVIEW

A story filled with mystery, magic, and secrets, The Forever Young Prisoner proves to be a most entertaining read ...singular and fascinating.

— INDEPENDENT BOOK REVIEW

PROLOGUE

"The following is a true story. Names have not been changed to protect the innocent, because the innocent are not always protected under the rule of law." Henry wanted me to start things off by noting that.

PART ONE
THE LOW SIDE

CHAPTER ONE

Prison. There's kinda more to say about it than just what you see on TV.

Speaking for myself, sure, there were cells back then, fights, lockdowns, and one's fair share of homies and hellies until, more than anything, we wanted to return to our real cribs. Even if that meant a cardboard box. Absolutely, orange jumpsuits, chains, and fences with sharp nasties sticking out of them restrained us. The barbed-wire fence, and the deer on the opposite side of it who stood eyeing yours truly instead of the inmate offering her an apple, attracted my gaze as I swaggered through the yard of my yesteryear prison home, in my orange threads, on my way to the chow hall to meet my destiny.

Two campuses standing side by side comprised Providence State Penitentiary. Normies and their TVs tended to equate them, when in fact they classed quite differently.

Nicknamed *Dracula's Castle,* the high side was an old, stone, fortress-type deal fronted by rows of razor-wire and electric fence. Very ominous looking from the outside, and inside, even more so, where dark corridors, metal, and cement prevailed. This architectural monstrosity governed the skyline as I kept along the path that cut through the grassy yard to the far side of campus. The Administrative Building in the fore looked like a hut in comparison to its backdrop. In the spaces between stood the fence, but no longer the deer with the dark, staring eyes who had since jetted, apparently.

"Whassup?" I said to my homies, extending fist bumps.

On their way to Admin, too—not to eat, but to mop—the Ferguson Twins ambled alongside me. They swabbed the decks on this ship of fools. When not swabbing, the twins spent their livelong day at the weight pile.

"Just chillin', Tommy. Just walking. What's over there at Drac's Castle you be staring at? You see Henry or something?" Fergs snickered. I could never quite tell them apart. Fergs and Fergs.

"Henry?" I said.

But Fergs fell back to either tie his shoe or massage his calve and his bro remained with him, and so I lost them in the orange throng. Still only a week into my sentence, I had my fair share of buds. Of course, this was just the low side, and shyness didn't much appeal to me. So far, all sunshine and lollipops compared to those two months in city jail and a week at Classification.

Sunshine, sure, but no lollipops just then, only a chance for some pops in the jaw, potentially. A commotion sounded. Guys hollered, and out of the corner of my eye I saw a few of them scrambling. My every instinct said, "Courtyard rumble," as followup to the morning's melee between the Southbangers and Santos Malos. Oftentimes, gangland rumbles spread and then everyone got into it. The TV said so. Time to fight or die, I told myself, as my street instincts kicked in and pulse surged.

Nobody bustin' it up, though, I noticed, finally, only a deer that had sprung the fence. Although the barbed wire layered fairly high up—they called it, in fact, "the deer fence"—this deer just didn't seem to care, and knew, too, how to use her legs. Maybe she had decided she liked apples after all.

The deer bucked, kicked, zigged, and zagged, offset by her

strange new environment, possibly, or to try to work up some clearance. Guys cleared away from her, all right. This spotted brown doe featured no antlers; still, no one wants to get rammed or kicked by a large, charging animal. Finally, she stopped prancing and kicking once she spotted her target. Slowly, with her eyes all over me, she padded the grass in my direction. With her ears leveled, the hairs on her neck bristled, and a stiff heavy walk, she let the fools around her know to stay away. They did. She slowed as she neared the walking path where a pocket of us stood gazing in wonder at the yard's newest visitor

"She's looking right at you," the voice of Fergs said from somewhere in back of me.

She was, indeed, looking right at me. She halted about five yards in front of me. The fur on her neck lost its spike, and her ears perked back up, as she calmed. Moments passed as she and I shared eye contact, while the others divided glances between us. Her round black eyes no longer feared and flared. Still, those midnight eyes sent shivers up my spine. They appeared almost human for what looked like a twinkle of sadness in them. And urgency. And appeal.

I resisted the urge to bolt. Living in the inner city for the entirety of my twenty-four years meant few encounters with deer. However, my guess would be that deer's eyes usually didn't have that much to say. A deer with eyes reminiscent of a woman's meant two things: that I needed to stop doping once and for all and get a grip, and get outta there.

Then, just like that, she turned and bolted. With a magnificent running leap, she cleared the fence and disappeared into the thicket of trees just beyond it.

I exhaled, long and slow.

"Maybe you reminded her of her previous owner," Fergs offered, as he stepped level with me.

"Deer don't have owners," I spoke in the direction of the trees. With another long exhale, I turned. "Nah, it's because chicks dig my feral, fancy-free style. Especially ones with four legs and spiky hairs on the backs of their necks."

Disturbances aren't every day in prison, but almost. However, life usually returns to normal in no time. Moments later, after someone asked aloud whether I was the "Deermaster," the low side resumed its usual habit of milling, chatting and playing participants. "Is that like Bassmaster?" I asked as we continued our walk.

The low side consisted of five dorm-like buildings surrounding a grassy yard. Here, inmates could participate in fun and healthful activities like hoop, toss horseshoes, entertain the one-in-a-million deer willing and able to breach the fence, or work out at the weight pile. Much of it lay in my rearview at this point in my trek.

But, yeah, the TV did overlook certain points besides just the entire existence of low-side prison "camps." And one in particular that's all-important: not all prisoners wear the same color. In most prisons, special sectors are reserved for those extreme *red*-suited offenders who have been locked up for a hot minute. These sorry red sacks dwell all alone; oftentimes they are holed up for twenty-three hours a day and cut off from the general population.

At Providence State Penitentiary, our beloved P-Pen, they referred to this special red sector as *Supermax*. It lodged deep within the depths of Dracula's Castle. No homie wanted to end up in *that* land of isolation, despair, and endless masturbation.

Even less did they in The Pit of Heck. Named affectionately after its legendary and lone occupant, this nightmarish realm could get a fool to lose his shit entirely. No fancy-colored threads down in The Pit. No colors, period. Darkness prevailed, along with roaches, rats, spiders, dust bunnies, and other Center of the Earth-type crap. The Legend of Henry Heck, The Forever Young Prisoner, sounded in bells and whistles, but its inception was with lonely groans and sighs in this dark, subterranean lair often referred to as simply The Pit.

CHAPTER TWO

I neither saw, nor sensed, any warm glow or rays from heaven as I flattened my palm against the Admin Building door on that fateful day in April 2022. Still, that was the day I first got schooled on P-Pen's local legend and experienced a kind of rebirth, to the echoing cheers of both the living and the dead.

Strange, how we recall those moments which at the time seemed so insignificant. It was a Tuesday. For chow that Tuesday, just like every Tuesday, my fellow inmates and I flattered our pallets with something called *rice and beans*—the rice was overcooked, the beans under—and pudding that looked like hair gel and tasted like dirt-flavored slime. In response to the morning's two-on-two rumble over in Building 5, the correctional officers—we just called them cops or C.O.'s—had called for a compound-wide lockdown, then a shakedown.

As a newcomer to things like lockdowns, shakedowns, and gang members tangling in tandem, my smile faded and I gulped as I strode down the long corridor leading to the chow hall. In the movies, all the big skirmishes usually went down here, and with the animals in this pen already stirred, I figured that might mean trouble. Then, I reminded myself this was the low side where fights were common but no one ever got stabbed, and if someone *was* gonna shank me they would need a damned good reason to do it. I regained my swag and crooked a grin as if to assure myself all was well.

I grinned at the gray cement walls of the long corridor and a gray-haired inmate along the way. I even grinned at the hatchet-faced guard on the other side of the chow-hall door whose steely gaze sought to inform me smiley faces were not allowed in these parts, or at least not on a new fish like myself. The pin on his uniform read "Officer Greeley." I snagged my tray from the hair-netted worker then weaved through a maze of tattooed faces, bad oral hygiene, and red, flaky psoriasis, to the northside of the chow hall. I halted in front of the table where my forever best bud and de-facto prison tour-guide, Danny Onofrio, sat waiting for me.

"Good times, good times." I sat down and let my sights wander. "Where's all the ladies at, though?"

Allow me to describe what I saw as I bit my fingernails and continued checking shit out.

Think high-school cafeteria, only more sterile; and by *sterile* I mean lacking any character whatsoever. No "Rah Rah Go Team" banners or "Under the Sea Dance" prom posters were displayed on the walls of this dump. Not that I experienced much of high school, but I'm just saying.

Standard gray linoleum floor. Standard paneled ceiling lights. Round tables like at a school, only metal. Five or six inmates to a table. A ragtag cast of characters sitting, milling, laughing, snarling. Two or three C.O.'s shootin' the shit like they were regular cowboys with their backs and taser guns leaned against the cement walls. A square opening in one of those walls allowed a kitchen worker to hand over your meal tray, and another square accepted it after you'd had your fill of frankenfood. The place sized bigger than Tony's Bar in Federal Hill but smaller than Al's Liquor Warehouse in Warwick. Of course, the low side only boasted 647 inmates, and its five buildings ate in shifts. Tattoos everywhere.

Orange everywhere. Goatees here and there. Not a window in the place.

Quiet, too.

Our table was quiet, the place doubled as downtown with its milling pedestrians and overlapping layers of chatter.

I could tell something was going on. As if spellbound, Danny silently stared off into the distance. Danny rarely mused or daydreamed like I tended to do, nor were there any ladies in the immediate vicinity, never mind doped-out ones—which, as a doper groupie himself, was the only thing that could spellbind Danny. That, and the dope itself of course. Following Danny's gaze to the far end of the chow hall, but seeing only the guard, Greeley, and a sea of inmates over that way, I settled into my chair, positioned my tray, then sprinkled some salt on my flavorless but free meal.

In between failed chomps of the under-cooked beans, I updated Danny on my latest foray into the world of short-story fiction. It was a light, Sunday afternoon reading affair I had tentatively titled "Attack of the Killer Zombie Rats from Hell."

Still the catatonic nonresponse from Danny. His eyes projected as stolid and impervious as his slicked-back dark hair.

I tried to divert Danny's attention by continuing our conversation begun back at the cell where I had wagered three Ramen noodles and a Cheez Whiz I'd get released on my first chance at parole. A three-year sentence hardly made me public enemy #1, I'd told him. Also, there was my alleged crime.

Guzzling some lemonade, I laid it all out for him. "The Place," I said. "Big Ben's Bar and Grille, over in Elmwood. You know the Place." Danny's spacey glare suggested he knew zip, but he knew the Place. I wiped my mouth. "The Crime: Okay, so, sure, I'd knocked that guy's front teeth into his brains after he'd told me to 'sit my punk ass down or he'd sit it down for me' because my head was blocking the Bruins game. But it was *Two-for-One Night* that put that fool in the hospital, not me. It's *Two-for-One Night* that keeps sendin' me into these uncontrollable fits of rage that make me wanna bash random fools' heads in then deliver them, bloodied and screaming, to the Killer Zombie Rats and their un-dead rodent brethren from hell."

I unfurled my fist. "Look, Danny, the parole board will know I was the victim—of the alcohol, and, well, the meth, and the... anyway, they'll parole me in exchange for counseling. That's their hustle. That's what they do." I shook my head in disbelief. "On-and-off dope buys for five whole years and they get me for a bar fight. Go figure." I continued to blather on, even as Danny kept his cow stare in the direction of wherever.

Finally it dawned on me Danny hadn't heard a single word I had said.

No one ever listened to Tommy McConnell. Not Fatts, Trixie, Danny, not even that pug mix named Fart Face whom I had shared that tore-up trailer with on the south side back in the summer of '19. Sure, deer along fences looked my way, and then bolted into the woods once we got too close, just like all of the other females in my so-called life. I plunged my spork into my beans.

Danny seized my arm. "Homie, see way over there?" Danny pointed to where his sights had been deadlocked. "Dirty blond hair. In his early twenties...from the looks of it." Leaning in, he whispered "And he's got the mark." Danny swallowed. "It's him. It's gotta be."

Danny's mention of *dirty blond hair* triggered a reminder that my light brownies, with their dry ends from one-too-many washings with Bob Barker prison soap, stood in desperate need of a trim. Unfortunately, haircuts cost money in prison: two stamps.

Danny's meal tray lay unchallenged as he resumed his stare. I grew curious.

"Say what?" I said, mimicking the phrase my foster dad used to use whenever I told him I had skipped school again.

"The question is not just what, but who," Danny replied.

I knitted my brows. "Who? What? Where?"

Danny squinted to focus. "A freak of nature. A mystery. A goddamn legend of our time. His own prolly, too."

Flicking a nod and with a general character description, Danny directed my attention to the white boy with blond woolly sideburns who sat alone at the far side of the chow hall.

"See Officer Greeley leaned up against the wall right behind our boy?" Danny cleared his throat. "Maybe he's standing watch while the legend eats so he don't try and mix with the other inmates." Danny rose. "He's got the mark. C'mon, this is our big chance. Let's go introduce ourselves."

I wasn't sixteen anymore, ever at Danny's beck and call because loneliness cut like a knife on mean streets and he was older and a friend. Sure, we tended to talk like sixteen-year-olds, but it seemed everyone in prison under the age of thirty talked a sour mash of street talk and early Millennial. The TV shows got that wrong, too: thirty-year-old inmates talking like grown men instead of kids who never wanted to grow up. Talkin' street set us apart from the normies with their normie-talk. Street bilingual, of course, I could choose. Others, like Danny, didn't have that luxury. Eyes on my tray, I said, "You're tripping. I'm starving."

"You're coming," Danny insisted. "I need a witness."

Groaning, I stood. My orange jumpsuit rustled. The cluster dangling from my belt-loop that included my prison ID and key clanged against the metal seat. "All right, I got your back." A thought flashed. "Wait, is this gonna be bloody?"

Danny grinned over his shoulder. "Bloody fuckin' awesome if this is who I think it is."

With Danny in the lead, we weaved through the obstacle course of tables, trying not to brush up against Kenny the Kidnapper, Garcia the Gangster, Fanny the Feezy, or Manny the Maniac, lest something apocalyptic happen. We stopped yards short of the table where, with a beleaguered expression, the blond-haired dude who had succeeded in spellbinding Danny sat eyeing us. For a split-second, it occurred to me Danny, with his obsessed gazes and all, might have since ventured a tromp into the shaven-leg land of the feezys. However, I dismissed the thought once I noticed Greeley surveying our approach with an icy stare. Clearly, something was up in P-Pen Land and it was likely not anything LGBTQ related.

I whispered in Danny's ear, "He looks like a fish."

Danny didn't respond. Too busy dividing his glances between the mystery man and the cop, it looked like.

I sighed. "What now?"

Danny took a deep breath. "Now," he mumbled, "we'll see if Clark Kent is Superman or if he's just some fish with woolly sideburns. C'mon."

Danny and I walked over and sat down as casually as buds at a poker table.

I sat to the blond guy's left, Danny to his right.

"So he can't blow for whatever reason," Danny had whispered on our meander around the table.

A moment of awkward silence passed as the blond guy gaped at us and we at him. Then, Danny bypassed the usual intros and began to make small talk.

The words sounded especially wack coming from Danny. "Hidely-ho, Ivanhoe," Danny said, winking at me. "How might things be going for thee, kind sir?" He smiled. "What's the good word, ol' timer?" Then, Danny stood up, and with a loud voice declared, "One small step for man, one giant leap for mankind." Snickering, he sat back down.

"Nice sideburns," I said, not knowing what else to say.

The face that stared back at us with its wide eyes, busted lip, and red swell on its cheek, spoke of a dude who had just got his clock cleaned. "Huh?" he asked, with his spork in his mouth and pudding dripping down his bloodied lip.

Danny snickered. "Just some old-fogy type talk there to remind a feller of the good ol' days." Danny peered in, focusing, studying. His eyelids fluttered and smile fell off. "Hey, are you all right? You don't look so hot, old man."

The blond guy shook his head and grunted something. On impulse, I glanced over my shoulder at Officer Greeley who looked as disagreeable as ever and stood eyeing us still. However, those eyes appeared more curious than scrutinizing at this point, relaying no message except his everyday one that he was one tough copper and didn't put up with no bull, so we'd better watch it.

The blond guy, too, glanced over at the officer. He whispered, "Y'all are with Tony, aren't you?" He straightened in his chair. "Okay, so, maybe I said something 'bout how Tony cheats at spades. But it's true—he cheats! Well, then your boy comes at me, see? I hit him once with my left, to fend him off..."

While the blond guy yapped on about some Tony character and the epic struggle had between himself and the same, Danny's expression morphed into that of Grumpy Cat. Squinting his eyes to focus, Danny inched right up to the blond guy's face until their noses almost touched. Storytelling, meanwhile, in the apparent direction of his lemonade, the blond guy continued his tale.

"And then I got him in an arm-lock, see, and then—" the blond guy jerked back from the greasy-haired Italian-American he'd discovered right up in his mug. The blond guy all but jumped to his feet.

The Spanish homies at the nearest table looked over in astonishment.

Danny just smiled, as if in amusement. "Whoa, now." He backed off, with palms out in a defensive posture. "Calm down, Rocky."

The blond guy lowered his fist.

Danny let out a breath. He groaned, and turned to me. "Upon closer inspection," he said, his eyes blank and glaring, "these are not the droids we're looking for."

I didn't know what Danny meant by that.

Danny's eyes bulged. "This isn't Henry Heck, fool!" He shook his head at me.

The blond guy's eyes lit up as he unfurled his fist. "Henry Heck? The Forever Young Prisoner? Wait, you thought I was that legend guy in The Pit?"

Danny nodded.

The blond guy narrowed an eye. "You guys pullin' my chain? Why me?"

Danny stood. "From across the ways, that smash-mark on your face kinda looks like a red birthmark." The red on Danny's own cheeks had meanwhile paled completely. The glimmer in his eyes had dulled to a listless stare. "Sorry to bother you, homes," he muttered, cheerlessly. "C'mon, Tommy. We out."

The blond guy asked us to sit back down. He said his name was Shawn Larson, Third Floor. Everyone called him Chopper. He asked what our names were.

Danny said it didn't matter.

"Tommy," I said, reclaiming my seat. "He's Danny. Who's this *Henry* guy everyone keeps talking about?"

Chopper touched his face here and there, maybe thinking he could rearrange it back into shape for his guests in this way. "Tell me, guys, straight up. You think that fool actually exists? The Forever Young Prisoner?"

"We're all forever young," I noted. "Teenagers trapped in adult bodies. Who's Henry?"

Danny sat down and curved a smile. "Your name's Chopper?" he asked, deferring my question.

"Chopper, like the bike?" I asked.

Chopper nodded. He said he rode the Narragansett coastline and sometimes as far as Connecticut. "Ever been to Danielson? Nice town, seems like. Though, kinda hard to tell when you're barreling through at ninety."

"Hells yeah," I said. "Ninety."

Danny bumped fists with Chopper. He flicked a nod at me. "Tommy here's got a hobby, too. He's a writer. I proofread his stories."

"Even though he can barely read," I put in.

Danny's glance over advised that I shut it about people's reading skills. "Oh, and what a coincidence. Actually, there's a story Tommy wrote with a character named Chopper in it."

I informed Danny the character's name was Wood Chipper Jones, not Chopper.

Danny explained to Chopper, "Tommy writes short stories," he cocked his head, "about, well, blood, gore, people getting put into wood chippers, and a long list of other atrocities. You know, the usual deranged ramblings of a wannabe prison author."

Grinning, Chopper gave me a fist bump. "That's bomb, man. I'm happy for you. I'm glad you are, you know, like, writing about people getting killed instead of going out and killing them yourself." Lowering his head, Chopper slurped his pudding. "My last celly had that problem." He looked up. "Hey, know what? Maybe you can write a story about yours truly. I've lived a pretty wack life so far. Three different fake names, four baby-mommas, seven felony convictions, addictive personality all *over* the place, two friends although one is imaginary—"

"Tommy's not writing anyone's bio, son," Danny said. "He's got better things to write about than your overall failures as a person."

One thing I always admired about Danny was how he could get away with saying things others could not. Surely, the slicked-back hair and badass Robert DeNiro vibe helped him along those lines. One of his many considerable talents was that, although Danny wasn't super smart, he could make you think he was.

Chopper listened as Danny continued, "Tommy's latest piece is titled 'Wood Chipper Jones's Baseball Bat Barrage of Death,' then something about zombie rats from the underworld. These are the rarest examples of high-brow literature you'll find in these parts, Chop. Besides, even if you do make it into one of his stories, it's fairly guaranteed you'll end up getting run through a meat grinder or pushed off a tall building or something fun like that."

I cleared my throat. "I had a character who lived in the end, once. His arms and legs didn't make it, though."

"Tommy's a wicked hot mess," Danny explained to Chopper, who probably cared less as he, too, was all that and more: it was a common affliction at P-Pen.

I said to Danny, just for clarification's sake, "Actually, at my sentencing hearing, Steve described me to the judge as 'a young man who simply lacked a purpose in life.' Ditto for my pretrial therapist. She said I needed to go to *war* with my bad habits, and that I'm at that age where if I don't find a calloused belly—or whatever the hell she'd called it—soon, I would risk the 'inevitable course of habitual offender status.'"

"Steve's his lawyer," Danny clarified. "What did that lady therapist say, homie? Those three things?"

I exhaled. "State your goals...which helps with purpose. Let go of the past. And show loved ones you care."

Chopper said, "You've got a purpose. You write."

"Writing about purposelessness isn't much of a purpose." Dividing glances between Danny and Chopper, I added, "Three stamps and a Slim Jim if *either* of you guys can come up with an even *halfway* workable story idea. Okay, so I tried writing this novel once, *Trouble at the Trailer Park*. But none of my characters seemed to wanna survive past Chapter 2."

Danny snorted. "Tommy had a hella bad childhood. See, Fatts and Trixie, the foster parents, got so pissed at Tommy one day after he'd cracked their bong, they dragged him outside the *trailer* and told him never to return until he'd hustled them up a new bong AND a dime-sack of H. After that, Tommy never wanted to see those fools again. And he never did. He never has. Facts. You were pretty pissed that day, weren't you, bruh?"

I folded my arms. "No sixteen-year-old was ever more. Yeah, I've had better days." I brightened. "Well, like that day a week later when I met *Danny Onofrio* under the Crook Point Bridge. He let me have a swig of his Johnnie Walker and a bite of his sandwich."

"And we've been best buds ever since." Danny looked at me. "Haven't we, G?"

Chopper twisted his swollen lip. "Um, idea. If you're gonna write about gruesome deaths and stuff why not write a prison story? You can draw from your experiences and it'd be more real life. Maybe that could be your purpose."

I shook my head. "I don't write non-fiction. Real life sucks sack."

After a long pause, over which half of me pondered Chopper's recommendation of a "prison story," and the other half wondered why I wasn't smashing people's heads in at that very moment for the mere mention of the words "foster parents," I suddenly realized how far off topic we had wandered. "Who, or what, is the Forever Young Prisoner?"

Chopper rolled his eyes. "He's a fish."

Danny patted Chopper's arm. "Be nice. You were new once, too."

Out of the corner of my eye, I saw an overly large blue thing headed our way. Officer Greeley. I figured he would stop over and make some cowboy remark like "Okay, gentlemen, let's keep it moving," and that would be that, but Greeley sat down with us.

He smiled. "The Forever Young Prisoner, I heard you say. I get goosebumps every time I hear this story. Don't let me interrupt you."

Chopper blinked. "Story time? And Blue's gonna sit in, too?"

Danny nodded. "Tommy and fish everywhere need to know. And Blue needs to be reminded," he said to the cop, who kept his smile.

I rubbed my hands in anticipation, feeling a bit shook with the C.O. seated right next to me like that, but not too much. I reminded myself this wasn't county or the high side. Although salty with the fishes and knuckleheads, the coppers *did* sit with the regs on occasion. But only on occasion. And Danny and I were hardly regs. This was highly irregular.

Over the following minutes, Danny proceeded to relay to us the supposedly non-fiction tale that every inmate at P-Pen had probably heard one-too-many times (but still wanted to hear anyway) about inmate Henry Heck, the poor sack forever locked away in The Pit of Heck. Danny shared the sketchy details of Heck's confinement, about the Pit of Heck itself.

~

After Danny finished his spiel, which, admittedly, left more questions than answers and was no more of a story than a sticky note with someone's grocery list on it, an energized quiet overtook us. This allowed me time to decide which follow-up question I might ask first.

The obvious one, of course. "You mean he hasn't aged since like the 1910s?"

Greeley shook his head.

Chopper snorted.

Sighing, Danny said, "I pretty much said that like twenty times, homie. He was arrested around the time of World War I. Remember that second bullet-point I just gave? About how he was supposed to go over on some boat and fight the commies or whatever but was arrested?" Danny guzzled some of Chopper's lemonade. He wiped his chin. "Third bullet point: no one knows the exact date of his incarceration or even his charges. There's no Henry Heck in the prison record. He's not there. Doesn't exist. All that's known is what's been told down through the years by C.O.'s and such who say there's this fool named Henry Heck who's got a red birthmark and has been locked in some hellhole for all of eternity and looks the same as he did when he got his mugshot and number back in the 1910s."

I frowned. "How old was he when he got his number?" I looked at Officer Greeley. "Do we know?"

Danny shrugged. "'Bout our age. Mid-twenties."

I asked, "What else do we know?"

The officer put in, "Well, you heard your friend's countdown just now. That's about the whole of it. No commies to fight in Germany, though. Or ghosts. At least I don't think so."

I looked warily at Danny. "You think he might be a *ghost*?"

Danny shook his head. "I didn't say that. Seventh bullet point: he *might* be a ghost, seeing as how there are ghosts, supposedly, over at Drac's Castle. So maybe—*maybe*—someone *thought* they saw a young-old man when really it was a ghost man. I don't know, fool. No one does."

I pondered. We all sat pondering. Finally, I stood, and sneaking a glance Danny's way, declared in a loud voice, "Three years, fellas. That's how long I'm here for. Don't worry, I'm your man, the detective you've all been waiting for. I'll snuff out the truth behind the mystery behind the legend of the guy."

Chopper mock cheered with a round of applause.

Greeley leveled his gaze with eyes that gleamed.

Danny sighed. "Stop stealing my thunder."

Stretching a smile, and taking a bow just like Danny used to do at the bars after announcements all his own, I sat back down. "Okay, okay, so, while here in prison, my two goals are...to not get laid, and to solve the mystery of The Forever Young Prisoner."

"Then you'll write a book about it," Danny quipped.

"I'll...write a book about it," I said, musingly. "Right. Exactly. That's a great idea, Dan."

"Slim Jim incoming," Chopper smiled.

"I can base the novel on my investigation," I said. "Then, when I find the guy, I can just quote him. He can tell me what happened, what the Pit of Heck was *really* like, and about his charges. I'm sure The Pit's got roaches. All pits do. So, maybe he had names for them. Totally can see that. I'll ask him when I see him. Remind me, Danny, to ask Heck about the cockroach names."

"That's straight, G. I will." Danny reached around Chopper to pat me on the back. "You'll be a regular detective, just like your hero, Sherlock Holmes, in that book you used to read, The Hound of the Basketballs."

"Baskervilles," I corrected.

"Old books," Danny said, kicking back a lusty lick of Chopper's lemonade. "Tommy reads 'em all the time. Used to read 'em by flashlight in that abandoned Buick we'd sleep in on the outskirts of Pawtucket, at the bars, in the trap houses, after he got laid. *Crime and Punishment, Moby Dickhead, Lady Chatterley's Lover...*"

I cued Danny to pass the refreshment. Reaching for it felt kinda like back in the day when we would pass the bong or some stolen bills until finally Danny got caught but refused to snitch on me. Anyway, flattering my reader ego wasn't going to get Danny anywhere on this particular day. More to the point, he was getting off-subject. "So, you think he was innocent?"

Danny looked hard at me. "That's what I said, about fifty-seven times." Crooking his thumb hitchhiker-style in my direction, he said to Chopper, "Three things I should've never introduced this guy to. Misty from Cranston. Meth. And the Providence Public Library."

"Meth's bad?" Chopper asked with wide eyes.

The officer glared at Chopper.

Chopper cowered. "I mean, ewwww, meth is so *baaaaaaad*." He returned the officer's brazen stare. "You know what annoys me even more than meth, though, Blue? It's when C.O.'s smuggle it into the facility—you know, for the right price or whatever." He said, weakly, "Think you can fetch us some meth?"

The officer replied, "Are you really as knuckleheaded as all that, Larson? You're in enough trouble as it is." He flicked a nod. "Now, these boys here look like they might have half a brain. And this one in particular," he leveled his sights at me, "might even be what they refer to as smart. I can see it in your eyes." He honed in on me. "You'll need that, along with a lot of luck, and all of your dumb questions, if you're going to succeed in your investigation."

Suddenly recalling that deer out in the yard with her dark, haunting, *smart* eyes, I glared nervously at Greeley with my own smart-ass ones.

"Investigation," he repeated, louder, answering my gaze. "Isn't that what detectives do?" He leaned back in his chair and eased a smile. "I mean, it'd be interesting to see how that would all pan out, your wanting to write a book and all."

Danny guffawed. "That's tight. I'm pretty sure he was just kidding, Blue. C'mon."

"Yeah," I said, nodding, dumbfounded. "Writing-wise, I kinda wanna finish up my rats story first."

Chopper plucked at his side-burn. "But maybe—*maybe*—Tommy, an investigation *is* your purpose. Maybe that's why you're here. If your investigation goes anywhere, you can write a book about it when you get out."

I nodded. Words of wisdom from Master Mutton-chop. Maybe that was where he *actually* got his name from, those chops.

"He's here because he's a homie with no purpose at all and a stupid ass for getting caught, just like the rest of us," Danny clarified.

Officer Greeley folded his hands. "At any event, just be aware, fellas," his expression returned to its former sternness, "that we in blue are just as curious and in the dark when it comes to Henry Heck as you all are. For this reason, especially, I'd advise you to be extra careful when you go around questioning witnesses like," he lowered his voice, "Monty Jenkins, Building 2, old school," he raised his voice, "or whomever."

Danny grinned. "Homie, I think you owe Blue a Slim Jim now, too."

Greeley's eyes widened. "Purely for research purposes for your man's book, you bet." He straightened in his chair. "Don't quote me on any tips, though, fellas. I'll deny it. Will they believe your word over a cop's?" he said to Chopper. "I can be an asshole, Larson. Don't test me."

"That would be *snitching*," Chopper said with huge eyes. "It's against code. I would *never* do that."

The officer studied him at length, then nodded. He ventured a peek over his shoulder. "Look," he said to Danny and me, "every inmate in Supermax is allowed a TV in their cell and an hour each day outta their cell. They're allowed newspapers, pens, paper, the occasional phone call and face-to-faces with their family and attorney." Greeley raised an eyebrow. "Not Heck. Rumor is he's locked down 24-7. A hole in the floor for a shitter, sink, dim lighting, bread and water, and we're pretty sure that's the way he's had it for the past one hundred years." A line creased the officer's forehead. "Unconstitutional conditions? You bet. But since few people know what goes on in the shadier regions of Castle Frankenstein..."

"How do you know all this, Blue?" I asked.

Greeley eyed me. "Clayton," he said, after a long pause. "Officer John Clayton. Born, whenever. Died, 1984. He passed away from a stroke just two days after spreading the original and only widely recognized rumor, Mr...." Greeley peered in at my name-tag "...McConnell. Clayton was a trustworthy source. He worked Supermax. No one knows where the Pit of Heck is, exactly. But assuming it exists, it would have to be over by Supermax, otherwise Clayton wouldn't have known about it."

Danny frowned. "A lone informant? Way back in the '80s?"

"There was another rumor, too," Greeley said. "Not long afterward. But it was proven false."

"False?" Danny said.

"That's what they say," Greeley replied in my direction. He said to us all, "Anyway, I'll bet my stripes this Heck guy was harboring some secret the top brass way back when didn't want anyone to know about, and today's crew, stuck with him, doesn't know what to do with him." Out of the sides of his mouth, he added, "Put that in your book, Irish."

"Was it the secret of eternal youth?" I asked.

Danny and Chopper turned.

The officer stirred. "Then there's that part of it."

Danny brightened. "What about that part, Greeley?"

"Yeah, Greeley?" Chopper chimed in.

The officer placed his chin in his hand. "Well," he said, "they say seeing is believing. And so far, no one's seen a damned thing."

Danny leaned in. "How about unofficially?"

The officer mulled it over. "Well, they say life's full of surprises, and so, you just never know." The gleam in his eyes suggested he knew plenty. "Well, Mr. Chopper, why don't you finish your meal so we can go for a walk to Captain Allen's office. Cap's got a few questions about that skirmish you got into this morning. That busted-up face of yours wasn't by accident, I'm sure."

Chopper returned to his meal. "Skirmish? What you mean? I cut myself shaving. I mean, I fell outta my bunk..."

Greeley folded his arms. "Save your tales for the Cap." He looked at us. "You guys and your damned inmate code of silence. I figure it had something to do with your nemesis, Tony Hernandez."

Chopper shoveled pudding into his mouth. "Tony Hernandeth? Whooth that?"

"Cap's not the kind who likes to be kept waiting. Finish your meal. If there's anything Cap likes less than waiting it's wasting taxpayer money." Greeley surprised us with pats on the back. "Good luck, fellas."

Danny blinked. "Good luck with what, Blue?"

The officer replied, "Your investigation."

Danny laughed. "Ain't gonna be no investigation!"

The officer paused for a moment, then sat back down, "Just out of curiosity, you fellas ever hear of the Black Hats?"

"Black Hats?" I said.

"Didn't think so. Upper management," Greeley explained. "Mid-management. Administrators. A few of the captains. Some officers, too. Fine men otherwise, but downright nasty when it comes to the prison's top secret. The White Hats counter, but all we can really do is assist. A C.O. couldn't do it, see; we'd lose our jobs—or worse. It would take an inmate. Some fearless, down-on-his-luck inmate with nothing to lose. Someone," he eyed us intently, "who doesn't care if he's written up for...whatever, catches a case for...whatever. For justice's sake; for the truth's sake; for freedom's sake." He looked at us. "For Henry's sake." He rose. "I mean, for the sake of that novel you plan on writing."

Backing off, furrowing his brow, the officer raised his voice, "Now, like I've been telling you boys, get it in order. No horseplay at the tables, or I'll haul you off alongside your friend!"

"Sorry, Blue," Danny declared as we rose.

Chopper brightened. "You leaving?"

"We gonna blow," I said. "We out."

Chopper bumped fists with me. "Good luck. Let me know the names of the cockroaches when you find out what they are."

Danny and I returned to our table.

"That was tight," Danny said as we sat down.

"Yeah. Only, I wish I had brought a notepad with me. And a pen."

Danny frowned. "Why?"

I swigged my lemonade. "To jot notes about what we just heard." I watched Officer Greeley key in and escort Chopper through the restricted metal door that led to Captain Allen's office. "Isn't that what author detectives do once they're officially on the case—take notes?"

———————

After Danny quit shaking his head at me for that, and returned to his cookie, we were confronted by some big-ass homey and his dogs who wanted to know why we had gotten chummy with a cop for five whole minutes.

"It was longer than *that*," I said, as Danny kicked me underneath the table.

"Are you and *Deermaster* cop lovers?" the leader of the pack guy said to Danny.

"Deermaster?" Danny said.

"Whose side are you on, anyway?" one of the dogs in back said, with a deadpan look on his face.

I raised my hand to tell Danny I had this. Coughing—as if to clear the way for something profound, all that came out was, "We didn't sit with him. He came over and sat the fuck down with us!"

Danny kicked me underneath the table again.

"We were telling this fool all about Henry Heck," Danny explained in an even voice.

This happened a couple of times over the course of the remainder of our meal, and over the days to come. Everyone's expression would change once Danny or I said that. Their scowls would level off, they'd bite back their words, or would look at one another as if with uncertainty. Some would even recite some of the rumors *they* knew. The head-of-the-pack guy stood blinking. "Oh, cool." Then, he and his dogs scampered off.

"Never, *ever* sit and rap with the cops," Danny advised me. "It's against code." He chomped his cookie and wiped his mouth. "Unless it's to sit and rap about that Pit of Heck guy. Then it's all good."

CHAPTER THREE

That I was clowning about that whole "detective" bit was no lie. As a semi-habitual drug user and sometimes alcoholic, I often talked out of my ass. It came with the territory. So I thought I was kidding. Like an open pack of cigs on the dashboard of an abandoned '93 Buick, certain things in life were just inevitable. My investigation into the mystery of the Forever Young Prisoner proved inevitable. But nothing ever happens all at once.

Danny made parole about a month later. This circumstance forced me to consider my own eventual parole, and that loathsome real-life world I would once again have to face. It encouraged me to set to rights my growing fixation with a prison world whose culture was slowly but surely laying its claim. Already within those first few months I had learned, like, twenty different card tricks. Cooking up a mean prison "spread" wasn't too difficult if you knew a few tricks like heating up the summer sausage first to bring out the flavor. I hustled up a tat on my left wrist in lieu of a haircut. Strip searches are regular in prison, and I was living proof a guy could get used to even this. Showing your bits becomes as everyday as combing your hair or tying your shoes. Prison grows on you. It slowly evolves into a love-hate relationship with keywords "home" and in this instance "camp." Anyhow, it sure as hell beat the Outreach Center on Fulton Street.

Danny's parole helped me recall one of my rashly-stated goals: to investigate the mystery of the Forever Young Prisoner.

Hearing about a *Forever Young Prisoner* really got me pumped at first, but over the weeks that followed, all of my enthusiasm kind of leaked out and left me with a flat feeling. Still, kidding aside, I had openly declared an intention, publicly stated a goal. Normies would probably call it "responsibility" to see a goal through to its conclusion.

"Screw it," I decided, finally, while shooting hoops out in the yard one day. "Let's just do this. It's a goal. It's something. Let's roll with it." I rolled to the basket for a layup.

"You always talk to yourself while hooping?" a white boy with a sleeved-out left arm asked. He must have been brand new because I'd never seen him before, nor had I seen him squatting in the grass with a ball under his business watching the showcase.

I tossed up a jump-shot. *Swish*. "It helps me play better," I said. I walked over. "The stakes are low, besides." I bounced the ball between my legs. "Yeah, like I'm really gonna *rescue* a homie from some dungeon—if he even exists, which he probably doesn't. And in the end, I can say—even if it's just to myself—I made a goal and stuck with it." I shrugged. "Though, it'd be cool if he did exist. And who's to say he doesn't?"

The tattoo guy eked a smile. "No idea what you're talking about, but your game speaks volumes." He laid his ball down and motioned for mine. He received my pass. "You and me, one-on-one. Let's go. Winner gets a stamp."

He took a few shots then handed me the ball. I handed it right back to him. "To 11," I said. "I'll give you an 8 point advantage. Make it, take it. Oh..." I rebounded the ball after his miss, "and I can even call Ms. Flounders, or whatever her name was—*Flanders* —my pretrial therapist, and tell her I made a goal and followed through with it." I swished a 3-pointer. "And in the meantime, I'll keep talking to myself and hustle up some stamps so I can get a haircut!"

Finally, in lieu of my big decision, I decided to make a phone call. Not to Ms. Flanders, save that for later, but to Danny. Who else on the outs gave a flip about Tommy Mac?

Danny's girl answered. Who apart from boasting the highest heels and dangliest earrings you ever did see, featured a girly lisp that could scrape an eardrum clear to shreds. But she was cool. Her name was Lilya. We all used to hang at that trap house in Mt. Hope. Good times, and so was she. She also happened to be Black. Dopin' good times opened its doors to all races, genders, and ethnic influences.

"Hi, Tommy," Lilya said. "What's good? How's the big house treating you?"

"Hi, Lil. It's treating me to the point I'll need treatment later. Is Danny there?"

Lilya cleared her throat. "He's, er, working at Stop & Shop right now," she said, weakly.

I rolled my eyes and pointed out it was seven p.m..

Silence.

Lilya sighed. "Alright, he's in the bedroom shooting up some...wait, is this line bugged?" She coughed. "He took the day off from work. He stocks shelves. Right now he's stocking up on some goodies ClownAround brought over. He can't talk right now."

ClownAround was Lilya's "real" boyfriend. In drug circles, sex and drugs went hand in hand. Lending out one's significant other didn't occur quite as regularly as the sharing of cigs or meth pipes, but almost.

Needless to say, I understood. "Okay. Well, tell Danny I think about him constantly. Love him. Miss him. Wanna have babies one day. Give him a kiss for me, 'k?"

Lydia giggled. "You're so funny."

"I know. A regular clown. And so, how is ClownAround doing?"

"He's well." Lilya giggled. "He's still pissed at Danny. Although, he did finally agree to let us smash, but only if he can sit and watch."

"Listen, Lil, tell Danny...tell him I've decided it's high time I go see Old Monty in Building 2. I thought to myself, heck, why not?" I blinked. "Yeah, tell him *Heck, why not?* just like that, those exact words. He'll know what it means."

"High times for sure!" Lilya said. "Got it. I'll tell him. Good luck over there. Get back to us in one piece. Hey, I was thinking, when you do get back, maybe you can write my life story. I've lived a very interesting life so far..."

The day hall. It was the main rec-area on the ground floor of Building 4 where an inmate could take a break from his cell and just chill. He could read, play cards, watch TV, use the micro to warm up his Keefe instant-coffee or Honey Bun, make a phone call, or just gaze out of the window at the rows of barbed-wire and Drac's Castle in the distance.

The day hall featured as an orangey abstract painting on this particular afternoon in early August, with everyone getting back from their gigs on the outside work crews or chow hall.

I ended my call with Lilya after her life story had progressed into her formative years, at which point I had told her some jacked ninja Nazi was gonna tear my head off if I didn't get off the phone, like, now.

Lilya, though, called my bluff. "I thought you said you wanna be a writer? Also, aren't you supposed to be showing loves ones you care? Isn't that one of your *stated goals*?"

She was right, my stated goals. "I do care," I said, but the words sounded empty in my ears.

"No worries," Lilya said. "We can finish the convo later." Instead of finishing her piece, she said, "Okay, peace," and hung up.

Crossing the day hall, I bumped fists with Tater, Chase,

LaChance, and some fellas at the checkers table as I tromped off to the stairwell. I had just passed the Prison Rape Elimination Act posters when I got called back—by Perez, a Northie. You could tell his affiliation by the falcon tat that would partially creep out of his sleeve whenever he reached to jut his dirty fingernail in your face then accept your commissary items.

"Tell your celly I want my rent money, Blanco," he said, with his twitchy red eyeballs all over me.

"Rent money. Got it. I'll tell him." I pivoted to retrace my steps to the stairwell.

"Make sure you tell him," Toro called over, staring me down. Toro was a Southbanger. For the life of me, I still couldn't figure how opposing gang-members who fought on the streets could be such casuals in the pen. On a side note, had Perez not covered his falcon tattoo there would have been hell to pay right then and there. This, per Danny, who said things tended to be even edgier over at Drac's Castle when it came to politics.

Although the PREA posters attracted their fair amount of attention—they were large and posted everywhere—they didn't attract mine so much as the new bulletin tacked onto the community board right next to them. Per statute such-and-such, beginning on date such-and-such, inmates were to be referred to as "offenders," no longer as "inmates." Words mattered to more than just wannabe prison writers, I guess.

The second-floor hallway. Think hospital: wood trim, concrete walls, linoleum flooring, but without the nurses, needles, or gurneys —although the gurneys would appear on occasion, too, after the brawls ran their course and the pools of blood had time to coagulate. A regular melee, and the Ninja Turtles would show up with their riot gear and pepper spray. Fights almost always happened in the cells, but sometimes the fallout would seep into the hallway.

I scuttled across the square linoleum tiles with my black government-issue shoes as I passed the bathroom and showers, trying to break my mother's back by stepping on every crack I could. "You're a mistake," I heard that mystery woman say with every crack mushed under my toes. But then I thought better of it and avoided every crack possible. Whomever they were, *wherever* they were, my real mom and dad were "loved ones" in my life, and I needed to show them, too, I cared.

I flashed a peace sign as I passed the open door of the Ferguson Twins's cell—fools who I had actually run with on the outs for a while.

One of the Fergses called over, "Hey, Tommy!"

I retraced my steps to peer into their cell.

"You gonna find Henry Heck for us?" one of the Fergses asked.

"I'll try," I said with a sigh, and kept walking.

I halted at cell B7.

I reached for the key dangling from my belt-buckle and keyed in. Home sweet home.

On the streets, they called him *Niño*. That's Spanish for "little guy." Not the sexiest name to have in prison; although certain offenders probably considered it super sexy. On the short side, slight, and with a freckling of pimples on his baby face, Niño's overall aspect let the prison-world know he was indeed a youngster, only twenty-one. You'll fill out, I'd tell him, even though that was probably bullshit. His second-cousin, whom we passed in the yard occasionally, referred to him as *Harry Potter*. I somehow didn't see the resemblance.

A pencil drawing of a donkey showcased on Niño's bulletin board. It let the prison-world know, too, Niño had money in the bank. Watson from upstairs had sketched it in exchange for three stamps and a Sriracha sauce. Dark clouds, whirling stars, words in Spanish over-top the donkey and archaic-looking symbols under-neath. I sometimes caught myself staring at this image. Niño referred to this humble beast as his power animal. I called it his "Big

Ass" or "The Ass That You're Not Getting." Bad jokes. The image was dark. He even had a name for his ass. Choco.

Niño lay on his rack watching *The Avengers* as I entered, just kickin' it after his five-hour shift in the kitchen.

He worked the slime-line, dishing out slop for the locals. In prison, reputation is key, and Niño's rep was that of generous portions and perfectionism in that he didn't just pile it on, he nestled it on, ensuring no sauce or crumb escaped its compartment on the tray. His reputation otherwise was *scrawny, unaffiliated little wuss*, and that was probably why the Northies had singled him out.

But I liked Niño. His snarky jab at that bus driver on the shuttle over from Classification was what had started it. His retort not only had me in stitches, but everyone, and it really broke the ice on what was otherwise an unbearable twenty miles with every movable part of you pinned down with chains. Talking smack like that required nerve, and that boy had it. Coming in on the bus together and being friends on the bus makes you friends for the duration: it's kind of an unwritten rule. Sure, his English sucked donkey balls, but at least he didn't snore.

This was my celly.

And this was our cell: a space about the size of a large bedroom. Metal beds in parallel on opposite sides of the room. Wood desk. Painted-over concrete walls. Flimsy green mattress—an exercise mat, basically. Through the window-slit one could see patches of grass, sky, and the north side of Drac's Castle in the distance. A clunky old-school TV reposed on a wood stand at the foot of Niño's rack. You had to get your name on a list for a television. It took months.

TV was Niño's domain. I made a beeline for mine: the desk.

"The place you like to be," Niño smiled, flicking a nod at my habitual abode as I pulled up my throne and sat down.

"I chill here and write because I like words," I said, repeating the line I so often used whenever he set the stage like that. "Books are an escape, and words are weapons fools use to quell kingdoms, climb a mountain, smash a vampire or...a sixteen-year-old's life." This last bit always raised Niño's eyebrow, but he never said anything. Maybe he already knew what that meant from overhearing my "active subconscious," as I liked to call it, mutter to itself while writing or sleeping. Also, what else was there to do in a cell but write, read, and shoot the shit? I didn't have a job yet and it would be another week before I qualified. There seemed to be a waiting list for everything: TV, shitter, shower, microwave, job. Niño got his job right away because non-violent charges did that for fools.

Niño's kitchen gig involved the dispensing of desserts. Pudding. Chocolate cake. Jello.

Ten minutes later, I felt like dropping my forehead into one of these, as the words simply were not coming. Finally, I set my pen down, and put my head in my hands.

Niño stirred. He clicked the volume down a notch and looked over. "You are dead?"

Face in my hands, I nodded.

Niño sat up on his mat, his elbows compressing its already skimpy cushioning down to pancake level. "Distracted? Daydream time? You are thinking about the girls? Hey, what ever happened to this one poem you are writing, 'An Ode to the Wet Ladies of the Wild, Wild West Side?'"

"Girls?" I said. "At a time like this? I'm thinking about a guy."

Niño shook his head. "Come now, you do this thing. The zombie rats from hell need Tommy's pen, paper and, oh, what is this word I look for here?" Niño curled his lip.

"Imagination? Creativity? Kick-ass writing style?" I offered.

Niño nodded "Yes, these things, to help the rats on to their next adventure of excitement." Niño stiffened. He lost his smile. "You are thinking of a guy?"

I lifted my head, opened my notebook, and tore out a sheet of paper. "I've been having some second thoughts about the rat story." I eyed the stick-figure sketch of an old man I had scrawled into the left margin of page 5 of my story. "Maybe the zombie rats aren't from hell. Maybe they're from Jersey. And maybe they don't wanna eat human flesh so much as they *have* to because their normal food source is unavailable or whatever. Maybe the rats are having a conflict of conscience."

Niño's blank expression said *no comprende.*

With the side of my hand, I slid the notebook clear off of my desk. That was my way of saying, *Yup, I've had it with the rats, bro. Also, I think I'm losing it.*

Niño eyed the notepad on the floor then Page 5 in my hand which he requested he see. I said, screw it, and showed him. Peering in, he studied it. He looked up. "Who is señor?" He pointed at my stick-figure sketch. "And what are these prison bars surrounding him?"

"Señor is sad," I explained. "Señor is in hell. Purgatory. The Pit of Heck. Wherever. *Mucho cucarachas.* Oh, I forgot. Perez told me to tell you you'd better get a move on that box of Nutty Buddys or he's gonna send *you* to hell."

Niño sat up. "It is not *his* box of Nutty Buddys. Ramens. Coffee shots. Stamps. Tortillas. And now, the chocolates. Why do I let him bully me? Is my commissary items, not his own."

"Maybe it's because you're a window thief who's now in this place called prison and well within range of the wolves. This ain't no chin check, celly. This be for realz. Didn't he say he'd bust you up and that you had until Friday?"

Niño laid back and flipped to the Red Sox game. "Do you know, celly," he said, as Chris Sale burned a fastball in for a strike, "you really should not do that. If you were my *amigo,* you would not."

I narrowed my eyes. "What, tell it like it is?"

Niño leaned in. "Pretend to be dead. It is bad mojo. You listen to me now...you chase after young-old men who are as good as dead, you read dead authors..."

I eyed my prison copy of Charles Dickens's *Great Expectations* on the corner of my desk, then placed a hand over it to harbor it from what was sounding like smack talk.

"...and now, you pretend to be dead. Have you ever hear of the Day of the Dead? It is a thing we have down in Mexico."

I crooked my head. "I thought you were Puerto Rican?"

Niño's severe glance eased into a smile. "I am kidding. Good for you. *Es bueno* you want to investigate the Henry Heck prisoner person you speak always to us of. Dead people do not bully for commissary, that is one good thing about them. Listen, you like words. Words are weapons, you say. *Si!* I give you words. To help you with your impossible mission into the realm of the dead ones. Words for to help you...and me. It is a mantra. I do this now. Summoning energies for you, and for me. I learn this thing after the airplane with my mamá down to Guadalajara. That is in Mexico."

"You're Puerto Rican!"

Niño leveled his brow. "Guatemalan. Half. My mamá was from Mexico."

I shook my head in disbelief. "We've been cellies for four whole months and I find out just now you're Pisa? Why didn't you tell me? No wonder the homies don't want anything to do with you." The Pisas stayed clear of him, too, strangely enough. Because he was half Guatemalan?

"You never ask, that is why not. Sometimes you must phrase the question. Make the words. To know. Here, I show you..." Niño stood. "My mamá had the very strong reputation down in Guadalajara." He cracked his finger joints. "Please understand this."

I curved a smile. "She put out?"

"Yes," Niño said, losing his. "Curses. Some of them worked, some no. Not all curses, reverse-curses, and blessings are a success. There is reason for this. Now, we do the thing..."

After stretching his lanky arms and warming up his vocal cords with a series of annoying, high-pitched screeches, or whatever the hell those things were, Niño clicked off the TV. Niño *never* killed the TV, and muted it only at night. TV was a part of our little world. All of those Liberty Mutual commercials I had to sit through while trying to write my *Wood Chipper Jones* story! Sometimes I wanted to smash the little bastard, but he was too nice. With the TV lights out, it was then I realized *this*—whatever it was—was gonna be no joke.

Niño began his mantra. He looked down at the ground. He spoke in Spanish, although some words didn't sound Spanish at all. A repetition of phrases ensued over those first few minutes, while he padded in a slow circle. Over time the words grew louder—and weirder, and Niño's feet moved faster, until he, yelling, began to whirl around like a top.

At one point he stopped, to wink at me. It sent shivers down my spine.

The second phase involved crooning, wailing, stammering, yowling, and foot stomping. With an amused smile, I just watched. A few times I wanted to laugh out loud, even though it was rather not funny. Frightening and disturbing would be better words.

The third phase involved some rather torturous-sounding guttural noises I would venture to say few human vocal-chords could produce, or would want to.

I heard the word "Nutty Buddy" spoken at one point, and a word that sounded like "excommunication." I'm not sure what else. "R"'s were rolling off of Niño's tongue like gumballs out of a candy dispenser. I almost wondered if his tongue might get stuck. Growing up, Trixie used to say that that happened with the "ispanics" sometimes, their tongues got stuck, and so maybe other things got stuck, too, and that's why they had so many babies. Good ol' Trixie.

One thing I'll always remember about Niño's showcase was he didn't blink the whole while. His eyes leveled downward and a darkish glimmer in those eyes matched every bit the intensity of his tone.

With one last, long, impassioned moan, Niño fell silent. He whispered, "*Consummatum Est. Consummatum Est,*" as he collapsed onto his mattress. His brow was wet with moisture and I was ready to hit the hay—or him, for acting like such a psycho and stealing away ten whole minutes of my Wet Ladies of the West Side fantasy time. My alarm-clock read 10:07. Lights out, that meant. Lockdown.

"Well, that was interesting." I fell back onto my mat and pulled the covers. I tucked the folded-up towel which featured as my pillow under my head. "Crack kills, celly."

Niño turned off the light and returned to his rack.

Outside, the crickets chirped. Next door, a freaky, bulbous, bearded sloth named Freddy kept banging on the wall telling us to "Shut the fuck up in there!" In the distance, on the high side, a siren wailed. It did that sometimes. Those rascally high-siders.

"You will be quiet tonight," Niño spoke over the sound of the wall poundings and siren. "You will have peace. No screaming and kicking like last night. And the night before. And the night before that."

Slowly, I sat up in my rack. "I talked in my sleep again?"

Niño nodded.

I exhaled. "What did Sleeping Beauty have to say this time?"

The poundings on the wall stopped, as did the siren.

Niño rubbed his chin in speculation. "Many, many things last night and the night before. This word 'Fatts' I hear. 'Trixie.' 'Danny.' 'Please, do not do that.' Um, what else? 'Who are you, and why do you seek us?' 'Can you see me?' 'Help me.' 'Seek us.' Oh, also you say, 'Enough of this, let's roll.'" Niño angled his dark eyes at me. "Enough of what, celly?"

I grinned. "Enough of that shit you were just pulling. Pulling my crank, more like. You were acting like a regular whack-job there, *señor*."

Niño laid down. "I have chosen that I will give Perez his Nutty Buddy."

I wiggled my hips around to face him. "Good. Now I won't have to hide under these covers here when Perez and his *amigos* stops by to smash you into salsa."

Niño's eyes widened. "I dispense the sweets to the others. That is my job. I give. I feed. Why should I not feed Perez the Nutty Buddy sweet? I will give him his *propio chocolate*. That is Spanish for *his just dessert*."

I snickered softly to myself.

Niño looked over. "Laughing time?"

Coughing, I remarked that *Nutty Buddy* was a damned funny name, if you really thought about it.

Niño retained his solemn pose; maybe he didn't get it. "A whole damned century," he said into the darkened stillness.

I lifted my head off of my towel.

"Something you say in your sleep, too." Niño smiled. Even in the darkness I could see that smile. "This refers to the young-old man, yes? The Henry Heck prisoner person you tell us about? The one you wish to free?"

"True that," I said. Laying there, I wondered what it would be like to never grow old. I stirred up mental images of a guy with a top hat and suit, lying around in some hell of a cell who was at that very moment staring at a wall and ceiling just like we were, and just like he'd done for over a hundred years.

"A whole century," I said, wistfully.

"*Si,*" Niño's voice softly replied.

"A whole damned century!" I closed my eyes. The words echoed off of the cement walls of our cell then ping-ponged around the insides of my brain. Ten minutes passed. A half-hour. An hour. The Wet Ladies of the Wild West Side had failed to make their appearance. My thoughts pinged and ponged to seemingly everything but the ladies tonight. With the exception of one.

"I had a real mom once," I said. "I never knew her." But Niño was sleeping.

Finally, the darkness, then dreamland, took me down with them.

Not even for one-hundred dollars would I go back in time and relive that one day when, after hours of gaming in my bedroom, I had decided to take a load off on Fatts's recliner in the living room and watch some porn on my phone. However, in this particular midsummer night's dream, there I was—my skinny ass all slung out on Fatts's chair with a shattered bong underneath it. Stamps are prison currency, and so ten stamps says dreamland Fatts was just then over in his bedroom hearing that glass shatter, and was on his way to kick my dreamland ass.

With my dreamland x-ray vision I could see through the walls into the foster parents' bedroom. Dressed to kill in his wife-beater and boxers, Fatts hefted the old lady's crotch off of his face as he swore bloody murder. Feet landed on the floor. Heavy feet. Thud! A heavy man. Considerably larger than my sixteen-year-old self. Stronger, too. And I knew this because, following Fatts's suggestion we arm-wrestle to determine who got the baked goods donated by the food bank, he always took the cake. Come to think of it, this was probably why Fatts got to be so *fatts* and I weighed in at 140 pounds even with my black hoodie and pajama-bottoms on.

Boy, was Fatts not happy then. I could tell by that baseball-bat he gripped in his hand as he stood in the doorway to the living room. "What is that!" He aimed the bat-head at the recliner and bong.

But in the dream it wasn't a bong.

"Sorry, Fatts, I think I broke your spectacles," I said, looking down at the smashed pair of glasses on the chair. They were old-timey with wire frames and circular lenses. In the dream, I referred to them as spectacles. I don't think I had ever used that word in real life.

Fatts narrowed his eyes at me until they were slits. He didn't wear "spectacles." No one in the trailer did.

With a coolness that would have made the likes of Danny Onofrio proud had he been *there* and not under the Crook Point Bridge with Johnnie Walker at that moment, I reminded Fatts that accidents happen. "A mistake," I said. "Like you've never made one?"

Fatts lowered the bat. He curved a cool smile. That smile, that mellow posture, proved infinitely more effective at getting my attention than all of that hootin' and hollerin' he'd barraged me with in reality. Fatts replied, just like he had that long-ago day, "No, you're a mistake, boy. Didn't your mother ever tell you that? Trouble's in your blood."

I winced as if struck. "Trixie never said jack."

"Not me," Trixie said, saddling up beside her man, the doorway just wide enough to accommodate the pair of lovebirds. "Ann, your real ma. She didn't want you, you know. That's why she left you for dead. That's why she left you with us. She said you was a mistake."

"And maybe we don't want you no more, neither," Fatts added.

It was the only time the foster parents, or anyone, had mentioned my real mother's name: Ann. A part of me felt sick at that moment, another part angry, another part betrayed—not only by my foster parents for mentioning nada up until that point, but by my real parents, whose imagined love for me stood as my last bastion of hope that life might mean something more than just waiting or wanting to die. Maybe real Mom and Dad had been too poor to take care of their newborn son. Maybe Dad had been too busy over in Iraq doing the soldier thing. Maybe I was kidnapped. Now, all of my hopes lay shattered like a pair of spectacles on a seat cushion. The truth cut like the jagged edges of a shard of glass. Those words: you're a mistake; your mother said so; Ann.

Those words—not the finger-pointing, the swooshing of the bat, or Fatts's threats; not even those very shards of glass festering in my ass that seemed to concern my foster parents not at all–was why I would make that fateful decision never to return to that trailer in Federal Hill.

With a hand on his arm, Trixie said to Fatts, "No, Frank. Let's teach the boy some responsibility by assigning him a task, a mission." She turned and said to me, "Find the owner of these glasses, bring him to us, and you will be named Liege of the Governor's Lands. Know that your quest shall not be without its dangers."

Dreamland Trixie said these exact words, I shit you not. At any event, Trixie seemed way more chill in the dream than she had been in real life. Like a normal old lady. Fatts, not so much; until with genuine concern in his eyes as the bat loosened then fell from his grip, he said, "Did you hurt yourself, son, sitting on that glass like that?"

Then I knew for sure I was dreaming.

"Would you like a spot of tea to help settle your nerves, Tommy?" Trixie said. Her eyes were large and caring as her slippered feet tempted steps towards the kitchen.

Dreaming.

No boggly, reddened meth eyes bearing down at me from either one. No snarling and swearing to high hell. No swooshings of the baseball bat to rid me of any sarcasm I thought I might have. No ultimatums or manhandling me out of the trailer with promises to sell me to the cartel if I didn't return with the bong and the H they so desperately needed. In retrospect, it was really all about the damned heroin, not a bong worth twenty bucks. Any tweaker and probably anyone with half a brain could've told you that.

With a bounce in my step, I padded to the front door to set off on my mission to find the owner of the broken glasses.

Then, things in the dream got kinda funny, I guess you could say.

Still clad in their bedroom attire with feet planted in the living room, Fatts and Trixie began to laugh. It struck me, suddenly, that no expression relayed an emotion more specifically than laughter. However, this foray didn't know what emotion it expressed. I had never seen this particular brand of laughter in real life. Neither amused, nor scornful, it sounded not so much inhuman as unreal. As this mock laughter grew louder, and more unsettling, their laughing heads morphed into donkey heads. I thought this was pretty damned funny until the reddened meth-eyes appeared. They were neighing, now. The donkey heads with their reddened meth-eyes— neighing, while their heads joggled like a pair of Bobblehead Dolls.

Instead of carrying me out the front door onto Penn Street, my steps landed me in a courtroom.

The laughter followed. More to the point, it grew. The sound careened to the very balcony seats tiered over the main gallery. A rowdy courtroom laughed, jeered, swore, spit at, and heckled me as I stepped down the aisle to take my place in the defendant's box. It was a box, with tallish mahogany sides just like the ones you see in that Victorian courthouse just outside of downtown in Governor's Square.

A man and a woman with donkey heads stood side by side at the witness stand, bearing testimony against me. Their testimony was laughter.

The crowd laughed, too. They pointed fingers and flung insults at the skinny sixteen-year-old accused of breaking a bong—spectacles, whatever.

The judge took his seat at the magistrate's stand. A dapper old gent with a bushy white mustache that pretty much owned the bottom half of his face, he could probably have hidden a small animal under that thing.

"All rise!" the clerk declared.

No trial. The judgment came predetermined and ready for delivery by Judge Mustache.

The crowd, in anticipation, let loose a raucous windfall of cheers and leers.

Not just the crowd, but the whole of New England.

With a hot-air-balloon vantage of the entire land of Oz, I could see Rhode Island, Massachusetts, Connecticut, Vermont, Maine...

I saw people. Crowds, convening on the steps of city halls, by newspaper racks, and a million other places. All of New England awaited the reading of the judgment, and while folks waited, they laughed. They laughed to mock or for joy at the administration of justice. They laughed because their neighbors laughed. But their laughter sounded like an empty chorus. In apparent disagreement with their mouths, their eyes shone lifeless. Dead.

Next, I saw a series of flashcard images portraying a series of men. The presentation of these images reminded me of the swipings of a phone to show off pics, say, of Block Island, or the hot-as-hell hoes you'd kicked it with at the club in Boston over the weekend.

Swipe. A snapshot of a man wearing a gray suit and a greasy

smile. Swipe. Another man in a suit with his eyes rolling in his head. Swipe. A man with his mouth open and tongue flailing as he whipped his head violently from side to side. Swipe. A man in a suit whose eyes displayed the reddened swell of one who hadn't slept in months. Swipe. A man with shit all over his face. Swipe. A man who looked like a demon. Swipe...

"It was a mistake," I mumbled, weakly, in the direction of the twelve jurors, each of them with donkey heads.

Judge Mustache rolled his eyes and neighed, loudly. He received the verdict paper from the clerk. The rancor from the peanut gallery subsided then ceased completely. Everyone eyed Judge Mustache, and the accused.

The judge curled a fiendish grin. That grin bespoke the words "Life sentence" or "Death penalty," but no such luck. Pointing his gavel at me, he pronounced the sentence through gritted teeth:

"You. Are. A mistake. Boy."

The dream ended. My eyes opened. Slowly, cautiously, still covered by my blanket, I peeked out of it. I scoured my sights around the darkened cell to see if there might be any donkey heads. I calmed. The coast was clear. No donkey heads.

I checked the clock. Just after 2 a.m..

On rare occasions, I did have lucid dreams, where in the dream I knew I was dreaming, but this one stood out like a souped-up pink Cadillac. I was shook. I had to write it down. I wrote many of my dreams down. That's what wannabe prison writers do, write.

The light filtering in from the hall provided insufficient light in the cell to read, but enough to write. I reached over and fumbled for the notepad on my desk, bumping the alarm clock and swiping a pen off in the process—then stopped.

A dark figure sat upright on Niño's rack, staring forward into nothingness.

"You are not a mistake, celly," Niño said, his voice calm to the point of death, his eyes looking straight on at the black and silent TV. "And I am not the only one who thinks this thing. Choco says so, too."

~

Perez died a few days later.

Details from the grapevine remained sketchy.

Understand, the prison grapevine is a real thing. Through the means of it, one catches wind not only of who's coming and going or what happened to Mick that one time the cops hauled him kicking and screaming to Solitary, but it's a way to gauge the atmosphere of the yard. Is the forecast stormy with a chance for gang warfare, or sunny with a chance for basketball?

Prison gossip is a grapevine that yields spoiled fruit on occasion, it's true. But in this instance two things were certain: a fight over a box of Nutty Buddys, and a man down.

Observably, the gangland affiliations dividing Toro and Perez on the outs did not extend, in the pen, to things like poker or spades. Not so Little Debbie. Perez came out the loser in the ensuing struggle over the box of dessert snacks. The rumors all leaned towards more of a skirmish than a fight. Sometimes fools land the wrong way or an underlying health problem ends up slamming harder than any fist. Perez's hands were found smothered in chocolate. He gripped those tasty treats until the moment he passed. Nice. Maybe that's why he lost. Death by chocolate, was the word on the yard.

Per the grapevine, this incident marked only the third time in the history of the low side an offender had said The Big Adios. It would go down in the annals as "The Nutty Buddy Knock-off."

The only good thing about the ensuing week's lockdown was the quality time it allowed me to spend with my celly, who went by the name *Harry Potter* now.

I slept, wrote and read. Niño watched TV. We made prison

spreads, Jack Mack, and burritos. They were bomb. "No wonder I'm such a good chef, Potter," I told him. "I learned from a Pisa."

"Potter!" Rinaldi from down the hall said after blowing into our doorway during one of the ten-minute pee and shower breaks. "Could you store me out some..." *stamps, deodorant, Ramens* "...I'll get you back, I promise."

"I know you will do this thing," Niño replied. "*Sí.*"

Freaky Freddy boasted a prison name, too. Sucrose. But I didn't call him that, no one did. Only *he* called himself that. He said, after stopping by to relay his message in person instead of yelling it through the wall, "Hey, Potter, think you can turn the volume down a little in there? Sorry about the racket the other day. Please don't curse and kill Sucrose. Sucrose is cursed enough as it is. Cassie his lady friend's been acting up and so is the hemorrhoid he and the guys discovered last week. Thanks."

Fergs and Fergs: "Hey, Tommy, think we can hang with you and Potter once lockdown's lifted? We'll help you smash some of that fish dish you guys made."

Rogue, our neighbor on the other side: "Whassup, Tommy. Whassup, Potter."

Readily receiving the ongoing gossip about Niño's "Magic Dance," and quickly making the connection to the death of Perez, the prison's gen pop merely acted in line with its recognized habit. Generally speaking, prison fosters belief. Boredom led us to read and think about things we had never read or thought about before. The chaplain told us to believe in a higher power. Our counselors encouraged us to believe in the most unlikely of all candidates: ourselves. We tried to believe in the greatest of all miracles: that we could change. Done right, a man will enter prison a man and leave a small, starry-eyed child filled with wonder at his brave new world.

The name "Harry Potter" meant Niño no longer classed as an outsider. It meant people had taken notice, and liked what they saw. It signified acceptance. Not every prison hotshot got dubbed, but it sure paid off in the currency of rep for those who did.

Toro kept his rep, sure enough. Toro means bull, love it or leave it. They loved it, and left him alone. Admin shipped him to the high side a week later anyway. Standard procedure. Fight. High side.

The one thing I did not enjoy about that one week of lockdown was, well, Choco. I gave that donkey bitch a wide berth. I stayed almost exclusively on my side of the room and avoided any and all eye contact with him, her, it, on pains of death.

CHAPTER FOUR

With lockdown behind us, my every intention was to pay a visit to Old Monty. It was high time I got with that fool. I was on a mission.

The problem with connecting with Old Monty was that he was housed in Building 2. Entry into buildings that weren't one's own was prohibited. It could mean a write-up. I was an angel when it came to shit like that, following the rules and whatnot, and so my plan involved meeting up with him on the yard during rec hours.

Monty always sat on the park bench at the north-side of the yard. Every day he arrived there around two p.m. after his shift in the kitchen had ended, then vegged like a heroin addict pretty much until sundown. The problem with Monty's bench was that in getting there you had to pass the b-ball courts. I would have to plan ahead, give myself a two-hour head-start knowing those courts were there, and homies would try to recruit me into their pick-up game or some cocky fool with half-a-brain and a sleeved-out left arm would challenge me to a rematch, guaranteed. I needed the exercise, anyway. I decided to just face the inevitable.

I set out with high hopes, a page-long list of interview questions, and already stretched legs. Passing through the day hall at noon that Friday, I noticed a new posting on the community board. Job assignments for the coming week.

"Tommy McConnell," it read about halfway down. *"Offender #173412. Work Crew 4. Start Date: August 8."*

Monday, that meant. Work Crew 4 put up fences for the county and dug in area graveyards. Digging holes to bury dead people. Wouldn't Celly get a kick out of that? Maybe he'd sic Choco on me.

But neither Choco, nor anything else, proposed to hold much sway once those courts came into view. Watson, our resident pencil portrait artist, owned the court, I noticed, as I set foot on it. He showcased some artistry there, as well, with his behind-the-back passes and sick handles. I had never played with Watson's homie before, but I knew of him. Pimp Daddy Mac. "A pimp on the streets," he clarified, as we bumped fists. I still couldn't get over how very chill fools seemed even though their reputation on the outs was killer. Things like encroaching parole-release-dates and ongoing applications to halfway houses tended to have that effect on people, I guess.

Pimp Daddy had a mean game, I could tell right away. His fade-aways and hard drives to the cup coursed as slick as a wet rubber. He was plain killin' it during warm-ups. But he was no Tommy McConnell, obviously. Still, he put his Rambo face on and thought he could beat me, just like a certain sleeved-out white boy did even after losing eleven games in a row.

We played rounds of twenty-one. I won the first game, Pimp Daddy won the second, I won the third, and Watson won the fourth. Wheh! I needed to get into better shape. Visoring my hand against the afternoon sun, I checked out the fools doing burpees over by the weight pile and along the walking trail; and it was then I saw him.

Old Monty.

I politely declined Watson's offer of a revenge game, bid the lads *adieu,* and set off to meet with Old School. I reminded myself this was it!

He didn't look seventy-four. His accompaniment slouched beside him on the bench featured wrinkles and spots aplenty, but not Monty. Black people aged well, I'd often noticed. How fitting. Maybe Greeley was right. Maybe this man really did harbor secrets.

Stepping closer, it became apparent Monty still looked old. Perhaps the angle of the sunlight on his face from that farther-off distance made him appear younger. I approached the park bench and just stood there, waiting for the old men to either notice me and pause their conversation or make me wait until it ran its full course. This process promised to take anywhere from five seconds to an hour. Once old timers got to shootin' the shit, there was just no stopping them. This was one of the many reasons why offenders over sixty were generally left on their lonesome. Prison is no country for old men.

Maybe their eyesight was dim. I chanced a step closer.

They noticed me, thank the gods!

I said nothing, at first, all the while I processed a quick character analysis. I studied the scraggly lines criss-crossing Monty's face, met with his brown eyes, and stood mildly amazed at how well his high cheekbones and salt-and-pepper hair had held out against the weather of years. Then I wondered what kind of brains might be hidden behind all of that, and what kind of man he might be generally.

He looked by all accounts like a decent man—for prison, anyway, to say nothing of his steam-pressed oranges and finely-combed hair. Bottom line, Monty appeared well groomed, and in prison there's actually much to be said about that. Besides, Old Monty had been a resident of P-Pen for a hot minute, and that he was now on the low side meant years, literal decades, of good behavior. Sometimes prison's worst turn out to be prison's best. Time heals. Time destroys. Time is a thing of wonder.

The next-door-neighbor man winked the sun out of his eye. "Cat got your tongue?" he quipped, grinning magnanimously at me. His blue eyes sparkled as he scanned me up and down.

I considered this odd old man then focused on Monty. I cleared my throat. "Henry Heck," I announced, all plain Jane like that, with my eyes on the Black man only.

Monty curved a smile that grew until his whole face was a smile. "Yes sirree. So, you're the one they've been telling me about. Come, have a seat beside me. Norm..." he said to the neighbor man.

Norm's eyes bulged as if he'd been struck. "You mean," he stammered, "you're gonna make me stress out my bad knee with havin' to get up then go knock off on the grass somewheres?"

"It would seem that way," Monty replied.

Norm kept his sights on me the whole while it took his rusty, angry joints to ratchet the rest of his members into their upright position. I supposed the purpose of that eye contact was to get me to physically assist him in his endeavor, but I just watched with feet firmly planted. I hate to stereotype, but I guessed "Norm" was a Chester Molester. Chomos didn't do particularly well in the prison system. However, the man's wrinkles and spots raised a standard in his defense. It was negative rep points to smash old people, and so the odds were probably in his favor he would die of natural causes and not otherwise.

Generally speaking, the ones who never smiled and the forever-smiling shit-eating-grinners wore the biggest warning labels. But none of that mattered now. Bad hip and wobbly knees took off at two miles-per-hour, and I claimed the man's spot beside Monty—after wiping the cooties off, of course.

"Well, then..." Monty said, his smile slackening a bit.

"Well, then," I repeated, at a loss for words suddenly. I reached into my pocket—not my prison pocket, my pants pocket—and withdrew my list of interview questions. "I have a few questions for you," I said, aware of some jitters. Maybe this was because I knew I might only have one chance at this.

Question #1: "I'm not going to take up too much of your time," I said. "So, I'll get right down to it. Does the Forever Young Prisoner really exist?"

Monty assumed a far-off look. The clouds overtop the Activities Building were showcasing in all sorts of original, funky, and puffy white ways. Maybe that was what he was eyeballing. I liked clouds, too, but this was no time for clouds. I coughed to try to get his attention.

Monty's hand twitched. I noticed this happened a couple of times. More to the point, it would tempt a lift upwards as if to steal a drag while he reflected. But, of course, that wasn't going to happen. "Well," he said finally, "maybe we should start from the beginning..."

Over the course of the next twenty minutes I learned a lot of things. I learned all about Monty's charges: he was a murderer, for realz. I learned that back in the late seventies offenders could smoke cigarettes, get girly mags, and introduce into their cells all sorts of items that nowadays would be contraband—"Like cigs!" he said, mentioning cigs for, like, the fifth time. I somehow got the feeling Monty had been a smoker. Truth be told, I was kinda jonesing for a cig myself.

I learned this Disneyland complex of ours—what they called the low side—didn't come into existence until 1983 and its original warden "was a major asshole." I learned the plumbing works and septic-tank systems in place in Drac's Castle were all replaced in the spring of '87, and that C.O.'s prior to, during, and since that time would sometimes disappear for months on end only to return with flimsy excuses like "took time off to be with my family. Speaking of families, it was the *Caniglio Family* that unofficially ran the joint back in the day," Monty noted.

No idea who *they* were, but that little bit of emphasis he placed on the words had me wishing I did. I opened my mouth to ask, but for my efforts got a continuation of Monty's spiel shoved down my throat.

I learned the warden who came in 1986 was a real sweetheart. All sunshine and lollipops at Drac's Castle. He was the one who ordered the overhaul of the plumbing system, re-caulked the castle's few windows, and relaxed the rules. He put the low-side warden in his place a few times then had him removed completely. He pretty much single-handedly ended the Caniglio Family's black hand of influence over the prison—for a time, anyway. Monty's few sources said these days it was actually "kinda hard to tell" who the string-pullers of the Guardians were. Overlap galore. The Family. The State. Special interest groups. The Feds, even, possibly. Everyone wanted to get their hands into this plate. "The old warden's name was Richards," Monty concluded by saying.

A sweetheart like none other, this Richards guy, to be sure. But Monty had yet to answer my question.

I repeated it.

He looked at me. "I don't know," he shrugged.

Question #2: "Officer Clayton," I said, reading from my notes. "Officer John Clayton. He died in 1984. Do you know—"

"Sure, I know Officer Harris," Monty said, flicking a nod. "Sam Harris, right o'er there. See him? And that's Officer Barkley standing right beside him."

I followed the direction of Monty's gaze. Sure enough, two cops stood in front of the Activities Building staring right at us.

Correction. One cop stood surveying the volleyballers. Officer Harris, Sam Harris, with his eyes gleaming underneath his blond crew cut, was the one eyeballing us. Naturally stout, and jacked in a measure that seemed entirely *unnatural*, he looked like a toad with a buzz cut.

With one-hundred yards between us, Harris and I exchanged glances. He looked displeased. He looked like The Hulk. Finally, slowly, he turned away.

Folding his hands, Monty said, "Yup, that's Harris. I've known that boy a whole lot better, and longer, than I'd known Officer Clayton. Clayton? That boy, he dead. Had himself a big ol' heart attack."

"Did he really, though?"

Monty shrugged. "I don't know. You tell me."

The interrogation of my chief witness was not proceeding quite as planned. In prison, everyone is a storyteller, and most every story is long and dull. But this particular string of answers in the form of off-subject banter and non-answers was starting to get on my nerves. The sun was shining, though. The breeze had a fresh, clean feel to it. It was a good day. I soldiered on.

Question #3: "You've been down for a minute, obviously. I've heard you're—"

"Getting paroled soon?" Monty lit up. "How'd you know?"

Good for him. Paroled. *You don't just cut fools off whenever they wanna say something*, I wanted to say. I could feel my rats-from-hell-side stirring around inside of me like a pregnancy. I felt like bashing, and smashing and...but Monty sat with his hands folded still giving me the time of day, and so what the hell was I thinking? Relaxing, I said, "You've been down for a minute, obviously..."

Monty didn't cut me off this time, he just angled his brown eyes.

I looked over.

Officer Harris again.

I looked away as soon as our eyes met. Something in his I didn't quite like.

Monty leaned back on the park bench. "His daddy worked the high side for three decades, you know. Retired in '07. If younger Harris o'er there knew what you and I was talking about right now he'd put your ass in the blender, just like Daddy Harris did mine. But, maybe you're made of better stuff than I was at your age." Monty patted my arm. "Oh, don't let that snarl of his scare you, son. Blue's just looking out. Ain't like he's gonna kill you." Monty scratched his chin. "Well, maybe. Black Hats gonna Black Hat."

"I'm not scared," I said, and wasn't. We weren't doing anything wrong, just black and white chillaxing on a damned park bench. "Kill me?"

"Well, it kinda mostly depends on how many answers you end up getting to these questions here..." Monty flicked a nod at my list. "I'm just sayin'." He leaned back. "Anyways, like I was saying, I'm gettin' out, sure enough. Paroled. Four decades and a lifetime later." He leaned forward and looked me in the eyes. "It's my little secret. Got a big one, too, and it's one I don't want leaving with me."

"Secret?"

"Look," Monty said, "instead of you asking your dumb questions, why don't I just tell you what I know."

Dumb questions.

I sat up on the bench. "That's tight, old school. Why didn't you say so?"

Monty said all at once, "Because I was too busy answering your dumb questions!" He took a deep breath. "But first, I wanna ask you some questions." He shifted around on the bench. "Question #1: Are you hard working?"

I blinked, repeatedly. This was highly irregular. "Uh, no. Well, maybe. On the outs I worked once for three whole hours at a Bed, Bath & Beyond. Another time I worked a construction gig through the temp agency for a day. I'm starting the work crew tomorrow. Properly motivated, I think I can do it."

"Are you honest, loyal?"

I laughed. "I'm here, dressed in orange. What do *you* think?"

"You're sayin' you're not motivated?"

I furrowed my brow. "Sure, I guess, when it comes to really important stuff like scrounging a meal or working up a good buzz."

"I mean, your investigation into this local legend of ours. Is it something you take seriously? Are you motivated about that? Purposed to see it through until the very end? At any and all cost?"

I said without hesitation, "Yes, fuck yes. It's the one thing I've got going for me right now. Maybe ever. I absolutely need to do this. It is my *stated goal.* If I fail, I'll be a homie without purpose, another Fatts. As much as lies within me, so help me God—"

"Good enough, although it sounds like you're doing it purely for selfish reasons."

He was actually right, in a way. But wrong in a way, too. "Besides, poor Henry," I said, and meant it. "A whole century in The Pit..."

Monty nodded as he turned to face me. "The library. Word from the grapevine back in the late eighties—this was a few years after Clayton—said that a man who fit Heck's description and whom nobody had ever seen before, and would never see again, made an appearance in the library. Not for very long." Again, Monty motioned to smoke his imaginary cig.

I sat silent for a moment. "Really?" I said, not sure if he was pulling my chain.

"Would I lie to such a highly motivated young man?" Perhaps the smile and tenor in Monty's voice hinted at sarcasm, but his eyes meant business.

I shifted around on the wood plank, anxiously. Libraries didn't kid around, and featured as my favorite places in all the world. Libraries and homelessness go together like cream and sugar, hip and hop, Wal and Mart. "What was he doing in the library?"

"Hanging out," was Monty's reply. "Reading. They held him there while a crew refurbished his cell. Library was under construction, too. We were shut down."

I probably could have asked a better question in response to that besides "Why was the library shut down?" but my mouth ended up saying that anyway.

"Plumbing issues," Monty answered, with a gleam in his eyes. He checked his watch. "Well, look at that time. I'm late for bingo." He rose.

Whether he was late for bingo was debatable; whether he was done rapping and ready to bail seemed clear enough. "Thanks, old school." I gave him a fist bump. "Did the grapevine say what he looked like?"

Already, Monty's spindly legs had made a break for it. He turned. "Blond hair. On the short side. Slim. In his twenties. Witnesses say he had a red blotch on his left cheek. Like a birthmark. That's all I can tell you."

I hesitated, then decided to get brave and ask, "Can you tell me who else is a Black Hat?" Suddenly, I remembered my other question.

"Oh, and who are the Guardians? You said something about Guardians. Are they the same as the Black Hats?"

But Monty kept walking.

"Thanks, old school," I said, keeping my seat.

"He had a difficult time talking at first," Monty hollered.

I hollered back, "What?"

Monty raised his voice even louder, "I said, that'll be five stamps for the hour of my time you just wasted!" He laughed. "Just kidding. Good luck with your mission."

He said it just like that: your mission.

I recalled my dream with its "mission" mandate from Trixie mama. Inconveniences, donkey heads, and dangers, be damned. Possibly, subconsciously, I had known all along it was time to get "motivated."

I scoured the premises for Harris, but he was nowhere to be seen. Sitting with my hands folded, it struck me I should have congratulated Monty on his parole. What a dick move not to. Maybe I really was a selfish bastard. A dumb one, too. I'd forgotten my pen again.

I stood. No worries, the implement in question reposed on the desk in my cell. I kicked up my prison tennies and headed home with renewed purpose. Writers write stuff down before they forget. Entering the day hall, I noticed to my surprise—or maybe not so surprisingly—none other than The Blue Hulk himself. Arms crossed, he stood convening with another officer whose building this wasn't, either. Harris kept his sights leveled on his cohort as I loitered by the micro for a moment then eased past, but you can bet your ass he knew the orange figure slipping by wasn't just anyone. Their conversation was all low tones, solemn looks, and nods, and difficult to figure. One word Harris kept tossing into the mix, though: *McConnell.*

CHAPTER FIVE

The Pit of Heck
The Year of our Lord 1943

Germany. The guards kept conversing about Germany. Germany this, and Germany that. The others contributed every now and again: anecdotes, questions, crude remarks, bouts of laughter, but the gangly jay with the hoarse voice did most of the talking. The knobby, hairy hand that slipped him his "meals" through the pass-through in the door twice a day belonged to this very man, Henry was sure. "Willie," they called him.

Germany, in a military context: tanks, bombs, machine guns, something called a "carrier," someone named "Himmler" or "Hitler" or some such.

Sufferin' catfish, is the war still on? Henry wondered, as he heard them blabber on about some island in Japan and an invasion of France.

The Germans took Paris it sounded like. Inconceivable.

Henry lay on his mildewed mat listening through the gloom of his cell to the guards in yonder staging area, corridor, or whatever it was out there. Honestly, he had no idea what lay beyond this reinforced metal door here. He listened, just as he had for the months, years, and decades prior. It seemed like only yesterday the judge had declared those forever words, "Guilty. Life without parole." But not yesterday. Ten-thousand yesterdays ago. Time stands still in prison, someone once said. No, the thoughts inside his own head had said that. Pining away in the shadows for years on end alongside roaches, spiders, and cold stone walls tended to produce in one's noggin quite the wonderland of thoughts, dreams, and fears. Henry could attest to that.

Now, Willie the Guard began talking about a "President Roosevelt," and that was when Henry stopped listening. Yes, President Roosevelt, but that was back in the days of Evelyn Nesbit and the building of the Panama Canal, back in the first decade. Simpler times, the Gilded Age, back when he was a boy. Surely Teddy had kicked the bucket by now.

Germany, Roosevelt, Nazis...never such banter as this before, Henry noted. Mind games, then. They were pulling the wool over his eyes, letting him overhear chatter about some never-ending war with Germany as a way to fiddle with him, crush his will, lower his mental capacities, and so maybe then he would forget what he had seen.

Henry ran his hand through his stringy blond hair. He slumped his narrow shoulders and breathed into the stale, musty air. He saw his breath. Chilly in here. Mind games. They're trying to fleece ol' Headhunter Henry.

OFF WITH HIS HEAD read the Boston Herald that one day.

SHUT UP AND PUT UP seemed to be the message nowadays.

But Henry could not shut up. His vocal cords, and heart, would flounder then fail if he didn't perform his daily ritual. He recalled a horse the family had once owned back at the farm in Smithfield that Father had named Blaze. Blaze came down with a rather debilitating case of colic and could hardly stand. When finally he could, his legs, wholly unaccustomed to walking, wobbled awfully until Uncle Jean had to put him down. *Horses are something fine, but are no more human than the rest of us,* as Henry liked to say.

"Mind games..." he winced at the sound of his odd, uneven voice echoing in the cement lair of cockroaches, cobwebs, and memories both good and evil "...are why these coarse fellows on the other side of the door grant me nothing but bread and water, why they leave me all alone in the dark, why they NEVER SPEAK TO ME FACE TO FACE LIKE MEN—" he said this part louder so the fellows out yonder might hear "—why they never let me see their guard faces, why...

"Why, why, *why*?" He stretched the curled ends of his handlebar mustache and peered up at a ceiling that fell flat and formless, the darkness obscuring any detail of it. Why me? Why this? Why...

Weren't his hair, mustache, or fingernails growing? Did his skin feel smooth and dapper after almost three decades? Did he never catch a sneeze, notwithstanding the dank and the chill?

Why had the governor and his entourage done this to him?

"Because I saw," he said, crestfallen. But such things were not to be dwelt upon. The past lay forever *in* the past. Not to suggest things like past, present, and future mattered so much anymore. Life, these days, featured as a never-ending Now. Henry's vocal cords felt loose and free at any event, and so maybe this was the time to say it. Henry sat up on his mat.

He breathed in, and out. He looked up. "And this," he said, "is all that I have to say in my defense this day."

"Slops up, murderer!" the hoarse-voiced one announced as his knobby, hairy hand pushed a platter of bread slices through the door. His captor spoke. How very queer.

Henry eyed his meal. *Oh, my, a slab of butter on the side*, he thought. A special occasion, that meant. Is it Christmas? Thanksgiving? The signing of some peace treaty with Germany? He squinted, his eyes straining to see through the semidarkness. He saw a note.

"Have a happy 50th birthday," it read. *"In hell."*

They laughed behind the door.

CHAPTER SIX

Lying face down with my nose mushed into my green exercise mat early the next morning, a thought struck me. Namely, that Monty's contributions to the Forever Young Prisoner legend hardly made sense.

The grapevine was sacred, tried, and true. Gossip was funneled down through a 647-offender-strong assembly line of truth seekers, devil's advocates, accomplices, and witnesses, all with their eyes peeled and brains switched on to determine whether a rumor was that and no more, or cold hard fact. The grapevine wasn't only inter-relational, but generational. Really important rumors got passed down. Here, the truth-seeking process forgave even less. However, over my nearly five months at P-Pen I had heard not a single mention about this library bit. Odd.

Sure, I'd ask around, but on the surface Monty's tip sounded sketchy. His hearsay presented me with one of three possible options: the grapevine had yet to clarify, the grapevine was wrong, or Monty lied.

Anyhow, time to rise and shine.

Niño said the weather lady on TV promised sunshine, so I donned my ball cap. After that, I slipped my work boots on, forgot to tie the laces, tied them, left the door open in the process, closed the door, woke Niño up, opened the door again and told him to leave the light on for me, closed the door, then down the hall I went for rubbery eggs and toast in the chow hall. After that, I was off to earn my keep in the fields of the Lord.

It wasn't just my first day on the job, but my first time outside the gates in five whole months.

I felt a surge of something—excitement, I guess—as I trod the path to a tin pavilion at the very edge of the property, our gate-side headquarters.

Names were roll-called and checked off on a list.

"Ferguson. Number 172934," the sergeant announced, scanning his sights.

Wiping the sleep out of his eye, Ferguson raised a finger in place of a hand. "Fuckin' here," he said, in a tired voice.

It was Fergs!

"Thomas McConnell. Number 173412."

I stepped forward and snapped a soldier's salute. "Here, *sir!*"

The others murmured and shook their heads. No sense of humor whatsoever.

I stepped over to Fergs while Sarge continued with roll-call. "You're new, too?"

Fergs shook his head. "Been here about a week now. Really liked mopping floors in Admin but...Every. Single. Fucking day. With my bro." He exhaled. "We needed some time apart. I'm my own person, besides."

"Damn straight," I said.

Then, just like that, we all hopped in a white van, no chains, no nothing, only Sarge with his 9 mm in case we tried to bolt, and cruised out of the gates and along Route 1 until we made it to some undisclosed location in the big, bright outside world. There were fields to see, traffic lights, trees, stores, towns, and of course, girls.

Even the old mangly ones promised to be hot stuff. And see them we did. One, on a bike, even waved back!

The guys seemed to warm up right away to my slick humor and snazzy retorts. No idea what they felt personally about my sorry ass, but anyhow they seemed to enjoy the entertainment. They were all stoked for me.

Low Key sat beside me in the van. He was, well, the most *low-key* about some Tommy fool's first day of pseudo freedom, although it was he who enlightened me as to the purpose of our stopover at the county building in East Greenwich, our tool and supply base. Here we donned our fluorescent vests and loaded up picks and shovels. We met some of the county workers there. No, we *saw* some of the county workers there. They didn't dare speak to the damned. Then, back in the van and off to the graveyard.

The gods only knew which one.

No matter, we were free!

As free as guys with a 9 mm on their minds ever could be, one might say.

As I gripped a shovel with my left hand, coffee with my right, and eyed the lands in front of us that were about to get all dug up by for-realz workingmen, I knew right then and there this was neither the time nor the place for those *slackers* back in their comfy cells.

Sergeant Brunansky served as watchdog extraordinaire, manager, and cheerleader. He barked, "Benson, Ferguson, McConnell, quit it with the joe and all that lollygagging. Get your vaginas out there and dig me some graves!"

Tools in hand, we got down and dirty.

The experience proved kinda dope, actually. Dividing my time between scooping up the land and scoping out the landscape for females, all the while talking smack with my new buds, was about as high times as it could get for a fool with a number. Although, it started to wear on me after the first hour, and so finally I took a break from scooping and just scoped.

"Which is cool," Benz explained, after he stepped over to check out my progress on the sun side of the hole. "It's okay to take a breather, Sherlock. No one can dig for five hours straight."

Twelve of us dug. Benz possessed that telltale brand of narrow-eyed arrogance and aloofness which was nothing if not Aryan. Hard to believe he wasn't affiliated. He wore the pants on the crew as the unofficial work lead. Joey was as pale as he was pudgy with soft, formless arms that fell off his shoulders like sausages. I knew his type, more crazy-weird than criminal. Think Freaky Freddy, but with a cowlick that wouldn't quit. Bad luck seemed to follow those guys. Felize and Diaz were Spanish homies, obviously. Felize kept to himself, but Diaz would shoot the shit with us. Cali was the only Black homie on the crew, and pretty chill, at least that first day. Lions and Fergs looked swole the one no less than the other, and were getting it in like bosses with that spade and rock-bar. Had I to guess, they were in for breaking and entering. They sure knew how to break up those rocks!

I was likely the only one with violents. The litmus which determined here was point totals, not the charge itself. I boasted only one violent in contrast to their six or seven, say, non-violents.

The remaining four offenders teamed up on the grave a few rows down. Fewer rocks over that way so less manpower needs. I didn't catch their names, except for Low Key.

Sarge stood watch and dallied us with snide remarks veiled as encouragement, all the while he sipped his iced coffee. From time to time he favored us with words of explanation about the task at hand.

The spring rains had taken their toll on Forest Cemetery, Sarge set forth, with all of the colorless formality of the military man that he had once been. And a toll, especially, on a few of the older, wooden coffins. The runoff had overwhelmed the drainage ditches and the water had seeped. These older coffins stood at risk of water damage. The interred residents hadn't the means to complain, so a local environmentalist had lobbied on their behalf. The county board agreed. Hence our task.

For five hours her headstone displayed in my face:

Margaret Ronsellier. Born 1895. Died 1917. Wife and Mother. Gone too soon, the gravestone read.

I had shitty coffee that was still coffee, homies to work the good earth with, sunshine, fresh air, a knobby old oak tree spreading its branches over us like an umbrella, and cars whizzing by on the road a ways off. This was special. The only thing missing was some females—living ones though.

The guys said the honeymoon would wear off by about the third day.

"Here's another boulder for you, Fergs," Cali said.

Fergs sighed. "This is gotta be the rockiest hole we've dug so far." He sauntered over with his rock-bar.

I laughed. "Maybe ol' Margaret lived a rocky life, or met some kind of rocky end. *Gone too soon,* it says."

It wasn't the rocks that bothered me. Of course, my task lay in scooping not smashing. It was the smoldering heat and humidity. Not to suggest the cool breeze from the ocean just a few miles away didn't make things slightly more tolerable.

Backpedaling from the hole to join Cali and the others, we watched as Fergs smashed away at a rock the size of a beach ball. Finally, after a long succession of strikes, it cleaved in two.

Fergs let out a breath and swiped his brow. I stepped over to stand alongside him at cliff's edge. "Two rocks now, instead of one," I said, with our gazes spiraling downward. "They're their own rocks, now."

A slow smile stretched across Fergs's face. "Damn straight, Sherlock."

I thought about Danny just then, and how this time apart was allowing me to be my own person, too, for once. Sherlock?

Lunch break was taken over by the van. Sarge swung the back doors open. With our fluorescent-yellow uppers seated in the vehicle and our orange legs dangling out, we enjoyed our bologna sandwiches and chips. The fools digging the other grave arrived late so they had to make do with seats on the water coolers or grass.

Was this what they referred to as livin' the dream? Pretty sure it was.

Benz rambled on about his adventures with Laura from Foxboro, the X-rated version, with no sight, sound, or smell detail left unrehearsed, when I saw her.

No, not Laura from Foxboro, who according to Benz had short dirty-blonde hair.

This woman had long black hair.

On the very verge of shooting some sly remark like "Target sighted: eleven o'clock!" I realized this woman seemed a little, well, different.

She stood stock still with her feet planted together, right beside that mound of soil and stone we had just shoveled.

Staring right at me, her pretty, young face looked devoid of any expression.

"What's the matter, cuz?" Diaz said, while Benz rambled on about motel rooms in Foxboro, which only Lions seemed to be listening to at this point. Out of the corner of my eye, I noticed the others dividing glances between myself and our worksite area.

"You see a deer?" Sarge asked. He took a bite of his chicken sub. "They've got the premises covered, those buggers do. They're everywhere."

She's got a long white dress on, I wanted to say. *Dark hair. She's standing right the fuck in front of us, not fifty feet away, looking at me with those dark, haunting, starry eyes. Don't you see her?*

They didn't, clearly. Seven or eight fools all staring in the same direction and all of them featuring the same everyday expression on their face.

I decided at length to plead the fifth, thinking they might stuff me into the back of the van with Joey otherwise. Crazy Joey. Crazy Tommy. Possibly, Sarge might even file paperwork requesting I be transferred to that special facility in Cranston for the legally insane. Crazy's the last thing you wanna be in prison. To see something wild is one thing. To see something wild no one else can see…yeah, those are the ones who end up in Cranston. The subject of "belief" aside, the line between Niño's "magical" and Cranston's "crazies" oftentimes proved razor thin. I wasn't about to test that line.

I swallowed. Addressing Benz, I said, "I think I just saw a deer."

I looked back—and the woman was gone.

On our slow walk back to the worksite, Fergs said, "Hey, maybe it was the same deer who hopped the fence that one time and stopped by to say hi to you. Remember?"

"Deers are hella common," I replied. "You heard Sarge." I scanned the premises for possible signs of disturbance as we neared but nothing looked out of place. I was shook. I could hardly shovel, my hands trembled so much. On a side note, peeps on meth sometimes claimed to see what are known as *shadow people*. Lilya saw one once, too. I never did. Then this happens.

You might not think that a guy who had once read *War and Peace* cover to cover, and mostly by flashlight, would suffer from a mild attention-deficit issue, but it's the straight truth. An hour later I was digging, laughing, and talking smack with the guys like nothing had ever happened. A deer, and nothing besides. However, and to be completely honest, the alternative made for all sorts of uncomfortable conclusions, and so maybe that also was why I blotted the lady in white clear out of my mind.

We struck wood an hour later. Lions lowered his spade. "You think ol' Margie will mind if we dig in around the sides of her coffin here? To loosen her up a bit? It's barely noon. I haven't even broken a sweat yet."

Sarge made known that once the veneers of Margaret Ronsellier and Guido Adinolfi's casements had been breached, our orders were to pack up our things and head back to base. It was the county's responsibility to dislodge and excavate the coffins then transfer the mortal remains to new coffins. Our job was simply to "clear off the crust."

"Bye, Margie," the guys joked through the back window of the van. "Rest in peace, Marge ol' girl."

"So, Sherlock," Benz asked, as we sped along Route 1 past fields, lakes, and a BMW with its top down and two ladies wearing sleeveless shirts in the cab, "what'd'ya think of your first day on the outs?"

Sherlock.

Fergs, Lions, Diaz, and now, Benz, had all called me that. It seemed obvious enough Harris hadn't been the only one who had noticed Monty and me on that park bench. The whole yard probably knew by now.

I marked it down on my prison calendar once I got back to the cell. *August 8th. Received new prison name.*

"One of the dopest days of my whole life," I replied to Benz's question. But of course, I often talked out of my ass. By tomorrow, it could be the worst day. No, my worst day had already staked its claim. Thanks, Fatts and Trixie.

"Hi, honey, I'm home," I said, bursting through the cell door and flinging my ball-cap to the four winds.

Niño sat with wide eyes on his rack. He wasn't alone. Seated at my desk, and engaged, seemingly, in a rousing heart-to-heart with my celly, was a personage I had seen around but didn't know by name. Actually, I wanna say his name was Weasel. Maybe not, but he kind of reminded me of one. Let's call him Weasel.

I plopped down on my rack. Untying then shedding my boot, I said to our visitor, "Henry Heck, I presume?"

Shifting around in his chair—my chair—Weasel blinked. "No, I am not Henry Heck." He looked hard at me. "Henry Heck...is a lie. A conspiracy. He doesn't exist. Only, the government wants me, you, and your mother to *think* he exists so they can control us."

I cocked my head. "How that?" I blinked. "Wait, what was that about my mother?"

"The criminal, deceitful, generational, crazy, *bloodsucking* powers that be," Weasel replied, eyeing the ball-cap on the floor by his foot, "wanna control you, me, everybody. *Control* is what they want."

I untied my other boot. "Right on," I said. "Ever been on the high side?"

Weasel lifted his chin. "I have."

"Ever hear of the Black Hats?"

Weasel said he had not.

I reached for my prison sneakers. "Ever hear a rumor connecting the Forever Young Prisoner to the prison library?"

The man pursed his lips. "No." He turned to my celly. "So, Potter, like I was saying...three stamps and three Ramens if you help me out. Listen..."

Proximity and chance forced me to have to listen in on their convo, too, unfortunately.

But first, a quick word about the Jesus peoples. See, although they were generally welcomed and respected for their oftentimes good intentions, the frequent ministry visitors to the yard with their tracts and free Bibles tended to yield results in one of two forms. One, offenders who received a sting of hope that lasted all of five minutes. And two, offenders who received a sting of hope that lasted all of five minutes then for five months afterward talked God smack. Weasel seemed to be the latter.

He explained his predicament and set forth his proposal. Roundhouse and Killjoy over in Building 3 had his ass in a wringer over non-payment of a poker debt, and so he was wondering if Potter, with his ways and means, might be so good as to "smite" them for him. "I could really use your help, Potter, please."

Folding his hands, Potter pondered. "This thing I cannot do," he said.

"Why the hell not? Look, once those fools get smitten, I can get back to the poker tables. Then, once I start winning again—which I sure as fuck will—I'll get those Ramens and stamps over to you. I promise, Potter. I swear on my kids!"

Two things: never swear on your kids, and never, ever trust an offender who swears on his kids. Ten to one this fool didn't even have kids.

With his head bowed, Potter said, "The curse could backfire."

"*Backfire*," I leaned over and repeated at Weasel.

Potter looked up. "I would say, and I think Choco would agree with this thing, that you should pay your prison debt."

"What if I can't?" the guy whined.

"Then pay in blood." I rose.

As much as I wanted to stay tuned for the riveting conclusion of "Potter the Smiter," I had some business to take care of. Potter could handle this situation on his own. He was the Big Man on Campus now.

"*Four* stamps and *four* Ramens..." the guy wailed.

"Cool story, bro," I said, closing the door behind me.

I noticed the showers were all taken. Tight. Just the excuse I needed to go for a walk to the Admin Building, finally. It was high time.

~

"Records department, please," I said, stepping up to the reception desk with a middle-aged lady with glasses and graying blonde hair seated behind it.

"Excuse me?" the lady said.

I cleared my throat. "Could you transfer me to your records department?"

The lady looked over her shoulder, "He wants to be transferred to our records department, Don."

A few paces behind the lady, a C.O. stirred. He stood beside a large filing cabinet holding a sheet of paper in one hand and a jelly doughnut in the other. Turning, Officer Shumpert revealed himself. Shumpert manned the library. He was the very copper who had recommended *Brave New World* to me. Not a bad read. I stood ever on the lookout for new titles. New old titles.

"That's McConnell," Shumpert said. "What sort of trouble you in now, McConnell?"

I stood straight and tall. "Henry Heck's case file, please. I want it."

The lady smirked and shook her head. "Don't we all." She returned to her typing. Moments later, she looked up. "He isn't going away, Don."

My eyes scoured the small office. Filing cabinets hunkered, with two of the largest ones standing sentry just outside of a doorless entryway that led to some back room. "Isn't there some little room around here..." I asked, looking straight at it, "with shelves, cabinets, boxes, and folders with offender case files in them?"

The lady pointed to her computer. "Right here. All information about offenders is in the system. If an offender isn't in the database, he isn't in this prison."

Shumpert closed the drawer of one of the filing cabinets and stepped over. "There *is* a room like that in back, McConnell. But like Muriel says, everything over *there* has been entered in *here*." He nodded at her computer.

"Can you look him up for me, then?" I shoved my hands in my pockets. "See, Henry Heck's the man of my dreams." I brightened. "The guy in my dream with the glasses—is him, I just know it. I have to find him. It's my mission. If I don't, donkey heads will attack and bite me. That is, if the Black Hats don't catch and slaughter me first."

Muriel eyed me, darkly. "I cannot," she said in a low voice. "For security purposes, we're prohibited from releasing information about other offenders. However, it's all public information. Have a friend or relative on the outs look it up for you."

"Danny," I said.

Muriel furrowed her brow.

"Onofrio—is who he probably means," Shumpert put in. "His buddy, and partner in crime."

Muriel sighed. She removed her glasses. "Actually, what I can tell you, Mr. McConnell, and off the record of course...Mr. Heck is not in the system. Believe me, you would not be the first who's punched those letters H-E-C-K into that database search field. Besides, Henry Heck, supposing he even exists, would be in Supermax. That's on the high side. The high side has their own records department."

Shumpert leaned in. "She's right. And if you don't trust computers, file what is known as a Freedom of Information Act request. You'll need someone on the outs do it for you. The prison's records crew will sort through all those folders you mentioned and photocopy the paper records you need. Write the offender's name, and say you want his full case file. The prison will mail the record to you. Federal law, under FOIA, requires we do so."

Muriel narrowed an eye at the officer.

"Tight," I said. "Maybe Lilya can do that for me."

Muriel cocked her head. "Oh, is she a little friend of yours, too? Such a pretty name. My sister-in-law's name is Lilith."

"Lilya," I said, "...is a crackhead. I'm a crackhead. Danny's a crackhead. We're all crackheads. All cracked up, too." I eyed Blue. "How about you, Shumpert? You a crackhead?"

"Watch yourself, McConnell." He chomped on his doughnut then wiped the powder off of his lips. "By the way, did you enjoy that book by Aldous Huxley I recommended?"

I nodded. "I liked that part in the end where the guy goes crazy and dies. Society, love it or leave it. He left it. Anyway, thanks." With my hand on the door, I turned. "May the Force be with you. Always."

More than just a human freak show, Freaky Freddy really knew how to hightail his fat ass. He snagged the last available phone in the day hall. Had I been there five seconds earlier I would've dialed that ass in and told him to go kick rocks, but he already had the phone to his ear. His path over from the micro spanned farther than mine from the stairwell, but he also knew how to play the jackass and make a dash for it. He sat talking to his girl. Waiting my turn, I got a lowdown on their convo.

Boy meets girl. Boy dates girl. Boy goes to prison. Girl gets lonely and gets some play on the side. Boy catches wind. Girl denies, says she can't wait for boy forever, when's he gonna get out? Boy says soon. Girl says uh-huh. Boy says no, for realz. Girl says see ya. Six months in the pen, and already I had heard this exchange maybe a dozen times.

Finally, Freddy got off the phone.

I dialed the number, entered my code, and sat sighing, forced to endure the automated connection process. "Danny," I said, "Need you to do something for me, bro. Is Lilya there?"

"Tommy! Where the hell's you been, bro? We be missin' your ass. C'mon over and hang. We got the whole crew here...Babbs, Rand, Remy, Sherry, Larry, Mephisto..." Danny lowered his voice "...and a few others you don't know but might wanna, if you know what I mean. We got skittles, bammies, pebs, brews—"

"Shut up, Dan," I said, "This line is bugged. Are you high?"

Dumb question.

"As the fuckin' sky, homes!"

"Well, is Lilya there?"

"Hi, Tommy," Lilya said. "We've got you on speaker phone right now."

"Lil, that you? Whassup? Listen, I was wondering if you'd be able to...hey, think you could get us off speaker phone for a sec so I can get in a word edgewise over Grand Central back there?" After some clanging, clamoring, and rounds of arguing, the background noise lowered. "Better," I said. "Look, remember that one night when ClownAround borrowed that convertible from that parking garage and even though you'd never driven before, you tried, and nearly ran me over and said afterward you owed me for that one?"

Lilya muttered something in the affirmative.

"Well, along Henry Heck lines, I was wondering if you could file on my behalf what is known as a FOIA. That stands for—"

"Freedom of Information Act. Been there, done that. Sure, I can do that for you, but not," she said, "because I owe you."

Arguably, it was because Lilya was the northside drug-world's answer to Betty White. But maybe, too, because she considered me a friend? "You have? You can? I mean, you will?"

"Sure. ClownAround's been in trouble a few times, as you well know. Once, his lawyer shared with us about FOIA. It's just a letter. So, you want me to write a letter to the prison and request copies of any paper records they have on Henry Heck?"

The gods were good, Lilya was on the ball tonight. "Yeah," I said. "Also, have Danny look up a website called the Inmate Locator. Tell him to punch in the name 'Henry Heck.' Also, see if there are any other Henrys at P-Pen."

"I already did all of that—I mean, he already did...all of that," Lilya said. "Danny already did all of that. Danny be looking out for his best bud, always. You know that."

My best bud, sure, who was seemingly wasted all of the time nowadays. Although, it struck me the sentiment cut both ways. A quick travel back in time with a look in the mirror might've told me that. Meanwhile, someone else—with dangly earrings and high heels—kept the ball rolling. "What'd you guys find out?"

"Henry Heck's not in the database, Tommy. Nothing. Now, there is another Henry at P-Pen. I don't remember his full name, but I have it written down, hold on..." the silence on the other end suggested Lilya went to go look; moments later she returned "...Ortego. Henry Ortego. Age 35. Brown eyes. Black hair. Burglary and menacing charges. I don't think that's the guy we're looking for."

We.

"Prolly not. Well..."

"I'll mail that request and let you know. It'll take me five minutes. Who wouldn't for a friend who's in prison? Hell, for *anyone* in prison I'd mail a letter if they went out of their way to ask. That's just the kind of person I am."

I pursed my lips and nodded at the phone. "Thanks. Lil, I know. We need more Lilya Jenkinses in the world. We're pretty good friends, though, too, right? How the hell you been, by the way? Gettin' some high times in?"

"Always." Lilya giggled. "Nah, just here to enjoy the scenery, more like. All these high times are starting to wear on me a little. I'm thinking of beginning a new phase in my life, maybe get a job."

Easier said than done, sister. But good for her, I guess.

Lilya went on, "There's a nail salon at Walmart that's hiring…"

I could think of nothing to say to that except, "Lil…"

"Yeah, Tommy?"

"Thanks."

CHAPTER SEVEN

Freaky Freddy cursed, moaned, and crashed his head against the wall late into the evening, dissing "Cassie," "Cass," and whatever other pet names for his girl he could sneak into the long strings of profanity he insisted on reeling off. *Ni modo*, Potter kept shrugging. Lucky for Freaky Freddy's fat face, hemorrhoid, and active vocabulary, he owed us one. However, Freaky Freddy's fluster had nothing on what was on its way to meet yours truly.

Fluster Friday started off innocently enough. I woke up, and opened my eyes. The clock read 4:58. Then the weirdness began when I realized it wasn't the alarm clock that had roused me but a dream.

In the dream I'd seen a clearing; in the clearing a deer, standing with its neck swiveled to scope me out. This was no ordinary deer. The deer's head, face, and eyes displayed in the form of a woman. I couldn't discern these features overly well, although I noticed she had dark hair.

"Not a deer," Niño said.

I cried out in fear. My dream had left an indelible impression upon my nerves. I looked over. Niño lay on his side: his eyes fell unblinking upon me. "Don't you ever sleep?" I asked.

"Yes, whenever you do not wake me from sleep with your loud voices."

Exhaling, I fell back onto my mat. "What did I say this time?"

"Not a deer. You cry out this thing, loud. What does it mean, this not a deer?"

"It means I'm wack, celly." I pulled the covers over my head. "Earplugs. They sell 'em on commissary. Order yourself a pair if my loud voices in the night bother you."

"Oh, no, they no bother me."

I was afraid he'd say that.

Fridays meant cereal for breakfast. You can't go wrong with cereal. Oh, yes, you can. Powdered milk, for one. Bad company for another. The Twins, Lions and I were joined by Low Key, who claimed he had the shits and planned to request a lay-in. Low Key offered some airborne test samples in case we didn't believe him. Fergs and I told him to get his ass on the shitter and the hells away from the cereal section.

So, we were down a man. And for this day's assignment that meant recruiting a volunteer from another crew with surplus work-ers, which turned out to be Work Crew 2.

The crew captain read the volunteer's name off of his list: D'An-gelo. That sounded familiar, but I couldn't quite pin a face to the name.

No worries. He recognized me straight off.

"Hey, it's Robin," Sammy called out. "Robin the Hood!"

Sammy D'Angelo, from way back in those dark days when I was still struggling to make ends meet with the carpet lint from Fatts's trailer still freshly wedged into the soles of my Adidas. Blow me. I had hoped my teenage street name wouldn't catch wind, and here it created a whirlwind, of knee jerks and laughter. The guys got a kick out of ol' Robin the Hood. There's a certain rep attached to that name, of course, and not a very grown-up one. I was a working man now.

"Yeah," Sammy told the guys, "Back in the day, Robin would slink around in his black hoodie and MJ shorts, scoping the alleyways for loose change, and dumpster divin' for chicken bones, Mickey D's leftovers, and most importantly, panties to whiff." The guys roared at that one, and although it fell far short of the truth, I decided to let it slide for the sake of their good time. "Those were the days, huh, Robin?" Sam said.

"Sure," I said. "Call me Sherlock."

Sammy clapped me on the back. "Okay, Sherlock." He'd been a skinny kid back in the day, and years later modeled the same wiry limbs and staggery gait. The goatee compensated, but only in passing.

In the van, Sammy asked if Work Crew 4 really got it in or was one of those pretend-to-work crews.

The question got spoken my way, so I answered. "Mon, Tues, and Wens we dug graves, yesterday we put up fences, and today we'll pick up trash on the highway. Right, Sarge?"

"Affirmative." Sarge gripped the steering wheel. "Can't tell you where, though." He adjusted his rear-view mirror to get a better vantage of my killer good looks. "Actually, I could tell you, McConnell, but then I'd have to shoot you."

I loved it when Sarge talked dirty.

We coasted for landing in the breakdown lane alongside the island sandwiched between the north and southbound lanes of I-295. Our requisite neon vests with the words "Providence Penitentiary - Inmate" stamped on the back was to inform citizen drivers we were dangerous criminals, not random luckless guys on the highway in search of an Uber.

Sarge dispatched us after sharing the details of our assignment. "Pickers and sacks are in your hands, vests are on your back, water's in the van, and bologna sandwiches are in the cooler. Now, stop actin' all brand new. Get your vaginas out there and pick up some trash!"

We plodded along in groups, scouring for beer cans, napkins, wrappers, and bottle caps along the way...and unofficially for un-smoked cigs, joints, batteries, and anything sex-related. Some of the guys like Joey and Cali journeyed alone. I paired with Sammy and Fergs.

As we coursed the fairway just beyond Exit 6, Sammy wanted to shoot the shit about old times, and all too often that meant rubbing me the wrong way with reminders of the foster parents. "So, how the hell are Fatts and Trixie?" he came right out and asked.

"How the fuck am I supposed to know?" I snatched up another scrap of newspaper with my pincers. "I haven't seen them in fucking forever."

"You never went back home?" Sammy asked. "Never?"

I indulged Sammy with some history, just to get him to shut his trap. Some of the history he knew, some he didn't. Fatts had issues, I explained. Fatts owned a baseball bat, I explained. My legs and arms got clobbered one too many times, I explained. My nose got broke three fucking times. Trixie was bipolar and a passive-aggressive who well into her thirties was still cutting. Fatts didn't shower.

Suddenly, a dark voice from behind us said, "Go ahead and say that word one more time, peckerwood. Just go ahead. Say it. Go right ahead."

I turned. Cali's eyes burned, nostrils flared, and forehead creased in rows of anger lines. He looked salty.

Fergs swallowed. "Tommy wasn't referring to you, Cali," he said, anxiously. "He was talking about his foster dad, not you, or your gang. It was a mistake. Tommy, you need to be more careful about what you say," he said to me.

It was then I remembered gangs have insult words for rival gang members. These are the absolute worst insults you can float a rival gang member's way. They act as trigger words, and perform like magic. Supposing the word "Fatts" featured as Cali's gang insult word, then damned if I wasn't David Copperfield ten times over.

I cleared my throat. "We weren't talking about you, Cal. That's my foster dad's name. Well, that's what I call him. For realz. I didn't even know you were in a gang. We cool?" I extended my fist.

Cali narrowed his eyes at me.

"I'm sorry." I extended my fist farther in his direction. "No disrespect. We cool?"

"I don't want your *sorry*," Cali said. "Sorry means you've got something to be sorry about." Visibly relaxing, Cali bumped my fist. He pointed his finger. "Say that stink around me again, though, and you'll have *red* to remember me by. Red dripping from your nose, your mouth, and who the fuck knows where else. Got it?"

"Sure, homes," I said.

It was a mistake.

Cali wandered off to hunt down a cellophane wrapper by the roadside, while Sammy, Fergs, and I ambled down the fairway back at it with our sacks and poles.

I tried to redirect the course of our conversation into some safe haven like how good pizza sounded just then or jokes about our mutual friend, Chet Broussard, who used to forage the same dumpsters I did, but this invariably led to talk again about the past and the very one subject I wanted to avoid.

The only difference between our present and previous convos was the labels "foster dad" and "foster mom" were used in place of the names themselves. Even Fergs joined in on the shit-show. He asked how my foster dad had fucked up my mind to the point I had chosen to skip the free meals at the shelters to go dumpster diving. Dumb question. A minor would get spotted, tagged, reported to the police, and returned to his caretakers. They made their remarks, and asked their dumb and dumber questions. With each round of Q&A my answers grew terser, and shorter, and my fists clenched tighter, until my nails burrowed into my palms.

The last straw came with Sammy's remark about seeing Fatts at a Dunkin' Donuts two summers ago with message relayed, "Come back home, son, your ass-kicking's long overdue." Fatts and sarcasm never meshed well, which told me he meant it.

All riled up, I saw my chance. A mistake, sure, yet a convenient one. Just yesterday, the idea had sprouted the seedling of a vague plan, and today, already, an avenue for its fruition. Thank the gods! Moments later, I rustled up some lame excuse to separate from the group. I tracked Cali down, approaching him from behind. His bald head and broad shoulders bobbed in time with his long, hunkering strides. I didn't need a tailor to tell me this man wore extra-larges. But no matter. My inner maniac kept screaming. And I knew of only one way to get the inner maniac to stop screaming.

"Hey," I said.

Cali froze in his tracks, but didn't turn around.

"Hey!" I said, louder, approaching.

When finally Cali did turn, I could tell straight off he knew exactly why I had decided to stop by.

"What the actual fuck is wrong with you?" I said. I let him know that common sense should tell a homey when other homeys are talking about a fool and when they aren't. I told him threatening people on a goddamn work crew was bad manners. I hadn't known he ran with a gang, I explained, and said he'd better watch his ass.

Cali smiled, especially at that bad manners bit. However, his eyes were not smiling. They just glared at me, while his lips remained sealed. Clearly no stranger to encounters of this sort, his cool flustered me for a second.

But only for a second.

I pointed my finger in his face. "Watch yourself."

"Get that shit outta here!" he said, slapping my hand away. I'd struck a nerve. I could see all of his coolness dissipate before my very eyes. Only fractions of time stood between him standing there and moving to do something stupid like swing—in which case I would have my excuse.

"Now, you listen to me," I said, "and I'm only going to say this once—"

"No, you listen to me, you punk ass little..." And then, Cali said the word.

In prison, this word spotlighted as the worst insult you could fling at another offender. It functioned as a call to arms, a battle cry, a trumpet call. The b word.

Sarge arrived on the scene like gangbusters. Never in a million years would I have dreamed that old man could run so fast. "Stop this, stop it, both of you," he hollered. "Break it up! You'll both be written up, I promise you."

A written warning would have seemed more appropriate. Nothing really had happened. Still, I understood Sarge's point of view. With maybe a dozen eyewitnesses from the community whizzing by, the program's reputation and effectiveness might be formally brought into question. Not that that really concerned me; I had myself to worry about. But the thought did cross my mind, for whatever reason.

Fergs, Sammy, and Benz waited for me by the van after we had picked up to head "back to base."

Fergs said, "You're not just gonna let him say that to you, are you, Tommy?"

"You're not just gonna take that lying down?" Benz narrowed his eyes at me.

No, and, no.

By this point, Cali and I looked slated to rumble. But when? I already knew where. My ticket to the high side lay all but in hand.

Hells, nah, not at the damned *library*. Libraries promoted the pleasant assurances of peace, sacredness, and neutrality. Still, Saturday morning meant a trip to the prison library for some fresh reads.

The library crammed its squarish frame into the east-side of the Education Building. The building's west-side housed the various classrooms where courses like "Intro to Construction," "GED," and the "Getting Out" program went down. A relatively new construction, the building showcased splashy bay windows and green paint.

Officer Shumpert greeted me at the door.

The elderly librarian, Mrs. Townsend, waved hello from her desk in her office.

Her chief assistant, Levesque, stretched his arm across the checkout counter to give me a handshake. Librarian positions were Cadillac jobs, and the more polite and clean-cut you presented yourself the better your chances of rustling one up. Levesque was that in spades. The gods only knew what he did to inherit his chain.

I felt wholly in my element, the king of the world, as I promenaded down the fiction aisle towards the Classic section in the way back. Who knew what adventures awaited me inside of whatever book I chose next.

I scanned the titles with their colorful, decorative bindings. Officer Shumpert passed by with his own suggestion, *The Great Gatsby*, but I'd already read that.

Finally, I decided on *Wuthering Heights*. Even though I felt like the king of the world just then, I knew by the end of the day I might be the king of pain. A gangster who wore extra-larges, Cali probably knew how to fight. Fights rarely ended in death, but sometimes they did. Ask Perez.

Wuthering Heights was chick lit, according to Lilya, and so what better way to try to atone for all of my crap treatment of women over the years by using not a few of them for sex and drugs, than to read their magnum opus or whatever you wanted to call it. A quickie read as atonement for all of my quickies, one might say. *Fuck*, I thought, scrolling pages. No quickie read here. Oh, well. Guess I had a lot to atone for.

Levesque processed my selection at the checkout counter. As he studied with curiosity its cover, it struck me I should ask him.

"Ever been on the high side?"

"Years ago." Levesque snapped my book closed and handed it over.

"Ever hear a rumor connecting Henry Heck to the prison library? Somebody I know told me someone saw him there once."

Levesque furrowed his brow. "I'd not heard that one, and I was on the high side for almost two years." He blinked at me. "Who told you this?"

"Just a guy," I said, "who was probably lying. Cheers." I walked.

"Wait—" Levesque called over, freezing me in my tracks by the magazine rack. I retraced my steps to the checkout counter. "Yeah," Levesque said, "I did hear something about that, now that you mention it. My celly in Pod 3 was old school. He said something about how back in the day some fool said he'd seen Henry Heck; although, I don't remember if it was in the library or not. But then he denied it a few days later. He recanted. He said he'd lied. He said it was a joke."

"Some joke. Remember anything else?"

Levesque shook his head.

Back at the cell, I dropped my masterpiece of 19th-century literature off on my mattress. *For later*, assuming I survived. I removed my sneakers and exchanged them for my work boots. Never wear sneakers to a fight if you've got an upgrade.

Niño lay on his rack. I hadn't even noticed him.

"Where do you go in your work boots?" he asked.

"I'm off to see the wizard." I tied my laces good and tight. "And you?"

Niño blinked. "Saturday, yes? No work time for Niño. I just watch TV. Look..." he pointed at the buttered rolls and reddened lobster tails with butter dripping off of them. Red Lobster commercials hailed as the purest form of misery, I had come to conclude. From time to time, Niño and I laid in our racks and chatted about what meals we might enjoy once we got out. Lobster always seemed to top the list. However, the convos usually bludgeoned the nerves more than settled them. "Oh, how I am wanting for a plate of these jumbo shrimps. The melted butter. The side of—"

"Shut yer trap, celly!" I blared. "Don't need that shit right now." I slammed the door.

Then, I remembered Choco and that pre-trial advice about showing loved ones I cared.

Opening the door, I said, "Sorry, Potter. You'll get yours."

Potter nodded and smiled. Such a good boy, who deserved ten jumbo shrimps.

I had told Benz "high noon, the park bench in front of the Activities Building." Ever on time for digging graves and scrounging for trash, he was late for the main event. I sat there, watching the world go by. The prison version of it anyway. Mostly, I watched the pickup game on the b-ball courts. Watson continued with his Globetrotter routine as the wannabees circled aimlessly trying to defend him. I'd forgotten, but Saturday meant ice cream sales in the Activities Building, and the long line extending out its front door not five feet away from me meant one too many "Whassups" and "Hey, Tommy's" for my nerves to rightly stand. So, I stood. And there he was.

"Had to get a Bomb Pop," he said, exiting the building while licking his treat.

"Benz, this is no time for Popsicles. Didn't you say the C.O. in Building 2 starts her rounds at twelve after twelve? That means we've got nine minutes."

Benz had volunteered to escort me to Cali's cell located deep within the keep of Building 2. Then, once the action started, he would act as my lookout. Truth be told, I knew at least a few others on the yard who lived in Building 2, but Benz insisted on being the one to accompanying me. Benz saw everything in black and white, was probably why. However, politics hadn't figured into my own calculus. Nothing personal, either. This was just something I had to do. Call it business. Cali had pissed me off just enough and had been in the right place at the right time to qualify as my excuse.

I sat back down on the bench. It was less than a minute's walk to Building 2, so we had a few.

Benz settled in alongside. "Sammy says you can fight." He licked his ice pop. "He says Robin the Hood should not be underestimated when it comes to combat. He says you eat Angry Energy Bars for breakfast and know what you're doing."

"I've been street fighting since I was ten," I replied. The words delivered smooth, calm, and collect, belying the true state of my nerves. I was rather glad I didn't have a Popsicle of my own just then or it would've been all sorts of quivering like that time back from the clubs in Beantown with that creative nymphomaniac, Shayna, Jewish Princess. No matter how many fights you've been in, nerves always show up.

"Well, forget all that." Benz winced in pain as he rubbed his ice-pop headache. "Cell fights are different. You're in a twelve-by-twelve box with little if any room to maneuver. It's flurry of punches versus flurry of punches. He's got long arms and is strong. My advice is to get in close, try to ground him, turn it into a wrestling match. Go for his legs. Don't play hero going for the knockout, get him to yield."

"Can we go now?"

"Personally," Benz said, as we started walking, "I think you're gonna get your ass kicked into tomorrow."

"Don't care if I win or lose." I let my sights wander off into the clouds. "As long as I survive, and get caught, and then shipped to the high side." I kicked a pebble. "Whatever happens, happens. I just gotta suck it up. That's how the universe rolls, homie. And that's how I gotta roll, too, from now on."

Benz leaned back to get a better look at me. "Are you on crack? You sound like you're on crack."

"Nah. Just all cracked up."

"You fight to win." Benz shook his head. "Anyway, you can't let him talk to you like that. Listen, you need to talk some smack yourself. Opening and closing lines are essential in any fight. You wanna get into his head.”

“Already got my opening lines,” I said, just to get Benz off my back.

Benz stopped. He turned to face me. “What? Tell me.”

I cleared my throat. “I’ll pause at first, right?” I said, as Benz nodded excitedly. “Then, I’ll pause a while longer. Then I’ll say…I don’t have any opening lines because your wack ass has left me speechless.”

Benz blinked. “No. Just no. Don’t say that, Sherlock, please.”

I shrugged. “Okay. I really hadn’t planned on saying anything.”

“Don’t wanna say nothin’, don’t wanna take this seriously, don’t wanna win, it’s your funeral.” Benz flicked a nod at Building 2 with its short shadows casting just shy of our toes. His eyes lit up. “Speaking of funerals, some of my peeps on the outs shared with me this morning about an article in today’s paper. Remember that old lady we dug up earlier this week, Margaret something-or-other?”

I winced the sun out of my eyes, then nodded, slowly.

“The county was transferring her body to her new coffin when they noticed some strange stuff. Signs she’d been poisoned. Official cause of death was kidney failure, but now it’s coming out she was a victim of foul play. Only twenty-two when that old lady died.”

“Body?” I said. “What body? She’d be nothing but a skeleton by this point.”

“The body was *preserved*, Sherlock. It was *intact*.”

“Not a deer,” I said, just like that. I don’t know who stood more amazed at these words out of my mouth, me, or him. “I mean, no kidding, really?”

Benz threw shade at me with his narrowed eyes. “Seeing deer again?”

“Nerves,” I said.

“C’mon. Let’s go.”

Benz went in first. I stood outside and waited. Seconds later he returned, waving me in. “The coast is clear. Move it.”

I moved it.

The day hall in Building 2 rather resembled the Building 4 one, only the geometry differed slightly with the microwave counter transposed with the reading nook; also, the poker tables appeared to feature a lacquer finish. The C.O.'s desk at the entryway to the lower hallway sure looked lonely without its attendant. We hightailed it through the day hall to the stairwell, meeting up with only a few suspicious glances along the way. *Offenders* didn't concern me. Snitching meant trouble on the horizon for the snitcher, and those who dared snitch did so only when their backs were against the wall. No backs or walls of that variety here.

We clambered up the steps to the third floor.

Benz explained, along the way, that Officer Bright always started her room checks on the first floor then worked her way up to the third. "That'll give us a good twenty minutes or so."

Benz inched open the door to the third floor and peered down the long hallway. Actually, three hallways featured on each floor, A, B, and C. They referred to these as "T" buildings.

We wasted no time with our brisk pace.

"Cell C34," Benz said. "At the very end of the hall."

About a quarter of our way down, the unexpected happened. A short ways ahead of where our footsteps landed us, we saw a cell door open and an offender push into the hallway hoisting a large, green, army-style duffle bag over his shoulder. Referred to as In-and-out bags, these duffle bags found employ only when an offender switched cells or planned to move Out. The offender, an old man, struggled mightily with the weight of his load that held all of his material possessions. I nearly dropped a load of my own the moment I recognized him.

My steps slowed and my pulse quickened as we neared. "You got that, old man?" We were in no position to be helping anyone but our own damned selves just then, but it seemed like the thing to say.

Monty dropped his duffle bag and divided glances between Benz and me. "Look what the cat dragged in." He eyed me, curiously. "You sure you're s'pposed to be here, son? This your building?"

I looked down at the linoleum floor tiles.

"I see." Monty picked his sack up off the floor. "Welp, all's well that ends well." He started walking. "Good luck. See you on the other side. I always wanted to say that," he said without turning.

"C'mon, Tommy," Benz said, while I watched Monty miniaturize with steps down the hallway.

"I was thinking..." I called out in a loud voice after him. "The grapevine..."

Benz seized my arm. "No time for that now."

Even louder, I said, "Was it you that saw Henry Heck? You were the one, weren't you?"

With his palm slapped against the door to the stairwell, Monty turned, slowly, and replied, "Sure was, son. As sure as I see you right here, right now, I saw that boy." Monty pushed the door open and was Out.

"Did you..." I said in a hollow voice to the empty hallway "...talk to him?"

I stood there without any breath left in me, as if in a stupor. Turning to Benz, I said, "But if he saw Henry Heck, why did he say he didn't? Why did he say he lied?"

"I dunno, Tommy," Benz said, after I had convinced my legs to start moving again and we ventured on.

Together, we stood outside the door to Cali's cell. The door featured a window slat across its face but I didn't dare peek in and risk Cali seeing me. I wanted it to be a surprise.

Pointing, Benz explained that Cali always kept the door slightly ajar whenever he chilled in the cell. "It was like this when I left, and it's like that now. He's in there." Benz looked over his shoulder to recheck the premises, no doubt. "Probably told his celly he'll be entertaining visitors and to go kick rocks. He's expecting you. You know how this works."

I nodded, even though I really didn't.

Benz said, "Listen. Three raps on the door means trouble, C.O.'s coming, get the fuck out." He punched me lightly on the shoulder. "See you on the other side."

Quelling the tremble in my hand with a quick shake and a clenched fist, I pushed open the door, not much in the mood for fighting all of a sudden.

Cali sat on his rack with his hands folded gazing out of the window. He was alone. His cell looked all in order. The desk and bureau appeared wiped clean of any decorative or household implements— probably all crammed into the doorless closet. The bed was made (although that was standard, only fish didn't make their beds, or didn't make them properly), and the floor shined clean and spotless. His stare over at me was the friggin' eye of the tiger. All Cali lacked was a warm-up robe and a trainer rubbing his shoulders. Benz said Cali would be ready and waiting. True that, and then some. The ring looked ready, too.

"I'm here," I said.

"No shit, Sherlock," Cali snapped.

That was a good one. A good opening line. So good, it made me almost forget my opening line. Oh, wait, I didn't have any. I pondered. Finally, I said, "Did you know you can save a hundred dollars or more when you switch to Liberty Mutual?"

Cali batted his eyes. "What the fuck's that supposed to mean?"

I cocked my head. "Liberty Mutual, love it or leave it. Hope you got life insurance, loser."

Cali removed his shirt to reveal a canvas boasting far more ink than skin cover. "Trying to fuck with my head like that ain't gonna do it. Get your sorry ass over here and let's get this over with nicccc-ccce and easy."

I took one step forward, and he came at me.

Benz was right. Flurry of punches.

Round 1: Defense. A temptation passed to flurry-punch right back—like in a catfight. But his arms stretched longer, and blows fell fiercer. Not advisable, unless you were cruisin' for a bruisin', as Fatts would say. So, I simply defended. Using my hands and arms, I shielded my upper body and mid-section against his punches. Able to absorb most of his blows in this manner, I did suffer one nasty wallop to the side of my head. My forearms and shoulder took their licks, but they'd live.

Round 2: Bob and Weave. His punches slowed as he prolly began to realize the futility of a direct attack. Still, I resisted the urge to flurry-punch back—still too far away for my shorter arms to hit him with any force and he'd shield anyway. So, I bobbed and weaved, baiting him into throwing some. He did, and I connected with some good counterpunches, mostly kidney shots. It takes balance and coordination to get off a good counterpunch. It's about rhythm. Often underemployed, kidney shots really deliver the hurt.

One of his strikes rocked my jaw. Luckily, it didn't have much weight behind it. I reeled a bit, and moved in for a hug.

Round 3: Knees and Elbows. Call it the dance, the clutch, the hug, moving in usually makes sense when you're fighting a guy with longer arms. You step in close where his arms can't extend, and give your man a hug—make sure to hold on tight so you can live to tell! Knees to the other guy's quadriceps work here, or if you can work some wiggle-room—elbows to the face. The knee strikes I got in, the elbows I did not with the exception of one glancing blow. For my efforts, I caught one of his elbows with my left ear. So far, I was getting my ass kicked. But it was still early.

The one downside to the dance, the clutch, the hug, is that it usually ends up on the floor. Floors are hard, unforgiving things. Dust, dirt, and hairs down there, too. Good thing Cali swept.

Round 4: Wrestling Match. Actually, the two of us ended up on Cali's celly's bed. Cali muscled me back and together we keeled over onto his celly's rack. Cali claimed top position, I lay prostrate underneath. Not a position of strength, as far as I was concerned. With him hovering over me like that, he seized my forearms and attempted to wrench them from my face to work some clearance so he could wreak havoc with his fists. He was stronger than most of those pretenders I'd fought over the years, and had my right arm almost pinned to the mattress in what would've been a crucifix pose. However, in order for Cali to extend his arm to pin mine, he had to lower his torso, and in turn, his head. Here was where the men stood out from the boys.

Headbutt. Why didn't fools ever see that coming?

Cali reeled backward, clutching his forehead. A streak of blood trickled down his rumpled, pain-stricken brow.

Round 5: Flurry of Punches. The course of Cali's blood flow and overall advantage went all downhill from there. He was clearly not himself with his big headache going on, and stood in no position to fend off my blows. I wailed on his face and midsection with my own flurry of punches. He backpedaled and got tripped up on the ledge of his rack, which didn't help him much. I sat cowgirl overtop him now on his rack. A haymaker right, a right jab, another right jab, and then, with one final left that rocked the side of his face and made a sickening smack sound, he was lights the-fuck out...well, as far as I was concerned he was.

Folks usually didn't expect the left.

Cali lay doubled-up, groaning, and all but immobile.

I backed up a few steps to the center of the room.

Through the window, Benz, smiling, gave me a thumbs up.

I'd done well. However, *well* in this instance meant getting caught, not winning. "C'mon, get up," I urged Cali. *Can't leave just yet*, I wanted to say.

Tommy McConnell rarely left a job undone. Cali remained conscious, and a man still conscious posed a threat. However, I figured I had proven my point. I didn't dislike Cali, but shit-talkers owned a special page in my book. Whole chapters, more like.

Three raps on the door.

Sweet. The cops.

I eyed the door. Benz, I noticed, no longer manned it. Did he knock then jet? Were the cops here already or on their way? I supposed it didn't matter.

Round 6: Bloodbath. In fact, all that mattered just then was the black-and-orange blur I noticed out of the corner of my eye. I saw it coming, but didn't have nearly enough time to dodge or lay down a front kick. Sensing my distraction, indecision, tarrying, Cali seized the opportunity to bull-rush me. Using the force of that run and his weight advantage, he barreled me over onto his celly's rack. The aftermath was all foregone conclusion. I tried to fend off his blows but the dude could wail. Cali had played possum. Damn him.

Smack, crunch, crash, as Cali's fists fell time and again. Liquid copper dripped from my nose down my lips. However, it was only when my head got rocked back by an especially vicious uppercut that the lights of my world spun, blurred, flickered, and faded to black entirely.

CHAPTER EIGHT

I could look a fool in the eyes and tell him the sewing together of my cheek-flesh with those four stitches didn't bring tears to my own, or the resetting of my nose was like a stroll through the Providence Place Mall, but that all would be lying.

I may talk out of my ass from time to time—well, most of the time, but I rarely lie. Once, while at a bar, I stole some BU student's change. He asked me straight out if I did it. I replied, "Yeah. I'm hungry, got a dollar to go along with that?" And when the red Captain John Allens stared me down and asked if it was I, Tommy McConnell, who had initiated such and such "confrontation" with Mr. Kensington, aka Cali, I looked him straight in the eye and answered, "You said it, Cap, would I lie to you?"

No lie, either—my vision wasn't the same after all of those slugs from Cali. The nurse practitioner said it would be blurry for a few days, maybe even a week. "Good times," I replied. Like my stopover destination was worth seeing anyway.

SEG would be my home for whatever block of time it took the coppers to complete my paperwork and scrounge up the available manpower to transfer me over to the high side. But solitary is a land of punishment, too, which meant they would be in no hurry to relieve me of my chain.

Actually, no chains rattled in SEG other than those intangible ones of bleakness, boredom, depression, and loneliness. These, though, rattled loudly.

The rusty bed-frame I reclined on to do one of three things an offender could do in a place like this—sleep, bust a nut, and admire the works of fine art on the ceiling and walls—bolted into the floor. No bother with slapping paint on the walls of this deal because this was solitary, and the offender was meant to feel that. Graffiti show-cased pretty much everywhere, although the overlapping patches of washout on the walls suggested there had been considerably more in times past.

The graffiti displayed in a medium of blue and black ink. Possibly, in time past, pens were allowed.

My accommodations otherwise bespoke nothing of the creature comforts. A metal toilet beckoned over in the corner. A small sink jutted out of the wall. Showers stationed down the hall, probably communal deals, the stuff of nightmares.

A yellow light illuminated the cell. The place had an abandoned hospital or asylum-type feel to it, even though I knew SEG sat housed in the Admin Building. Opposite one of these art-gallery walls, our beloved chow hall catered the masses.

The veins of liquid streaming down the face of my door indicated Solitary wasn't exactly that. Out of boredom and maybe stupidity I ran a taste test. Urine—though not mine. Set into the metal door, a window slat displayed its grinning teeth which were those inglo-rious iron bars. My viewing port into the SEG hallway, for better or for worse.

My neighbor across the hallway favored me with a visual only once or twice, although I heard him often enough. He screamed, cried, sang, cursed, spat, and flung urine and feces into the walkway. I'd given up on telling him to shush. Solitary welcomed both those who had misbehaved and those who were a bit too, shall we say, rambunctious for the gen pop. This fool seemed to be the latter. Truth be told, my fart-slinging neighbor could well have been straight out of some '80s hair band with that long, stringy shag of his. But enough about Bad Hair Day.

The only neighbor who concerned me inhabited the cell directly adjacent to Bad Hair Day's.

"Hey, Cali," I called over.

No response.

"Hey!" I said, louder.

My former adversary made an appearance at his window. "What it do, Tommy?" he said, in a low, tired voice. "Excuse me, *Sherlock*."

Cali and I had since made up. This should come as no surprise, really. In prison, it's not uncommon for ring participants to throw shade on their previous gripes and return to peace once their scores were settled.

"Hey, Cali. What's the high side like?"

Cali's face in the window lost every whit of expression. "It's a place where someone like you don't wanna be."

"But we're goin' there," I said. "There's no stopping us now." I gripped the steel bars, and lifting up on my toes, mashed my face against them. Lofty, these windows were. "Honestly, I feel there's something's waiting for me over there. Something big."

"Yeah, big." Cali smiled. "Bigger than you know and you'll be feeling for realz you keep acting like the NAC you is." Non-Affiliated Caucasian, that meant.

I looked far off. "It was the best of times," I said, wistfully. "It was the worst of times." I looked at Cali. "That's from a book. I forgot which. Hey, Cali, super important question. Where's the records room on the high side and how am I ever gonna get over there?"

Cali looked at me darkly. "You can't. You gotta get a pass, and no cop's gonna give you a pass to the records room. It's off limits."

I frowned. "But on the low side fools can just waltz right up—"

"High side's different, Sherlock."

That was bad. Fucking awful, actually. We addicts don't just talk out of our asses, we act impulsively and without thinking some-times, too. I probably should've asked first. Still, other things awaited me over there. Big things.

"Listen," Cali said. "I heard you ball. So do I. Just don't get out much. Bum knee. That knee was one hundred percent, you wouldn't have anywhere *near* pulled off what you did in my cell the other day. Anyway, there's homeys I know on the high side who ball. Sliding into a pick-up game's not like on the low side, you gotta have connections."

"Sweet. Hook me up."

Moments later, Bad Hair Day made a cameo in his window with his reddened eyes, imbecile smile, and wild Axl Rose hair. He swore, crooned, cited long verses of nonsense at loud decibels, made animal noises, and threatened to throw "kaka" at my door again.

Again? No *wonder* that smell.

"Shut up, asshole!" Cali growled.

I said to Cali, "I've tried that already. Don't work."

But it did work. On cue, Bad Hair Day retreated into his cell and ceased and desisted with all of his badness.

Soon afterward, I retreated into mine. Lying down on my rack, I could feel it. The aches and pains. My face didn't hurt so much as the bruises coloring my shoulders and arms. But no biggie. *Takes a lickin' and keeps on tickin'*, as Fatts used to say.

"Where's my *Wuthering Heights*?" I complained to the graffiti on the walls. At least the graffiti had something to show for itself: personality. I thought for a moment about the long line of sorry asses who had occupied this wasteland of cement and steel prior to my arrival.

Louder still, I blared at the walls, "I could sure go for some old-school British chick reads right about now!"

If walls could talk.

They didn't. But who knew if they weren't listening. It almost felt like they were.

In Solitary, time kinda loses its rep. It's not a big badass like everywhere else in the universe where it lords over matters like celestial orbits, work schedules, and days served in the city jail that one can credit against their prison term.

Lights in the cells cut out at ten, switched back on at six, and so these were the only times you knew the time.

Without any masterpiece of 19th-century literature by my bedside to read, then quickly tire of reading, then try to read again, because I'd promised myself I would—I hadn't lasted very long trying to read all of the bad bathroom humor on the walls instead. I dozed off.

When I awoke, darkness. After 10 p.m., that meant.

Effuse light from the hallway eked in through the hairline cracks of the door and that window slat stationed a bit too loftily for us average-height guys. The effect created more of a gloom than a darkness. The hallway filtered just enough residual light that an offender could venture out late at night to piss in the bowl, or drink from the sink, and not trip over his shoes or walk into a wall.

Into this gloom I so often stared during my time in SEG. No choice, once the lights cut out. Except in this instance, I did have a choice. I could stare into the gloom, or I could stare at the shadowy figure clad in orange taking up space over by the sink.

Still groggy from sleep, and my vision still blurry from Cali's wallops, it didn't fully register at first I had a visitor.

Considering he stood only seven or eight feet away from me as I squinted at, studied, scanned him up and down, I remained surprisingly calm and in my element. Although my vision stood impaired, I was hardly blind. We made eye contact.

"What's in a name, Blanco?" the visitor asked.

It was Perez.

"Hey, Sherlock," a voice said from over by the door.

I whipped my head around as if on impulse to see who it was. Here, the slightly farther distance, and lesser familiarity with the speaker, presented more of a challenge to my blurry vision. The round face peering in through the bars belonged to a C.O., but which? Officer Machado was the guard on duty, but if this was Officer Machado then I was Shakira. The man's face featured inside of a big head topped by a bristly, blond crew cut. I knew that face, but couldn't quite place it.

"Have a blast over there at Drac's Castle, Sherlock," the C.O. said, the words drenched in sarcasm. "He isn't over there, you know. Drac isn't. It's just a name, Drac's Castle. All you're gonna find over there is what you got over here. Headaches, heartaches, pain, pain, then more of the same. Don't end up another casualty, little man, 'k?" Flashing a snarky smile, the C.O. waved goodbye with his fingertips and exited stage left.

After blinking away my confusion, I scurried to the door, raised on my tiptoes, stuck my nose out, and angled my sights beyond the bars into the walkway. I could see Blue sauntering off as he whistled. More of a form, really. But a decidedly large form. More than just husky, it was The Blue Hulk, Officer Harris.

Harris was an odd one, damn straight. Maybe his sideways glances and less-than-encouraging send-offs meant he wasn't particularly fond of me. It was not uncommon for cops to favor offenders they liked and make life difficult for those they didn't. Perhaps he didn't like me—or perhaps he liked me very much. I hadn't thought of that. That little fingertip wave of his? I shook my head. Where was Bad Hair Day at a time like this, sound asleep when he could be helping a neighbor deal with stalkers?

The other more likely scenario featured Harris as a blood brother in some secret society who had sworn an oath to preserve on pains of death the secret of the Forever Young Prisoner. A Black Hat. One of Monty's so-called "Guardians." I rather preferred my stalker assumption.

Suddenly, I remembered I wasn't alone.

With my nose stuck up against the door, I sucked in breath. Pivoting my feet, I willed the rest of me to turn around.

The cell lay empty.

Was he hiding under the sink—no. Under the toilet—obviously not. Under the bed? I walked over and squatted. Nope. Nowhere.

I flung myself on my rack.

Gazing up at the ceiling, I entertained a great many thoughts over those hours which followed. My thoughts tend to bounce, be it known. And, no, Perez didn't figure much into them. Actually, I made every attempt to block him out. Already I felt half-crazy just being here, and the last thing I needed was visual proof that this was exactly where I needed to be. *Perez was a just figment of my imagination*, I told myself. My sights were blurry. My thoughts had been all here and there. I had just woken up. Maybe it was Officer Harris's shadow on the wall I had seen, or my own.

Instead, I amused myself with fantastic thoughts about basketball, Lilya, Lilya's FOIA request, Cali, Sammy, and that big boss man, Harry Potter. I thought about my real parents.

Real dad? Was he maybe some high-level exec in search of a long-lost son to help him spend his multi-million-dollar fortune? A semi-pro basketball player? A MMA fighter? A fun-loving contractor type in need of a little buddy to drink beers with on his porch?

You're a mistake, the words invaded my daydream.

Suddenly, that daydream morphed into a nightmare. Fatts was swinging for the fences and my real dad sampled in turn as a Mafia boss, hit-man, junkie, con man, and a Nazi collaborator. Was I part German? Doubtful, as *McConnell* was about as Irish a name as you could get. Fatts used to say *trouble* was *in my blood*, whatever that meant. I probably should have asked. Nazis, *hell-o*. Talk about crackheads. Ironic they were the ones who had created meth. Why was I even thinking about those German clowns from yesteryear? Maybe that big swastika inked on the wall had something to do with it.

I raked my fingers through my hair and then stood. While trying to wrap my heart and mind around some make-believe Daddy Warbucks and Nazi villains, my mind had failed to register the return of the cell lights. Past six a.m., that meant. I dragged myself over to the sink to wash my face and brush my teeth with my rubber toothbrush.

After an entire night of tossing, turning, and thinking, I returned to my one solace: the scribble on the walls. I decided to begin my day with a light spell of reading.

It was gang lingo, mostly, that a fool couldn't rightly understand without a fifteen-year-old translator.

That dynamic duo of larger-than-life female C.O.'s, Bernardi and Bright, received not a few flattering mentions on this wall of shame.

Other highlights included:

"Kiss it, boyyyyyyyyyyyyyyy."

"Go fast, don't die."

"HATE."

"For a good time call…"

I hadn't actually scoured much of the wall that faced opposite my rack. I checked it out. Just to the left of the sink it showcased. How had I missed this precious pearl, right by the sink like that?

Blurry vision? Claustrophobia and its blunting effects on awareness?

Wedged in between "I WANNA DIE" and "GET ME OUT OF HERE!!!!" three words penned in black ink let me know something *big* maybe really did have me in mind.

Hmm, that's not wack at all, I thought. This Easter egg read:

"Perez was here."

Below it, on the floor, lay a pen.

CHAPTER NINE

The Pit of Heck
The Year of our Lord 1963

Hitler lost the war. The never-ending war with Germany and its so-called "Nazis" was *finis*, as the French would say. This much was certain. All of that banter about tanks, carriers, invasions, came, and went, and in the twenty years since not a single word was spoken in that regard from the gents on the other side of the metal door. *America was still the land of the free...* Henry rolled his eyes, then finished his thought... *the land of apple pie, hamburgers, hangovers, and the home run. Innovators like Thomas Edison and the ever-enchanting Maude Adams.*

By this point, Thomas Edison's lights had surely flickered out, and Henry could all but envision Maude retired from the stage and knitting quilts at an old folks home in a resort city like Newport or Miami Beach. Henry's vintage, in other words. This much was certain.

What remained less certain was what the name of this one cockroach with the black stripe might be. He looked like a Rutherford.

However, to call the pest Rutherford might be disrespectful to Henry's cousin. Rutherford Ronsellier, a no-good blackguard—in Henry's humble opinion—had insisted on using Uncle Jean's emporium in Woonsocket as a front for his gambling adventurism. Still, he was family. Henry decided on a compromise. He would call the pest Rudy.

Woonsocket, Rhode Island. Ah, the memories. Henry's extended family had all lived over that way, as did many French generally. French Canadians had poured in from the north over those first few decades of the century to work the many textile mills in town. Uncle Jean and Henry's father, Michel, had found employ at the Bernon and Social Mills, respectively, until fortune led them their separate ways: Uncle Jean to his entrepreneurial endeavor, and Father to buy the family farm in Smithfield. Henry, of course, grew up in Woonsocket, until moving to Smithfield with his parents as a pre-teen. But well into his twenties he still visited. He first met Margaret there.

A bird of a different feather, Gerdie would've never made do in Woonsocket, nor likely anywhere but the Big Apple or Gay Paris. Through her veins ran only the noblest of blood and upon her choosing, only the ritziest of locales. Ever on the up and up, she had *panache*, as the French would say. *Good ol' Gerdie*, Henry thought, as his smile slackened then fell off entirely. She, too, had certainly run her farewell trot around the bases by this point.

Certainly, they all had.

"And so why do I dwell on them?" he asked himself.

Possibly, because there was so little else to dwell on here except maybe this hunkering excuse for a washbasin bolted into the wall that served no purpose whatsoever except to collect rust and serve as the only eye candy in the cell. Just then, he saw two of his friends scurry across the stone floor.

"Why, hello, Beatrice. Hello, Arthur. A good day to you both."

Henry made sure to name each and every one of his cockroach friends. Without names, they existed as mere shadows. Naming gave them an identity. The act of christening made the vermin, the pests, his enemies otherwise—his friends. Also, saying their names out loud proved critical. That it consummated a near familial bond between himself and the beasts was a fact not lost on the little buggers, Henry could tell.

Henry lay back on his mattress and rubbed his aching, creaseless brow. Their "medicine" baked into the stale bread they had given him earlier in the day seemed to be working its effect. But he still had time.

Henry wondered—again, for the millionth time—why they didn't just bump him off him once and for all, instead of putting him, and themselves, through this whole rigmarole. If their plan involved preventing others from knowing what he knew, why not just eliminate the source? Because a dead body wheeled through a prison on its way out the front door could create problems. Because someone, somewhere, maybe had a morsel of conscience. Because killing was wrong. Because they wanted to see if Henry might stay young forever. It could have been any of these things or none of them. Henry didn't know, and hardly cared anymore.

However, a pen and paper would've interested him. He would soon declare this wish to the ceiling. Naming mattered. Declaring, just as much so. In fact, naming and declaring went together just like pen and paper. In order to declare something you had to first identify what it was, and no point in giving something a name if it you didn't plan on saying that name.

The act of declaring kept Henry "engaged, sane, and young." Aloud, Henry stated in addendum, "It strengthens the vocal chords, if nothing else." Ditto for schedule: it kept him mentally on the level. Henry pondered his schedule for that day. *Better get all of my declarations in before the lightning strikes*, was his exact thought.

"I still have time," Henry spoke into the darkness.

As he lay on his mat, Henry rummaged his thoughts as to the many would-be advantages of a pen and paper. With these, he could record the names of all of the cockroach and spider friends who had skittered his way over the years. He could scratch down his remembrances of Gerdie, Margaret, his own adventurism as a farm boy in seeking out employ in big-city Providence as a butler, and that fateful day at the mansion. He could sketch pictures: it didn't matter what of. Horses, certainly. And rolling green hills with ladies holding parasols and men in straw hats with canes picnicking in the foreground. On second thought, mental images like that spit rust. He would probably end up sketching portraits of his roach friends.

With pen and paper, he could write in gut-wrenching detail about his adventures here in the land that time forgot. He could share about that time a stone in the wall got dislodged back in '33, or when the wall opposite sweated those few days back in '24. He could share about when the upper door-hinge rusted clean off and how the guards had ordered him to take his medicine "right now, right now!" so they could move in to make repairs. He could share about when the bread got so moldy it began to squirm.

He could share, too, about that gent who looked like a banker standing in the corner, stretching his fist at Henry. A weird aftereffect of his medicines? Doubtful, because four or five times this happened. Once, he even held a conversation with the banker. The banker asserted he was innocent, too, and offered Henry a penny for his thoughts. Entertaining his delusion, Henry spoke at length of Margaret and that day at the mansion. The next day, Henry discovered a penny on the washbasin. He kept it there as a reminder. Of what, he could hardly say.

Certainly, Henry would scratch out his recollections of the guards themselves. Who could forget Pelligrini, whom the others called Greeny, or Guido, with his Boston accent, or the guard who kept jesting about someone named "Ike," or that guard in these early sixties who kept beckoning through the door "Peter Pan, Peter Pan...who or what the fuck are you, Peter Pan?" His recollections of the guard with the hoarse voice held a special place in Henry's book of memories. The frog in his throat grew into a toad until it forced him to retire. "I've had it. I'm going fishin'" were the last words

Henry heard garbled through the iron door. Willie, they called him. Willie planned to go fishing!

Oh, the memories were so very many, and so very dear, Henry could nary process even these few without a tear in his eye, as he lay there. But, yes, pen and paper. No matter that the light seeping in through the cracks in the door provided the only light in the cell. Henry's eyes had adjusted. If not read, he could anyhow write. The memories listed so many that Henry reckoned, all told, they would fill a ledger as voluminous as *Arabian Nights*.

Now, time for some declarations.

Today's slate promised to be short. The meds were performing their magic; he could feel the tingling in his hands and his growing inclination to swoon. Progress, that meant. These meds were stronger than last year's meds, and last year's meds stronger than the ones the year before. In fact, Henry had learned to determine the course of years simply by these yearly druggings they doused his meals with as a means to knock him out so they could sweep his cell, bathe him, and God knew what else…run a medical exam, study him, maybe, too. His record on file probably featured as long and voluminous as *Arabian Nights*. By Henry's calculation, it was the Year of our Lord 1963.

One of the guards on duty named either Matt or Mel just over the past week called it The Space Age. Speaking at the other side of the door, he said the entirety of civilization had since launched off into "The Great Beyond" to populate Mars and the moon. Those left behind faced the challenge of a nuclear winter all on their own. But Henry already had challenges to face. *Whatever a nuclear winter is has to be more tolerable than my present lot,* Henry considered. But Henry didn't much believe what the guards said anyway. Mind games. It was like that never-ending war with Germany.

Henry was purposed to not to let the endless riddling and enigmatic silence of the guards make him lose his marbles. Was it their purpose to make him lose them? Henry had an inkling. No, a vision. A remembrance of what he saw that one day. The Caniglios. The governor. The whole darned truth. The credibility of local government stood at risk if that truth got out. Hence, his chain, and these efforts by the guards. His marbles were his own, and not one would be lost. More to the point, Henry remained fixed in his grand purpose to remain forever the same man.

And declaring seemed to help with that.

Four declarations only for today. Henry's eyelids kept forcing themselves open. He was fading fast. Every day over the course of the entirety of his confinement he'd declared these four baseline declarations. Others, too, but these four every day.

Henry raised his chin up to the ceiling. There existed a prison up yonder where other inmates, guards, and administrators dwelt. The ceiling above lay drowned in darkness, wholly obscured by the lack of light in the cell. In his mind's eye, Henry imagined a mining shaft, like the ones he used to read about in the newspapers. Up, up, up into darkness the shaft rose. Surely there lived and worked folks up there who might hear—as might the guards, but he didn't trust the guards. Henry was quite certain he was underground, under the prison proper.

For one, it never got too hot or cold in here.

For another, his journey here had followed a downward course. Of course, nearly five decades had passed since Day One, but he could still remember it.

He remembered...the neighing of the horses as the carriage ground to a halt in front of the gates. The rows of razor-wire. The prison entrance with its great oaken door set into its ornate, cathedral-like frame. The black-and-white-checkered floor of the processing area. The side door they promptly slipped him into after his stint at the processing counters while all of the other inmates shuffled into the waiting area. The long spiral staircase. Steps down, down, down. The passageway with its lone lantern and dirt floor he wasn't supposed to see but for a second saw anyway. The tying of the blindfold. The trek down the dark passage. The guards who ignored his continued inquiries as to where they were taking him.

The untying of the blindfold. The kick in the seat of his pants to encourage him into the cell. The slamming of the door behind him.

Down. Down. *Down.*

And so that was why Henry always looked up, up, up whenever he said,

"*Help* me."

Second declaration. "I am guilty," Henry said, "but not like this."

Third declaration: "Pen, please."

Fourth declaration: "And this," Henry said, "is all I have to say in my defense this day."

Henry lowered his head. The room spun and blurred. The usual moments he afterward allowed to pause and reflect were ones he did not now have. Only a fresh round of oxygen stood between himself and the floor. He took a deep breath, then zigzagged towards his mat and nosedived into it.

Henry's world faded to blackness. Soon afterward the door opened and the men in blue entered to haul him away.

CHAPTER TEN

I can't say I was happy when my cell door in solitary clicked open, and Officer Machado stepped in. I didn't smile when Machado fastened and secured much too tightly the cuffs around my wrists and ankles—then ran a chain from my wrists to my ankles to secure the cuffs. I didn't break into dance when, like a friggin' mummy, I instead had to shuffle down a long hallway to the staging area by the Deport bay doors. I kept my cool when they led me into a room to strip-search me, and when Machado proceeded to chain me up all over again.

What *did* make my day, though, was the greeter, with greeting, who received me upon our exit from the pat-down room.

"Well, well, well," Greeley said, smiling. "If it isn't Mr. Sherlock Holmes himself."

Penning his signature on my transfer papers, Machado handed them over to my seeming lone ally. "McConnell. He's going to Pod 2. He's trouble, but not big. You shouldn't have any problems."

"Thanks, Blue," I said, giving Machado a thumbs up. "I'll forever cherish these special times we've shared. Your face in the window.

That little stash." I turned to Greeley. "You gonna be my limo driver?"

Greeley had yet to take his eyes off of me. "No. I ride shotgun. Your official escort will be Officer Bernardi."

And here she came.

Holy hell, the humanity. Swaggering down the hall with her chin up, chest out, game face on, summoned the image of a pro wrestler on her way to the ring. Pretty but...thick, big, and tall. "I'd hit that," I'd heard so many offenders say. Yeah, if they survived the foreplay.

Greeley and Bernardi flanked me on our walk out to the van.

It was a nice van. It boasted red lettering on the side—that I barely had time to read because the blues seemed wholesale intent upon fast-tracking me through this "unsecure" region of parking lot to their wheels parked on the far side of it.

The inside of the van looked not so nice. A metal shelf along the wall provided me with my seat. Officer Bernardi secured my belt buckle. Buckle up, it's the law. Click it or ticket. Sectioned off from the cab where the Blues chilled by a partition that showcased a viewing slat with those inglorious iron bars filling the spaces between, this belly section of the van featured not a single window. I squirmed in my seat. "Hey, do you guys offer in-flight movies?"

"Just sit tight," Bernardi replied. "Count your blessings you're here and not where you're headed."

"Off to Drac's Castle," merrily, I sang. I cocked my head. "They say Drac isn't over there, but I don't believe that for a sec."

From the passenger's seat, Greeley swerved his neck just enough to give me a look out of the corner of his eye.

Bernardi gunned the ignition.

"Wait." Greeley looked down at something in his lap. "I've, er, got his Check Out papers, but not his Check In papers." He rifled through my portfolio in apparent search of my Check In papers, whatever those were.

Bernardi took her hands off the wheel. "Processing on the high side doesn't require In papers, Ryan," she said with an edge in her voice. "Intake is their responsibility, not ours. We check him out, they check him in."

"I know that, I know. Still, I printed out a copy just in case they ran out of forms or their printer was down or whatever. Why don't you go run and get them, Sue? I believe I left it on the counter by the pat-down room."

Bernardi's eyes widened. "Would you perhaps like to go fetch them yourself?"

"Um, not really." Greeley cleared his throat. "Actually, doesn't procedure state the driver's accompaniment is to stay with the vehicle at all times? While the driver's responsibility is to focus on driving. But you're not driving yet, so..."

Bernardi furrowed her brow. "Does it say that?"

"Yup, that's what it says," I offered from the back, not knowing if it was true or not.

Bernardi flitted me a look then blinked at Greeley. "Would you like Officer Bernardi to fetch you some coffee while she's at it?" she asked, sarcastic as all hell.

"No," Greeley smiled. "Just the papers. And a Sprite."

"A Sprite?"

"From the machine. Here, why not grab yourself one, too." Greeley dug into his pocket and handed her a bill. "Gotta stay hydrated. It's a long haul."

"It's two-hundred yards!" Bernardi narrowed her eyes at Greeley. "I'll go." She switched off the ignition, and wrenching the door open, hopped out, then slammed it.

I figured what the deal was here so I wasted no time.

"Greeley," I said. "Question. Why did you tip me off to Old Monty that one time if you knew he was lying?"

"Lying?" Greeley craned his neck to get a better look at me through the viewing slat.

I nodded. "Everyone I've spoken to says Monty confessed afterward to lying about seeing Henry Heck that one time at the library."

Greeley sighed. Shaking his head, his neck lost its lean and he disappeared behind the partition. He said, after a long pause, "They didn't wanna ship you to the high side, you know. Couldn't justify keeping you, but sometimes no reason can be reason enough if the right people choose to look the other way. I hung around just long enough to make sure they didn't." Greeley shifted in his seat to face me squarely through the viewing slat. "I just hung around, was all."

"Thanks," I said, not sure if I meant it or not.

"Sure, Monty lied," Greeley answered. "Short answer...officer's intuition. Now, listen, McConnell, and listen good. I've worked the high side. I know Monty, well. For example, there was this time we discovered a razor blade in a cell we knew Monty frequented. It wasn't his cell, but he was over there. So, we questioned him. I questioned him."

Greeley's face took on reddened shades of fervor as he pressed it up against the bars. "Monty denied any involvement in the matter. At one point, I asked him, 'Are you lying to me like that time you lied about seeing the Forever Young Prisoner?' Monty looked me square in the eye and replied, 'I confessed to my murder charge, Blue. I could've lied and said I didn't do it. We had a bunch of defenses laid out. I could've taken my case to trial, and won. I could be home right now bowling ten-pins or connecting with kids and grandkids sprung out of my younger, tiger days whom I never knew existed. Why would I lie about *this* after what I chose not to lie about?'"

I shook my head. "I use lines like that, too. It's called talking out of your ass."

"McConnell, after years of dealing with criminals I can tell straight off who's lying and who isn't. There are two types of liars. Those who lie to save their hides, and those who lie just because. Monty never struck me as the *just because* type."

I asked, "If Monty saw Henry Heck and shared it with the grapevine, why did he turn around and say he didn't?"

Greeley turned to face the windshield. "I can't tell you that, McConnell."

"You can't, or you won't?"

Greeley looked back. "I can't. I don't know. Two things." Greeley darted glances out of each of the side windows. "And very quickly. The birthmark. The original intel provided by Officer Clayton mentioned nothing about a mark. I don't know how the birthmark rumor started, but from what I gather it started around the time of Monty's venture in the library, and so it's safe to assume Monty added in that detail himself; and for whatever reason, it stuck.

"Also what stuck was the name, Henry Heck. Not his real name, I don't think. Again, Clayton mentioned nothing more than just generally about some young-old man who had been locked away since the 1910s. Blond hair, blue eyes. Drafted during WWI. Life sentence. No mention of a name or charges."

"Kinda wack Clayton didn't know his charges," I said. "Or even his name."

"Clayton wasn't in the inner circle, that means. He got his information secondhand. He might have spilled more but never got around to it with that surprise heart attack days later."

I suddenly recalled Harris's warning: *Don't end up another casualty, little man, 'k?*

"Someone's coming," Greeley said, with his eyes on the driver's side window. "You have literally fifteen seconds to ask whatever else you've got. After that, my lips are sealed, and I will deny this conversation ever occurred.

I racked my brain. "Fifteen seconds?"

"Ten," Greeley blurted.

Finally, I had one. "Okay, okay, so, there's this one officer, Harris—"

The van door snapped open.

A heavy load plopped onto the driver's seat. The whole chassis leaned over onto its side from the additional weight. My immediate thought was Bernardi must have smashed a few grinders on her way to the soda machine, until I saw the blond crew cut.

"Hi-ya, Greeley," Harris said, "long time no see." More earthquake shiftings around in the driver's seat. "Officer Bernardi had some emergency business to take care of over at the Activities Building. Some knucklehead whom we've yet to identify unplugged the network cables and the whole system's down. I was fortunate enough to be over this way and so I volunteered to escort Little Man here."

"Hi, Sherlock." Harris smiled and did his fingertip wave through the window. "Paperwork all in order?" he asked the co-pilot.

"Yeah," Greeley replied in a low voice.

"Cool beans." Harris gunned the ignition. "Highway to hell time." He footed the gas.

Our "two-hundred-yard" drive ended up taking no less than than twenty minutes with all of the sliding fences we had to wait for to open, to close, to open. Only one of those gates courted us on the low side, but no less than five on our approach to the high. Not that I saw any of it. Greeley gave updates.

Harris said nothing, meanwhile. Still, I could almost see him gripping that steering wheel as if it were my neck and with a monstrous grin stretched wide across his meaty mug.

Undoubtedly, his silence doubled as mind game, and it annoyed the fuck out of me. Finally, I just came right out and asked, "Are you one of the Guardians?" Hell, why not? What was the worst he could do, murder me? The high side lay outside of his domain anyway.

Greeley groaned. Too fucking bad. Why mince words with the likes of a Beast on Wheels?

The beast just grunted and wheeled on to the next gate. Remaining for the most part silent, he did afterward offer a few dallies with reference to the "charcoal rain clouds" overhead that threatened to "unload their purchase at a moment's notice once the time was right."

Lines like that kept me in line. Harris might simply have meant the weather. Or he might have meant that someone's gun planned to unload its purchase into some sorry sack's head when the time was right. No wisecracks from the sorry sack on *this* highway to hell. Meanwhile, I tried to gauge Greeley's own opinion on Harris through their interactions, but there was little to go by. Greeley kept decidedly quiet. If I could conclude anything otherwise, these two were not friends.

Our somber journey continued its silent course, to say nothing of the dashboard radio that Harris switched off no less than three times after Greeley had attempted to lighten the mood with some tunes.

Finally, the van ground to a halt, the engine died, and the officers stepped out. The back doors of the van sprung open. The light of day shone in the young mummy's face as he stepped out into his brave new world.

I stretched my neck to look up at Drac's Castle. "Day-um," I said, eyeing the towers, intricate stonework, gargoyles (what-the-actual-fuck?), huge front door, and the sheer height and breadth of the place all up close like that.

Two C.O.'s stood sentry by the great wooden doors. They traipsed the steps downward to intercept our slow trod upwards. Raindrops fell as the low-side cowboys handed me over to the high-side cowboy and cowgirl. What color might *their* cowboy hats be? I wondered. The storm clouds overhead lacked only flashes of lightning as a finishing touch to this epic-scale portrait of doom. Then, that happened too.

"Let the games begin." Harris patted my shoulder nicely with his giant's hand. Punching my shoulder would have been more welcome, way less freaky.

"Good luck, McConnell," Greeley said.

PART TWO

THE HIGH SIDE

CHAPTER ELEVEN

While its gaudy exterior of gargoyles and stone seemed to possess all of the distinction of a medieval fortress, the insides of Drac's Castle lent themselves to humbler colorings, though no less historic. It felt like entering a time machine and walking out into those bygone days of Dickens and Poe.

While standing out in the rain waiting for the coppers to key in the code to Drac's front door, my mind's eye envisioned a large banquet hall replete with tapestries, chandeliers and maybe even a knight or two...or anyhow some large hall like at the capitol building or Grand Central in New York. Of course, donors and distinguished guests required incentive. But this was no lollapalooza like all of that.

The ceilings hung low. Black-and-white tiles overlaid the floor. The lime-green paint splashed on the stone walls bore a stark resemblance to puke, but that wasn't what I felt like doing when my sights passed their way. Green also symbolized the luck of the Irish. *Big things*, I kept telling myself in spite of my nerves, as I continued under the ceiling with its sags, cracks, and light bulbs in metal cages hovering over me like fangs.

Dead ahead sat five teller booths. Was this the Loan and Trust on Page Street? I sure as hell hoped so; maybe Harris had gotten his addresses wrong.

Aside from the windowed booths, the atmosphere reeked of age. It reminded me of one of those Colonial-era museums in Boston. You could feel the past creep up your damned pant-leg—or was that a roach? Did they have those here? I sure as fuck hoped so; talk about atmosphere! Granted, main lobbies of old prisons needed to make a statement. It's what the donors, bigwigs, and visitors saw first.

"Ma will be awfully impressed when she stops by for her visit," I told the officer standing to my left. The pin on his lapel read "Officer Rooney." The female officer's name looked to be "Weldon." She was plain Jane, about forty, and really on the ball about correcting fools.

"Visitors and guests enter through the *main* gate," she clarified. "This is just the prisoner entrance."

Just the prisoner entrance? Sure, no lollapalooza like all that, but still.

"Can I look at that?" I asked, pointing to the bronze plaque framed on the wall.

Officers Rooney and Weldon exchanged glances. "Go ahead," Weldon said.

I mummy-walked over. The officers kept on me like glue the whole way.

Horatio S. Barr, the plaque showed, along with the guy's head, in relief, in profile, engraved in bronze. He of the bald head and sweeping Santa beard. He of fortune, and fame. He of the imperial congress—or whatever the hell the plaque had called it. He of the state senate, the U.S. Senate, the storied advocate of thousands of working-class immigrants. He of the American Legion. He of the J.P. Morgan ring of trustees. These very prison walls, the plaque set forth, were dedicated upon their completion in 1889 to the memory of this great man. Hence its name—

"The Horatio S. Barr Correctional Facility," I read aloud. I cocked my head at Weldon. "I thought it was called P-Pen. Is that just its prison name?"

Weldon tempted a smile then lost it entirely once Rooney looked her way.

I read on: *He of conspicuous gallantry and heroic deed; he who fought bravely and auspiciously; he of robust charge and towering intellect...*

"He of the wilt and the worm," I said to Rooney, adding my two cents. "The guy's dead. This was a long time ago."

"Okay, field trip's over," Rooney snarled.

"And look," I said, as Rooney grasped my chain and tugged, "his dearest son, Theodore Barr, would ascend *no less* to the heights of public affairs, serving as the state's fifty-second governor." The officers ushered me onward. "Little Rhody wouldn't be the Little Rhody it is today, Blues, if it weren't for the hard work and sacrifice of such fine and noble men as these."

"Don't believe everything you read," Weldon said under her breath.

Rooney eyed her.

The officers dropped me off at the first teller booth, possibly because the lone teller sat there.

"Do I have to?" I whined.

"Sit down," Rooney commanded.

The nice lady received my Intake information: age, sex, height, weight, shirt and pant size, sexual orientation, medical history. "Any tattoos?" she asked.

I told her tattoos cost money, right?

"I'll take that as a no," she said.

I flipped my wrist and showed it to her.

She leaned in to study the evidence. "Question mark...on...left wrist," she said as she typed.

"Means I don't know," I said, "but I wanna."

The nice lady reached to flick something on her desk. "Curiosity and cats," she said in a low, not-so-nice-sounding voice. She clicked her mouse. "Any identifying marks? Birthmarks, scars?"

I sat up in my chair. "Birthmarks?" Suddenly, boredom took flight.

"Well, do you have them or not?" she asked, looking at me.

"Not personally." Shifting in my seat, I added, "What is a birthmark, though, really? Is it like love? Which you don't know you have it til it's gone? Or is it more like a mosquito bite, which on Monday is an itchy mound of slaughter on your forearm but is going, going, gone by late affy on Friday?"

The nice lady fluttered her painted lashes at me. She scribbled on her form. "No, then," she said.

"Is everyone here as nice as you?" I asked.

"No," she replied. "Gang affiliations?"

Next, she instructed me to follow the yellow line on the floor that extended beyond the row of bank-teller booths. First stop, the Unshackle Room. I looked over my shoulder at the nice lady. Nope. She pointed. Keep going, that meant. Next, I passed the Strip Search Room.

I looked back.

"Walk the yellow line," the nice lady yelled.

I kept walking.

The yellow line led me along an arched stone passageway. I made a right turn, a left, and then straight on for a ways. The door I ran into clicked open upon my approach. The small antechamber beyond the door lay bare except for a narrow metal bench for offenders to squat on and a plexiglas window set into the far wall.

It reminded me of a Ticketmaster window. Maybe that was where all the cool kids bet on the races.

Behind me, the door clicked shut. That sound it made wasn't kidding. Click-lock doors, as opposed to slammer doors, always seemed to trigger something in my psyche. Tangible things you could see and hear, slammer doors at least made sense. If slammer doors were a gun then click-lock doors were a gun with a silencer. Ditto for the black-and-white floor tiles. Something about the patterned contrast in color seemed to mess with a fool's head.

The dour clerk at the ticket-window handed me my navy scrubs. "You're all set," he said. "You can change in this room here," he said, pointing to the door directly across from me. The door buzzed and popped open.

Quiet, here. Talk about graveyards. Where was everybody?

The dour clerk instructed, "Once you're suited up, I'll clear you. Just keep along the yellow-brick road. Your case manager is Ms. Ragazzino. You'll find her at the very end of Case Manager's Row. She's expecting you."

"A key," I said. "How am I supposed to get into my cell?"

"All locks are electronically activated," the clerk explained. "Keys and doorknobs are apportioned to low-side offenders to adjust them to life on the outs. They are a privilege."

Brains are "apportioned" to fools, too, but they don't always use them, I almost replied.

"Love it," I said. "More click-locks. I demand to speak with Governor Barr at once!" I leaned in. "Is he in there?" I straightened. "How about a medical exam?"

"Completed at your intake six months ago," the clerk said, and slid the window closed.

"Hey!" I shouted at it.

The dour clerk slid the glass back. "Do we have a problem?"

"We do. How am I s'pose to change into my new threads when I'm still wrapped up like a Christmas present in these chains here?"

The clerk bit his lip. "Oh. Oh, dear. That was Officer Rooney's charge. It must have slipped his mind. I'll buzz him." The clerk tapped some buttons on his phone and spoke into it.

No less than three hours later, the door clicked open and Rooney swaggered in. "Oh, would you just *look* at this poor little devil with his hands folded and head down," he said, eyeing me all slouched on the ledge like that. "Did someone forget about you?"

"Maybe on purpose," I said under my breath.

"Hey, what kinda op you think we run here, anyway?" Rooney looked down at the keys dangling from his belt strap. "Just for that…"

The process of unshackling proposed to be straightforward enough, but proved far from straightforward, and far from painless. "I'm tightening, not loosening again, aren't I?" Rooney kept saying. "Where did that damn key go now?" was another of his favorite lines. The unlock key kept slipping out of his hand and mixing with the others, which meant he had to test all twenty of them time and again. At one point Rooney cursed, "The pin's stuck," and tried to *pull* the cuffs off.

After the unshackling process paid its wages on my ankles, wrists, and overall well being, Rooney patted me on the back. "You did well," he said. "You didn't scream once."

My forearms, especially, had seen better days.

Rooney fumbled into his pocket and pulled out a pair of rubber gloves. "Strip search time. Afterward, you can go suit up in the changing room."

"Right here, right now? What are the gloves for?"

"Body cavity search, McConnell."

I snorted. "That's only if there's a suspicion of contraband or a foreign object stuck up theres. Coming into a new facility shouldn't require—"

"I know, Clayton. I mean, Sherlock. I mean, I know." Rooney grinned. "Everything off."

It hurt, a lot, but I survived. The clerk, at least, had the courtesy to draw whatever shade he had over there behind the ticket window.

"Follow the yellow line," Rooney said, pointing to the out door. "Don't look back. Don't ever look back. Forward, not back. The future, not the past!" He stood with his feet firmly planted and arms folded.

No escort? This was highly irregular.

The door clicked open upon my approach.

I swallowed, and cradled gingerly my left wrist which seemed to have taken the worst of the thrashing.

I supposed this unsavory episode should have weighed more heavily upon my mind, but for whatever reason I just blotted it out.

It was like those black-and-white squares. Study them long enough and your mind flies away, never to return. Here on the high side I would need to get hard anyway. I needed to stay positive. I thought about Ms. Raggazino.

With a name like that, she's gotta be hot!

The next corridor along the way appeared altogether unsure of itself. Padding along, I noticed the ceiling lofted rather than hung. Higher, brighter, and cleaner, it lent a more pedestrian, albeit institutional type feel to my route. Hopefully, my luck hadn't run its course with the passing of those green stones walls. The paint on these *cement* walls appeared to be an off-white. Here, modernity seemed to have more of a say. But the scenery still had an aged feel to it. The ceiling still sloped in a few places, the white walls farted yellow and brown stains here and there, and the grime embedded in-between the black-and-white floor tiles looked to be the kind that never went away and took years to accumulate.

I continued to put one foot in front of the other along the yellow line on the center of the floor.

My new blue scrubs felt good to walk in. The elastic waistband snuggled me in just right. My shirt fit not too big, not too small. The dour clerk had allowed me to keep my undershirt and black tennies.

Not a soul in sight. Special hallways for special boys, maybe. Probably.

Any number of doors caught my attention as I passed by, but these looked more like utility or storage compartments than ways in or out.

Right turn ahead.

I skidded my wheels around that turn, and eyed another long hallway.

No different than the first hallway with one notable exception.

About midway down, sitting all by his lonesome on a metal bench, sat an offender.

Notably, the color of his prison scrubs was red. A dark, blood red.

I kept my pace. There was a Ms. Ragazzino to get with. Would she let me call her Rags? Her friends probably called her Rags. Maybe some teased her and called her Raggedy Ann. I wondered if Rags had red hair. Of course, it was entirely possible red might be my lucky color at this particular moment in time.

I wondered if I should try to talk to the man in red.

The fool looked straight shot, I noticed, as I neared. His shock of blond hair sat atop a remarkably oblong head in a jumbled mess. Talk about Raggedy-friggin'-Ann. His shoulders slumped, while his legs and arms appeared to twitch. The man looked to be about thirty, although his disheveled appearance made him appear older. Ganglylooking. and bony, his skinniness appeared more along the lines of refusal to eat than lack of provision—just judging by the food stains on his shirt and the posture he maintained with his arms crossed and torso pitching forward and back. Once meth peeps got crazy restless like that, food pretty much no longer mattered. His lips moved, evidently in convo with either himself or some invisible acquaintance.

Closer still, I noticed the man featured a reddish-brown mole on his left cheek.

That got me thinking. Until I stopped thinking along those lines once the man veered his sights my way.

Those eyes. Sure, they were blue but...

"You're here," the man exclaimed. "It's you. It's really you. You've come to rescue me!" He stood.

My tennies ground to a halt yards short of his bench.

"Don't you know me?" he screeched. "I'm Henry Heck."

I fainted on the literal spot, so overwhelmed, overjoyed and happy was I.

Just kidding.

"Bullshit," I said, although I half-regretted it the moment the words exited my mouth. What if it really was The Forever Young Prisoner? Granted this hadn't been my expectation: to meet a hot mess seated on a park bench in a deserted hallway in the middle of the prison. Although, maybe my expectation should've been to meet a whack-job. Hadn't Heck spent like a whole century in the hole?

His huge, boggled eyes widened all the more as he stretched, slowly, probing, grasping, in what looked like an attempt to fondle my face, maybe even hold it in his hands. "You's the one..." he garbled.

I sidestepped his hug attempt.

Suddenly, I noticed, off to our side, a pharmacy-style window with a ledge. Med-line, where offenders were doled out their daily prescriptions.

"Are you waiting for med-line to open?" I asked.

"Med-line," the man said, backpedaling, slowly, unsteadily, shakily, then plopping back down on his seat. His face twisted in a mask of pain. "My Seroquel, they won't give me—"

"They won't give you the meds you so need for your severe schiz-ophrenia, mental-healthia, and million other afflictions you've got going on right now?" I asked.

The man lolled his head all the way back until it bumped against the wall. "Seroquel," he moaned, with his neck jutting out and Adam's apple protruding like a walnut. "800 mg dose, not just 400...not just a 400 dose..."

Angling one's noodle up against a wall like that suggested little in the way of smarts, if the integrity of a wig lay at stake. The perfect angle for something like that to slide right off. And that's why his probably did.

"Your hair's falling out," I told him. "I mean—off." Stringy brown hair draped en masse from the head where a jumbled blond rug once perched.

On a whim, I drew closer, and reached for the reddish-brown mole on his cheek. It appeared much too defined around its edges to be anything but suspicious. It peeled right off.

I studied this bit of costume jewelry. How curious. After a moment's reflection, I stickered it onto the tip of the crazy man's nose.

"Better," I said, thumbing it home with a press of my finger.

The man jerked up on the bench. Stepping all over the wig on the floor, he looked at me with huge eyes. "I am the man, the myth, the leg—"

"No, you're not," I said. "But someone, somewhere, with a black hat on, wants me to think you are." Weirdos were everyday in prison, but the full-on crazies all lived over at Cranston. Someone had invested time, resources and planning to invent this deception. Wigs and mole stickers did not list on commissary. These had been provisioned.

I scoured the grounds for cameras. I didn't see any, but they were here, certainly.

A part of me felt scared, truly frightened, as I resumed my course along the yellow line. What were the boys in blue up to now? But as I neared the next marker, the door at the end of the hallway, I had regained much of my redolent Tomboy swag. Tomboy, another of my street names. They called me that back in my late teens when I was flat-out killin' it. As I was now. I was on a mission. Momma didn't raise no quitter.

"Momma, as if," I said, reaching for the door.

The door clicked open at the mere raise of my hand. They certainly hadn't forgotten about me!

～

The next hallway seemed to have a better idea of what it was. An unremarkable, institutional-style passage whose walls, floor, and ceiling would meet the standards of any twenty-first-century building code. Benches lined the walls. Offenders in blue sat on them. One of the offenders wore canary-yellow scrubs. Sumptin' different. Speaking of yellow, here also was where my line ended.

This was Case Manager's Row, surely, as referenced by the clerk in his decidedly dour way before his homie, Rooney, had his way with me.

Right or left? I hung a left, because to the right a staircase ascended, and to the left a hallway dead-ended with a placard displaying at land's end: Case Manager's Row.

An officer along the way whom I bet spoke Spanish appeared to notice my befuddlement, because he stepped over to greet me. "McConnell?"

I nodded.

"Right this way."

I followed Officer Silva down the hall to the last door on the left.

He showed his face in the window and directed me to do the same. I could see her in there, but not well. The door clicked open.

Usually, irony got the better of me in these types of situations and in exchange for the buildup of my expectations I was rewarded with Lizzie Borden's evil twin or Grandma Moses. She was hotter than I could've ever imagined. On the outs, a six, on a good day, with the help of some make-up and a new nose. But here in the pen she scored a fifteen. No, a fifty.

Short, lustrous black hair, blown eyes, lips that could suck a blow-pop down to the bazooka in seconds, dress pants and a suit. Of all of the females at Providence State Penitentiary I had encountered so far, this modestly-scaled woman fared, by my own estimation, I decided, as we stood eyeing each other, sizing each other up—about as close to my type as it was ever gonna get.

She angled those brownies at me believin' I was all that, too, I could tell.

"Have a seat, Mr. McConnell," she said.

"Gladly," I replied, and meant it.

She folded her hands atop her desk. Black nail-polish. Kinky. "Mr. McConnell, my name is Mandy Ragazzino. I'm your case manager."

"That means you're gonna manage my case."

"Yes, very good," she replied. "I'm the one who bears the greatest responsibility, apart from yourself, of course, to see that your time with us runs as smoothly and uneventfully as possible. Also, I'm here for any questions you might have, and to recommend courses, work programs, as well as the many other options this prison has available for offenders. I'm here to help you prepare for your eventual parole."

"Good times, good times," I said, reaching for the rubber stress ball atop her desk then withdrawing after a flash of warning from her brownies.

Mandy straightened my portfolio until it was flush with the edge of her desk. "So, let me ask you, because it's a question we always ask newcomers, how would you rate your experience so far here on the high side?"

I shifted in my chair. "A negative ten," I said. "A misadventure for the ages. Headache. Heartache. Dishonor. Despair. Honestly, I'd like nothing better, at this point, than to just settle down with a good woman and retire."

"To your cell, presumably," Mandy replied, squelching a smile. "But before you do, there are a few things you and I will first need to go over." Flipping pages, reading, Mandy scanned my record. "Well, we are certainly a low-level offender, aren't we?"

"We sure are," I agreed.

"First time in prison. Three-year sentence. Only one write-up. Your latest venture on the low side raised your point total to seven, which technically still places you in the low-side category, but for your own benefit, and that of your peers, we've placed you here for the next eight months."

"Eight months? That's it?"

Mandy blinked at me. "Unless you get into trouble again in which case your point total will be raised."

I leaned back in my chair. "Well, we'll just have to get ourselves into some trouble, then, won't we?" Smiling, I leaned forward. "How often do I get to see you?"

"Offenders meet with their case managers every six months."

"Well, that sucks."

"Mr. McConnell—"

"You know who you kinda remind me of? Lilya. She's fun, adventurous, hotter than a Hot Pocket, paints her fingernails all kindsa wacky and wild...hearts, rainbows, smiley-faced skulls..."

"Focus, Mr. McConnell."

I added, softly, reflectively, "And her heart's the purest gold."

Mandy clicked her pen as she scanned my portfolio. "I'd really like to get you out on a work crew eventually. You'll qualify in three months. I think you'd do well, all things considered. Classes are out of the question due to your limited time with us." Mandy touched the curled ends of her dark hair as she looked over. "She's a friend of yours this...Lilya? You like this girl?"

Like her? I never really thought about it like all that. Actually, I did like Lilya, in a kind of way. Maybe in a whole lot of kinda ways. "A really close friend, that's it," I said.

"Do you have any questions for me?" Mandy asked.

Any big plans for this Friday night? I wanted to ask. Instead I said, "My scrubs are blue, but I've noticed different colored ones, like yellow."

Mandy brightened. "Yellow means low-risk. You might be in yellows sooner than you think. Yellow means work crew, just think of it that way."

I tapped my fingers lightly on her desktop. "How 'bout red?"

Mandy's glowy professionalism fell off a bit. "Red?"

I nodded.

She tilted her head. "Very well, I'll tell you. But first, why do you ask?"

"Because it's my favorite color," I said, trying to keep a straight face.

Mandy cleared her throat. "Red would not prove a flattering look on you, Mr. McConnell. No red around here, not without an entourage of blue surrounding it. Red means Supermax, not any place you would be allowed to go or would ever want to."

"Why not?" I said. "I could look around, scope out the place. Maybe there's some dope stuff over that ways. Is there a tour or something like that I can take?"

Mandy furrowed her brow. "You're serious."

I nodded.

She blinked. "Well, that's an incredibly odd thing to say, Mr. McConnell. I don't think I've ever heard that one before, and I've heard plenty." I could see the gears inside of Mandy's head wheeling as she studied my face and particularly my eyes. Seconds later, she started typing on her computer. "Which reminds me. There was an email I'd received shortly before your arrival that I hadn't had time to read. Hold on..."

"From your boyfriend?"

"No, Mr. McConnell."

"Is it about anyone I know?" I lifted off the seat cushion in an effort to see.

All I did end up seeing, as Mandy read, were those wheels inside of her head spinning, faster, faster, until finally she clicked her mouse and fell back into her chair. Afterward, she indulged dark glances my way.

Rubbing her chin, Mandy said, "Mr. McConnell, I can tell you're going to be a very difficult case."

I fell back onto my seat cushion, all the way back.

She wasn't finished. "Your original charge was violent. You were involved in an *extremely* brutal boxing match over there on the low side. You lasted only four days on a work crew..." Mandy kept rubbing her chin in that weird way. A ring: she was married. "Also, your record indicates you are insubordinate, sarcastic—"

"Is there a law against that? Prison's *made* me sarcastic, ma'am. Coming in, I was this shy, quiet—"

"—insubordinate, sarcastic," she went on, "and most significantly, *most significantly*, Mr. McConnell, it states that you *poke your nose into affairs it has no business poking itself into, into business this prison can* well enough *handle on its own.*"

Oh. Oh, dear, I thought, to quote the dour clerk.

"Keep poking your nose into affairs that aren't its own, and it's liable to get *broke.*"

"My nose already got broke," I said. "Like four-hundred-and-nineteen times."

Mandy exhaled. "Mr. Sherlock—I mean, McConnell, you'll find it's going to be a long, difficult road for you should you at all decide..." she angled her sights down at my hands which were splayed on her desk. "Oh, my God. You're bleeding!"

The hands themselves looked fine, actually, even though they didn't feel fine. And the wrists and forearms weren't exactly bleeding, just hella chewed up. Nope, two or three of the scratches were oozing red life fluid, she was right.

"You've been trying to hurt yourself!" Mandy rose from her seat.

I didn't quite know how to respond to all of that other than, "Well, not exactly."

Mandy froze in mid-step on her way to the door. "Not exactly? *Not exactly?* Would you please care to explain what *exactly* you mean by *not exactly,* Mr. McConnell?"

I sank into my chair. "Black Hats gonna Black Hat," I muttered. Damn. Scratches were nothing. Everyone got them.

"Officer Silva," Mandy called into the hall. "Officer Silva! Would you please be so kind as to stop by for one moment?"

Officer Silva stood in the doorway with his arms folded, as Mandy returned to the business side of her desk.

"Suicide watch," she said. "This man has been trying to harm himself. Please escort him to the Isolation Room, immediately!"

CHAPTER TWELVE

Known by its many designations such as cool down room, safety room, isolation room, padded-cell compartment, unofficially as "paddies," and colloquially as "The Lizard Room," this segregated chamber with its padded walls and floor might well have invoked other names, as well. Personally, I would have called it *The Place Where They Got You, Really Got You, and You Can't Get Away.*

The big issue, for me, lay not in the padding stuck up against the walls and floor, or the straightjacket which assumed the form of a giant, green puffer-jacket that enveloped everything but your face. Nor the lack of any air conditioning inside of this dreaded Lizard Suit which made one feel almost as hot as Rags had feigned to be before she had turned to the dark side. Nor, that the cops fed you by hand.

It was the fact that a pair of black-hatted cops could talk smack *while* they fed you by hand.

Rooney and Perry, their name-pins read. As things would turn out, Perry, whom I called Captain Baldy to his face, seemed like the more darkly motivated of the two. He'd level the spoon up to your lips, pull it back once you snapped for it, then call you all sorts of dastardly names for spilling gravy all over your damned self again. Mind games, mostly, that played on one's patience, and all the more when one couldn't so much as twitch a finger inside of his suit. I think their intentions geared less towards injuring or threatening me as to make me go crazy. The word "Cranston" was mentioned once or twice, but I guess it didn't fly in the face of my continued forbearance. I had lived on the streets, mind you. Living Hell was my middle name. We'll not discuss that little episode involving myself, Perry, and the egg roll. It doesn't figure much into the story otherwise and anyhow I survived.

Finally they decided I mustn't be as crazy as all that and let me loose; although, I *would've* been as crazy as all that had they kept me in that reptile suit a day or two longer.

The one long-term downside to a Lizard Room visit was the devil green scrubs they dressed you up in afterward. Penned by my captors in black marker just above the shirt pocket of my greens read the name "Clayton." Allowed to roam freely, so to speak, I still listed on Suicide Watch. This allowed the prison's "chain of command" to keep an official eye on me.

Everyone else eyed me, too, as I made my way into the Pod 2 commons area.

A guy who looked about as Aryan Brotherhood as could be catcalled as I mounted the zigzag staircase to the third floor, "Is it as bad as all that, Greeny?" By the color of his scrubs, which were brown, my best guess placed him as either a trustee or maintenance. He, the pod officer, and two others, filled out the place.

My worry up until this time had been to arrive to cell-wide, deafening chants of "Fish, fish, fish!" therefore this colorful, soft greeting elicited every bit a sigh of relief.

"Green is the new black," I said to Brownie, weakly. Just then, my army-style duffle bag slipped out of my hand onto the second-floor landing; the bag tipped over, and one of my shower-shoes fell out. With a shake of my head, I kicked the bag. With my shoe in hand, I took a moment to admire the view.

Those documentaries on the Discovery Channel didn't lie. The floor of the commons area caught my attention first. Seamless, a burgundy-brown color, with a sheen you could almost see your reflection in, the floor extended to the four corners of the earth. And so truly was this our earth, our little world, this square of space they called *Pod 2*. Rows of cell doors populated three out of the four walls. The front of the pod owned the fourth wall. It featured the main entrance and a control tower. Not really a tower, more like a control *center*. They called it the "podium." Here, an officer sat behind an array of screens and switches and monitored the goings-on. Two pay phones showcased on the wall. Tables populated the commons area. The commons area was just that: an open area in the center of the pod comprising the whole ground level. The face of the individual cells featured those inglorious iron bars. This meant you could see in. See-through worked for dresses, not prison cells, was my own opinion.

Three levels, or tiers, overhung one another, each with its own mezzanine walkway and shower room. The mezzanine walkways jutted out ten feet or so from the cells. Railings sided all transit areas which included the walkways and staircases. No less than five rows of railing raised a defense against any would-be accident. Gravity, love it or leave it.

Sure, there were words spoken at me as I passed the first few cells on my trek along the third-floor mezzanine, but just the usual jailhouse bullshit, no biggie. Thumping and bumping sounds issued from the fifth or sixth cell. Grunting, thwacking sounds, too. Two homies absolutely *wailing* on one another, I verified, as I looked in. Either the angle of the walkway with respect to the face of their cell hid their beef from the officer downstairs, or he simply didn't give two shits. Probably the latter. No matter how many fights you've seen or been involved in, they are always awful, awesome, fearful things to behold. The sound alone of a fist against a face leaves an indelible impression—and not just for the guy getting whacked. The present ruckus sounded like a damned symphony. My sights redirected and feet marched on.

I peered through the bars at my new celly.

He sat slouched on the lower bunk. He raised his head.

"Fuck," he said, dropping his book onto his mattress. "A loon," he said, loudly. "They've sent me a goddamn loon!"

"Green is the new black," I said, as the cell door clanked, rattled, and rolled open. "Watcha readin'?"

"He's crazy," my new celly shouted, seemingly at the top of his lungs. "He wants to know what I'm reading!"

My greens had in no way assisted my rep thus far. Probably, that had been the point; and presumably, the luck of the Irish extended only so far.

I hoisted my duffle bag and crossed the threshold into my new prison home.

The cell door clanked, rattled, then rolled home behind me.

My new celly stood. "Look, fella, if you're gonna off yourself, don't do it on my rack, anywhere but on my rack."

I dropped my bag off by the desk. It landed with a thud. "Guess I'm on top," I said, eyeing the top bunk.

"Damn right you're on top," my celly replied. He sat down and folded his large, pudgy fingers while he took a deep breath. He scanned me up and down. Narrowing his eyes, he said, "All right, loony bin. Some quick ground rules before your crazy ass gets too comfortable and you end up losing it. Listening?"

Scouring the place, I stopped, looked over, nodded, and kept scouring.

"Fail to keep your area clean," he said, "you get slapped. Walk around the place half-naked, you get spanked. Mess with my rack or any of my things, you'll find your head in that toilet over there." He pointed to it. "Capeesh?"

Standing with my reddened arms and wrists at my sides, I asked, "What, exactly, might I have to do to get you to murder me?"

My celly's eyes widened. "You *are* crazy, then."

Smiling, I loosened the drawstrings of Santa's sack and began to rummage. "Nah," I said. "You've got me confused with everybody else in this joint."

The wide eyes of my celly blinked at me. "That's a sure sign of insanity, when you think you're sane and everyone else around you isn't."

"I know," I said. "That's why I said it."

My celly pursed his lips as he resumed his probe. Folding his hands behind his head and laying back, he watched as I unpacked my things. "You're a young squirt. Fresh fish, if ever there was."

I turned. "And you're a grizzled old man with a beer belly and dark, sad eyes." He wasn't a small man, and looked like he could throw his weight around, too, if push came to shove, and so I opted not to get any more colorful with my observations than simply this. In so many ways he actually reminded me of Fatts.

As a general rule, offenders were paired with others their own age, or around their own age. This specimen looked to be about fifty. As I withdrew my plastic cup, container of Keefe coffee, fingernail clippers, and comb, and set them down one by one on the bureau, I wondered why they had assigned me to this old fart. I could almost see the same query in the old fart's eyes as he watched me unpack and refold my boxers.

"How long you been down?" I asked.

"Long enough," he growled. After a longish pause he added, "...to get all gray, grizzled, and grow a beer belly."

I smiled at that. We were bonding already. "What were your charges?"

He sat up in his rack. "Extortion. Armed robbery. Evasion." He smiled big. "And maybe a murder or two."

I glared at him out of the corner of my eye. A few of his teeth looked missing, but that was to be expected. Prison dentists pulled teeth, and made you wait six months to pull your teeth, and that was about it. No yearly cleanings in prison, and the rubber toothbrushes they sold on commissary worked only slightly better than the use of one's thumb.

"I thought they put murderers in *Supermax*," I said, placing my own rubber scrubber atop the shelf in my open-faced closet.

"Super's for *dangerous* murderers," my celly replied.

A temptation passed to inquire into the difference between a "murderer" and a "dangerous murderer," but I decided to save the subject of Supermax for another, more opportune time.

"And you?" he asked. "Your charges? Forget to file your taxes?" He laughed.

Setting my alarm clock, I said, "Put a guy in the hospital for getting too chippy with me."

That shut him up.

Five minutes later, while arranging my mattress, I looked down at my celly. "What's your name?"

My celly narrowed his eyes up at me. "Sal Caniglio," he said in a hard, but tired voice. "What's yours—Clayton?"

"No. And not Sherlock, either. Not here. Not now." Sal looked at me. I looked back. "Tommy McConnell."

"Nice Irish boy," he said. "I like that. Maybe you'll bring me luck." He flipped a page in his book. "Why did you write Clayton on your scrubs then?"

I replied, after a moment's pause, "They did. They wrote it."

Sal sat up in his rack. "Clayton? As in *John* Clayton? Do you know who that is? He died, under suspicious circumstances. Some say he was killed. You did *something* to piss them off. That writing means you're a marked man. Possibly a doomed one."

"I'm not worried about the cops," I said. "All bark no bite."

"Yeah, until their bark gets you to bite the bullet. Or maybe you've tried it already. *Green is the new black*, he says," Sal said, mockingly. He jostled in his rack. "Look, that label's not just to warn you, but others, not to associate with you. They're not gonna just *off* you. That would look suspicious." Sal thought about it. "Well, maybe, if you *really* pissed them off and the situation presented itself, but more likely they're gonna isolate you, make you go crazy, find every excuse to ship you to Cranston. That's how they roll. And don't even *think* of telling me what you did to trigger them, because I don't wanna know."

"I'm not actually Irish," I said, changing the subject. "My real dad's ancestors or whatever—"

"Fuck, you think I'm stupid? You don't think I know that?" Sal returned to his book.

Folding my towel into a perfect square, I craned my neck to read the front cover: *Wiseguy* by Nicholas Pileggi. "These days," I said to no one in particular, placing my makeshift pillow at the head of my mattress, "everyone wants to be a gangster. Even old men with dark, sad eyes."

No response from the peanut gallery.

Last but not least, I withdrew from my duffle bag my paperback copy of *Wuthering Heights*. The Inspection peoples on low and high sides had let me keep it. I climbed into my rack and began to read.

Page 1. Day 1. That's how every great story always begins.

What Sal Caniglio lacked in congeniality, he more than made up for in quirk. He featured every whit as the clean freak and schedule junkie. Longer sentences did that to even the gnarliest offender, the grapevine said. And here it was. Clean living, ironically, was all but code. It *was* code.

Bed time varied, but with lockdown in effect, Sal turned in at nine o'clock. Not a minute later or sooner. Beddie-bye for me would have to be the same, at least for these first few days.

Sleep swept over me like the swelling tide up a Narragansett beachfront. Lizard suits don't breathe too well nor can one breathe especially well in them, and needless to say I hadn't slept well over the previous two nights.

Deep into the night I had a dream. It's vividness brought me to the point of wanting to pinch myself, but I couldn't, because my arms were deadlocked. A large, pale-faced man stood beside my rack. He kept slapping me. He grabbed my arms and began to shake.

Fighting back, I yelled, "My butthole's mine. It's mine, you son of a bitch. You can't have it!"

Finally, I opened my eyes.

Sal Caniglio showcased right up in my mug in all of his sweaty, fleshy glory.

This was no dream. Rather, dream and reality had merged.

Sal muscled my forearms in a vice grip as I fended him off with swipes, punches, elbows, whatever I could muster if only I could muster up some space to do so first.

"Cut it out!" I blared at the round face up on me. "Just. Cut. This. Shit. Out!"

"No, *you* cut it out," Sal said, endeavoring to pin my arms.

His words walloped me harder than even his fist would've. All at once I relaxed my arms, legs, neck, and just let him pin me. "What did you just say?"

He released, as well, and backed off.

Breathing heavily, Sal retreated. I could hear the bed creak as he laid back down on the lower bunk. "We'll have no more of *that*," he said, sputtering the words in-between belabored breaths.

Still groggy and lost in the deep well of catch-up sleep, I tried to wrap the few, jumbled scraps of awareness I had around the situation at hand. "No more of *what*?"

Sal paused to let his asphyxia or whatever subside. Breathe in, breathe out. Breathe in... He sputtered, "Did anybody ever tell you you talk in your sleep?" He sucked in another breath. "Did anybody ever tell you you talk *loudly* in your sleep?"

Suddenly, it struck me that sleep-talkers might not fare well on this high side, and even less well for those with "Clayton" penned on their damned green shirts.

"Talk in my sleep?" I laughed. "No way. How do you know it was even me? You were probably dreaming."

In my mind's eye, I could see Sal's eyes roll. "Who was it then," he said, sarcastically, after another deep breath, "the boogeyman? Bet you're gonna tell him it was Ol' Morgan."

A neighbor, maybe? His old celly? His imaginary friend? "Who's Ol' Morgan?"

"Resident phantom. We're getting off subject." With the slow return of Sal's normal breathing came a wave of negative energy wafting up from the bottom bunk like heat. "Listen, you *writhing, moaning, loud-talking-in-your-sleep son-of-a*—"

"What did I say?"

Sal swore. Swore again. He took a deep breath, then replied, "You was flailing back and forth on your rack, moaning, writhing. You kept repeating 'Help me...I'm guilty. Help me...I'm guilty. Help me...' then something else I couldn't quite figure 'cause you were mumbling that part. Listen, fella, even if you *wasn't* guilty of whatever crime yours was, I ain't gonna help ya. No one is. Don't you know what 'do your own time' means?"

I nodded, even though I knew Sal couldn't see me. "Of course," I said. "It's another way of saying mind your own business."

"It means do your own fucking time! It means, when you hear your neighbor gettin' worked over, don't pay a visit. When you overhear a plot, turn a deaf ear. When you're in the showers and see someone's ass get taken to the cleaners, keep showering—and don't drop your own damned soap. It means don't make other people's problems *your* problem."

All of that sounded super encouraging. "What if it was *your* ass, celly? Wants I should just walk away?"

"Yes, the fuck, yes," Sal declared. "Just keep walking. That's what you do, that's what I do, that's what's done. It's *code*. Don't make everyone else's problems *your* problems. And stop it with the damned sleep talking or you and I are gonna have a problem."

"Do your own time, celly," I told him with a smile in my voice.

Sal quieted after that. Only he said, "It's late. Go to sleep, Tommy McConnell."

Lockdowns came in two flavors: hard and soft. The similarities between the two listed numerous, and included...23 hours in the cell and one hour out of the cell to do things like shower and stretch legs, no rec activities, no classes, no family or friend visits. The lone differences? Eat in the chow hall versus eat in your cell.

This was a hard lockdown, so breakfast was taken in the cell.

Over rubber eggs and burnt potatoes, Sal spilled the tea about the smack-down had two weeks earlier between the Northies and Southbangers, a three-on-four match in the commons area of Pod 5. Gangland rumbles meant the whole facility had to pay the price. The grapevine hinted that lockdown would be lifted within the next few days.

Two weeks earlier, I thought, *was when Niño had done his crazy dance.* Those sirens right afterward. That must have been that.

Two weeks earlier seemed like a hella long time ago.

The night of my donkey dream.

You will be quiet tonight. You will have peace. No screaming and kicking, like last night. And the night before. And the night before that.

"How we doin' up there?" Sal asked from the bottom bunk after we had cleared our trays, settled in, and returned to reading.

"We're *dying* up here."

I heard Sal stir. "What do you mean *you're dying*? You did it? I mean, you're doing it? What the hell's going on up there? You doin' the dutch?"

Dangling my arm, I waved my 19th-century masterpiece of English literature volume down at him. "It's a rough read. This flowery English prose is just *killin'* me. I'm thinking it's gonna be a romance. It's starting to look that way."

The flipping of a page in his Roberto Saviano novel meant Sal had calmed. "Then why read it?"

"Because, I'm a man of my word."

Sal quieted. "You promised someone you'd read it? Who?"

"Myself."

Sal leaned over the side of his rack to look up. I leaned over the side of mine to look down. "Yourself?" he said. "That's admirable. If you were my son, Tommy McConnell, I'll tell you I was proud of you, right after I kicked your ass for talking in your sleep."

Sal's words made me smile. "Haven't you ever made a promise to yourself?" I asked.

"Sure, a million times. To go rogue, to break ties with the Family. To just walk away. But they keep pulling me back in. They keep *pulling me back in.*"

"Isn't that from a movie?" I eyed my book's front cover with its strange lady in white.

"*The Godfather,*" Sal replied. "And it's not just a movie."

Nor were Sal's words just words. The way he spoke this last bit suggested Sal wished to discuss no further this subject of his family. Good, spare me the long, boring details about the legal issues with the wife or the kids who keep borrowing Dad's credit card while he's away on vacation here. Do your own time. Besides, more pressing questions loomed.

I said to Sal, "Spill the tea about Old Morgan, your resident phantom."

Sal grunted. "Spill the tea? What the fuck's that s'pose to mean?"

"Tell me about Old Morgan, your resident phantom."

Sal asked, "You wanna know about Old Morgan, our resident phantom?"

"Tell me about Old Morgan, your resident phantom."

Sal exhaled. "After I finish this chapter. The main guy's about to go ballistic on this other guy who keeps asking dumb questions."

Minutes later, Sal slammed his hardcover closed. "You believe in ghosts?"

I placed mine aside, too. "Nah. Maybe. Does it matter? Who knows. Tell me."

I could hear Sal shuffle around. "You don't believe in ghosts, but you wanna know about one? I thought you said you weren't crazy?"

"I lied. Tell me. I want all the gory details. Like, what did he die from?"

"He didn't. They say Old Morgan lives here among us still. Offenders, cops, even an orderly have seen him."

"I mean, what did he die from when he *died*?"

"The thing that gets us all in the end. Old age."

"Possibly not all of us. Anyway, tell me."

Sal did.

Apparently, the Horatio S. Barr Correctional Center, erected in 1889, home to gargoyles and stone edifices, to one too many of those inglorious iron bars, and lizard-suited peoples, was home also to more legends than one.

Morgan Pennington was about as telltale a name as any. Pennies were Morgan's business. A moderately successful mid-level banker at the downtown Loan and Trust, he was indicted for his involvement in a racketeering scheme, which, curiously, took down none other than himself and a clerk—all of the other higher-level homies were eventually acquitted. Those who knew him best called bullshit.

While in prison, money remained Morgan's business. He collected pennies, back in the days when hobby practices were allowed, even if unofficially. *A penny for your thoughts,* and *if I had a penny for every time* were two of Morgan's favorite sayings. However, not even Morgan's estimable collection of 517 foreign and domestic pennies could save him from the renderings of time.

On his deathbed in the prison infirmary in the gentle Year of our Lord 1936, Morgan pronounced a curse upon the whole of Horatio S. Barr Land. Declaring himself subject to a power loftier than the judge and jury who had sentenced him, he admonished the guardians of the land for their malfeasance, reaffirmed his innocence, then flipped a penny in the air. *Heads,* he told the guard to his right, and you boys got it right. *Tails,* he said to the nurse on his left, "then whenever you see me a month from now, a year, or in fifty years, you'll remember Morgan Pennington and know he was innocent."

Sal must have been nodding because the whole bed-frame seemed to jangle. "Legend has it Morgan's penny came up tails. He died hours later, gripping his penny. They say the sightings began just a few days afterward."

"Tight! When do we get to meet this penny guy?"

Sal slapped his mat, hard. "You're not listening, there's more!" He breathed. "Okay, so the legend states that only those who grip a penny in their hand and are pure of heart may call forth the Ghost of Morgan Pennington. Over the years a few have tried it, and there have been sightings."

"Isn't it dope when the universe does stuff like that?"

"*Dope*?" Sal jostled about. "Listen, McConnell, I've been down for eighteen years and have known more than a few guys who have made the Morgan Penny Promise while nearing their end. I knew some of those boys were at least partly innocent of their charges. But no one's ever heard from the likes of...Johnny Dee...Sharpie...Old School Bellini..."

I thought of Niño.

Curses. Some of them work, some no. Not all curses, reverse-curses, and blessings are success. There is a reason for this. Now, we do the thing...

"Where's the Penny Man at?" I asked.

"Pod 1, cell B19, middle tier," Sal replied. "That's where all the activity is said to take place. Two or three times he was supposedly spotted in the infirmary and once or twice other places."

"Pod 1, cell B19. Got it. How do I get over there and where the hell am I gonna get a penny?"

"You *can't* get over there, and pennies are *contraband*."

"You let me deal with the penny. Why no Pod 1?"

"Chomos and rapists over in Pod 1. They wouldn't let you over there besides."

That sounded fairly dead-endish, for sure. "Has the Penny Man ever swung by this way?"

Sal snorted. "I thought you didn't believe in ghosts? Use a button in place of a penny, that's what some clowns do. Grip it in your hand

and call for him, see if he comes. If ghosts are anything like dogs…" Sal grew quiet. "I had a dog once," he said, gloomily. "A pittie named Corleone. Those were the dark days, way back in the day, when all of my hopes and dreams started to shatter all around me."

I bit my lip, debating within myself. For what it's worth, a bit of sound advice that often goes unheeded is to never underestimate the influence of a tight space, lengthy stay, and engaged audience. Oftentimes they may yield the revelation of what are known as "prison secrets." Unsolved crimes are confessed, dirty laundry is hung out to dry. As if unthinkingly over the course of a conversation the words just flow. I swallowed. "I have a dream."

"And what might that be, Tommy McConnell?" Sal asked in a tired voice.

I took a deep breath. "To solve the mystery of The Forever Young Prisoner. They called me Sherlock on the low side. I'm not Sherlock *here* because I don't want anyone to know. This is something I'm hella serious about, Sal."

Sal lay silent for a very long time. Finally, in a low, almost inaudible voice, he replied, "You don't say?"

CHAPTER THIRTEEN

The grapevine got it right this time. Two days later, lockdown lifted. Master Control made the announcement. The cell doors clanked, rattled, then rolled open, and all of Horatio S. Barr's creatures, great and small, tattooed and scarred, ripped, jacked, and beer-bellied, green, blue, and black-and-blue, emerged from their burrows to greet the great outdoors.

Quite the sight, everyone storming out at once like that! Kicking up our heels like horses out of the stall, we clanked down the zigzag staircases to converge on our greener pastures, the commons area. I received my fair share of glances along the way, although it did less than deter my sights away from the pay phones—all claimed within seconds, though, with a queue of ten or twelve stretched out behind.

No worries. In prison, time doubled as friend. Time, then, to do some people-watching. Standing forlorn aside one of the tables in the phone area, I scanned the premises.

Not much in the way of eye candy here. Correction: there was good and plenty. A few Suckers out yonder; Dum-Dums over this way; Milk Duds, Zeros, Hubba Bubbas; the one with the glasses standing by the far table looked to be a Nerd, with that Jolly Rancher getting cute with him. That Whatchamacallit sashaying down the staircase looked to be a Sweet Tart, on his way to that table of Sugar Babies. A Goober or two. A Smartie. Nut Rolls and Mars Bars roamed the place freely. Chunky yapped on the phone. Not a Mr. Goodbar in sight. Oh, and a Swedish Fish. Myself.

The population as a whole looked decidedly older and rougher than on the low side. More eclectic, I would say, too. The spread spaced wider here when it came to types of criminal charges. Druggies and thieves populated the low side, but not so much here at Drac's Castle. Not all high-level offenders are tough guys; some are pseudo-tough; some are tough nuts; others are just plain nuts. The full demographic appeared to find representation here.

I didn't recognize a single face.

Although, one seemed to recognize me.

From behind me, a voice said, "Hey, you made it!"

I turned. The face didn't register for me at first. However, the blond mutton-chop sideburns rimming the sides of it sure did. "Chopper. Fancy seeing you here. What it do?"

"Congrats on your promotion." Chopper smiled as we fist-bumped.

"Go for the gold, mamma always said," I told him.

Chopper introduced me to his buds, Mike and Slider.

"Mike & Ike," I said, smiling, but they didn't get it.

An older offender, Mike boasted about thirty years on Planet Earthquake, if I had to guess, and Slider looked a few years older than that. They weren't so much big dudes as hard looking. The narrowness in their eyes, in most everyone's eyes, made sharpened flint look like the rubber end of a prison toothbrush. Happy-go-lucky Chopper featured as the lone exception, but his six months here was Laffy Taffy to some of these old timers.

"How's your writing going?" Chopper asked, while his buds sized me up.

"My writing?" I coughed. "It's not." I hadn't written in weeks. "I mostly read now."

"You'll have plenty of time for that!" Chopper said.

"Ever been to prison before?" Slider said with his eyes boring into me.

"Low side," I replied.

"For what it's worth, it's not the same," Slider noted. "You'll discover that soon enough."

Chopper laid down some of the ground rules for me. Yard time was every day from one to three. Body counts, knuckle-body checks, surprise inspections, were routine here. "Make your bed, watch your back, do your own time—"

"And ditch the green," Mike said, leveling a stare.

"Yeah, that too," Chopper said, then turned and walked away alongside his buds, finally heeding the call of their elbow nudges.

To blame Chopper for bailing like that would mean to turn a blind eye to the fact that associating with fish in green logged negatively in prison rep points. Eye contact appeared minimal, too, I noticed, as I angled a look around. The few forays in my direction ogled, leered, and bit back. However, my trusty ally, time, would ensure the Pod 2 boys warmed up to me eventually. In time, they would see the gold behind the green.

Segregation seemed a thing here, too. Not that I planned to be the one to rouse them, but these homies probably needed to wake the fuck up. Whites banded with whites, Blacks with Blacks, ditto for Hispanics. Even the feezys cliqued together. With their shaven legs and flimsy wrists, they maintained a six-foot shield of space wherever they roamed. The LGBTQers registered as a protected class. To mess with them meant the long arm of the law tapping on your shoulder; to hang or even yap with them meant the strong arms of your homies strung around your neck. Not that too many of *these* LGBTQers looked like they needed protection. Flimsy wrists aside, some of them stood over six feet tall, featured muscles aplenty, and assuredly knew how to get their kicks in while in places other than just the shower room. Just because his name was "Filippa" didn't mean she couldn't *filippa* you over and body slam your ass. Mental note.

After ten minutes, I grew tired of waiting for the phone and retired to my cell. Sal asked if I might do him a favor and pass along a message to "two guys, one with a mohawk" in cell C12. But I wasn't anyone's FedEx guy, I told him, and besides, I was busy doing my own damned time.

"Good boy," he said in a voice that belied the sentiment.

No less than an hour later, the long line at the phones petered out, and I made my way over.

Connecting through the automated system didn't wear on my patience so much this time. Anytime was a good time that wasn't spent moping around lonely and awkward in the commons area.

Lilya answered, and agreed to accept my call.

"Tommy," Lilya exclaimed. "I've been waiting for you to get back!"

I, not we, she said. That Danny had fallen on rough times seemed obvious enough. He didn't seem particularly anxious to talk to me, either, but that was probably for the best. Drugs and monitored convos didn't mix too well. Danny would get his shit together. Maybe.

"Have you really, Lil," I asked, "been waiting for my call?"

"Well, duh, that FOIA request you'd asked me to mail out. Anyway, it came back. Hella quick turnaround time."

"Quick turnaround sounds bad," I said.

"There's no one named Henry Heck at the Horatio S. Barr Correctional Facility. No record exists. The handwritten message at the bottom of the letter they mailed back said *Get a job*."

I snorted. "Figures. I don't think Henry Heck's his real name anyway."

"And so, guess what? I did get one. A job. How you gonna find out his real name, Tommy?"

I dug into my pocket and pulled out a scrap of paper. "No one to help me out with that so...maybe I'll ask the dead."

Lilya didn't respond.

Unfolding the paper, I read aloud, "We've braved its ghosts often together, and asked them to come. But, Heathcliff, if I dare you now, will you venture?" I refolded the paper and returned it to my pocket —my pants pocket.

Lilya said, in a puzzled voice, "Is that code for saying you're high? I've heard there's a lot of *stuff* in prisons. Not the hard stuff. Pills."

"Pills? Nah," I replied. "I don't go to med-line. Lil, that was an excerpt from that book you recommended, *Wuthering Heights*. I thought you said it was a chick book."

"It is. A ghostly romance. Kind of."

I nodded at the phone. "I'm on Chapter 13. Gonna keep reading to find out how that girl ghost floated her way over to that guy. In the first chapter she visited and banged on his window. That part was dope." I shared with Lilya about our resident ghost, Ol' Morgan, his pennies, and how one might call for him with a penny in hand.

From her intermittent giggling, it appeared Lilya didn't think ghosts were entirely snoreway. Then I remembered she saw shadow people.

I finished by saying, "Still, they say only the *pure of heart* may call upon Old Morgan. I'm thinking if I can get mine to be even *half* the 24 carat yours is, Lil, I just might have a chance."

Lilya snorted.

"Hello?" I said, interrupting the awkward silence which followed.

"Get an EVP recorder, Tommy," Lilya said, excitedly. "It's a sensitive audio recording device that picks up ghostly voices. You can call for your Penny person, press record, and see if he answers. It'd be wicked cool to have one, right? Look, someone I know's got a birthday coming up..."

I laughed. "Mail me a card. The inspection boys and girls *might* let that go through. Your ghost recorder will boomerang, I assure you."

"How about a penny?" Lilya asked.

Suddenly, a loud, grating noise sounded over the wire. Our

connection would appear to have been compromised. The screws were screwing with the line, there could be no doubt.

"I think I've lost you," Lilya said, her voice coming through in spurts.

"No," I spoke loudly over the interference. "You haven't. I'll be out soon enough. We'll get together and rap. You and me we...we're worlds apart, and yet in so many ways we're like the very same soul."

The line went dead.

"You sound really good, Lil," I spoke into the dead phone.

I redialed the number when I heard a voice from behind me say, "Don't even go there."

"One and done," a Hispanic guy with facial tats next to the first guy said.

I swallowed. "My girl was...just about to tell me all about her new job," I said, weakly, and hung up.

My girl. Had I called Lilya that?

Ascending the staircase, I noticed an offender with a mohawk standing at the entrance to our cell. I didn't feel quite up for the usual meet and greets, so I decided to just chill for a while in the commons area until he bailed.

Now, we won't delve too greatly into the details concerning the "shower" I had received while in the Lizard Room. Things got pretty hectic, enough said. Suffice to say, I had received but a partial cleansing, and needless to say I hadn't showered in just under a week.

Not that this fact alone offered much incentive against having to face the dreaded community shower room. Per the rules, showers calendared a minimum of twice a week. Time, then, to face the music. Shower shoes on, a towel over my shoulder, and my Bob Barker soap in hand, I ambled my way down the mezzanine to the wet and wild room.

Nearing, I heard the sound of screams. Nope, just some fun-lovin' light banter from the fellas. Images flashed before me of girls in white t-shirts at the car wash, spraying each other with hoses while laughing. No girls here. Just murderers, rapists and the like.

My intention was to make the guys think this shower deal was the most hum-drum, everyday thing Tommy McConnell had ever experienced. And so while dipping my foot in the pool I began to whistle. If I had to face the music, so did they.

"If you're gonna pull that shit, at least play something good," one of the old timers snapped.

I said, "Like what?"

He replied, "'80s shit."

Deciding to pass on my theme song, "18 and Life," I whistled some Bananarama for him. Before I knew it, the guys were all sway-ing, swinging, and humming along to the bad beat of "Cruel Summer." And a cruel summer it was; although one not without promise.

Chopper was a latecomer to the pool party. He slipped in just as the others began wiping up. With regards to Chopper, let's just say life's occasionally full of surprises: things don't always measure up the way you would expect. Anyway, while lathering up, Chopper recited some of the ground rules of Shower Land for me. "First rule," Chopper said. "Don't ever, EVER, drop your soap." Chopper snickered. "Just kidding." The feezys had a corner on that market, he explained. Their cells acted like revolving doors in many instances. Why force it on one when you can get it free and willing from another? Also, there was PREA. The long arm of the law had gotten a whole lot longer since the program's inception a few years earlier.

All of this "long arm of the law" talk suddenly got me feeling about as clean as a whistle. I flipped off the shower and wiped up. I never did get around to hearing what Ground Rules 2 and 3 might be.

"Got any meth?" Chopper called over on my way out.

Two steps out onto the gangway I halted, closed my eyed, and let out a long, slow breath. Returning to stand on the threshold of the shower room, I diverted my gaze as Chopper flipped off his shower. "No," I said. "Do you?"

Yard time was good times. In prison, it was the best of times.

Count happened every day at 1 p.m.. The cell doors clanked, rattled, then rolled open, and we all stepped out. Standing in front of our cell doors, the C.O.'s, well, counted us...just to make sure no one had skipped town between then and morning count. For those interested in yard-time, the door now stood open to them. We roamed in packs, that way our overseers could keep tabs on us. To venture anywhere on your own like to a case manager or the mail room required a signed pass. Blue roamed the highways and byways in search of strays.

The Pod 2 through 5 buildings, and the Activities Building, framed the grassy *yard* in a perfect square. That magnificent stone castle they called Drac's own stood at the fore. Granted, it was all a front. From the outside looking in, it presented as some fantastical, medieval fortress that conjured the spectre of thousands of cloistered chambers and narrowed passageways. The reality was more akin to a walled city with an overly large frontispiece. Business all took place in the backyard.

Not to say this frontispiece towered unimpressively. Doubtless it boasted chambers and passageways; although perhaps these numbered in the low hundreds, not thousands. Its chiseled peaks and precipices loomed overhead, dimming out the midday sun as they cast forth their shadows beyond the bench presses all the way to the cornhole area. Four observation towers dominated the skyline at each corner of the yard. Cops with sighted rifles manned them. I wondered what an offender would have to do to get one of those cowboys to pull the trigger.

It occurred to me just then that Supermax must be underground, under Drac's Castle. The castle proper no doubt laid claim to the administration and classroom sectors, and the library. I already knew Case Manager's Row and the Lizard Room found their homes there.

The yard itself featured two basketball courts, a wraparound walking path, benches, a few play-areas, and a weight pile. Standard prison-yard fare. I doubted very much they had ice cream here.

Sure, I kicked up some dust and wandered the grounds. But my eyes never seemed to leave Drac's Castle. The stonework on the building's facade looked just as stunning as those splashy peaks and precipices. Overlarge, chiseled blocks of stone layered atop another in a roughened display. The grandeur of the place reminded me of those turn-of-the-century municipal buildings or old churches you see downtown. It hearkened back to days of old.

My man sat chilling in there, somewheres.

It just blew my mind to think he was as nearby as all of this.

My afternoon stroll in the park transitioned quickly enough into a sit-in affair on the four-on-four basketball game between what looked like rival gangs. No, not rival gangs, but homies who were definitely affiliated. You could tell by the tattoos. Or maybe not. It was hard to tell with the sun in my eyes. Just then everyone seemed like a shot caller, predator, or gangster. I rose to go relax on one of the benches along the path.

And that's when I saw him.

The gash under his right eye and the bruises around his left appeared to have healed well. At least his mug didn't look like a smashed pumpkin no more. The same might've been said for my own.

Cali had been watching the game, too. I hadn't noticed him because even though he wore extra-larges, the homies sandwiching him no doubt wore double-x. The trio stood just off to my left.

"Hey, Cali. What it do?"

Cali turned to look. His eyes bulged when he saw me. He shook his head. His expression darkened. He narrowed his eyes.

"My, my, my. If it isn't Look Who the Fuck That Is," he said.

I didn't know what that meant; although, it had sounded—fairly, maybe, hopefully—tongue-in-cheekish, and so I flashed a smile and walked over.

"Get that shit outta here," Cali exclaimed upon my approach, all hellbent, "or I'll work you over like I did the last time."

Cali relayed to his homies about the epic beat-down he'd delivered to me on the low side. "The only reason I got this," he said, pointing to his facial scrapes, "was because of the four or five others he brought with him who came at me, too. I beat all they asses, but they got in a few." Cali's homies smiled and nodded, evidently impressed with their bro's prowess.

I realized, suddenly, that reminders about b-ball hookups was probably not gonna be a thing, and now, more than ever, the dark reality of high-side rules.

I chilled on a bench with my hands folded and head down for the remainder of yard time. Chopper required meth. Fuck, who didn't?

I felt the bench shift as someone joined me late into my pity-party session. "Yard time's over in five, McConnell," a female voice said. I looked up. It was Officer Weldon. "Feeling the heat?" She peered up at the clouds. "It'll start cooling down soon. Labor Day's come and gone."

"Feels more like Halloween." I rose. "Thanks."

CHAPTER FOURTEEN

I slapped my book closed. "It's a slow read, ghosts or no ghosts. And right now, they're all are on vacation: the ones in this story, and everywhere else." I kicked my legs out and dangled them over the sides of my rack.

"Still looking for ghosts?" Sal asked from down below.

"They're never anywhere when you need them." I hopped out of bed. "I need a breather."

I clanked along the steel mezzanine and down the three flights of stairs.

Poker. Crazy Eights. Texas hold-em. Nothing settled the nerves quite like a good round of cards at those times when the blues or boredom came at you in spades. Shyness be damned: it was time to make some friends, and poker headlined as one of the few ventures where Joe Prisoner and even the most luckless of fishes might share some quality time. Or so I had figured.

Ah, an empty chair, repining all by its lonesome under a table clear of humanity except for a smidgen of an old man with his nose up in some Stephen King. "You won't mind if I steal this," I said, snagging it.

The old man threw daggers at me with his eyes.

I slid the chair over to the adjacent table. Here, a solemn gathering, all with that telltale Aryan Brotherhood look about them, sat playing spades. "Hey, bros. Need an extra player?"

Not a single one of this colorful crew lifted their eyes my way.

"Go kick rocks, Clayton," the long-bearded one said.

"How about when y'all start up the next round?" I asked.

A fool with a snake tattoo crowning his bald head leveled a finger at my chair. "This seat's taken," he said, and yanked it out of my hand.

My eyes bulged. "Taken? I just dragged it over from another table."

"Run, Forrest, run!" smiling, the trustee in brown said. I knew his name now. Breaker.

I yielded up the chair, found another straggler, and ushered it over to another poker table that looked to have available seating.

The results played out in similar fashion, only this time I was advised to "Take a long walk off of a short dock, greeny."

To this I replied, "It's actually been a while since I swam in the ocean. *Green Fish at Sea.* Maybe that'll be the title of my next book."

"You're a writer?" one of the guys at the table asked.

The others stared him down until he dropped his sights back onto his cards.

My colorful remark appeared to have lightened the mood, anyhow. No more slack from the boys at Table #2, but nor were they willing to cut me some slack and let me play in.

All out of options.

Nope, one other. The Blacks ran a card table. It was likely, probably, against code, but what the hell. Already a black sheep, I moseyed on over.

They saw me coming from like a mile away.

The tall, lank homey seated at the far end of the table rose. With a smattering of coarse language and bedeviled looks from one and all, the tall guy expressed in no uncertain terms that my presence among them was not gonna be a thing.

I hooked a u-turn. "Green is the new black," I said, in the middle of my turn.

The tall guy's eyes nearly popped out of his head. "What did you just say about my momma?" He said to his man seated beside him with the do-rag, "Did you hear what he just said about my momma?" Smiling, his man nodded.

I ascended up the staircase to calls of "I dare you to come back here and say that again about my momma. Get your ass back down here, now! I dare you, I double dare you, to say that again about my momma..."

"At least you have one," I sputtered.

I collapsed onto my mattress and slapped my arm over my face. "I give up."

Sal snickered. "You're brand new. You're green. You have penned on your shirt reminders of the blood of John Clayton. What do you expect?" I heard Sal lay his book aside. "Lots of folks have been asking about you, you know. I tell them *he's a fucky little rascal, but okay in my book.*"

"Thanks, Sal." I sighed. "I just hope when they do end up liking me it's not because I'd agreed to join their gang."

"They may never like you while you're in green." I heard Sal scratch at something in his pants. "Not a big fan of these lowbrow prison gangs here."

"Same."

The bunk creaked as Sal sat up in his rack. "*Same?* Is that what you just said? What the hell's that supposed to mean? You're supposed to say, yes, I agree with you, or I feel the same way too, not *same.*"

I grinned. "Same."

"Why..." he was gritting his teeth now, I could just see it "...you fucky little...if I was your father I'd..." I heard Sal sigh, then lay back on his rack. "Never mind," he said.

"Hey, Sal, why no TV in here?"

Sal paused a long moment before answering, probably to allow his blood pressure to lower to non-lethal levels. "The TV belonged to my last celly," he answered in a forced, even voice. "When he left, it did too."

"Why did your last celly leave?"

Sal scratched his head. "Dunno. He put in a move request a year ago. They didn't wanna move him. Now, they move him. I'm not complaining. Hope that SOB never comes back."

"I'll rustle up a TV for the cell, bruh. I qualify. I'll get us on the list."

I could hear the bed-frame rattle and sheets rustle down below. Sal screeched, "I don't need some *fish* like you to get me a TV. If I wanted to get a goddamned TV I'd just..." Sal went on about TVs, the minding of one's own goddamn business, and something about little Irish fishies trying to bite off more than they could chew. Finally, Sal told me to scram, he had to take a deuce.

I didn't feel much like getting up, but of course, did.

The tall drink of water smiled as I passed by. "Look, Cam, he's back," one of his bros said. But Tall Drink didn't say anything. He just nodded and smiled his big, toothy grin at me.

A smile meant...happiness, joy, peace, goodwill towards men, that sorta thing. That's what I kept telling myself as I maneuvered past the poker tables to the podium where Officer Gaetske sat manning the controls.

"Got a question, Gaetske," I said. "How would I get over to the library?"

Gaetske explained that library hours were such and such and that the rules required a written pass from an officer for the granting of a one-time twenty-minute visit.

"And where might this library be located?"

Gaetske pointed to the door. "Myself or Officer Tate will buzz you out. You hang a left out the Pod 2 door, out the front, and go through the yard. Go into the main back entrance of the Barr Building. Once you're in, down the hallway, second door on your left."

I cleared my throat. "And the records room?" I asked, all casual like.

Gaetske eyed me. "Same." Sweet, another Gen Zer. "Records room is in the Barr Building, too. But you're not allowed over there."

No harm in trying. "Wow, this Barr Building sure sounds like the place to be."

"Not really." Gaetske looked down at his console, scanning its impressive array of video screens. "Be thankful you're over here. The castle's where Pod 1 and Super are."

"What else is over there?"

"Okay, McConnell," Gaetske said. "We're gonna have to cut this convo short 'cause I gotta take a deuce."

No one wanted to rap with me nor look my way except to throw daggers, and when they did, suddenly they had to take a shit!

Not exactly excited about having to retrace my steps, I took a deep breath and pushed my tennies along anyway. I didn't know if Tall Drink of Water was still smiley-facing it or not, and didn't want to know. With my head down, I made my way up the stairs.

I heard grunting sounds as I neared the cell. Wasn't it a full five minutes I had given old school? Jeez. Dump, wipe, flush, not that difficult. I decided to check in anyway, maybe Sal was just finishing up.

Grunting, sure, I verified, as I stood in the doorway. Although, maybe this had less to do with his bowels and more to do with the two fools who had him pinned, balls to the wall, while they delivered kidney shots. One of the miscreants sported a mohawk.

I stood with my arms folded, sizing up the invaders. "Need some help, sarge?" I asked. "I can handle these fools." I didn't know if I could or not but maybe.

"Tommy, is that you?" Sal screeched.

"Your knight in shining green armor has arrived."

"Tommy," Sal exclaimed. "Get outta here. Do you hear me—out! Do your own goddamn time! Remember? Don't worry about me."

"You heard what the old man said, celly," the mohawk man's friend advised. "Do your own time. He wants you to leave him alone. He's busy right now."

I took a step forward.

"Do you hear me, Tommy McConnell—out!" Sal shrieked.

I bailed, then sat stressing on the stairs until break ended.

That night, just after ten, marked my first participation in a knuckle-body check. During standing count, Sal decided to fall to the ground and groan while clutching his sides. After further review, Officer Gaetske and the third-shift crew noticed significant redness and swelling and determined foul play. The cops ran an inspection of all Pod 2 cells to probe offenders for reddened knuckles, elbows, or knees. Nothing came of it. Kidney shots are like punches to the gut. They don't redden knuckles very well.

Sal was still feeling it the following morning. All night long he had tossed, turned, moaned, groaned, and writhed in agony. He never did say anything with regards to his little tossup with the Mohawk Indians or whoever the hell those guys were. In prison, Code operated like a hard-line religion. Opening one's mouth to "tell" was like breaking one of the Ten Commandments.

To ease Sal's mind but more to get him to put a sock in it down there, I offered to read aloud excerpts from my book. Actually, I didn't offer. I just started reading.

"*Wuthering Heights* isn't a damned book," Sal swore. "It's a song. Stop it with all that flowery, long-winded jabber or I'll climb up there and jabber your face in. Say what you mean and mean what you say, my father used to say. And it's what I'm telling you now."

I snapped closed the book. "If Miss Emily Bronte can't put you to sleep, no one can. Your funeral." Just about to hop out of bed, his words hit home. "You had a dad, huh? Lucky bastard. Sounds like Pops was a good man."

"No, Pops was not a *good man*," Sal spat. "I'd kill that asshole if he wasn't dead already. No one in the Caniglio family ever was a *good* man. You've never heard of the Caniglio family?"

"No," I admitted. Although, maybe I had. It sounded familiar. Old Monty that one time in the yard had rambled on about some "Family." Maybe this was the one.

I heard Sal roll over onto his side. Fools down the hall probably heard it, too. "Keepin' it secret ain't just code here, but other places, too," he explained, in between moans.

I suddenly recalled that social worker who had stopped by the trailer that one time to inquire about my bruised arm. Fatts stared me down, and so I ended up telling her I had gotten whacked with a baseball while playing catch. Not a baseball, in reality, a baseball *bat*.

Sal went on, "I could go on about the Family's dirty laundry but I won't because you'd probably shit your pants up there. Not that we're nearly as powerful as we used to be. Did you know the Caniglio family used to basically run this prison?"

"I heard that." Yes, this was the family Monty had mentioned.

"Well, see, everything was going just dandy with all that until one day this hotshot warden arrives who thought he could turn the place right-side in. Richards, his name was. And he did. They called it a renaissance. Can you believe that, a fucking renaissance? The '87 Renaissance."

"I didn't know they called it that," I said.

"Maybe one day when I've got absolutely nothing to lose I'll write a book. Spill the beans. Name names. It'll be payback, redemption and a dream come true all rolled in one. Only, it's the very steep price I'd have to pay afterward that keeps me from ever trying. I would have to be at my very wits' end. This is my one great dream, Tommy McConnell."

"It's good to have dreams," I said, softly. "Unless there's donkey heads in them."

Sal exhaled. "How's your investigation going, by the way?"

"Into the mystery of the Forever Young Prisoner?"

"That one," Sal said

"It's not. Though, I'll be heading to the library in a few."

"What's at the library?"

"Books. Also, they say Henry Heck stopped over there once, decades ago. I'd like to scope the place out just to get a feel for where he'd been that one time."

"Good luck with all that."

"Thanks." I hopped out of bed and pulled on my shoes.

Sal blinked at me. "You talked in your damned sleep again last night." He grimaced in pain and held his side.

"What did I say?" I stood by the cell door for an uncomfortable long while awaiting an answer. Sal looked me dead in the eye. That look signaled a message, but for the life of me I couldn't make out what it was.

"I forgot," he said, holding my gaze.

I penned my name, the time, and applied my signature to the check-out sheet, then Gaetske buzzed me out of the Pod 2 door. With my library pass in hand, I followed the hallway until it led me outside.

The yard lay empty: it was still early. Blue roamed the grounds on the lookout for anything out of the ordinary. As I neared the entrance to the Barr Building, Officer Weldon stepped over and stopped me.

"Where you headed, McConnell?"

"Library." Grinning, I showed her my pass.

Weldon read it then nodded. "You getting along okay?"

"It's all good." I flicked a nod. "So, which door do I take?" No less than seven or eight entrances advertised along the backside of the castle. One looked like a main entrance, another said "Visits," another led to the chow-hall, and the others might have opened their doors to maintenance, administrative, or storage routes. None looked very promising in the way of dark passageways to the hidden mysteries of the past.

"The middle one, obviously," Weldon said. "The main entrance."

"And where might those other doors lead?" I asked, as if offhandedly. "Supermax?"

After shaking her head, Weldon squinted her left eye to either get the sun out of it or wink at me. "The library is the second door on your left, but if you keep going down the hallway you'll hit a T. Left is Pod 1, right is Supermax. You won't be allowed over there. It's monitored. Your pass says 'Library' so best you stick to it. Venturing any farther will get you a warning or write-up, depending on how far you choose to go."

Lacking no basic essential except maybe a pair of shades to get that little squint out of her eye, and pretty damn chill for a cop, Weldon sure got down.

"Thanks, Blue," I said, and made my way in.

I resisted the urge to pad at least a *little* further along the black-and-white floor tiles, but pressing my palm against the library door, I opened it and entered.

It wasn't the Providence Public Library, that was for damned sure. The room was long and rectangular with end-to-end bookcases lining its walls and a few tables in the center. Against the wall opposite me a check-out counter and Information desk greeted patrons. The librarian seated behind that whole works greeted me, too. He flashed a smile at me as I entered.

I mean, he *smiled* at me.

I couldn't help but curve a smile of my own as I approached.

"What can I do for you?" the librarian asked.

Inwardly, I sighed, and brainstormed a smart reply to this loaded question. The penciled eyebrows. The glossed lips. The sloped shoulder. The rolled-up sleeve and velvety arm. The bandeau around his noggin. The eyes—had it. Mascara, totally. This offender, clearly, was what they referred to as a feezy.

"One million dollars...is my going rate for the shower room," was my response to the librarian's question.

The librarian blinked, repeatedly.

I cut a glance at the clock on the wall behind Mr. Librarian. Fifteen minutes to get my shit done then back over to Pod 2.

"Got a name?" the librarian asked.

"Cookie Rooster," I said, hearing that name somewhere, at some time, and liking it. The librarian brightened. I coughed. "Just kidding. Call me The Stranger."

"Okay, Stranger, but I'll still need a name. They'll wanna be sure you're here and not anywhere else."

I gave him the name two wholly unknown, probably rekt some-ones had christened me with twenty-four years earlier.

"What can I help you with today?" the librarian asked.

I wheezed out a long exhale. "Okay, I want all the books you got on the subject of ghosts, and one book, you know, just for reading. Fiction. Any suggestions?" I always liked to ask the librarians on duty for recommendations before I perused. What other fools liked might be something I ended up liking, too.

The librarian stepped over to his cart. Leaning way over, he rummaged. "I'll have you know we *just* got the newest John Grisham in yesterday—"

"Classics, my man. The classics."

"Literature, you mean?" the librarian asked, pivoting and swaying back to his station.

I nodded. "I don't mess around."

"Well, well, *well*," the librarian said with eyes that gleamed. He twisted his lips as he pondered. "Well, Stranger, why not read *The Stranger*? It's a classic by a French author. Ooh la la. Think that's something you might be able to handle?"

"I'll try."

"Don't try. Do." He pointed. "Paranormal's against the west wall, and Literature's way back south wall. Any questions, you come see you know who. I'll be filing my nails and trying really hard not to be bored while a fellow avid reader is away."

I'll bet you'll be thinking about me, I thought. "How many books can I check out?"

The librarian showed his palm with fingers splayed.

Not long afterward, I returned with my five selections.

"Ever read Kurt Vonnegut?" the librarian asked, as he stamped my first book.

"Nope. Just stamp these ones right here, please."

Stamping my fifth book, the librarian asked, "Ever read *The Metamorphosis* by Franz—?"

"Kafka," I offered. "Yup."

The librarian looked at me. "Really?"

"Yes." Then, I remembered what I had wanted to ask. "Hey, you happen to know anything about the history of this library?"

"Not much," the librarian said, with the grind of frustration in his voice. Probably ticked for not getting his invite to the shower room yet. "I know it dates back to days of yore." The librarian snickered. "That sounded kind of Tolkienesque just there, didn't it?" He cleared his throat. "I believe this place has been refurbished a few times."

"You've...read Tolkien?" I asked. "Not just watched the movies, but actually read the books?"

The librarian nodded.

"All *three Lord of the Rings* books?"

Smiling, the librarian nodded. "*The Silmarillian*, too."

I snorted. "Damn, that sucks." I cleared my throat. "The book, that is, not the fact that you read it. Which is impressive." We exchanged glances inside of a moment of awkward silence. I shook myself. "So, this is the original structure but maybe just painted over a few times?"

"From what I gather. Look, Stranger man, I've only been here four years. The head librarian, Mrs. Carter, can tell you all about—"

"Any other way to get into the library than through this main door?"

The librarian pointed a long, pink fingernail at the unimpressive-looking half-door set into the wall over by the New Release section. It bore all the distinction of an air shaft or HVAC access-way. More of a hatchway than a door. "I don't know what that there is, and I've never seen anyone use it before." The librarian leveled his brow. "You planning an escape?"

I shook my head. "A rescue. *Au revoir.*" I waved good-bye as I turned and exited, and with some fire in my step because I had only four minutes!

~

So harried was my pace I just missed bumping into Officer Weldon on my way out of the castle.

"You're welcome," she said, as I breezed past.

I retraced my steps and showed her my pass. "I have only two minutes, that's why I'm stormtrooping it. It's not because I'm on meth or running to get some or anything like that."

She took my pass and signed her initials to it. "There. You've got another five minutes. You're welcome."

"For what?" I said with a furrowed brow.

"Your new celly." Weldon peered in at me. "Greeley's idea, but we were the ones who pulled the strings to make it happen. For the truth's sake. For Henry's sake." She lowered her head and kicked a pebble. "Be aware, Sherlock, that Sal's on the fence. He's been like that for a long while. He may break, and talk, who knows." She looked up. "Listen to him."

"What are you talking..." I started to say, but stopped with one look at Weldon's knowing smile. Ah, the mysterious and elusive White Hats, then.

"There's a small band of us here," she said, with a gleam in her eye. "We look out for each other, and others who wanna help, too—like yourself. Not everyone in blue is thrilled you and Sal are cellies; we kind of caught them off-guard. There may be countermeasures. Now, you'd best be off or you'll be late."

CHAPTER FIFTEEN

Gaetske examined the pass upon my return. "Met up with Weldon, huh?" Smiling, he nodded. "Good for you. She's one of the good guys."

Sal remained laid up on his rack. I didn't know if this latest hammering cataloged for him as the latest in a series, or simply as a one-and-done. Either way, it seemed to have taken a toll on Sal's psyche. When I entered, he lay staring bug-eyed at the wall.

"Anything I can do for your sorry ass?" I asked, with reference more to his mohawk-boy problem, generally, than to his present condition. I didn't know how to play psychologist any more than I knew how to play golf.

"Do your own time," Sal said in a thin, reedy voice, with his eyes on the wall.

No rage. No profanity. No threats to jabber me to death. Not much in the way of movement, either. This wasn't like Sal at all. I grew even more concerned. I needed to bail for a while to be alone with my thoughts.

"I'm taking a shower," I announced

Alone in the shower room, I thought in particular about that lingering gaze Sal had dropped on me earlier. Clearly he had something on his mind, and in response, quite possibly, to whatever sleep words I had spoken the night before. Maybe it had to do with the library. No, this morning I'd mentioned the library. Well, it didn't matter, and in the meantime, Sal looked to be dialing it in.

As I flipped off the shower, I wondered why I cared even at all Sal had fallen on hard times. A fish in a pool of sharks, I had my own problems.

I wiped up and got dressed. Shower sandals on, towel over my shoulder, and with my shower caddie in hand, I hooked a turn out of the wet and wild room onto the walkway.

I actually heard it before I saw it.

The jeers. The commotion. The laughter. The "Oh my God, he's gonna fall!"

Midway down the walkway, gangway, mezzanine, whatever you wanted to call it, right in front of our cell, stood Mohawk Boy and his friend. With their heads stooped, they gazed through the safety rails at some curio below. My heart skipped a beat. Nearer still, I noticed what they were looking down at. What the assembled crowd in the commons area stood looking up at. What the offenders in the doorways to their cells kept howling about.

I saw two pudgy hands positioned along the ledge of the gangway. Whomever those pudgy hands belonged to had somehow worked his way up and over the five rails, and then, either climbed down the far side, or fell down, only to catch hold of the mezzanine ledge. Dude was dangling.

I knew those hands. I'd felt them slap at me and saw them in my dreams.

The Dangling One was Sal.

Suicide attempt? Doubtful, because Mohawk and Company appeared to be in on it. They couldn't have slid him through the rails or pushed him over-top of it because Sal tipped the scales and that would've required one hell of a push. Maybe he clambered over to escape because they'd threatened to kill him.

C'mon, Gaetske, where you at?

Probably in the bathroom on his phone with his fucking earbuds in. Damned Gen Zers.

I stopped a few yards short of where Mohawk Boy stood. Looking down at the pudgy hands, I greeted their owner. "Hey, Sal. How's it hangin'?"

"He's not gonna get up from this one, I'm afraid," Mohawk Boy said with mock-sadness.

Lowering my shower caddie, I inched along as if to get a closer look. "Look who's talking," I said, and straight-punched the fool right in the solar plexus. Talk about getting hammered. Gasping for breath, that boy was down! Along with his shank, which tumbled until it settled just outside of our cell. Mohawk's friend lunged for it. I kneed for his face but connected with his shoulder. We scrapped, but no serious blows were landed. Just then, Officer Gaetske sprung open the bathroom door and came running full throttle. Mohawk's friend scampered hurriedly to his cell, but not before jutting his finger in my face. "You're next, Clayton."

"Yeah?" I called out after him. "My place or yours?"

I decided, on the spot, to do it. But I would need to act fast.

I climbed those five rails like nobody's business, straddled that top rung then swung my legs over. I descended the forbidden side of the fence.

Gaetske hollered on his way up the stairs, "You get down from there now. Do you hear me, McConnell? Now!"

The next part would require some doing. Had the fools downstairs never been to a circus before, they were about to be in for a real treat. I inserted my legs up to the knees in through the space between the second and third rails. "Hold my legs," I ordered Gaetske, who stood on the safe side of the fence now. "I'm gonna flip back, like a trapeze artist. Hold them!"

Gaetske stirred, but didn't move. He stood blinking, reluctant.

Finally, he squatted and pinned my lower legs against the second rail.

Just like skydiving, I told myself. Not that I'd ever skydived before but because skydiving was straight fire and something even average people could do if they were dumb enough. *Just let go, and fall*, I told myself.

The marble floor down below would show little kindness in the event of even the slightest mishap.

Skydiving, I told myself.

I fell back. Free fall.

Scariest moment of my life, I won't even lie, when the whole world flipped upside-down like that. Even scarier than that time when Danny overdosed on Oxy and we, higher than the heavens in our own right, had to drag him three city blocks to the hospital.

The top part of my back, and shoulders, smacked up against the mezzanine ledge. I was dangling too now, only upside down.

Now, for some real doing.

The whole pod went quiet. I heard Gaetske gulp.

My face leveled with Sal's elbow. Side-wise, we spaced less than a foot apart. That he faced in, and I faced out, seemed to be our biggest problem.

"Doesn't matter, Tommy," Sal said. "Nothing matters anymore."

"If it didn't matter you wouldn't have held on this long. C'mon, I'm gonna grab you, and once I do, I want you to grab hold of me." I twisted my torso and reaching, slipped my left arm across and under Sal's left armpit. I worked the same with the right arm.

"You're gonna need to let go," I said. "When you do, chicken wing your arms. Fold them down over mine and I'll cradle you by the armpits. Then, hold on for dear life. Ready?"

"Okay, Tommy McConnell," Sal said, and let go.

We dangled there in a sort of lover's embrace. A secure enough posture, albeit uncomfortable and highly awkward. With my arms wrapped tightly around his upper torso in a literal bear hug, and with his arms chicken-winging it for all they were worth, and the whole of his weight hanging in the balance, I wondered how long, realistically, I could squeeze the Charmin like this. All of his weight rested on the muscles in my upper back, arms, and shoulders—and the back of my knees, of course.

Finally, as a matter of course, I twisted back around to face the commons area, no longer in the direction of the railings—the result of my initial twisting to reach for Sal. Not to suggest I could in any way *see* the commons area. My face lay buried in the soft, sweaty flesh of Sal's upper back.

In twisting, I had to roll Sal over with me. But it happened. Now, we both faced away from the mezzanine: an upside-down, backwards bear hug.

Downstairs, a door clanked open. The main pod door. Moments later, an officer's boots clanked up the zigzag staircase.

"What the hell is this?" the new cowboy said.

Damn. *Rooney*.

"We've got two offenders dangling off the rampart," Gaetske explained.

"I can see that, ass-clown. No, what's *this*. You holding the man's legs like that? The rule states, and I quote, that no officer shall at any time interfere with—"

"And common sense states that if I let go they'll drop and splatter like tomatoes," Gaetske said all at once.

"Tommy," Sal spoke in a low voice. "Gotta tell you something."

"What, that your pits smell like onions? You should've told me that *before* I decided to do this."

"First, thanks. Second, you're the stupidest son of a bitch *ever* to do what you just did. Third..." Sal breathed in, out, in "...yeah, he exists. The Forever Young Prisoner does."

This caught me entirely off-guard. About to tell Sal this really wasn't the time, I considered this might be the only time he would be willing to share. "In Supermax?"

"No, way down below. Secret passage. Cops were paid off for decades to keep quiet. One of the many favors the Family paid to the governor—a long ago governor. Your boy knew too much. Couldn't just kill him. No one wants blood on their hands. The Family's superstitious, too. No one wanted another Old Morgan: ghost going around telling people he's innocent. Henry's on record with the prison, but not on record, if you know what I mean."

I didn't at all know what that meant.

"I never saw him. But I knew. We all knew. Anyway, he's here."

Rooney called down, "What's goin' on down there, fellas? Enjoying a nice chat? It'll be a few before the crew with the lanyard and rope find their way over, so just sit tight for a while, 'k?"

"Just pull us the hell up!" I hollered. "Three or four guys could do it. Just haul us up!"

"That actually sounds like a good idea," Gaetske said. "We can pull him up by hand. Working the lanyard over and securing them will take no less than ten minutes, and that's if the equipment was here already. I don't think they'll be able to hang on that long."

Rooney called down, "Think you boys can lovey-dovey for another twenty or so?"

"Fuck you, Rooney!" I wondered why the special forces, the Ninja Turtles, hadn't arrived yet: they usually hit the scene of an emergency one-two-three. They logged membership in the Black Hats, too, arguably. They would delay until Sal and I fell.

Sal said, "Only reason he was in the library that one time was 'cause of the new warden."

I rocked to and fro to work some space between my flattened nose and Sal's shirt. I couldn't see them, but I knew they were down there. I yelled, "Don't just stand there, ass-clowns. Get up here and help us!"

I heard pockets of chatter at first; then, prison shoes clanked up the flights of stairs. It sounded like a small army.

"Oh, no," I heard Rooney tell them. "No, you don't. Back off. All of you."

Gaetske said, "You, you, and *you*, hold onto his lower legs.

Romero—you, Mendez, and Rodriguez help me grab his legs then we'll pull McConnell up and through."

Moments later I began to rise.

"You stop this right now, do you hear me?" Rooney wailed. "You'll be written up, the whole lot of you!"

"Gonna write Gaetske up, too?" one of the offenders asked, although I barely heard it with the feezys downstairs performing their cheerleader routine: *Tommy, Tommy, he's our man, if he can't do it, no one can!*

With something like ten sets of strong arms gripping and hefting me up, up, up, my head and outstretched arms were soon all that remained of me on the forbidden side of the rails.

I kept my arms outstretched, continuing to grasp Sal merely as a precaution. Once his head cleared the second rail, not a few of the beefiest arms in Pod 2 fastened upon him and wrenched upward. Once he grasped the rails, I let go; he hoisted himself into a standing position along the ledge. Sets of arms reached beyond the bars to make sure the old timer didn't go nowhere.

The guys set my feet gently down upon the floor. I don't know how many fist bumps and pats on the back I received just then, but I would have assuredly failed a knuckle-body check had it been administered afterward. Like a walk-off home run in a game seven, the applause across the pod reached a deafening decibel. The cheerleaders' rant reached a crescendo that sounded almost orgasmic. I'll never forget the looks on the guys' faces.

Sal's barrel chest and belly refused to fit through the rails. He would have to climb or be lifted over.

Rooney barked, "You five men secure him until the infantry arrives." Which would end up being ten minutes later. "The professionals will get him over the top, sure as you can say *pile of horseshit*."

I never did see Sal Caniglio after that. Word through the grapevine spoke of an escort to the infirmary then a transfer to PC, Protective Custody. I never got the chance to thank Sal for putting up with the greenest fish on God's green earth. I never got the chance to tell him he was the closest thing to a father I'd ever had even though I tended to talk outta my ass with regards to shit like that. I never got the chance to tell him I cared. I never got the chance to tell him I hoped his dream to spill the beans would one day come true. I almost wondered if it hadn't come true already.

CHAPTER SIXTEEN

The Pit of Heck
The Year of our Lord 1987
May 17
7:44 a.m.

There was an expression they used back in the day, and maybe folks still used it in whatever day happened to exist beyond the confines of Henry's cell. Another day, another dollar. By that logic, Henry figured he should be a millionaire on par with those elegant folks in top hats and billowy gowns he used to open doors for and serve breakfast in bed to.

Margaret envied the wealthy, Henry reflected just then. In the cloistered kitchen of their humble, third-story mill-worker's apartment, whenever the cheap wine moved her, Margaret would pad around the place with her nose in the air just like the richies did, sip with her pinky-finger pointed out like she was a regular at tea, and say to the dog, "Thank you, my good man," whenever he'd fetch her the newspaper.

It was Margaret who had recommended Henry apply for the

position of butler. "You can hold a tray, can't you? You can open a door, can't you? You can speak politely, can't you?"

The one thing Henry could not do was be British. "Non-British accents need not apply" so many of the classier job postings read. Europe boasted as the cultural capital of the world, and a European staff meant you'd made it. Meanwhile, the governor's ad stated nothing of the sort. With no experience other than farming and livery work, they hired Henry on. Rumor had it the governor's daughter was fond of him.

"You even look like a butler!" Margaret said.

"And what might the wife mean by that, dare I ask?" Henry replied into his newspaper.

"Sound like one, too," Margaret snickered. "You sure you grew up in Smithfield?"

No wonder, then, Margaret had ventured out of her way that one afternoon those millions of years ago to attempt to *know* her dearest Henry in the study closet of one of Providence's wealthiest?

Poor Margaret.

Gertrude Barr, on the other hand, was many things, but poor she was not. Besides just the governor's darling daughter, she was every whit charming, cultured, statuesque, and featured as the city's unofficial ambassador of sophistication and couture. Active in state and social affairs, she regularly visited the Vanderbilt mansion in Newport. Rumor had it she dined with French aristocrats and took her tea in a bejeweled medieval goblet. Margaret would have admired that young woman to the very ends of the earth had she but known her. Had she but known, too, what Gerdie had meant to husband Henry, or the role she would play in what fate had in store for them, she would have chased that uppity tart to the very depths of hell. Margaret never knew, then kidney failure took her.

Poor, poor Margaret.

"Kidney failure, my foot," Henry swore into the musty darkness of his cell. "Traumatic kidney failure, my foot," he swore yet again. A vigorous, hale woman of twenty-two years, Margaret had never complained about any such ailment before. Henry recalled that gentleman identifying himself as "bailiff" who had out of the blue delivered a complimentary cup of tea to Margaret during pre-trial. "For madame, the Defense's lovely and chief witness," he had said, with a greasy grin stretched all the way to his hairy ears.

Poor, dearest Margie.

Henry in some ways envied her, though. At least she was at rest. His circumstance forever prevented him from being at rest, even though rest was all he ever seemed to do.

Even more than the roaches—that numbered so many over the years, Henry had quite run out of names for them and now had to number them...even more than those cherishable memories of his youth, and those intolerable memories of the trial with those angry men eyeballing him, and those bitter-sweet memories of Gerdie; even more than the fillings of his mind with counting to 10,000, then counting backwards from 10,000, then reciting every word of the English language he could think of—so much more than all of that put together, he thought of Margaret.

Quite certainly she spoke to him in his dreams. Her message to Henry five years earlier, and two years earlier, announced, "He's coming." Last night, the message came yet again.

Who's coming?

It was the year of our Lord either 1986 or 1987. Henry's one-hundredth birthday lay just around the corner, wasn't that exciting? Maybe those coarse fellows behind the door would honor him with a slab of sour butter again.

For better or for worse, he'd eat it. Just like he had eaten Wilbur XIII, Tess Anne IV, and Alfred XI that one time the guards failed to serve his stale bread for a week back in the seventies. Henry had to ask their roach relatives for forgiveness afterward. It was a bad time.

Henry stood.

Time once again to declare.

Angling his chin up, Henry said,

"*Help* me."

Second declaration. "I am guilty, but not like this."

Third declaration: "Pen, please."

Fourth: "And this," Henry said declaredly, "is all I have to say in my defense this day."

Henry heard a knock at the door. No, more like a knocking up against the door, along with a clink, clank, the jangling of keys, and curse words from the other side. Meal time?

Certainly not. The door began to creak open. Herein sounded the ghastly shriek of rusty metal hinges. They spat orange-red dust as the light, by degrees, grew brighter.

Henry curled into a fetal position to protect his eyes, as well as the rest of him, potentially. The shafts of light streaming in from wherever *out there* was proposed to blind Henry's perpetual night vision.

A man dressed in blue stood in the doorway. Tall, stocky, and with graying red hair, he sported a holster at his side with the butt of a gun sticking out of it.

One of the guards.

An actual, living human being.

"Greetings, Mr. Ronsellier," the guard announced with a loud voice. "Welcome to the land of the living."

Even if Henry had within himself the voice and courage to speak, he wouldn't have known what to say.

The guard studied for a space of time Henry's crouched form tucked up against the wall. "The men who put you here are all dead, Mr. Ronsellier," finally, he said. "Warden Richards wants you taken care of properly now." The guard paused, perhaps expecting a response which he didn't then receive. "Captain John Harris, sir. At your service, in a manner of speaking. Pleased to make your acquaintance. I've been granted the rare privilege of seeing to it the Forever Young Prisoner is provided for."

Officer Harris chanced a step into the cell, wincing at the foul odor and breathing deep what little oxygen the stale air had to offer. "It's a different world than way back in your day. Civil rights is much a thing nowadays. Section 1983 lawsuits, the Civil Rights Act, et cetera, et cetera." Wetting his lips, clearing his throat, Harris declared, "The Eighth Amendment is all too often construed as apples for oranges. A prison sentence should be measured in mileage, not calendar years."

Clarifying, Harris said, "That's from *Heck v. Harris*, 1985, a recent court case in New Hampshire that changed the life of a prison inmate named Cheryl Heck. See, her sentence was reduced because of lousy prison conditions perpetrated in large part by my very own brother, Stan Harris." Harris stepped out of the cell to steal a breath; he returned "We're not making the same mistake any longer with you, Mr. Ronsellier." Harris stepped closer. "Think we can stand to our feet?"

"Who you talking to out there?" a voice from out in the hall said. A pause. "Oh, did you pop the door open?"

Harris yelled into the hall: "I decided to open it. Wanna swing by and ask him what the correct pronunciation of his name might be or are you still gnawing on that bagel?"

"Hold on!" replied the hall voice.

Harris said to the crouched figure, "Officer Day insists your name is pronounced Ron-sell-*ee-ay*. I say it's Ron-sell-*eer*. Officer Speck pronounces it Ron-sell-*ee-er*. Maybe you can clear the matter up for us."

Moments later, two men stood in the doorway.

"My God. Look at him, Cap," Officer Day declared. "His record says he's 94 years old. He looks...college aged. How is this possible?"

"Welcome to today's exciting new episode of Ripley's Believe it or Not," Captain Harris said with a smirk. He addressed the crouched figure, "Maybe Mr. Heck here—I mean, Mr. Ronsellier here—can enlighten us on these many uncertain matters."

"If he can talk." Day squinted into the semidarkness to get a better look.

"He can," Harris affirmed. "We hear him babbling all the time. More like robot babble. The same thing, every day, over and over.

Maybe he doesn't think anyone's listening, but someone's always listening. Every word he's said over the past seventy years has been documented." Harris smiled. "We keep a ledger."

"You hear that, bud?" Day called over. "We's keepin' a ledger on you. Gotta watch what you say, the walls got ears."

"Doesn't matter now," Harris said. "You know that. The new warden wants transparency. Besides, Governor Barr's long gone. Commissioner D'Antoni was the last of the lot, died in '82."

Day stooped as if speaking to a child. "You hear that, Ronsellier...all those people who testified against you, who said you did it..." Blinking, Day stood. "Wait, was he...maybe kept down here this whole time as a way to keep him from saying stuff about all of those bigwigs?"

Harris frowned. "Not in our job description to know that, officer."

"Nor are hellholes like *this* a part of our job description," Day said, surveying the cobwebs.

Harris stepped over to the nearest one and plucked it down. Wiping his fingers clean of the stick, he said, "I'm surprised they kept this up for so long. Thank God for this new warden, get some common sense into this place. No more ledgers, either. No more having to record his rants every morning."

"What does he say?"

Harris said to the crouched figure. "Hey, old school, Officer Day wants to know what it is you recite every morning. In the mood for a rehearsal?"

Henry's face remained glued to the back of his elbow.

"Nothing too special," Harris said.

"Is he gonna get up or what?"

"He's been down for seventy years, officer. Give the man some time." Gazing in wonder at the living relic crouched before them with half an eye peeking out from behind its elbow, Harris said, "Year after year his medical exam comes back a-ok. One liver enzyme is slightly elevated, and his blood pressure's always low but that's to be expected. Of course, he's under sedation during the exam. Otherwise, perfect bill of health."

"You know his whole medical history?"

Harris leveled a brow. "This is no ordinary inmate." He placed his hands on his hips. "Look, I've worked this detail for the past twelve years now, and this man's test results are the exact same every single year. Hair don't grow, fingernails don't grow, twirly mustache don't grow. Nothing changes. It's like he's on pause."

Day swabbed a finger along the grimy plaque layer mucking the stone wall. "I heard they send his results to the NIH."

Harris nodded, slowly.

Day wiped his finger on his pants. "So what do the feds have to say?"

"*That* is classified," Harris said.

"But you know. You've worked this detail for the past twelve years."

Harris raised his voice, "They don't have any fucking clue, okay? Cellular regeneration, who the hell knows? Maybe he's a vampire, a zombie, a saint."

"Like," Day gulped, "one of those saints who don't decompose even centuries after they've been buried?"

"*Worthy sirs, I...*"

"Look, he's trying to say something. Is he afraid of us? He looks scared to death." Day turned to his captain. "When do you think was the last time he saw a living person?"

"Seventy years ago. Old management said no human contact, pretty much no to everything when it came to Mr. Heck here—I mean, Mr. Ronsellier here."

Officer Day chanced a step forward. "We are your friends...friends...we come in peace..."

"Maybe if you hold out a cracker that might work," Harris said, rolling his eyes.

"Or my leftover bagel," Day exclaimed. "Sure, it's worth a try.

Better yet, some Reese's Pieces, like in the movie *ET*? Hold on, I think there's some in the machine, I'll be right back."

Captain Harris folded his arms. "Well, Mr. Ronsellier, so what's it gonna be? Come with us so the boys can fix the place up nice and pretty for you—put in a sink, toilet, electricity—or stay, and the cell remains the same crappy way it is? C'mon, let's do this, fella."

With every ounce of courage in him, Henry stood.

"That's my good man," Harris said. "There you go, one foot in front of the other, very good, just like that..."

CHAPTER SEVENTEEN

CHAPTER 17

Never underestimate the value of a word spoken in its season. My English teacher in junior high, Mr. Plourde, had said that, with reference to that wicked cool masterpiece of 20th-century literature, *The Catcher in the Rye*. The right words, at the right time. J.D. Salinger's portrayal of teenage angst through his novel's protagonist, Holden Caulfield, found no better time to state its reasons than in the early 1960s. *The Catcher in the Rye* signaled my initiation into the realm of literature. For me, Mr. Plourde's words were the right words at the right time.

This, too, was a time kinda just like that. The right words at the right time.

Seated at the desk in my single cell, I copied the words verbatim from Chapter 16 of that masterpiece of 19th-century literature, *Wuthering Heights*:

"Catherine Earnshaw, may you not rest as long as I am living. Haunt me, then! I know that ghosts have wandered the earth. Be with me

always—take any form—drive me mad! Only do not leave me in this abyss, where I cannot find you!"

In the middle of writing "take any form," I heard a surprise visitor at the door grunt "Uh-hmm" to try to get my attention.

I raised a finger. "Just a second, let me finish this sentence."

"The warden wants to see you."

Officer Gaetske.

"The warden?" I looked over.

"He wants you in his office. Not tomorrow," he said, as I finished penning my sentence. "Not when you finish writing your thesis. Now."

I wedged a tab of paper into my paperback and closed it. Also, I bookmarked then consolidated *New England's Best Ghost Stories* and *Rhode Island at Midnight,* stacking and sliding them against the wall. I rose. "Am I in trouble?"

"My opinion? You're either gonna get spanked or they'll give you a medal. Good job out there yesterday, McConnell." Gaetske patted my shoulder on my way out.

That seemed to be the going phrase this morning. On my traipse down the stairs they all kept saying it, in its many variations. "You the man, homie," one of the Spanish homies said. "Way to go, dog," one of the Black homies sang. "That's what I'm talkin' 'bout, bro," one of the AB fellows extended a fist.

Gaetske's directions to the warden left little room for error, unfortunately. Now, any attempt to deviate like an "accidental" wrong turn down a T intersection into the forbidden zone, Super-max, might prove less than excusable. Then I remembered Sal's mention about Heck's *underground* chamber.

That mysterious air-shaft in the library, then.

Mission Impossible music sounded in my brain as I breached the Barr Building and peered down that long hallway with its zebra flooring. But, no, I hooked a quick left and ascended the spiral staircase.

The second floor.

Here, another long hallway stretched with offices all along, most of them with their doors closed. A left turn funneled in the direction of Case Manager's Row. That wasn't the way. I hung a right into yet another hallway. At the very end of it, an office situated whose magnificent, beveled wood doors winged open in welcome.

"Gateway to his excellency's chambers," I muttered upon my approach.

Warden Samuel R. Press, the nameplate on the side of the door read.

I entered.

Samuel R. sat with his hands folded atop his desk, smiling, as I stood before his excellency in my greens. Smiles meant things like happiness, joy, goodwill towards men. Smiles, not shit-eating grins. More to the point, smiles had little business on the kind of face that met my gaze with its burrowing anger lines, stern brow, protruding chin, and jittery, piercing brown eyes. The warden's jet black hair parted meticulously off to the side and spared no expense in the matter of grease.

The warden rose.

I could think of no better greeting than "Whassup, Ward," while I processed a quick scan of the premises. I noticed a bay window with a birds-eye view of the yard, pencil sharpener, pics of the wife, brass knuckles, all kinds of dope stuff. "Livin' the dream, huh? Nice place you got here."

The warden rounded his desk to greet me. "Congratulations on your heroic deed, Mr. McConnell. Thank you, it is nice here, yes. Call me Sam." He shook my hand. "Saving a life is a wonderfully big deal, and shall not go unrewarded."

"Oh, you've heard?"

The warden pumped my hand. "Of course I have heard, Mr. McConnell." He released my hand. "Paperwork was submitted yesterday on your behalf requesting that Providence State Penitentiary recognize you, Thomas McConnell, for your achievement of saving a life. Do you know what happens if the board agrees? Sit down, please."

I did, and shook my head.

"150 days off of your sentence." The warden grinned, broadly. Then didn't. "You don't seem particularly pleased, Mr. McConnell."

"No, that's tight. 150 days is, like, half a year."

Slowly, the warden stepped back to the business side of his desk. "They will vote your way, I assure you. There were eyewitnesses. Video footage. Believe me, Mr. McConnell, this prison wants you out as much as you want out." While leaning in, he slipped his palm over the brass knuckles atop his desk. "And I do mean that most sincerely."

I nodded, even though I didn't know what that meant—or didn't want to know what it meant.

The warden sat down. "Now, I'm going to make this short and sweet. Afterward we'll meet the press and have a photo shoot, okay?"

"Photo shoot?"

"The taxpayers, sir, will want to know." The warden reached into his desk drawer. He extracted a cigar, and lit it. "You see, back in the day," he said, puffing, "when Rhode Island still had the death penalty, we would grant doomed men a last meal. They named the meal, we got it for them. Of course, this was a very long time ago. The state of Rhode Island has since abolished the cruel and unusual practice of execution. Plenty of other ways to make an inmate suffer for his sins, if you know what I mean." The warden grinned, broadly, again.

"The last man to be executed in the state of Rhode Island was a gentleman named Gordon. Irish fellow." The warden's grin grew. "So, what'll it be?" he said, leaning back in his chair and puffing. "Sirloin steak...filet mignon...cheesecake...wine, women, anything your little Sherlock heart desires...as a reward, additionally, for your service to our prison community for saving a man's life."

I raised an eyebrow. "Wine, women?"

"Not on your life. Your last meal, what'll it be?"

Although this phrase "last meal" did for the record strike me as suspicious, all my mind's eye could see at that moment were those Red Lobster commercials on Niño's TV.

"I do like lobster…"

"Lobster," the warden said, scribbling on the notepad in front of him.

"Filet mignon's hella good, too."

The warden scratched off the word "lobster" and wrote "filet mignon."

"On second thought…"

"Yes?" The warden raised his head.

"Thank you for the offer but…whatever could I want more than a penny?"

The warden snorted. "A penny? We'll see what we can do about that."

"It's for a ghost."

"So I assumed. You're not the first." The warden squashed his cigar then put his fingers to his lips and whistled, loudly.

Moments later, two women and a man dressed in business attire entered the warden's chamber through a door set into the side wall. The man held a large, fancy-looking camera.

The woman shook my hand. "Mr. McConnell, my name's Linda White, so glad to meet you. I'm associate editor of The Northeast Prison Quarterly, and this is Maggie, our intern, and Jordan, our photographer. We'd like to ask you a few questions about yesterday's rescue and maybe get a photo or two…"

I leveled my brow at the warden. "My going rate for interviews is one penny."

Remarkably, Warden Press laughed at that.

Later that afternoon, about an hour before chow, tired of chillin' in my single cell with ghost stories and the old-timey writings of Ms. Emily Bronte, I decided to get some fresh air.

The feezys started up again with their cheerleader rant on my descent down the staircase, so I gave their table a wide berth. This ran me straightways into the Hispanic homies' table, who requested I come hang with them; but this crew looked to be all birds of a feather with their shot caller perched at the helm, so I offered some lame excuse and kept walking, not entirely with my eyes on where I was going. Finally, I looked up, and seated at the table where my feet landed me sat Tall Drink of Water.

We eyed each other.

"Come to get your ass whooped, dog?" Tall Drink asked.

He called me his dog—which meant it was safe, at least, to sit down. I did. "One-on-one," I said. "You and me. The court in the yard, in the gym, no matter where. You name the place, I'll name the time."

Tall Drink rolled his eyes. "*Basketball* is a game for *clowns.*"

"C-lowns?"

"How's 'bout a real game?" Tall Drink looked down at his chess board, with its pieces all lined up and ready for battle.

I made a face. "Ch-ess?"

"Ready to get your ass whooped, dog?" Tall Drink slid the chessboard my way. "You go first."

I scratched my head. "I've only played this game, like, once or twice before."

"Chess is a mind game. It's all 'bout strategy."

"Like basketball," I said. I studied the black and white pieces on the chessboard. "Me, though, I usually just put my head down and ball. Don't know nothin' about *strategy.*"

Tall Drink burst out laughing. The whole commons area looked over. "You could've fooled me. You's a bad man. Your move."

Chopper stood in my doorway the next morning. "Where'd you get it?"

I flipped my penny, caught it, slapped it down onto the back of my left hand; flipped it, caught it, just like I'd been doing all morning long.

"Pennies from heaven," I smiled.

"That's contraband, you know," Chopper advised.

"Nope." I placed my penny down on the front cover of *Here a Ghost, There a Ghost*. "It's a magic penny. A great, mighty wizard gave it to me."

"A great, mighty—"

"Wizard, warden, whatever."

"Are you serious, the friggin' *warden* gave that to you?"

I nodded.

Chopper pondered. "Okay, so, maybe *that's* why Captain Perry stopped by earlier. To drop off that penny. Then, he got into it with Gaetske over the new moves."

I flipped my penny. "Captain Baldy? New moves?"

"Gaetske moved Mohawk Man and his celly to another pod."

I batted my eyes for a moment then stepped over to my desk. "And moved *this* guy in." I dangled the dead rat by its tail. "Found it right beside the coin."

Chopper's eyes bulged. "Perry put it there. Beside the coin? Not good, Tommy. No ways."

I nodded. "Well, if ever I *do* end up like Professor Ratsworth here," I said, in a low voice, "you guys can rest assured I died knowing..."

"Knowing what, Tommy? What?"

I thought about it. "Knowing, that I followed my stated goal and dream to the very end." I looked at Chopper. "Donkey heads and dead rats be damned." I tossed the latter into the trash.

Chopper continued to eye the rodent, even with it lying face down on its funeral bed of snotty tissues and Honeybun wrappers.

Joining my sights with his on the burial site, I said, "I think that's a great place for it, actually." As the undercover Sherlock, I needed to keep up appearances. This was no time to act scaredy by focusing on things that might make me lose my overall focus. I returned my sights from my dead visitor to my living one.

Chopper breathed. "So, the mohawks are out," he went on. "Perry threw a shit fit over it, too. He wanted them to stay and play. Gaetske said *no way*. Perry's the cap in Admin, though. This isn't his turf. What does he care if…?" Chopper stopped in mid-sentence and looked down the hall. He turned to face whomever was approaching. "I didn't do it."

"At ease, Larsen," Gaetske said. He poked his head in. "McConnell, you're wanted in the mail room."

"The *mail* room?" I said, in sudden search of my tennies.

The mail room situated directly across the hall from the library.

"What you got for me?" I asked the inmate worker seated behind the mail counter. I handed him my pass. After studying it, and scanning the list of names on his clipboard, he called for one of the C.O.'s in back.

"Roommate request," the officer clarified, after sorting through some paperwork on the counter.

I didn't know what that meant.

"An offender has requested to cell with you." Blue handed me a form. The form looked already filled out, only a line at the bottom with an "X" next to it appeared to be lacking its signature. For my own sig, in the event I agreed to cell with the requesting individual.

"Who is it?" I said. "I don't know anyone here."

Then, I saw the requestee's signature and the name in print.

I didn't know whether to shout for joy or slam my fist down on that mail-room counter.

I signed.

The officer reviewed the signed form. "We'll get this approved then your friend can move over from Pod 4 to your cell in Pod 2 as soon as tomorrow."

"Fuckin' clown," I kept saying on my way back to the cell. However, had anyone asked me to erase the smile I had on my face the whole ways, I would not have been able to.

At lunch the following afternoon, I barely got down one bite of my mystery-meat stew. The dozen guys who over the course of my meal had joined me wanted a lowdown on some of the finer points of my "Daring Dangle," as they kept calling it, but my heart just wasn't in it. My heart felt stuck down in my shoes; all the while my spirits soared. I felt pissed, shook, and giddy all at the same time. I bailed without even touching my apple-crumb dessert.

On my way back from lunch I had a feeling, like the vibes those dowsers get in their rods when they near metal, or so my ghost books claimed. Tackling the zigzag staircase, I could see flits of shadow, of movement, from inside the cell. Someone was in there. I held my breath as I stood in the entryway, watching him unpack the few items of his In-and-out bag onto the bottom bunk.

"You lazy, scum-sucking, pipe-smoking parole violator," I said.

"Tommy," Danny exclaimed. "Long time no see." He sat on his bottom bunk. "And how have we been?"

I entered. "Good, 'til now."

"Recidivism, love it or leave it, as Tommy Mac always says. Ah, homie," Danny said, giving me a fist bump then a hug. "It's gonna be just like old times."

"Sure," I said. "Just like that."

"What's with the greens?"

CHAPTER EIGHTEEN

Coincidentally, my "greens" found their final resting place in some refuse or recycling bin, too, the very next day. Officially, I no longer listed as a suicide risk, and so they issued me my blues. Unofficially, their eyes would remain ever on the lookout, of that I could be sure.

Gripping my magic penny, I listened while Danny rambled on about life on the outs. His parole officer classified as a douche. His drug dealer as backstabbing slime. Lilya's landlord wanted money every damned month. Lilya didn't have much along those lines, so she hooked up with WalMart—instead of with Danny, Clownaround, and whomever else; she said she was through, finally, fucking around. ClownAround bolted soon afterward, prolly to Boston to schmooze up to that tweaker chick from Fairlawn with the third-story apartment. Johnny Rizzutti whacked Dan in the jaw in the backseat of their borrowed Silverado and was due one.

"Wait," I said. "What was that about Lilya?"

After relaying the magical adventures he had shared with some half-dozen or so others, Danny caught his breath. He explained that

Lilya had applied at the nail salon at Walmart, but no go. They'd liked her enthusiasm and Beyonce style but not her "no certification and non-existent work history." So, she decided on a Plan B: be a Walmart bagger then let the nail people watch from a distance how she showed up on time every day, smiled bigly, dealt courteously with customers, painted her nails a different color every hour on the hour. "She's crazy about nails," Danny said in summary.

"Tell me about it. It's good to have dreams. As long as there's no donkey heads in them." That was my new favorite line.

"What's with the penny, fool? You've been fondling it non-stop since I got here."

I proceeded to tell Danny about the legend of Old Morgan and the power of pennies, when he stopped me. "Hold on. Speaking of ghosts, I got something for you." He rummaged through his duffle bag.

"You know, Dan," I said, clenching my penny as I watched him fling shirts and underwear over his shoulder. "You're my homie, my best bud, but I've gotta tell you something, and maybe this is the time to say it. And it's not because I don't care, but because I do." I took a deep breath. "You've gotta be the laziest, stupidest, most worthless, pathetic junkie this crazy world has ever laid its eyes on."

Danny froze mid-search to shoot me a nasty look.

"That's right. I call. You're lights out. I call. You're *busy*. I call. You *can't come to the phone*. I call. You answer, but you're so high and off the chain it risks getting us in with the po-po. While Lilya's researching and filing stuff on Henry's behalf, you're too wasted to so much as say whassup." I walked over, dropped onto my chair and opened one of my ghost volumes. "And now, don't even tell me—"

"There," Danny said, slapping a black, plastic, rectangular widget down on my desk. "*Now* you tell me who's not looking out, homie."

I studied the mystery object on my desktop. Some digital apparatus. A screen, black housing, buttons.

Danny explained, "They call it an EVP recording device. Lilya said you needed one. She says Happy Early Birthday, Tommy."

I couldn't believe my eyes. "How'd you get it in here?"

Danny curved a smile. "I kiestered it. Tucked it up where the sun don't shine as far as it would go. Don't think it didn't hurt, and don't think my prison pocket won't be feeling it for any less than a week. Coming in, I made sure to get constipated so the x-ray couldn't tell the difference between—"

"I don't wanna know." Danny knew every trick in the book. It was a lovely, touching gift, but... "Did you wash it at least?" I asked, grimacing.

Danny glowered. "Did the best I could."

"That's encouraging."

Danny turned around and leaned way over. "There's a penny somewheres up in here, too, that Lilya wanted you to have..." he twerked his moneymaker back and forth "...but it just doesn't seem to wanna come out."

I smiled. "Tight."

"Exactly. Way too." Danny turned to face me.

"What if there's a shakedown?" I examined the recorder. "They toss cells every so often here."

"Stick it up where the sun don't shine. They'll pat you down, but no strip searches during a shakedown."

I shrugged. "Thanks, Lilya. Thanks, homie." I handed over the recorder to Danny who tucked it into my duffle bag.

"No problem, fool. Now, finish telling me why all these ghost books, pennies, EVP recorders. Lilya shared some, but I wanna hear it firsthand. Does it have anything to do with your investigation into Henry Heck?"

Around the ten-minute mark of my "long version" answer to Danny's question, we received a visitor, whom Danny received into the cell.

Mendez presented as a high-strung, sleeved-out Latino in his late twenties, but in arriving at our cell without invite, arms folded, and with a snarky smile on his mug, he presented as Pod 2's official get-it-for-you man.

Or so I had figured.

"Whassup, dog," Mendez greeted Danny as he entered. "Good to have you back." The two fist-bumped, hand jived, joked around, then Mendez sat down. Danny's second stint on the high side meant he knew fools, and evidently Mendez numbered among them.

"It's dope to be back," Danny said. "I was in Pod 4 for like two days when I heard the news about Tommy's rescue of Old Sal. Didn't surprise me none. I kept tellin' fools, *Yup, that's my boy*. Anyways, I figured Old Sal might've gotten roughed up hella bad and in which case Tommy might've hustled him a single."

I turned to Mendez. "Hey, can you maybe tell us what the deal was with all that? With Sal? I mean, who were those guys, Mohawk Boy and the other who kept hounding and pounding him?"

"Sal Caniglio went rogue," Danny assumed the reins. "Any white boy can tell you that. If those fools weren't Family, they were hired by the Family to straighten Sal out, maybe even off him." I liked how Danny could talk authoritatively on subjects he knew absolutely nothing of—that was actually his rep. On the other hand, possibly Danny did know, as he'd been on the high side his last go-round. Anyhow, Danny hadn't known Mohawk Boy. You never really knew with Dan.

"Yeah, but there's more." Mendez looked at me. "The latest rumor has it those Devil Coyotes were messing with Sal to try to get him into PC. They wanted him to check in."

"Check in? Why?" I furrowed my brow. "Devil Coyotes?"

"To keep Sal from talking—to you, Tommy, to you," Mendez said.

"Me?" I mulled it over. "Sounds about right," I sighed. "Black Hats gonna Black Hat. Great, now they've got some hair-boy band doing their dirty work for them. They've been threatening me over my investigation since day one."

Danny leveled a stare. "It might be *you* over those rails next time, homie."

"Investigation?" Mendez said.

Danny cleared his throat. "Into the ghost of Old Morgan," he lied.

"No such thing as ghosts," Mendez said. "Why waste your time?"

"'Cause time's all we've got," Danny replied. "Not sure if I believe in them, either. Or for that matter, homies who are a hundred years old and stuck in prison basements. *Believe* is what you do when you've got nothing better. If Tommy asked me to help him investigate the goddamn man on the moon, I'd go there, 'k?"

Mendez asked Danny, "You've been here how long?"

"Third or fourth day," Danny replied.

Mendez frowned. "Prolly got no money, then."

Danny turned to me. "Mendez was at that party at Remy's pad that one Fourth of July, remember, Tommy?"

I remembered the party. Although, Mendez I did not, nor much of anything else that happened that one day.

Eyeing me and me only, Mendez said, "So what can I get you? I got uppers, downers, lefters, righters, upside-downers, pebs, cigs, joints, nudies, oxy, fentan... You name it, I can get it. What'choo want, what'choo want?" He snapped his fingers. "C'mon, c'mon, I haven't got all day."

"Wanna place an order for us, Tommy?" Danny said.

I shrugged. "Don't have anything to trade for. I haven't worked in forever. I smashed my last pack of Ramens last night."

Mendez sat blinking at us for like ten seconds. "*Adios, amigos,*" he said, standing, then bailed.

"Disappeared." Danny smiled. "Just like one of your ghosts."

"Yeah," I said. "So anyway, like I was saying, and in summary..."

Just over a week later, I sat at my desk gripping one of those prison pens that ran dry after like ten days. I shook that son of a bitch. Tested it. Nothing. Fortunately, it's lifespan coincided exactly with my project needs, so I didn't throw it into the trash so much as dropped it in. Turning to Danny, who sat chillin' on his rack, I handed him the page I had moments earlier torn out of my notebook.

"This is the *for realz* summary right here," I informed him. "Forget what I told you last week. Updated version. Revised summary. And my plan of action."

Danny received the paper. He read, and read, and…I could tell by the lines in his forehead and the vacuousness in his eyes that Danny wasn't reading *shit*. Not only a lousy reader, the dizzying effects of barbiturate were muddling his brain at this particular moment in time.

I snatched the paper out of his hand and handed it to Chopper.

Let's all get high over at Tommy and Danny's place while we listen to Tommy talk about his ghosts, the Three Musketeers—Chopper, Mike, and Slider—had offered.

Chopper's reading skills looked to be worse. He kept snickering and then, started laughing as he flitted his sights up and down, side to side, across the page. "This is good, Tommy," Chopper snorted. "Dope short story. I like it. So, what happens, exactly, to the rats at the end here?"

"Rats? They've since packed up and moved back to Jersey." I reclaimed my essay. "I don't write stories anymore, I live them."

A temptation passed to hand it over to Slider. A jailhouse lawyer, I knew that he could read, notwithstanding that swollen black eye from his morning meetup with Rodriguez, Second Floor. However, he looked far too busy staring off into some starry infinity; besides, I wanted everyone to get this.

Mike folded his legs on the floor alongside Chopper; Danny paired with Slider on his rack; and I chilled at my desk. Cleverly bundled and camouflaged inside of a Slim Jim wrapper, the goodies situated at various midway points throughout the soiree, passed between our eager hands in between darted glances at the cell door. "Quality prison reefer," Danny said, with a puff.

After Chopper poked his nose into the hall to verify one last time the coast was clear, no cops, I announced, "Okay. I've finished reading all my books. I've finished thinking all my thoughts. This is what I've come up with. Read it, and weep. I mean, listen and weep." The following is what I read for Danny and the boys:

PARANORMAL FINDINGS
by Tommy McConnell

<u>Patterns.</u> *Ghosts rarely appear in physical form, and when they do they quickly bail. However, they may appear to children under the age of six and adults who are hours or days away from their death; with these they may even hold convos.*

Anomalies include the flipping on and off of lights, opening and closing of doors, switching on and off of electrical devices, tappings, rappings, muffled sounds, and voices—not a hell of a lot else though. Ghost messages caught on EVP are usually hella short and cray-cray; although, they will at times be clear enough to render a possible meaning. That ghost messages only deliver in the form of semi-coherent partials and riddles—suggests something. Think filter, *and that not by accident.*

Ghosts are territorial...they rarely haunt a place not associated with whatever unfortunate incident had led to their demise or downfall. "Connecting" with a ghost requires a stated desire to connect, some come on line, and a physical presence in said locality. The longer and more earnest the effort to connect, the greater the chance of hooking up.

Ghosts will appear in the form in which their unfortunate incident occurred. If a homie got all tore up when he was young he will appear after his death as a young man, even if he lived to old age. His unfortunate incident locks him into that particular time and place. Frozen in time, frozen in place, forced to relive the incident over and over for all eternity, or until justice is served.

Once justice is served, viz, once the mystery behind the reason for the existence of a ghost is solved, the haunting ceases, the ghost fades, it dies, it moves on.

Objects may invite and/or allow for a "point of contact" to be made with a ghost. A doll, a painting, a penny, a do rag, anything that once belonged to the deceased and had meaning to them.

Ghosts never kill. This is especially poignant considering ghosts can move stuff and many were in their day murderers, wackjobs and the like. This raises questions as to the free will of ghosts. They have the power, opportunity and arguable desire to smash fools—yet never do.

<u>*Other Observations.*</u> *In the novel* Wuthering Heights, *the protagonist, Heathcliff, unleashed a ghost by digging up her grave. In Chapter 27, it is stated that he beckoned that hella fine Cathy ghost day and night for 18 years. Only at the end of this time she came to him. At the moment of her death, Cathy, for her own part, expressed her wish to haunt Heathcliff.*

In the novel The Stranger, *which presents a counterargument to the existence of ghosts, to the existence of everything—of any meaning or purpose in life, a man reacts without feeling to the death of his own mother. Here, the dearth of feeling corresponds with the absence of meaning. Men are mere animals without souls. The philosophy of "existentialism" was this French author's whole selling point. Tommy McConnell, convict, addict, and asshole extraordinaire, is however gonna call bullshit on this one. Not givin' two shits that Mom died? C'mon, homie.*

<u>*General Conclusions.*</u> *Ghosts have free will, but only in a restrictive sense. Their will is constrained by any number of unseen laws of the universe. Their version of free will lies only in their ability to express that will, not carry it out.*

Living peeps over the age of five nor nearing the moment of their death, as a general rule, may not face-to-face with the dead. Why? Who the freak knows. But it's a thing. However, as in law and order, there are exceptions to every rule—but only upon the meeting of certain rare conditions. For a hookup to happen, the desire and stated intention of the dead must be made before death; this intention must correspond with a living person's desire for the same. But that's not enough. The universe must ensure this mutual desire of both living and dead meet up to some designated standard. To this end, time and testing is required.

The afterlife is as much Prison World as is P-Pen. Restrictions, rules, and overseers are the norm. Postings on otherworldly walls might very well say that count is at ten o'clock, chow is here, never over there, and inglorious iron bars stand as warning that one shall proceed no further. Ghosts cannot breach the walls of their otherworldly realm any more than an offender can his. Their "visits" are monitored, regulated and with permission. That laws of the universe are no bullshit may be verified by the overwhelmingly numerous, trans-generational, trans-cultural, altogether consistent, patterns of ghost anomalies which presuppose any number of limiting factors.

Grand Conclusion. When beckoning the ghost of Old Morgan, and gripping that point of contact in his hand—a copper penny, Tommy McConnell shall not say "Morgan, come forth to me," but rather, "Grant that Morgan may come forth to me," not unlike the manner in which one might petition a judge.

So it is written. So it shall be done.

"I like that last part." Danny yawned.

"You read books for two whole weeks just to come up with *Grant that Morgan may come forth?*" Chopper shifted to refold his legs.

"No." I snagged my pen and scratched a note in the margin of the page. "Actually, I would have to petition Morgan. He has to *want* to come."

Slider stood. "I don't know anything about *any* of that BS you just wrote there, Mac," he said, looking far less stoned all of a sudden, "but, for what it's worth, I can appreciate your mention of exceptions to every rule. It's true," he turned to explain to Danny, Mike and Chopper. "A statute of limitations can be extended if you have a reasonable excuse for tardiness. A qualified immunity defense can be overcome if the officer had acted outside of his official capacity. Arguing those rare exceptions in the fine print is what separates the good lawyers from ones like the asshole that I had."

Danny nodded. Chopper shrugged. Mike sat stoned out of his mind, appearing not to hear or understand anything.

Slider asked, "Why do you wanna see Old Morgan so badly, Mac?"

Danny put in, "He wants to ask it where Henry Heck is."

I nodded. "That. But also, I'm just kinda interested in finding out, you know, more about ghosts."

"Why?" Danny asked. "You were never into ghosts before."

"I dunno. Just, you know…'cause." Then I knew what to say. "If I can't solve one mystery, dammit, I'm gonna solve another. I'm not leaving this joint without solving *something*." I slammed my fist on my desk.

"Mommy, mommy…" Danny said, laughing.

I sighed, deeply.

Danny addressed Chopper and Slider. "That's what Tommy used to say in his sleep back when we were roughing it in that abandoned Buick. Mommy, mommy…" Danny kept laughing.

"Like hell I did."

"You did, homie. Sorry," Danny said.

We hadn't noticed up until that point—or maybe we had, but it didn't quite register with all of the dope in our veins and my ghost essay blowing everyone's minds the fuck away—but Mike lay crashed out on the floor staring at the ceiling. "Fuck," Slider said. "Lightweight. If we have to drag him back to the cell we'll get caught."

The smoke in the cell had already started to dissipate. Even if a C.O. had passed by at that very moment there could be no certainty that ours had been the cell in violation. Not only did the smoke appear to be clearing, but Mike had just inhaled the last of the evidence.

Danny and Slider made a spread after that and talked about cars —which ones were the easiest to borrow, then we all played Spades to fill in the time until Mike came around. For the others, ghost talk was something they could listen to, enjoy, get stoked about, then walk away from. I couldn't, not now.

While the gang assisted Mike—still dragging, but on his feet—out of the cell, clenching my penny, I declared, "Morgan, come forth to me." I paused, just to make sure the universe and Morgan got that, and maybe for my own sake to let it sink in. Then, I said, "*Grant* that Morgan may come forth to me."

CHAPTER NINETEEN

No less than a dozen times a day, every day, over the course of the next month-and-a-half, I recited the same spiel. Petitioning, invoking, summoning, declaring, whatever you want to call it, I kept doing it. And not only myself. Whenever I grew tired of clenching that penny, I would pass it along to Danny, Mike, Slider, or Chopper, and they would invoke on my behalf:

"*Grant* that Morgan may come forth to Tommy."

Damn, if I wasn't gonna connect with the ghost of Old Morgan.

At the very least, I wanted to *hear* from him. So, the very day before what would turn out to be the mother of all lockdowns, Danny and I decided, finally, to try our luck with the recorder.

Thumbing the record button, I voiced my now familiar mantra. We waited. While Danny circled the cell waving his arms and chanting to try to invoke the spirits (I had made the mistake of telling him all about Niño), I asked, "Is anyone here? Can you hear me? Speak if you can hear me."

Once or twice Danny took a break from dancing to say things like, "You got nothin' to say to Tommy, fool? C'mon, let's go, ghost homie!"

We played back the recording and listened closely. Nothing, except for the sound of our own voices and Danny panting because that was probably the most exercise he had gotten since Sally Brooks of Warwick. They didn't call her Meth Surge Sally for nothin'. Red-faced, and laid to utter ruin after their five-hour rodeo, Danny splayed on her bed afterward like a dead man—and still she kept poundin' the saddle.

Speaking of poundings, there was lockdown. Unlike a sledge-hammer, which hits you hard but once, a jackhammer is death by a thousand thrusts. Lockdown didn't last a thousand days, only thirty, but it felt like a thousand, with Danny complaining the whole while about no TV in the cell.

Neither of us qualified, as it turned out. My altercation on the low side had moved me to the bottom of the waiting list, and Danny's tenure listed in weeks not the required four months.

I recommended that Danny make the most of his free time and work to improve his reading skills.

He was all about that, at first. With the library closed during lockdown, the librarian wheeled his cart from cell to cell for offenders to select books from.

My selections topped fifteen after the first week: I was set for the duration.

Danny selected any number of James Patterson books. These proved easy reads with their short, simple sentences, and Danny did well. He read aloud for me, and although the flatness of his tone suggested a lack of recognition as to the meaning of the sentences he read, his ability to read those sentences was at least there. Danny enjoyed true crime. All criminals do, it seemed. Not that Danny made any attempt to read these.

I kept encouraging Danny to challenge himself with more diffi-cult reads than just James Patterson. And so, when the cart rolled by one fine afternoon midway into the month's lockdown, I spotted an opportunity. A prison story. Danny would dig that. By a French author. That caught my attention. A classic. That meant it would be challenging. The book was titled *The Man in the Iron Mask*. I wedged the paperback out from between two hardcovers, and thanked Mr. Librarian.

"Think about it," he replied, grasping the handles of his cart with his long, pink fingernails decked out in glorious display, as he wheeled off to the next cell. "I don't bite."

"Think about what?" Danny asked, as I returned inside.

I flung the paperback at him. "About getting a clue. Homework assignment. Book report—is what I want when you're done. I wanna know what happens. I'm in the middle of *The Amityville Horror* right now and you better believe I plan on finishing it."

I flipped open to the page where I had left off. It proved easy to find, now that I had a bookmark. No longer relegated to mere tabs of paper, I owned a Governor Theodore Barr Memorial Library business card.

I read the handwritten note on the back of the card:

I'm a secret admirer of the classics myself.
Let's hang sometime when we get out, talk books.
Ever been to the Providence Public Library?

You bet I had. Below his message, the librarian scrawled his phone number and name "Jeff." He had sneaked this free gift into one of the ghost books I had checked out.

Jeff, I thought. An everyday, average name for an everyday, average guy with long, pink fingernails who liked books. A guy with hopes, dreams, and ideals possibly way different than the ones I had naively attributed to him. And even if he *did* bite and wanted to smash, so what? It didn't mean we were gonna. Maybe one day I would get a clue myself.

"Why you so quiet up there?" Danny said, from the lower bunk. "I haven't heard you flip a page in the last ten minutes."

I wedged the card deep into my book. My ass would be grass if any offender besides Danny saw it. "Just thinking," I said.

Danny whined, "I don't like all of these jerky names."

"They're French," I explained, "Don't try to pronounce them, just read them for ID purposes."

Ten minutes later, Danny said, "The book's about a guy in prison who's not allowed to talk to anyone, and no one's allowed to rap with him, and he has to wear a mask so no one can see him. Hey, that sounds kinda like someone we know."

"Yeah, us," I said. "Lockdown Us." *And maybe Henry Heck, too,* I thought. "Also, Dan, you can't just read the blurb on the back cover. That's called cheating."

"I give up," Danny groaned. I heard a *thump.*

I leaned over and looked down, and in very deed the book lay splayed on the floor. "What page are you on?"

Danny sighed. "Four."

I sighed, too. "Well, let's maybe take a break and try the recorder again."

We did.

This time we got a bite.

"Help. Weed," Danny said, repeating the muffled phrase coming from the recorder. "The dude wants weed, homie!"

"I don't think that's it," I said, "I think what he's saying is *help me.*"

"No, homie," Danny insisted. "He wants weed. *Help. Weed. Help. Weed,* he keeps saying. Homie, if we don't get this fool some weed, and soon—"

"No," I snapped. "No weed. It's lockdown. No money on my books, anyway, bro." I climbed back onto my rack. "Welp, that was super helpful."

We returned to our tales.

"Do I have to?" Danny moaned.

"Yes!" Frustration's chain continued to rub red, and bloody, my patience; although not so much because of Danny.

I exhaled. It suddenly occurred to me that ghosts, all of them, classified either as evil like the ones in *The Amityville Horror* or as waste-of-time riddlers like Old Morgan, as I continued reading about the infamous Red Room. Why didn't they answer? Why didn't they ever come around? Even if Old Morgan's message had been *help me* not *help, weed*, so what? That didn't help *me* much. Help him with what?

"Check this out." Danny rose, then splayed open his book for me. He pointed at the handwritten words scribbled into the margin of page twelve:

HR was here. 5/17/87

"H&R Block?" Danny proposed.

"Someone's initials." No sooner did I come to this riveting conclusion than I recalled those words scribbled onto the graffitied wall in solitary *Perez was here.*

"Keep reading," I told Danny. "Your assignment is to read the first twenty pages, then you can go back to Dr. Seuss or whatever."

Our cell underwent its first shakedown during this time. Turns out, the rub of frustration's chain stood of little consequence next to the yank of worry's noose. Danny stood ready to confess. While I distracted the officer with continued questions as to when he thought lockdown might end, Danny deferred, though, and shoved the contraband item way up yonder. It wouldn't fit. He stuffed it into my duffle bag.

Danny and I sat with our hands folded and hearts thumping at a table down in the commons area while Gaetske tossed our cell.

We returned about an hour later.

Smiling, Danny waved my recorder. "Right where I left it."

"Gaetske," I said.

"He let it slide. Why?"

"Dunno." I straightened the stacks of books on my desk. *Weldon and her little band of helpers. The mysterious and elusive White Hats.*

Finally, lockdown ended.

"Anywhere but here, anywhere but in this damned cell," Danny kept saying. So, whenever we had the chance, we cruised on over to TV Land.

Mike and Slider's pad.

Chopper usually made his way, too.

It happened three days after lockdown ended. Slider sat at his desk in search of "rare exceptions" to include in the post-conviction challenge he had agreed to exchange for the mother-load payment of a Cheez Whiz and eight stamps, while the rest of us watched some janky '80s movie called *Hello Again*. The others watched only at my insistence. A ghost movie, with no ghosts. Even on TV, they were never around.

Officer Gaetske poked his head in.

"I didn't do it," Chopper said, dropping my penny onto Mike's mattress.

"McConnell," Gaetske said. "Mail room."

I sat on Mike's rack with my eyes glued to the dead lady brought back to life on the TV. "Er, I already got a cellmate, Blue. And no one ever sends me mail. How's about I stop by the mail room tomorrow? I'm watching this movie right now—"

"You have a visitor request," Gaetske said.

Lilya Jenkins, maybe? Until it struck me Lilya's history might be a bit too checkered for her to risk the ever required background check.

I clenched my fist and tapped my toe as I began to grow moss, mold, and Jeff-length fingernails, waiting in line in the mail room for those five minutes which felt like an hour. Shifting impatiently from one foot to the other, I forced myself to tarry while some wack-job recited a for-realz *treatise* as to why he thought books shipped in the mail from friends shouldn't be contraband. The officer kept telling him, "I don't make the rules, Nowacki. I don't make the rules, Nowacki..."

I wanted to scream, "He doesn't make the rules, No*wacki*, now GTFO!"

The human caterpillar which featured me as the butt squirmed an inch closer to the mail-room counter upon Nowacki's vocal, red-faced departure.

"Hurry it up," I spat under my breath in the direction of the guy afterward with the beard who wanted to know why "more than half" of the package mailed to him by his baby mama hadn't arrived yet.

The officer studied his clipboard. "Because it won't."

"Because it won't," I echoed from behind. "It's contraband. They sent it back. Have a nice day."

Beard-o slipped me one hell of a nasty look on his way out. You bet your ass I returned the favor.

After three others were granted their moment to rub even redder my patience, I stepped to the counter and flashed my pass. "I'm here for—"

"McConnell," the officer said. "Okay, so, we have *this* for you today; and then...there's *this*."

The enveloped item looked to be a Hallmark card. A birthday card. The return address read "Lilya Jenkins." Thanks, Lil! As for the second item...

"Sign here if you agree to a visit with this individual," the officer said, pointing at the blank line at the bottom of the already-filled-out form.

I peered in. The requestee's name read 'Andrea Weiss.' "Who that?" I said. "Andrea Weiss, Andrea Weiss..." Nope, nothing came to mind. "What if I don't wanna buy Avon?" I scratched my head as I studied the name and loopy signature. "What if I already renewed the warranty on my vehicle? What if I already got counted in the year's census?"

The officer tempted a smile. "You don't have to sign if you don't want to."

I bit my lip. "No, I will. Not like I got anything else going on this week."

"That is correct, this week," the officer said, watching me sign. "You will meet with your visitor in the visiting room at three o'clock this Friday. You, however, will need to be over there at 2:30 for processing."

Processing. A body-cavity search, maybe. Sweet.

Andrea Weiss.

That passage of time between Monday and Friday felt almost as long as that month in the winter of '19 I spent sleeping in a cardboard box. The days just dragged on and on.

My rack served as my habitual abode over this clip. I tossed, turned and racked my brain while lying there. Who could she be?

That Tuesday I returned from my shower and found a Bible on my desk. Danny said a "Reverend Brother Someone-or-other" dressed in a suit and a tie had, alongside his escort, Gaetske, stopped by to hand out bibles.

Sitting at my desk with my head in my hands, I decided out of sheer boredom to open the thing.

"Bible Roulette," I said, and jabbed my finger at the first words I had caught sight of after a random opening. I read:

Take with you words, turn unto the Lord, and say...

I sighed.

"What's the matter?" Danny said from his rack.

I wet my lips. "The *Lord* just told me..."

"What?" Danny sat up.

I snapped closed the volume. Bible study, over and out.

"You're trippin', fool," Danny said with a quick shake of his head, then returned to staring blankly at the wall.

Gripping my penny, I said, "*Grant* that Morgan may come forth to me..." And then, "Morgan, come forth to me..."

I climbed onto my rack while Danny sat grinning. "Guess whose birthday's coming up this Friday, homie?"

Friday was no day to have a birthday. Friday was the day of my visit.

"You gettin' good and ready for your birthday bash?" Danny said, with a smile I couldn't see but knew was there by the way he said it.

I had forgotten about the infamous prison birthday bashes.

Tradition held that all close friends were to stop by on your special day to wish you a happy b-day. As their birthday present, they "bashed" your arms and legs. Afterward, while you lay immobile on your rack, in pain, and icing up your battered limbs, your buds would cook up a spread or some yummy dessert for all to enjoy.

In prison, birthdays meant bruises, and birthday bruises meant love. So often fools hid on their birthday, or hung out at the library all day. Tommy McConnell, though, would suck it up. Still, with visits came strip searches. Bruises all over one's body would almost certainly raise a red flag.

I asked Danny if my birthday bash might be postponed until Friday evening. Danny said he would talk it over with the fellas, but probably they could swing that.

"I dig this version of Danny Onofrio. Livin' clean and sober. Thinkin' clean and sober. Sober looks good on you, Dan."

But Danny was all about staring at the wall at that particular moment.

Slung out on my rack on Thursday afternoon, I said, "I think I know who she is. No, I *know* who she is."

Danny stirred. "Who?"

"A medium," I said, calmly. All anxiety had since exited out of me like the castings out of some evil spirit. I felt at peace. I knew this was it, just like I'd known Misty from Cougartown—Cranston, rather—was a bad idea, but decided to go through with it anyway over the promise of free meth and hoary gray pubes. "A medium, like the ones I've been reading about in my books. One who's got a message for me from Old Morgan."

"Maybe," Danny said.

"No, not maybe."

I spent the remainder of that evening checking out Lilya's card. *See you soon*, it said, the words surrounded by a thousand colored hearts she had drawn herself.

CHAPTER TWENTY

The big day finally arrived.

"I'm off to see the wizard," I announced, tucking my shirt in and tying my laces extra tight. "Sorceress, medium, crazy black-cat lady, whatever you wanna call her."

Danny said, "You know you're just gonna have to untie those tennies when they strip search you then tie them up all over again."

"It's the thought that counts," I told him.

Danny watched as I made further high maintenance preps.

"Brushing your teeth for a visit?"

"Sur," I said, with foam dripping down my chin. "I want to make a good impression so the lady can tell Ol' Morgan I'm all dat."

"Oh, you'll make an impression, all right," Danny replied. "The crazy cat lady will *definitely* think you're as crazy as she is."

The strip search was nothing, really. Perhaps a tad more exploratory than the work-crew searches, but no round-the-world, butt-pirate quest for treasure. "No need for a body-cavity search," Officer Vasquez said in answer to my question. "You'll be seated at your booth behind a glass panel. Communication with your visitor will be over a phone. It will be monitored: cameras all over the place, so no big worries from our end. No funny business, though, okay?"

I nodded, then followed the officer into the prisoner's side of the visiting room. This narrow plot of real estate consisted of an aisle fronted by a row of booths not unlike those cubicles you see at the library, or at a school where you take those hearing tests with the chunky headphones and beeps. You chilled on one side of the glass, your visitor on the other.

I was stoked. I didn't know why. A meetup with the damned Vice President, sure, some jitters, but not with some witch lady or wayward sales rep. Maybe hers had been a mistake, and she had the wrong Tommy McConnell. Still, I reached around and patted myself on the back. Books, naps, walls, and those inglorious iron bars, would all still be there when I got back.

A tall Hispanic woman opened the door leading into the small sitting room on the other side of the glass. She darted glances around to get her bearings in this strange, new prison environment. She looked as nervous as all that as she wobbled in her purple pumps towards me.

I swallowed. I was nervous as all that, too.

The path of her pumps didn't quite make it, though. Her purpled course deviated until she disappeared behind the side partition of my cubicle. I heard a voice from my side of the fence say, *"Que Pasa, Momacita!"*

I leaned back, then swerved my neck as far as tendon would allow to peer down our side of the aisle to see how many of the booths had offenders in them. Three or four. Also, I noticed at least two spy cameras bolted into the ceiling. I waved hello at them along with the muttering of a few choice words, then flashed the thumbs-up sign at Blue standing at aisle's end there.

When I turned, I saw a woman seated in the chair opposite my window.

Shook, I emitted a girly little burst of surprise. Recovering, I pointed at her. "You magic," I said. "Don't even tell me you isn't."

However, it seemed clear from the woman's widened blue eyes and bewildered expression she hadn't heard me. Then, I remembered convos took place over the phone.

However, no phones just yet. For a short, awkward span of time we did no more than eye each other through the glass. She featured short, curly brown hair feathered here and there with streaks of gray. She looked to be on the shorter side, although it was hard to tell with the two of us seated. She wore thin-rimmed glasses. Her white ruffle blouse and designer blue scarf—neck wrap, whatever you called those things—suggested efforts on her part to look sharp. All in all, she looked well maintained. Her manner, judging by any number of little things I noticed over those few moments—like the efficiency of her movements, and the deliberation of her gaze—suggested this middle-aged lady classed as either an A type personality or someone who regularly associated with the highfalutin alien life forms of that sort. In a word, she was a normie, maybe even a super normie.

Andrea Weiss gazed at me with a kind of sadness in her eyes. I could have sworn I noticed a tear in one of them. Although I had never seen this woman before, she looked strangely familiar. Then, suddenly, I knew what this was: some cougar washed clear from my memory by the ill effects of the dope. A witch lady, then, it would have to be. Letting her be otherwise would mean having to sit through a long storied build-up that would conclude in an askance for money. No money for her *or* her bad habits. Dick, neither. It belonged to the State now.

"You have your father's eyes," she said, finally, over the phone.

A creative, unique, and surprising opening line, certainly, but two could play that game. "I was raised by wolves, ma'am," I confessed, speaking into the phone. "My wolf daddy's eyes are reddened slits and mine are big, bright and blue. You're oh-for-one so far. Nice try, though."

Andrea smiled. "And your grandmother's sarcasm."

I shifted in my chair. "You're clairvoyant? Is that what you're trying to tell me? As a pretext to getting me to believe and receive your message to me from Ol' Morgan? I'm Tommy McConnell, by the way. I live in this place called prison."

Andrea wiped the corner of her eye. "I'm Andrea Weiss, by the way. I live in a blue colonial just west of West Warwick. Very nice to meet you, Tommy McConnell."

I rested my elbow on the counter and placed my chin atop my fist. "So, you knows all abouts my family tree, then, eh, Miss Andrea Weiss from just west of West Warwick? Let's see here… my daddy is a werewolf who moonlights as a lumberjerk; I have his eyes, and my grandma's woof! My sign is Sagittarius…possibly Pisces…or maybe Leo. My future is bright, although cloudy with a chance of meatballs presently. The lines in my palm suggest I'll marry a lass with a unibrow." I leaned back. "Let's skip all that, though, okay? I believe you. You don't have to prove you're believable, reputable, whatever. You're here. You're all I've got. You don't have to try to prove you know all about me. What does our mutual friend Morgan have to say, ma'am? That's the bottom line."

"But I *do* know all about you, Tommy," Andrea said.

Frustration kicked in with a sigh and a roll of my eyes until I leveled my sights on my visitor. "I don't give two shits, ma'am. We have like thirty minutes here. Do you have a message for me from Old Morgan or not?"

Andrea cleared her throat. "Well, yes, I do. Among a great many other things, and for starters, is the message—hello. You know Morgan?"

Holy hell, maybe she really *was* a witch with a word. *West of West Warwick*, she had said. Was that code, maybe, for the Wicked Witch of the West? With the line bugged, maybe the whole of it would be in code. "Yeah," I said, calmly, in spite of my surging adrenaline levels. "Sort of. Morgan says hello then, huh? What else does he have to say?"

"She. Penny Morgan is a *she*."

Penny Morgan, I liked that. There was definitely something cookin' in the micro here never-minding this one mistaken ingredient of gender. No telepathist ever hit the nail one-hundred percent dead nuts. The law of percentages was what mattered, or so said all of my ghost books. I shrugged. "Okay, what else does *she*, Penny Morgan, have to say?"

"She wants very much to see you."

"Really?" I brightened.

"Why, she's the one who discovered you. She couldn't make it today because of a family emergency. It's your birthday; at least one of us had to come. So here I am."

A little weird, this last bit about ghost families, but who was I to judge. "Tell me more." I folded my hands atop the counter.

But Andrea Weiss said her mouth felt dry, and would I mind ever so much if she got something to drink? No, I wouldn't. I pointed at what looked to be a soda machine over against the back wall. She made a beeline for it.

Holy crap, I thought, sitting there by my lonesome. *Old Morgan for realz wants to see me! Wait until the guys hear about this. They'll go ballistic.* "C'mon, c'mon, hurry it up..." I muttered at the female form struggling with her bills at the soda machine.

Finally, she returned.

"That figures," I said, eyeing her mineral water. "Okay, okay, okay, so, tell me more about Penny Morgan."

Andrea sipped her water. "Penny is a student at URI, presently," she said, re-capping her beverage. "She's a sociology major, but her roommate, Maddy, is a criminal justice major. Maddy receives bulletins in the mail every so often which tell about the goings-ons in jails, prisons, and criminal justice just generally here in New England. One day Maddy came across an article about an offender right here in Rhode Island who had saved another inmate's life. The rescuer's name was Tommy McConnell."

I tapped my fingernails on the counter-top, loudly. I thought I had told crazy cat lady here to quit it with all the prognosticating about irrelevant matters in an effort to prove herself reputable. I hoped to hell she wasn't a scammer. A scammer might know nothing about you, or everything. Either way, no money. Or pre-scheduled favors. Some form of blackmail, possibly, even?

Andrea went on, "Penny Morgan's actually her first *and* middle name, but I'd always call her that growing up: 'Penny Morgan, you come downstairs right now!' that sort of thing, and the name stuck. Penny started liking the double name, and her friends all started calling her that.

"Anyway, Penny was shown this article and so we all wondered if rescuer Tommy McConnell might be *our* long lost Tommy McConnell. We eventually came to the conclusion it was. Photos don't lie. That part in the hair. The Langford chin. The McConnell eyes." Andrea clasped her hands together. "Oh, Tommy, Penny wanted so much to come see you today but unfortunately she had to attend her great-grandmother's funeral."

I nodded with mock enthusiasm. "I've used that line, too," I assured the missus. "Grandma in hospital. Wife pregnant. Can you spare a dime, mister? It's called talking out of one's ass. Are you talking out of your ass right now, Miss Andrea Weiss?" I asked her straight out.

Andrea ignored my quip. "Penny's great-grandmother, Old Miss Ronsellier, lived a long and eventful life. Why, just last month we helped celebrate her 100th birthday. Isn't that something?"

Meh, I thought. Plenty of fools lived to be one hundred years old and looked every minute of it. It was the centenarians who *did not* look like their age who got *my* attention.

"Old Miss Ronsellier was an orphan just like you, Tommy," Andrea said. "Her own parents got into some big scandal around the turn of the century. Her father went to prison for it and her mother— yours and Penny's great-great-grandmother—passed away during the course of his trial, from kidney failure. Recently, the newspaper wrote an article about her. Turns out she didn't die of kidney failure: she'd been poisoned."

This lady had for realz done her research, and could spin a good yarn no less. The question was, what did she want, and why venture down this precipitous family-matters road to try to get it? I narrowed my eyes. "Margaret Ronsellier," I said, just to see what else she might know on the subject.

"Yes, Margaret Ronsellier. That's exactly who I'm talking about. She was the one who was poisoned those many years ago."

I looked up. "I saw her once, you know."

Andrea blinked. "You saw Margaret Ronsellier?"

On second thought, talk about ghosts and graveyards required a pretext, and frankly, this woman didn't look the part. She was no witch, dammit. Actually, now that I thought all the more about things, no woman would *ever* arrive all neated up in faux pearl earrings and designer threads if she intended to ask for money. Still, there was something unholy going on here. "What's Penny Morgan doing attending college, is what I wanna know? Penny Morgan's dead, Miss Andrea Weiss. He died like eighty years ago holding pennies in his hand."

"Penny Morgan is not dead. She is very much alive, and wants very much to see you. Penny Morgan is your sister, Thomas."

I decided I might need some water, too. Maybe even a bucket of it poured over my head. "First off, Miss...whatever your name is, if that's even your name, I don't have a sister. Second off, my name's not Thomas."

"Of course your name's Thomas. It says so right on your birth certificate."

I looked at this woman with her frank expression seated on the other side of the glass. "How would *you* know?"

"Because I was the one who named you...after Tom Cruise, the movie star. Your father wanted to name you Arthur—after Arthur Conan Doyle. Can you believe that?"

No, I couldn't, which was why the shit hit the fan just then. I stood. "Who put you up to this?" I said, pointing. "Who are you working for? Danny? Did Danny put you up to this? Lilya?"

My Angry Tommy side planned to do its best Hulk impersonation and supersize, then did. "No practical jokes about my real mom, okay?" I said, with my finger twitching like a tweaker on Day Two. "Don't fuck with me along those lines, okay? Penny Morgan? Penny *fucking* Morgan? You're telling me I've got a sister named Penny *fucking* Morgan? Are you *fucking* kidding me? Do you honestly expect me to *believe* that?"

"Watch your language," Andrea said, batting her eyes as she inched back in her chair.

Just then the officer stopped by. "Mr. McConnell, I'm going to have to ask you to please settle down. If you want to end your session, you can end it, otherwise please sit down."

"I'll sit down when I'm damned well ready to sit down," I screeched. Then I sat back down. I took a deep breath, then another. "Okay, *Mom,*" I said to Andrea Weiss, "tell me, if you really are who you say you are, why did you *ditch* me those many years ago and never once checked up on me since? Hmmm?"

Andrea groaned. She suddenly looked not well. "Your father and I did not *ditch* you, Tommy. You see—"

"I'm listening," I said, leaning back with my hands folded behind my head. This was gonna be good. "Go on..."

"You see, when Frank and Trixie Lutz agreed to adopt you it was because...it was because, well, I was only fourteen at the time—*fourteen*, and your father was *fifteen*." She exhaled. "Does that answer your question?"

I shook my head. "Nope. But it's a start."

Exhaling again, and again, then slamming her water until there was barely any left, Andrea Weiss explained how the girls on her cross country team had encouraged her to get rid of it, how her parents encouraged her to keep it, about Ken's neighbors—Ken was the father, apparently—who couldn't have a child and wanted one desperately; about their parents' insistence that it not be Frank and Trixie, anybody but those slimeballs; about Ken's insistence that it be Frank and Trixie: they were good customers on his paper route; about the many updates she and Ken received over the years by phone from Frank and Trixie...about the yellow-and-blue bike Tommy had gotten for Christmas one year and the A grades he kept getting in his English classes—"and without even trying, it sounded like," Andrea added; about the injury he'd suffered to his knee one summer when he was six or seven.

Andrea related about the surprise visit she planned to make to Tommy's fifteenth birthday party at the Fun House Ice Cream Shop in Warwick; however, her "Forever Failing Ford" ended up breaking down on the highway and so she had to turn back.

Andrea drained the last of her water. "We didn't...want to confuse you when you were young, about who your parents were. We didn't want you to be faced with two sets of parents. Our plan was that when you got to be *of age* we'd stop by...and we did: I did anyway, your father was in Oregon at the time; he now lives in California. Anyway, you weren't there. Frank said you had upped and disappeared. To this very day Frank and Trixie don't know where you are. They've been worried sick about you, Tommy."

Frank and Trixie knew how to talk the talk and wear the right masks when they needed to. That, too, was probably how they had succeeded in convincing whatever adoption board. Nor had they been nearly as far along in their bad habits back in the day. But none of that mattered now.

On the verge of a sniffle, I said, "I knew I'd see you again. I knew you'd come visit me here." That part about the yellow-and-blue bike was what put me over the edge.

Andrea set her bottle aside. "How did you know that, Tommy?"

I wiped my eye. "I wouldn't have thought about you every day over these past many years, and cried out in my sleep at night if, you know, I didn't think I'd ever see you again." I gulped. "Mom?"

"Yes, Tommy," Andrea Weiss said. "Mom."

Words failed me as I tried to recount, afterward, the narrative of my visit with the mysterious Andrea Weiss. Danny, in like manner, sat speechless.

"That's fucking incredible," he said, finally.

I exhaled. "Yeah."

Later, after the next phase of dawning realization—acceptance, with its bouts of chatty excitement—died down, and we returned from dinner, Danny ventured to share about his own forebear, Vicky, whom he knew all too well, he said, and who had since run off with some contractor type on an "extended vacation" down at the latter's beachfront property in Florida. Danny's dad lived somewhere in Mass. Danny didn't know where, and didn't want to. I didn't mention Penny Morgan. It was best Danny Onofrio didn't know I had a college-aged sister.

Meanwhile, words did less than fail me with regards to the aftermath of my birthday bash. With the big news about my brand new fam, Danny and the boys wanted mine to be the biggest, baddest, birthday bash ever. They didn't fail to deliver. I spent the three days afterward laid up in my rack. But it was all good, because these were my peeps. Peeps everywhere, now.

One good thing about paralysis is all of the sympathy visits you get. Everyone—and I mean *everyone*—stopped by to congratulate me on my reunion with my forever mom, and then laughed their asses off as I groaned a pain-stricken "thank you" or "okay, thanks" from my rack.

Even the feezys stopped by. "We wanna be moms, too, one day," Filippa and Chantelle said, poking their noses into my cell. Attempting to raise my arm in reply, but with my peace sign making it no farther off of the mattress than one or two inches, I cried out, well, pretty much like I was being murdered. Those boys blew a nut at that, and kept giggling as they tromped down the gangway.

But things weren't entirely the rose garden that Mom's backyard supposedly featured. Laid up for days in a row sure got my thoughts rolling, and not all of them smelled like roses. At the tail end of my convalescence, I hobbled down the stairs and dialed her number.

"Hello, young man," Mom answered. "What's good?" She laughed at her clever use of a slang reference. But *clever* could swing both ways, as she was about to find out.

I took a deep breath. "Hey, Mom, you know that song 'I Just Called to Say I Love You?'"

Mom quieted at the sound of my darkish tenor. "One of the songs I grew up with. Yes, I know it."

"Well, I just called to say *fuck you.*"

I hung up.

Back at the crib, the homies gave a unanimous big thumbs down to my sour salutation.

"Did you really say *fuck you* to your mom, homie?" Danny snickered. "And the way you said it, too. You really said it like that? You're goin' to hell, bro."

"We'll send you there *ourselves,*" Slider added, "if you don't call her back and apologize. Only ten-year-olds talk like that, Mac."

"Well, then, that's to make up for what I wanted to say when I was ten, but couldn't because she wasn't around," I replied, folding my arms and tucking my chin into my chest.

"Listen," Danny sat beside me on his rack. "When you call, say stuff that's gonna make her feel like a million bucks. Like the way you talk the honeys at the clubs, only not like that. Ask her about her job, pearl earrings, damned garden, even. Old people like that shit. She's your *mom,* homie."

"Ask her for some advice," Slider put in. "She'll like that even more."

"All right," I said. "When the time's right, I'll go talk her up."

"You apologize *now,* asshole," Slider ordered.

Sighing, I stood. "I'm going. I really didn't mean it. It was just something I had to get off my chest, I guess."

~

"Apology accepted," Mom said. She let out a breath. "Well, then. So, would you like to speak with your sister?"

"Sure would," I replied. I coughed. "Hey, er, Mom, one last thing before you bail. I just wanted to say that I really liked those earrings you wore at my visit—I mean, at your visit. They were super nice. I liked 'em. Hey, so how's that ol' rose garden been treating you? Roses are red, violets are blue..." I racked my brain "...I got a new mom...guess who?"

I heard a snort at the other end. "That's sweet, Tommy," a young woman's voice said. "I sure hope your writing is better than your poetry."

I did more than just *speak with* Penny Morgan; she came to me. We met in the visiting room three weeks later. She sported red hair, freckles, and the widest, whitest smile the light of day had ever dropped its rays upon. She'd inherited my killer good looks and sparkly bright eyes. Also, she thought Sandbar Hot House's suicide wings were straight fire. But these seemed to be the only similarities between us, thank the gods.

Was it talking out of my ass to tell my new kid sister she was my "*real* lucky Penny?" I don't think so. For her part, she kept repeating time and again how "wicked awesome" it was to have a brother. She said she would always be there if I needed someone to talk to. "When's your parole review?" she asked.

"Soon," I replied. "I dunno."

She said she could help me find a place once I got out and that she and her friends could even help me move in if I was "open to that." She went on to say she enjoyed skiing, listening to 90's music, and hanging with her friends on campus or at the beach. She asked what I liked to do in prison.

"Read and try not to get killed," I replied.

"Read what?"

"Books. Classics. Literature," I told her.

She mulled it over, then asked if she could make a recommendation.

"Sure."

"*Anne of Green Gables.*"

"What's it about?" I asked.

Penny smiled her heavenly smile. "It's about an orphan who moves into a new home. There, she's warmly received by her new family who help her to grow up and go on to do great things."

Over the weeks which followed, Penny even mailed a few letters. Granted, this did have one downside.

"Who's this...Penny Morgan McConnell person?" Danny asked, framing one of her letters between the pinched fingers of his leveled hands.

My heart sank at Danny's discovery. I shrugged. "Just someone."

"No, not *just someone*. She has your last name, homie. Also, you wouldn't have hid it in your bag if she was *just someone*. It was sticking out: I went to go unstick it in when I noticed the name. Who is she?"

I shrugged, flipped on my shoes, and sailed out the door for a revenge game of chess with Tall Drink.

"Penny...Morgan...McConnell..." Danny announced the next morning at chow. "Tommy's got a new mystery woman in his life, fellas. Who is she, Tommy?"

"Yeah," Chopper said. "Who's the hoe?"

I dropped my spork into my beef stew. "I'll tell you when we get back to the cell," I told the drama queen.

"She's my sister," I said to Danny, plainly. "But she lives way the hell over in California so you're never gonna get to see her, okay?"

Danny flicked a nod at the letter. "The return address says Kingston, Rhode Island, homie."

Perhaps, just perhaps, I could've ripped out of my ass some magic words to get me outta that one. Frankly, though, my ass had grown tired of talking on my behalf, and so I just told Danny Penny attended URI. "She's one broke-lookin' bitch, though, Dan, gotta warn you."

Danny shrugged. "Wouldn't be the first time I've had to use a paper bag. When do I get to meet this beast?"

"Things are different now," I said. "They're just...different."

"Lemme have a peek, at least," Danny pleaded. "Any photos? Does she like to get high? You would never say that about your own sister, fool. I bet she's hella fine."

"Here—have a peek at this," I said, and offered him my Bible.

Dad got down, for a dad. He wrote me a few times. He lived just outside of San Diego with his old lady Kim and their dog, Moby. Ken McConnell sold insurance for a living, played golf, and cycled the "Pacific Coast Highway" on the weekends. He was some sort of regional manager. He was some sort of nice guy, judging by his letters.

In them, Dad always referred to me as "bud." How's it going, bud? Sounds like you're getting along fine in stir, there, bud. Hey, bud, maybe I can fly on over and meet up with you, Penny, and Ann once you get out of the slammer. Never Tommy, always bud. The way I figured it, Dad had originally wanted to call me Arthur, and still wanted to call me that, but couldn't, and so maybe "bud" signaled as his little revenge against the birth name I had been given. Or maybe he just liked calling people bud.

I wrote back and told Dad I wanted to see him. My letter sounded, in all honesty, way too generic, like I had simply filled in the blanks in some "Letter to Father" form I'd printed out in the prison library. This was probably the result of my trying to overcompensate for my inability to speak on my new dad's level. At first, I had encouraged myself to communicate with Ken McConnell in the same shoot-the-shit manner I'd spoken with the closest thing to a father I'd ever had—Sal, but somehow this just didn't seem workable with a regional manager who cycled Pacific Coast Highways on the weekends. So, I stuck to janky old platitudes, and in language without color.

I grew concerned that Ken McConnell would stand wholly ashamed of his new son. I spent more than a few sleepless nights with this in mind. I kept envisioning him dressed in blue with a holster on his hip. Big, bad Ken the Pseudo Cop, getting his groove on to kick his new son's ass into shape. Not to suggest I didn't need that.

Mom wrote a few weeks later to tell me she had just deposited one-hundred dollars on my books and that calling one's mom classified as one of the greatest requirements and privileges an adult son had. I made the rookie mistake of sharing this inside information with at-risk parties.

Not ten minutes later, Mendez stood in the entryway to our cell. "What'choo want, what'choo want? C'mon, c'mon, I haven't got all day," he reeled off in his usual sales rep refrain.

Sidling past Mendez, Danny sat on his rack then motioned for Mendez to get his ass out of the cold and come in. Smiling, Danny asked, "You gonna place an order for us, homie?"

Sadly, the greater part of me wanted to. More than just wishful thinking, my wish list existed as a living, breathing reality penned by that addict beast inside of me. Fentanyl topped the list. Oxy ran a close second. Or even a joint, hell. But then I thought about my lucky Penny. I thought about that biggest, baddest pseudo cop of them all, Ken McConnell.

The conflict within reached the level of gang warfare as I stood bouncing glances between Mendez and Danny: Dad will be ashamed of me, I told myself. *Ken can go to hell,* that other part of me replied. It would be a betrayal of trust, I thought. *Nobody's perfect,* came the reply. This will cause problems. *Life's full of 'em,* the beast replied. I can't. *Yes, you can.* What kind of son would I be? *You're your own damned person, fuck 'em.*

I opened my mouth with plans to say *Fentanyl, oxy, weed, nudies* when the words "I'll be right back" dropped out instead.

I whizzed outta that cell then down the stairs to go cry to my mommy.

Andrea Weiss could tell right away I was dialing it in. "What's wrong, Tommy?" she said. "You sound distraught."

"Mom," I said. "Could I, er, ask your advice about something?"

Her longish pause suggested a nod and a smile at the other end. "Sure, Tommy, that's what parents are for."

"Really? I thought they were for birthing you then bundling you up for the stork to deliver to whomever." Inwardly, I kicked myself for saying that. "Anyway, did you ever have a time when you wanted to do something *really* badly but you knew it would prolly be not good for you in the end?"

Mom grew silent for a moment. "Count to twenty."

"What?"

"Whenever you're faced with a temptation to do something you know you shouldn't do, or say something along the lines of that one outburst you had during our visit, or that dilly a few weeks back, or the one you popped off just now, stop, and count to twenty; or ten; or slowly to five."

"Count? What if that doesn't work?"

"Pray, quietly to yourself."

"I'm not religious."

"Neither am I," Mom replied. "But you can still pray. You never know who, or what, might be listening."

"I gotta tell ya, Mom. That kinda shit is *really* not my thing."

"And no swearing. Recite a mantra, a favorite line from one of your books, some positive word of encouragement for yourself."

"Mom," I said, "I wanted to ask you...remember you told me about Old Miss Ronsellier, who died recently, whose mother was Margaret Ronsellier? You said Margaret Ronsellier had a husband, who went to prison. Do you know his name?"

"I don't," Mom said, after a moment's reflection. "There was some controversy with Margaret and her husband; he went to prison for it, and no one in the family ever talked about it. That's all I know. Your great-grandmother was born just a few weeks before Margaret died. Why?"

I sighed. "Even back in the day there were probably hundreds of prisoners. I was hoping it might be one in particular, but without a name, there's simply no way of knowing."

Back at the cell, Danny stood with his hands on his hips as I entered. "It makes the both of us look hella sour, homie, and hurts our rep big time, when you fucking bail like that. Mendez stomped outta here. He was pissed. He might not do business with us ever again."

"Damn," I said, and meant it. But only a small part of me meant it by that point.

CHAPTER TWENTY-ONE

Had she, Ms. Ragazzino, filtered through the mill of my thoughts even at all over those previous four months, I might have recognized the name. But she hadn't, and so I didn't.

Gaetske rolled his eyes. "Your case manager. McConnell. She wants to see you."

"Why?" I asked.

Turns out, it wasn't because of anything I had done wrong, but what I was going to do: get a job on the outside work crew.

"You'll begin your work detail next week," Ms. Ragazzino said, with her head buried in her business of filling out my assignment form. "Your name, number, and start date will be listed on the bulletin board in your pod. You will report to Sergeant Daniels downstairs in the west lobby at six a.m. on your start date." Ms. Ragazzino's pretty face with its deadpan expression kept level with her desk as she signed and dated line after line on my forms. "You will be assigned yellow scrubs. Between now and your start date you will go down to the laundry room to exchange your scrubs. I would suggest you do this sooner rather than later. Officer Gaetske can write you a pass for that." She raised her sights, but only high enough to study her fingernails. "Any questions?"

"Nope," I said.

Rags swiveled her chair and began typing. "Your parole review will take place in…" she peered in at the computer screen, "five weeks. The 150 days off of your sentence pushed your itinerary up quite a ways. You'll receive further updates about all of this from me. Do you have a parole plan in place yet?" she asked, looking at me finally.

"My new fam agreed to take me in so that I can grow up and go on to do great things," I said, stretching a toothy smile.

Rags returned to her typing. "Be nice if they could set you up with a job, too. We'll keep in touch about all that. Historically, violent offenders don't get paroled on the first try. Have a nice day."

Short. Sweet. No bullshit. Both from my end, and hers. All told, I felt rather proud of myself. "No rabble-rousing," just like I had promised Mom. And this wasn't just any rabble-rouse candidate, either. Not only the phattest piece on the yard, Rags identified as the Lizard Room sendoff lady herself!

When I returned to the cell, I noticed Danny wasn't alone. He introduced me to his visitor, a roughened, old-school cat who sported a forehead streaked with a scar and a shadowy cast to his face indicating his snarl as I entered was just a sampler of the beef he had with the whole world. He looked damned grumpy. I'd seen this fool around. Definitely not homie material.

Bypassing the usual pleasantries, I checked my look in the mirror then was out the door like The Flash.

Danny summoned me back—to ask where the hell I thought I was going, and why.

I returned wearing my reluctance on my sleeve as I dallied at the entryway to the cell. "B-ball game. Gym," I replied. "Just because."

Danny shook his head. Folding his legs as he sat on his rack, Danny resumed his lecture titled "High-side Basketball and its Effects on Low Tolerance Individuals." My title for it, actually, Danny just rambled. "What you gonna do when you drive to the basket and get hard fouled?" he asked.

"I get hard fouled," I shrugged.

Danny unfolded his legs. "What you gonna do when you get hard fouled like twenty or thirty times?"

"Suck it up," I said. "Wipe the blood off. Keep playing."

"What you gonna do when you start crossing fools over and scoring on them and they start not liking that a white-boy fish keeps making them look bad until finally they decide to do something 'bout that shit that's very outside the rules of the game?"

"I'll tell them," I said, "God bless you."

Our visitor cackled.

"Danny," I said. "I got this. I know some tricks now I hadn't known before, to help me stay calm and keep from going off on fools."

Danny stood. "Tommy, while you're still here in one piece, not all bloody, cursing and crying yet, I want you to meet someone. This is Charlie. You may know him by his prison name, Skeletor."

"I don't answer to that name," Charlie growled.

I stepped over and extended my fist at Charlie. "Hey there, sarge. What's good?"

Charlie's waxen glare back at me then down at my fist suggested nothing was good, never had been, never would be. "You damned kids and your *fist kisses,*" he growled. "You either shake my hand or you kiss my ass. No fist kisses! Damned kids. A good thing I don't have my 12-gauge *or I'd blow every last one of you to hell!*"

Danny cleared his throat. "Chuck's not used to being out of his cell. He agreed to come over here only upon the promise of three stamps and a Ring Ding."

"And I better get that shit," Charlie swore. "Or else!"

I told Danny this might present a problem seeing as how we did not *have* three stamps or a Ring Ding.

"No, but you, Richie Rich, can get them," Danny said, leveling a stare. "You can order them today, and pick them up at commissary next week. Then, Skeletor will have them."

"I'd better," Charlie growled.

I winged a hurt, nasty look over at Danny as might some fool who had just caught his best homie stealing from his own dear mother.

Danny said, "You'll thank me later." With his sights far off, Danny said, "Remember that time, homie, when you got all pissy and whined that your celly wasn't helping you with your investigation into the Forever Young Prisoner?"

Narrowing my eyes, I nodded.

"Well, so Charlie here says he worked for a while in the records room, as a janitor. This was about a decade back, isn't that right, Charlie?"

"Right as rain, fucker," sounded the reply. "Motherfucking worst job I ever had in this shit-hole of a penitentiary. I had to clean the goddamn piss on the floor whenever Blue would miss the goddamn toilet bowls, scrub the coffee stains outta the goddamn carpet, straighten all of them manila folders sittin' atop them crooked fuckin' shelves—"

"Tell Tommy here what you just told me," Danny said.

Blinking, Charlie scratched his head. "What, about those feezys having sex in the storage closet and jizzin' all over the bleach containers?"

"No, not that. The other thing you told me."

"What other thing, those rats that were..." Charlie watched Danny shake his head "...that dick cop with the..." Charlie watched Danny shake his head "...that straggly hag at the reception desk who wouldn't...?"

Assuming the reins, Danny ventured to explain that inside of a dusty filing cabinet somewhere deep in the bowels of the records room was a drawer containing inmate case files not entered into the computer. The drawer was labeled "Non Sequiturs." It stood off limits, and locked: the key hung in the office, but Charlie never got bold enough to try it and so he never did poke his nose in to see the actual files. However, there was enough whispered discussions over the years to warrant the conclusion that these were files not in the registry.

"Is that true, Charles?" I asked.

"Damned right it's true, shithead," he replied. "Are you callin' me a liar? Those fuckers got some kind of racket going on o'er there. I kept telling those pigs they wanna play with fire they're gonna end up in the joint right here along with…yeah, and so that's when they fired me." Charlie squinted at me. "Hey, what are you doing?" He turned to Danny. "Whatever the fuck is your friend doing?"

"I'm counting," I said. "Hold on…"

It had been a long time since someone had called me a shithead. One of Fatts's fave names for me. Twenty seconds later, I exhaled, slowly. "So, you think those files were removed on purpose from the system, Chuck?"

Charlie slapped his thigh. "Are you stupid? Is that what you're telling me? They weren't entered in the first place, asshat. The words *Non Sequitur* signifies these were older files that didn't get processed whenever the change was made from paper to digital records, maybe back in the late sixties or seventies. Damn, son," he said, "if you had brain cells to match the number of nuts you had then maybe, just maybe—"

"That'll be all for today, Chuck. Thanks. You can blow," Danny said.

"Word," Charlie said, pumping his fist. "Isn't that what all the kids say nowadays? *Word*?" We heard him snicker and blather to himself all the way down the gangway to the stairs.

Danny raised an eyebrow after he had returned to his rack and I to my desk. "Helpful?"

"Maybe." I put my chin on my fist. Minutes later, I said, "I've been thinking…" and then I asked Danny if he still had that book *The Man in the Iron Mask* with the writing in the margin of one of its pages.

Danny went to scour for it. Finally, he found that puppy.

I noticed as if for the first time the handwriting's married letters and slanting style. Cursive. Those words: *HR was here,* and then that date: 5/17/87. Fancy cursive, too.

"Someone writes like my grandmother," Danny said, evidently noticing the same thing.

"No one writes in cursive like that anymore, especially if they're writing their initials." I set the book down. "I have an idea."

I explained to Danny my idea, and how I had come to figure it. The contributing factors listed five-fold. One, Officer Greeley's mention that "Heck" was likely not the Forever Young Prisoner's real last name. Two, Monty's mention that Henry visited the library back in the '80s. Three, that novel *The Man in the Iron Mask.* It captured Henry's whole predicament in a nutshell. It would've totally made sense for him to have selected that book off the library shelf. Four, Sal's mention about some '87 renaissance. This time-frame jived with Monty's sighting of Henry at the library; also it jived with that date in the book. Five, Mom's mention that Margaret Ronsellier's husband had been a prisoner. Lastly, Charlie's mention about the secret files and these initials here penned in cursive: HR.

I didn't share with Danny about my encounter with the ghost of Margaret Ronsellier. However, it, too, had figured into my analysis. I *wanted* Henry to be Margaret's husband, if only for the selfish sake of justifying her visitation that day at the graveyard as truly that and not due to some other factor like temporary insanity or insanity period.

"Yeah, *and...*" Danny said, after I had finished my spiel.

I took a deep breath. "And so maybe what all of this means is Henry Heck is actually *Henry Ronsellier.*"

"*And...*" Danny said.

"Which means, now we've got a name. With a name we can file a records request."

"Lilya?" Danny asked.

"Lilya," I affirmed. "FOIA. Lilya. Henry Ronsellier."

Snorting, Danny stood. "You honestly think the prison's just gonna hand over to *Lilya* some top-secret file in some top-secret filing-cabinet just because she had asked them to?"

"Not top secret," I said. "More like an open secret. All that stands between that file and the world at large is a key in an office." I frowned. "Still, you're right. Lilya will have to get creative."

"Creative?" Danny exclaimed. "Sure, she's a rock star with those fingernails of hers, but this might be a *little* over her head, don't you think?"

"No, I don't think that," I said. "I think Lilya's a rock star in all *kinds* of different ways."

Danny glared at me.

I went on: "I have a feeling about that girl."

"Oh, do you now?" smiling, Danny put in.

"Anyway," I said, "I'll have to get creative, too, in sharing all of this with Lilya over the phone." I eyed the photo pinned to my bulletin board of Mother and Daughter with Roses. "Think what I'll do is share with her Mom's cell number instead of saying the name *Ronsellier* over the megaphone—I mean, the prison phone. If she's game, and finally over pretending she's not still upset with me, she'll tell Lil the name." I stood. "You did good today, Dan. You get an A for the day. C'mon, let's do this."

CHAPTER TWENTY-TWO

The Pit of Heck
The Year of Our Lord 1987
May 17
8:34 a.m.

"C'mon, let's do this, fella," Captain Harris said, beckoning Henry forth from his dungeon. "That's my good man. There you go, one foot in front of the other, very good, just like that. Once the boys get this dump of yours all fixed up, you won't hardly recognize the place. That's it."

The officer eyed the Forever Young Prisoner with no small wonder as the latter drew level with him. Looking straight into the boyish face of his commission, Harris said, "You've made it—to the door. But we've still got a long way to go."

Henry wondered, as he stood there on the very precipice of the known world, if he should bid his cockroach friends farewell, but then he thought better of it when he noticed the no-nonsense look on the officer's face and his military stance with feet spread apart and arms folded. The world stood an open door now; the roaches might as well scurry back to the past where they belonged. The future lay within walking distance—if he could only walk. His knees and ankles felt as wobbly as those spinning tops he used to play with as a boy back on the farm.

Harris led Henry, without chains and mostly without assistance, down a corridor that shone only degrees brighter than the cell they had just exited. To Henry, however, those dangling cage-lights blazoned like the firmament itself. He shielded his face with his arm. Through the filter of his sleeve, he could see a low-arched corridor of mortar and stone.

"You'll get used to the light," Captain Harris encouraged Henry who plodded alongside him.

Henry flexed, stretched, and extended muscles and tendons he had not flexed, stretched, or extended in literal decades. The spaces between his steps around the narrow confines of his cell had measured in inches; but these, walking strides, seemed to measure in miles. He had to *think* of each step—every swing of motion came with studied deliberation: the bending of the knee, the extending forward of the foot, the landing of the foot. It felt like learning to walk. Henry stumbled at one point, but recovered with the flattening of his palms against the cold stone floor. Harris just looked on, seemingly afraid to get too close—even though closeness was inevitable. Eventually, the wobble in Henry's knees became such that Harris had to offer his shoulder as a support.

Harris shouted, "Day! Forget those damn Reese's Pieces of yours and get over here. We've got stairs coming up!"

Out of one of the few lighted chambers along the way, Officer Day burst forth clutching an orange and altogether curious-looking scrap of paper in his hand. How long had it been since Henry had seen the color orange? His eyes fixated on the vibrant color in the younger officer's hand. Wondrous, bright, flamboyant hues of a miniature sun. Orange!

"Want one?" Officer Day asked, thrusting the opened package of chocolates Henry's way.

"Not now," Harris barked. "Let's get him to the library first."

Day pocketed the chocolates then pulled out a Sharpie pen. He flashed it at Harris. "What about this? Now, or later?"

Harris slammed his fist against his thigh. "Damn it, Day. A *red* magic marker?"

Day pursed his lips. "Sharpie's only come in red and black, Cap. No brown Sharpie pens that I know of."

With his face tempting to turn almost as red as Day's marker, Harris stammered, "You could've gone to CVS and bought some...some, I don't know, brown-colored makeup, shoe polish, *nail* polish. You might've taken a trip down to your friendly neighborhood costume store."

"Costume store?" Day held up the pen. "Do you want it or—"

"Gimme that." Harris snatched the pen out of Day's hand. "Okay, Mr. Ronsellier, this might tickle a little..." he uncapped and extended the pen tip to Henry's left cheek. "The whole intention here was to give you a mole, a *brown* mole, but instead your left cheek's gonna have a big red dot on it."

"You're incognito now, old timer," Day smiled as he watched. "None of those rumors mentioned anything about a mole on The Forever Young Prisoner's cheek. No one will suspect you now, if we end up coming across anyone."

"We won't," Harris said, applying some finishing touches. "Those plumbers got the place cordoned off well enough, and we got lockdown in effect here. This little transfer to a secure location should work out fine, assuming our guy's legs hold out. There." Harris leaned back to get a view of his masterpiece. "Looks like someone just drew a big red circle on his face. Hell in a handbasket. Well, let's keep moving."

The stairs did prove a problem for Henry. The officers sandwiched their man and hoisted him up and along as best they could.

Knee joints popped, crackled and protested while muscles ached and strained against the down pull of gravity. It wasn't that Henry's muscles and joints couldn't do it, but that they were wholly unaccustomed to doing it. Officer Harris himself noted this when he said, "He'll get there, sure enough," as the trio ascended the spiral staircase to the landing three levels up where they stopped to take a breather. "With every flight I feel less of his weight on my shoulder. His legs are getting stronger."

There, on that stony landing three levels up, was where Henry Ronsellier said his first words. The single word "Date."

The officers froze as if the very voice of God had spoken to them.

Day backed off. Leaning flush against the stone wall, "He wants a date, Cap," he said to Harris. "And he was looking at you when he said it."

Harris nodded, slowly. He spoke at Day in a low voice, "Well, not that I would know, personally, how difficult it must be for a guy like Mr. Ronsell...Ronseal...Mr. Henry here...who's been down for forever and a day and all alone the whole while..." He turned to Henry, "But I'm married, old school. I've got a wife and kids."

"The date," Henry said, louder, clearer.

"He wants to know what today's date is," Day said.

Harris cleared his throat. He straightened some imaginary coptie at the base of his neck then said to Henry, "May 17th, 1987. What else you wanna know? How many more steps we gotta climb? None, we're here."

Henry didn't reply just then. For now, his interests remained solely in listening, absorbing, learning, gauging, and locating an aspirin if at all possible.

Captain Harris heaved Henry up, and then, packed him into the opened hatchway-door set into the wall there on the landing. This opening gave way to a crawl space extending into darkness. It reminded Henry of a horizontal chimney. So far, this new world of the future seemed less like greener pastures and more like a road to nowhere. Henry felt a lancet of fear as he mused whether this tunnel might lead to somewhere, alright. Not a library, but a cliff, and at the bottom of the cliff a basin filled with lava. That, or surprises far worse. The fact that Officer Day had climbed in first didn't ease this particular worry one iota.

"Sorry we have to do this to you, old school," Harris said, climbing in lastly. "But we can't just waltz down the main corridors of the prison with the Forever Young Prisoner jangling his chains alongside. Can you crawl? Will you be able to cra-wl," he asked Henry who just stared back. "*Comprende?*"

"The man speaks English," Day elicited from inside the passage. "And crawling's easy."

It *was* easy, for Henry anyway. Captain Harris, meanwhile, a far huskier man, had to paw along the narrow delve which proved only slightly larger than that chimney Henry had in mind. Henry could hear Harris curse from time to time from behind. Day led the charge with no small abandon, maybe thrilled to be leader of the pack for once. The light beams from the officers' flashlights zigged and zagged as the men struggled to crawl and see at the same time.

"I want to know everything," Henry said, after moments of mostly silent crawling.

"He says he wants to know everything," Day said.

"I heard!" Harris hollered. Then, the captain cursed even louder as his head knocked up against the ceiling once again.

Knockings came from inside of the walls, as well.

Harris said, after fumbling his flashlight and mumbling something about claustrophobia, "Those contractors are gettin' 'er done. Finally, some real modern plumbing inside of this stone-and-steel dinosaur."

Quiet ruled for a space of time after that, until Day quipped, "We're sure in a tight spot, aren't we, Cap?"

Harris breathed, heavily. "Not as tight as the one my brother's in right now. Keep moving, Mr. Henry," Harris hollered forward.

"I heard he lost his job," Day said over his shoulder.

"More than this job," Harris said. "That Heck lady wants to sue him now. *Heck v. Harris.* That New Hampshire court case will go down in the books as the black swan event for us proud men in blue.

I told Stan to appeal but it sounds like the county doesn't want to. Of course, that Heck lady's time will be up by the time the appeal even goes through. Thing is, he really was a lousy cop. Cheryl Heck's rights were indeed violated. My son wants to be a cop and work in a prison just like his dad. I hope to blazes he doesn't get his grandfather's genes like Stan did."

"We're here," Day said, halting, as he steadied his light beam on the hatchway door dead ahead.

The square-faced, metal panel that measured all of maybe three feet high featured a clasp and a latch on the tunnel side, but nothing on the business side, and so the hatchway door had to be left ajar. *Just like a life sentence—a way in, no way out*, Henry thought, as he clambered out of the narrow passage with the help of some over-assistance from Day. Or maybe life was like that just generally. Not that Henry knew much about *life* as he'd experienced only twenty-four years of it up until the time of his little mishap. He did know what a library was, however.

Not to suggest he saw much of it at first, with that Glory-level brightness shining in his eyes.

"You'll get used to the light," Harris said, as he dusted himself off and gulped down breaths of fresh oxygen.

"Feel free to look around," Day said, wandering his own sights around after Henry's eyes had come to bear. "We've got books over here, and paperbacks over there, and big tall books over this way, and magazines in this corner here, and…" Day scratched his head then stepped over to stand and sightsee alongside Henry who stood gazing at the plaque on the wall.

"Governor Theodore Barr Memorial Library," Day read the words at the top of the plaque. "That's this place. He was governor a long time ago. Bushy eyebrows, dang. Did you know him?"

Slowly, without taking his eyes off of this esteemed once-governor featured in bronze, Henry nodded. He narrowed his eyes.

"Oh, you don't like this man?" Day stepped back and pinched his nose.

"Be nice," Harris said from his spot behind the reception desk, noticing Day's maneuver. "It's not his fault. It's yours, and mine. Of course he doesn't like him." Squatting, Harris disappeared behind the desk. "Governor Barr was one of the witnesses at Henry's trial, there at the very scene of the murder. He testified for the prosecution. He's dead now, if that's any consolation to you, Mr. Henry. They all are. All those guys."

Henry simply could not tear his sights away from the rigid, stern, hairy features of this demon face cast in bronze. So many memories lived here: good, bad, and horrific. So many emotions.

"We can take it down if you'd like," Harris offered.

"Down?" Day said, turning to him.

"Possibly," Harris said, with only the top of his head visible behind the desk. "The new warden's got a soft spot for The Forever Young Prisoner. I think he's in large part fascinated by him. I'll powwow with Warden Richards. Seventy years in a hellhole and a man has a right to request the removal of a damned plaque. Would that please you, Mr. Henry?"

Henry turned to Harris and nodded.

Officer Day escorted Henry to one of the tables. The carpeted room featured nothing more than the desk, the plaque, a trash can, and a few dozen bookcases with rows of volumes on whose pages lay the pure-gold fingerprints of this future world.

Harris, meanwhile, unearthed a web of chains from their hiding spot behind the desk. He ushered them forth.

"Do we really have to?" Day asked. "The door's locked. No one's here. No one will come. It's lockdown. He can't escape, and even if he does—it's prison. I'll be here the whole while, too."

"It's that last part that worries me." Sighing, Harris lowered the shackles. "Shucks, I forgot. Mr. Henry, you have *five* minutes to pick out any *five* books off of these shelves here. After that you will be secured to this table for the next twelve hours or however long it takes that small army of workers to remodel your cell. Officer Day will be with you the whole while. There's a bathroom in back and water there, too. You can rest your head on the table if you get tired. Five minutes, starting *now*."

Five minutes later, Henry returned with his selections only to be bound to his station like a regular Harry Houdini—whom Henry had never actually seen in person; although, a friend of his did attend one of his venues at the Hippodrome in NYC once. Chains, chains, and more chains, sounded the report back. Here was another memory Henry had all but forgotten until just now.

Looking wistfully at Day seated at the nearest table, Henry made a scribble motion with his hand.

"No pens," Day said. "Or paper. You heard the captain. Here— you can have some of these." Day drew out of his pocket the color orange.

Day's "Reese's" candies tasted as pure and sweet as the Seventh Heaven. Not quite as crackerjack as those Belgian chocolates he and Margaret used to enjoy at the Corner Emporium in downtown, but better, certainly, than stale bread.

Henry so wished over the passing of that next hour his twelve hours here might be twelve-thousand hours. This was so utterly beyond words, even though it was all and only about words, and photographs, and orange candies. Flipping those pages of *The History of the 20th Century* with his chocolaty fingers was bar-none the best time he had had since Tess IV had given birth to Johnny Wise II, Alfred Jr. III and Bob Jr. V. The book, overall, painted quite the gloomy portrait: wars, assassinations, revolts, protests, communism, great depressions, bombs flying, bombs exploding; but the information listed endlessly. And the photographs—those marvelous modern inventions—and the clothing and hairstyles, stood unparalleled by anything he had ever seen before. Scotch tape: what a wonderful, novel, revolutionary idea. *Ingenieux*, as the French would say.

Henry propped his elbows on the table and flipped pages. The chains extending from his wrists to waist had been slackened for this very purpose. Henry flipped those pages with a flourish, in order to get a gander at all of the photographs, some which displayed in color!

"Gonna go use the powder room," Day said, interrupting the magic silence as he lowered his spy novel and stood. "Isn't that what you all used to call it back in the day? The powder room?"

But Day's foray to the library powder-room didn't appear to go as planned. He exited no sooner than he had entered, exclaiming, "Those plumbers need to learn them some manners, if you know what I mean." Day studied the tangle of chains strung around his charge like lights on a Christmas tree and the legs of Henry's table which bolted to the floor. "You sure as heck won't run off. Be back in a few," he said, and out the library's front door he went.

Henry returned to his history lesson. His eyeballs nearly flew out of their sockets: they'd put a man on the moon!

No more than a minute later Henry heard the library door swish open. His eyes stayed glued to the photograph of some ex-president named JFK and so he hadn't the slightest inkling to turn around to congratulate Officer Day for a job pulled off in record time. Had he done so, Henry might well have seen an inmate dressed in blue gaping at the curio seated at the center of the library. Only after the inmate began his rounds of loading books off of the shelves onto his cart did eyes meet.

The two men exchanged cat-and-mouse glances over those first few moments as would a boy and a girl seated at opposite ends of a soda-fountain counter. The man was clearly an inmate, and clearly a library worker—what with his cart; and so, Henry's first thought was *why ever in the world they would have allowed a negro to be a librarian. Silly willy*, ran the gist of Henry's follow-up thought. Still mired in the past, he had failed to consider the world had changed.

Stretching the chain secured to his wrist as far as it would go, he extended the man a salute.

His cue received, the man walked over wheeling his cart. His slow approach looked wholly cautious, as if he feared Henry might have a stick of dynamite underneath the table.

Finally, the man did more than just stand and gawk. "Hey, why they got you all chained up like that, man?" He scanned Henry up and down. "And those scrubs, gray-and-blue striped. Those be old school. Way old school. Like, my granddaddy type old school." He peered in. "What's that on your face? Not the fancy mustache, that red thing?"

Henry touched his cheek.

"You a transfer from a different prison or sumptin'?" the man asked.

Henry shook his head. He paused, meeting the man's brown eyes with a knowing little glimmer in his blue ones, and pointed his finger downward.

"Down below? Downstairs? Underground?" The man furrowed his youngish brow. "Can you talk?"

Henry nodded. It wasn't that Henry couldn't talk. Every day for seventy years he had spoken words aloud in his cell—but the same words, usually. His word association just wasn't up to par yet. He knew what a mustache was, of course, and he knew that word, *mustache*; however, his mind seemed wholly unable to connect the image of a mustache to the *word* mustache. For his mind to construct whole sentences then transfer that information over to his tongue Henry sensed the need for a level of patience, and planning, he hadn't the least inkling for at this very early stage in his exposure to his new world.

"You just can't talk very well, maybe?" the man asked.

Henry nodded.

"What's your name?"

Henry swallowed, then forced the word out, "Hen-ry."

The man winced, no doubt at the awkward sounding of the

word. But then he flashed a toothy smile. "Hi, Henry. I'm Monty Jenkins, the library assistant here." Monty stepped forward to offer a handshake but quickly recoiled. He grimaced. "No offense, man," he said, backpedaling, "but you smell like sumptin' the cat dragged in. Look like it, too. What have those boys in blue been doing to you? You smell like you haven't showered in weeks."

Weeks? Henry was tempted to say. Instead he said, "Pen," all the while he made a scribble motion with his hand.

"You want a pen? Is that it?"

Henry nodded.

Monty slipped over to the front desk and returned with a pen that he handed over to Henry.

Henry looked down at the pen, up at Monty, then at the cart directly behind Monty. Henry pointed at it.

"What?" Monty said. "You want a book off of the cart?" Monty watched Henry nod, then said with a subtle shake of his head, "I'm your damned butler now, is that it?"

Henry gave a start. He gaped at the librarian assistant with wide eyes.

"Just kidding, don't get all excited." Monty eased a smile. "My whole job is to play fetch. Which one?"

Henry cocked his head.

"What book do you want?"

Henry thought about it, then shrugged.

Monty shrugged, too. He turned to scour the shelf.

With Monty's back turned, Henry quickly scribbled his initials and the date into the margin of one of the pages of the lone novel he had selected.

Monty returned from his cart with the March, 1986 edition of *Popular Mechanics* in his hand. "Will this work?"

Henry nodded emphatically.

A bit too emphatically, Henry thought, as Monty's sights dropped instantly to scan the other selections Henry had laid out on the table in front of him. "Oh, a history buff," Monty said, with his librarian instincts no doubt in full swing as he pondered a possibly more appropriate offering.

But Henry shook his head. He nodded at the magazine in Monty's hand.

Monty understood, and handed over the magazine.

Henry accepted the magazine and gave back the novel.

"You don't want this one? Wanna exchange it? Okay." Monty examined the cover. "The Man in the Iron Mask." He looked up. "What's it about?"

Henry replied with a long stare at Monty. It showcased that same knowing glimmer in his eyes as before, only this time Henry held the look, refusing to let go. This time, too, Monty seemed to catch on. He returned Henry's eye contact with studied curiosity then dropped his gaze to examine the book in his hand. He flipped it and read the synopsis on the back cover. His eyes grew large, larger, and larger still, as his sights scanned the text. When he finally looked up, Monty's eyes were the size of silver dollars.

Henry nodded at this show of recognition.

"I knew it!" Monty said, slapping his hands together. "It *is* you. Hot *damn*."

Suddenly, Henry heard the library door swish open behind him. Monty quickly did an about-face and wedged the paperback into the top shelf of the cart.

Henry heard a voice by the door gasp. He lowered his sights to catch one last glimpse of this Marilyn Monroe dame on the page in front of him.

Monty busied himself with straightening the books on his cart.

"Who in the Sam Hill is *this*?" Day blared. "Who are you? What are you doing here?"

Monty turned, slowly, and pointed at himself.

"Yes, you," Day barked. "Didn't you see the sign on the door: *Off Limits, Under Construction*? How did you even get in here?"

Monty extended the key dangling from the lanyard attached to his belt buckle. "I work here. I'm Mr. Sharpe's assistant. And the bathroom—is a done deal. Those plumbers finished up a whole two days ago. No construction going on here no more, Blue."

Day stood silent for a moment. "It's lockdown," he wailed.

Monty swallowed. "Lockdown's the very reason I'm here. See this cart?" He pointed at it. "During lockdown the boys can't make it here to the library and so the books come to them."

Henry heard Day curse under his breath as his shiny cop boots scuffed the carpet on their approach to the table. Day alternated wild, fretted glances between Henry and Monty. He said to Monty, "What did this man say to you, anything?"

Monty shook his head. "He can't talk, sumptin like that. He didn't say two words."

Day said, "So you spoke to him then—you tried to communicate with him." Day flattened his hand against the table as he leaned in. "This inmate here, Mr...Mr. *Heck*, is a transfer from another facility. Can't you see he and his mole want to be left alone? All right, now, take your cart and get outta here. I don't want to see you back in here today."

Monty nodded. And with one last peek over his shoulder at The Forever Young Prisoner, Henry Heck, he pushed open the library door and got outta there.

Day groaned, loudly, as he sat with his head in his hands.

Not long afterward, the door swished open again and Captain Harris entered.

Day recounted for his captain the entire episode; only in this version, Day had performed his business on-site, not in some yonder off powder-room which would have necessitated the desertion of his post.

Harris fumed, cussed, and turned bright red. At length he calmed. This rather relieved Henry as the veins in the captain's neck looked to be on the verge of bursting.

"Monty Jenkins is no dummy," Harris said, wiping the sweat off of his forehead. "He'll figure out what it was he saw here. However, he'll too know what the word 'repercussions' means, probably knows how to spell it even." Harris said to Day, "You track Jenkins down. Take another officer or two, guys who can be *persuasive*. You find that boy and tell him to forget everything he saw here today. It never happened. By now, probably half the yard knows the Forever Young Prisoner was in the library."

"I'll go get Tibbetts," Day said. "He's *very* persuasive."

"No, not Tibbetts!" Harris barked, freezing Day in his tracks on his way to the door. "Tibbetts is not on board. We want someone who is *on board*. Persuasive and *on board*."

Day brightened. "Moretti."

Harris frowned. "No, not Moretti." His countenance darkened. "Do you hear me, Day? Not Moretti." Harris curled his finger to beckon Day to come to him. Day walked over.

Harris said in a low voice, "I disagreed with the old warden about offing guys who had discovered about the Forever Young Prisoner." Harris cut a peek over at the Forever Young Prisoner—probably to see if he was lending an ear, which of course he was. Realizing, probably, though, too, that any secrets overhead by Henry would proceed no further than the walls of his lonely cell, Harris's voice regained its normal decibel. "Clayton was a good cop, Officer Day. Nosy, prying, ratting, but good. The same might be said for Baker. Luckily, we were able to keep the removal of Baker a secret."

"Don't forget Tremblay," Day put in. "Black Hat Special. Knife to the throat."

Harris noted, "Did you know it was *Tremblay* who first came up with that name *Black Hats*? Bleeding to death, he swore he and the *White Hats* would prevail. Whites Hats? Black Hats? Who would've known they had their own little group going?"

Day furrowed his brow. "I thought we were *The Guardians of the Mysteries of the Clock*?"

Harris gritted his teeth "*The Family* with their fancy names to flatter us with can, go kiss my ass. Ditto for Moretti, with those *removal* instruments of his." He batted his eyes. "Just don't tell them I said that, Officer Day. I have a son."

Day snorted. "Yeah, like they'd mess with your son. He's tops on their list of recruits."

Harris grew silent.

"Kearney," Day proposed.

Harris raised his head and nodded. "You go get Kearney. He's on chow detail right now, but you pull him off. If Captain Clay makes a fuss, tell her Harris said so."

"What about you, Cap?" Day said with his hand on the door handle. "Can't you be persuasive?"

"I plan to have a little chat with Mr. Henry here while you're away," Harris said, seating himself on the chair directly across the table from Henry. "Now go."

Henry heard the click of the door behind him as Day left.

Henry hadn't noticed at first, but Harris held in his hand a curious white bag with handles and the words "Stop & Shop" imprinted on the sides. Out of this bag Harris drew a half-dozen cylindrical metal cans. He placed the cans of Pepsi on the table, setting them down all in a row. He folded his hands. "Never did recover from that New Coke debacle," he said, eyeing the arrangement. "I'm a Pepsi man now. So, Mr. Henry..."

Henry snapped his book closed.

Harris raised an eyebrow at that, then flicked a nod. "Those books are yours, by the way. Yours for all eternity—which is how long you're gonna be around, you keep aging the way you do." Harris leaned back and placed his already folded hands atop his capacious midsection. "And so, what's all of that about, anyway, if you don't mind my asking? You're not aging. Just curious, a question between friends. I mean, you were around when Theodore Barr was governor. Hell, and Theodore *Roosevelt* was president. But man to man, I gotta tell ya, you look hardly older than my son who's in high school."

Henry just stared back.

"Don't wanna talk about it?" Harris said.

Henry shrugged.

"Does my black hat scare you?" Harris pushed a can of Pepsi

across the table at Henry. "Look, I know you can talk, fella. I've been in law enforcement a long time. I notice things. For example, your lips don't move but your eyes are all over the place. Your body-language responses are all in the moment, never delayed. Your mind is there. Maybe not all there, but there. Listen, we're all gonna be here for the next," Harris checked his wristwatch "ten hours or so—"

"Would you like to hear," Henry asked in a throaty voice; he wrestled with the words until finally he was able to push them out, "what really happened?"

Harris's smile grew and grew. He leaned in. "Yes, I would very much like to hear what really happened, Mr. Henry," he said, snapping open his Pepsi.

CHAPTER TWENTY-THREE

"The 1910s..." Henry said, in-between sips of his soda, "was an era that was...was really two worlds in one, you see." Henry scratched his head: he knew what he wished to say next, but how to say it was the problem. Finally, his eyes brightened and he said, "The world of the Haves, and the Have-nots..."

Providence, Rhode Island
The Year of our Lord 1917
August 24

At no other time did this become clearer to Henry Ronsellier than when he, alongside his wife, Margaret, walked down Valley Street on that late August afternoon under mostly smoggy skies. The sun's rays filtered through the coal smog from the nearby Rising Sun Mill to settle on the young couple. Side by side they strolled the lanes fancied up in their Sunday best: he, in his tuxedo—but only because his job required it—and she, in her white work blouse and long navy dress.

As the couple made their way out of their duplex apartment, they

255

noticed a group of dirtied boys stare at them once they hit the main dirt road. They noticed otherwise—at their leisure, for theirs was a leisurely stroll at first—the many mill houses just like their own standing like dumb, begrimed soldiers all in a row. They saw clothes lines, chickens, stray dogs, and the occasional horse and buggy. Further along reposed the great mill itself: a monolith of brick not unlike the mill where Henry's father had once worked and where Henry had promised himself he would never work. Valley Street. Home sweet home.

However, as Henry and Margaret footed along, the scenery began to take on new life. Hooking a left onto Westminster Street, which positioned them now on the outermost edge of downtown, the scene offered early clues as to why some referred to Providence as 'The Beehive of Industry.' The Corner Emporium stood here, most prominently.

Once they breached the Huntington Line rail tracks, the real Downcity began. Throngs of businessmen in gray serge suits and bowler hats strolled the walkways. People drove cars. Colorful marquees advertised of clothing, groceries, dry goods, and jewelry. Raising a din along street corners, groups of women held signs that read "Prohibition NOW" and "Buy War Bonds." The entire population of the city walked, talked, and shopped here, it seemed—even a few in uniform, which was Henry's soon-to-be fate, as well. Henry tried not to think about the war.

Way off in the distance, the couple could almost see the Providence River with College Hill just on the other side of it with all of those beautiful Victorian mansions and the Brown University buildings consorting just shy of the riverfront. There their journey would complete its rags-to-riches course and its course entire.

No need to take the trolley on this fine afternoon; although he and Margaret still had to dodge them. One whizzed by just as Henry got to mentioning about the Brooklyn Dodgers, who had acquired their name from their fans who so often had to dodge trolleys on their way to the ballpark. Margaret replied she had never been to New York City.

"You've never been anywhere," Henry said. "That's why I wanted you to come with me today."

Just then, Margaret stepped over to tell Bob the grocer, "To the governor's ball, that's where we're going!" And afterward to Mildred, the owner of the flower shop, "We're off to the big ball!" Of course, one might well have guessed the couple's destination from the manner in which they were dressed, but not at all from their slow, meandering course. Henry's every intention lay in making a scene. Although his wife trod this path nearly every day to shop at the dry goods stores, she never did so alongside a husband in a tuxedo. Margaret must have felt like a regular Cinderella just then, which pleased Henry ever so much. Herein stood his great chance to make up for his endless thoughts about Gertrude Barr while he lay awake in bed beside his wife night after night.

So rare are these occasions, anyway, we leisure together, Henry thought, after tipping his hat to another of Margaret's friends as they resumed their course.

While passing the tall and majestic Turks Head Building, Henry and Margaret made one final stop as Margaret leveled off Henry's collars as well as the curls in his mustache. "They're uneven," she said, as she pulled at his whiskers. She asked if Henry had forgotten his gloves!

Henry patted his coat pocket. "Never until the show starts, dear."

The mansion situated on the crest of a hill overlooking the river and the whole of Downcity. "It looks like an English manor on the outside," Henry told his wife as they footed across the river bridge. "But on the inside it's like a French chateau."

Margaret liked the sound of that. Both she and Husband were second-generation Quebecois, the children of mill workers imported from Canada in the 1880s. The couple, although French Canadian, did not consider themselves French per se, and certainly not French chateau material. As the Americanized son and daughter of immigrants, they knew every word to "Take Me Out to the Ball Game" but not a single word to "La Marseillaise."

The governor's yearly ball boasted as one of the city's bragging points. Anyone who was anyone in the state of Rhode Island, and beyond, would be in attendance. Henry's invitation extended not because he was someone, but staff. Margaret did not share this distinction, but as the kitchen stood in need of extra help for the big event, Henry had referred her. Henry's boss, the maitre d', had asked, "Can she chop onions?" Henry rolled his eyes and asked if a cat had whiskers. The maitre d' took that for a yes.

For Margaret, the day held the promise of rubbing elbows with dignitaries and scenes reminiscent of the ones in her flighty novels where all of those aristocratic trysts happened: Lord So-and-so wandering off into the nether regions of the manor house to rendezvous with Lady Such-and-such to do Lord and Lady things only Europeans knew about. More likely, Margaret would remain holed up in the kitchen all afternoon with her onions.

"Wouldn't it be something," Margaret said, eyeing the mansion as they passed under its iron gate at the foot of the hill.

"If what?" Henry smirked, still thinking about Lords and Ladies. "If you and I could perhaps wander off during the course of the festivities to some secluded spot inside of this place and...?"

"And, what?" Margaret asked, with wide eyes, halting their trek along the pebbled path with a hand on her husband's arm.

"And, you know." Henry smiled.

"Oh," Margaret exclaimed, "let's! Wouldn't that be exciting? Yes, our child would be something like, well, *nobility* if you and I were to...right here." She angled her sights up at what must have looked to her from this vantage like a castle.

Henry knew his Margie well enough to appreciate her taste for adventure, but surely these words had been in jest no less than his had been. Cinderella needed to keep her slippers on, along with everything else, if Henry intended to keep his job.

Likely it had been a mistake to think about, and then mention about, Lords and Ladies and such, because now into his thoughts entered Gertrude Barr. No doubt she would make a showing at the state's biggest shindig as hosted by her very own father. Gerdie (as she had asked Henry to call her) had seemed rather on the make lately with her continued flirty looks his way. This was *plum-plum-pullaway*—as they used to call it back on the farm—at its finest. Maybe Gerdie sought to fan the flames because she knew Henry would be off to the front soon. Though, Henry did owe her in a sense. She had effectively gotten him this job—payback in its own right, quite possibly, for what he had done for her at the first.

The party proceeded well, at least from a butler's point of view. The front door swung open and closed smoothly as Henry allowed guests in and out. He checked off Senator Cartwright's name on the guest list, and Marie Doro's, the actress. The afternoon's lone homage came from State Senator Roberts, who actually looked Henry in the eyes when offering his "thank you." The textile and jewelry union leaders arrived in their customary simple suits and tight smiles, but this time their names didn't show up on the list. Henry had to whistle for muscle to escort them out. Even Duffy Lewis, the Boston Red Sox outfielder, stopped by.

More than a few of these esteemed guests wanted to know when the reception ended and the ball began.

"Foxtrot and Charleston in the ballroom starts at seven," Henry answered each time. Short and sweet. Henry had not been hired for small talk, but to offer straight answers and recite pleasantries as he fulfilled his domestic tasks.

The guest list was actually Henry's least favorite part of his job. "Robert Frost...Robert Frost..." he said, squinting as he scanned its pages. He wished words everywhere were bigger. "Ah, there it is. Welcome, sir."

Afterward, when the incoming traffic slowed, Henry took up a tray and served hors d'oeuvres, all the while Margaret chopped onions and carrots in the kitchen.

Henry so wished Margaret could join him out here among the swells.

They had both wished the Vanderbilts would be in attendance, but Henry hadn't seen them yet. The governor, meanwhile, again donned the dubious mask of a social pariah. He kept failing to notice, never mind acknowledge, Henry, every time he passed. No great surprise there, but nor did he greet numerous others whom he normally went out of his way to make small talk with. He kept ignoring his untied shoelace, too. The governor didn't dislike Henry, or at least Henry didn't think he did. Simply stated, as a busy, burdened—and of late, distracted and stressed—governor, he was a man with priorities. During the weekdays, which calendared as Henry's usual schedule, he catered primarily to the governor's wife and her circle of progressive friends.

Serving hors d'oeuvres placed Henry directly in the mix of this great company. In the process of pouring a Scotch for Mayor Leffler, that personage whom he feared—and adored—met his wandering gaze. She looked stunning, as usual, but so much the more gussied up in that layered party dress, as she saluted him from her spot on the Louis XV armchair. Henry didn't know why he, of all people, should attract the attentions of Gertrude Barr. His looks and charm certainly didn't recommend themselves to the point of such high regard. Might it simply have been because of that one time...no, but that was silly.

"I want to thank you, once again, and oh so sincerely, for returning my coin," Gertrude said upon her arrival in Henry's space, as her gloved hand pinched a Hershey's Kiss off of Henry's platter. Hershey's Kisses hardly classified as European delicacies as did so many of the other do-dads on Henry's platter; in fact, this was food-stuff mass produced right here in the States. The governor had titled his newest initiative Changing with the Times. Hershey's Kisses fit.

"Europe is passé," the governor once said to Henry while reclining on his immaculate chaise longue. "That's why I agreed to hire you finally. Because you're a regular All-American boy."

Gertrude went on, "Why, you could've just walked off with that coin and I wouldn't have known the difference. You're hardly well off. Tell me, why didn't you?"

It had been Henry's second day in the big city. He had resolved himself to a walk around Roger Williams Park, still rather depressed about Bunker Lane Buggy's refusal to hire him on as a driver. "You know horses well enough, but not the city yet," they had informed him. Some aristocratic gal in a fur coat and her dog dallied on a nearby park bench. As she rose, a $20 gold coin fell off of her person onto the bench. She walked off, seemingly unaware. Henry retrieved the coin and returned it to her. "That's swell of you," she had said, using the common vernacular that was hardly her style. Then, when Henry applied for this butler position, this very Governor's daughter had caught sight of him in the foyer, and afterward he received word back he had the job.

Henry shrugged. "Returning that coin was the thing to do, I guess."

Gerdie nodded. "Well, I think what the thing to do *now* is to let you have that coin back. Finders keepers, yes? Would you not like your $20 back?"

For a man whose yearly income totaled just over $500, $20 wasn't exactly peanuts.

"Your coin," Gerdie said, "will be ready and waiting for you, upstairs. Won't you come and get it?" Gerdie cocked her head. "You're leaving soon, are you not, Henry? I may never see you again after today."

Henry deigned a nod.

Gerdie snapped a soldier's salute then laughed in that polite, socialite way of hers. "Kiss," she said, unwrapping then popping the chocolate into her mouth. "It shall be upstairs waiting for you. You know where."

Henry did not know where, and he sure as heck hoped Gerdie didn't mean her bedroom. But it was probably too late to ask, because now she stood swirling her Bourbon alongside that baseball player. Moments later, Henry watched as Gerdie made her way for the stairs, smiling at him as she ascended.

Henry sighed. He couldn't just traipse up those stairs in the wake of the Governor's daughter in front of everyone, now, could he? He didn't know what to do. He lowered his tray onto one of the fancy French console tables and set off in haste for the kitchen.

"Margaret—" Henry said.

Margaret lowered her cutting knife. "Your wife chops, Henry, then chops s'more. She's malcontent," she said, sighing loudly. "I have yet to see anything today except for this god-awful kitchen."

"We're all malcontent, dear. It's some kind of plague upon humanity." Henry bit his lip as he glared pathetically at his wife.

Margaret looked at her husband. "Well, what is it? Why are you here and not out butlering?"

Henry swallowed. "We, er, we need money, don't we, Margie? We could use some extra money, is what I mean to say."

Margaret nodded, slowly. "Yes, yes, we could sure use some extra dough…" She placed her hands on her hips. "What is it you mean to say, exactly?

Henry rubbed his fingers nervously. "What I'm trying to tell you is that, well, I'll be going upstairs soon…" Henry cleared his throat. "I have to go upstairs…for something."

"Upstairs…" Margaret repeated. "Upstairs…" Her eyes brightened. "Oh, upstairs!" She smiled at her husband. "Oh, very well then. That sounds like a plan. Good idea. You go on up those stairs." Margaret winked at him.

Henry furrowed his brow. About to ask Margaret what the meaning of her wink might be, the maitre d' burst through the swinging doors with a bucket of shrimp-on-ice. Margaret quickly returned to her chore.

"You will be pleased, dear, when the matter is all said and done," Henry said, patting his wife's arm before leaving.

That Margaret didn't try to talk him out of it stood as reason enough for his continued steps in the direction of the stairs. Not exactly granting permission, she had anyhow agreed they needed the money. Point in fact, that Gerdie had in mind more than just a coin transfer appeared likely, and Henry wasn't altogether certain he could resist the offer of a kiss, maybe even multiple, breathless kisses, from the likes of Gertrude Barr.

Henry's foot literally landed on the first step of the staircase when he got called aside. Councilman Adams wished to know where the lavatory was. Henry forced a smile and with a few, probably overstated anecdotes about the labyrinthine quality of palatial residences, led the councilman to the lavatory beyond the drawing room, along the North wing, just past the conservatory. Adams didn't understand the toilet's operation, however. Henry explained the chain which required pulling, and the toilet seat which required the sitting down of his big rear end upon. Henry's patience had run its course: Gerdie was waiting.

"Did you just say something about *my big rear end?*" the councilman spoke out of the doorway at Henry, who was by that point long gone.

The second-floor hallway presented only slightly less palatial than the splashy downstairs. Persian runners stretched across the mahogany floorboards. Candelabras lit up the wallpaper, even though electricity *did* run here. Rococo-style carvings adorned the door frames. The door to the billiards room begged notice and praise in particular. Henry could hear voices and commotion from in there. If anyone asked, he could say he came upstairs to cater to those fellows in the billiards room. The door to Gerdie's bedroom situated at the end of an adjoining hallway. Other rooms advertised along the way: the study, a tea room, a wash closet, and the library, but these all looked empty. Henry halted midway down the hall to straighten his mustache and the suspenders underneath his jacket. Did he know what he was doing?

"Pssst," Henry heard from inside the study.

Henry stepped aside and poked his head into the darkened room. "Who's there?"

"Pssst." The voice came from the study's closet.

Henry saw a thin arm extend out of the closet. A finger beckoned for him to come.

As he entered the governor's study, Henry reminded himself that a $20 coin served as reason alone for his acceptance of this little invite. Gerdie's brains stood matched only by her charm. Passing by the billiards room would rouse suspicions against Henry. This was indeed the better way.

Henry footed closer, and closer still—then got yanked into the closet and quite smothered with kisses. Henry kissed back, only because it seemed like the thing to do. Gerdie smelled like onions, strange. Even her breath smelled like—onions.

Henry nudged the woman off himself. "Wait," he said, "it's you, isn't it?"

Margaret snorted. "That's an odd thing to say to your *wife*? Who else would it be? Who did you think I was?"

Henry stammered, "I, er, what...what are you doing here?"

Margaret guffawed. "What do you think?"

"Oh," Henry said, remembering his wife's romantic mentions on the way over which never in a million years would he have thought...or maybe he would have thought...until Gerdie had muddled those thoughts.

"Oh *what*? What does 'oh' mean?"

Henry cleared his throat. "Well, I—just didn't think you would have the nerve to go through with it, is all."

Margaret wrapped her arms around her husband's neck. "Well, I'm here. You're here. We're both here..."

And so, there they were. Had Henry's hitherto purpose been to amend for his nighttime fantasies about Gerdie, then this little foray deserved a ten-times reprisal. The next part, then, came easy. And, boy, did it ever come. The walls rattled. The earth shook. Buttons popped. Vestments dropped. Hair flailed all over. Moans sounded. Sweat dripped. Oaths of a forever love were declared.

Henry exhaled afterward as he fell back against the rear wall of the closet. Finally, he said, "You'll be in dutch for this, you know. You're supposed to be chopping those onions."

"No, sir," Margaret lilted. "I'm on lunch break."

Henry shook his head. "No such thing as lunch-breaks in *this* house."

Margaret bobbed her head in an emphatic form of nod. "Yes, required now. This past week the new state labor law came into effect: mandatory half-hour lunch breaks. Jillian down bakery ways told me then we both demanded our lunch breaks. Old Lady Hanson could do nothing but say 'very well.' Your Governor friend signed the bill as a part of his new *Change with the Times* thing."

"Friend?" Henry winced. "The state legislature passed the bill, Margie, but the governor has yet to sign it. He will, though. It's his bill." Hankering for a smoke, Henry closed his eyes and just enjoyed the moment, the silence, the cool feel of the sweat on his skin. He reckoned he probably shouldn't fret about his job. He would be off to France soon anyway. This was his going-away present to his wife, then. Maybe that's what she had in mind, too.

But things weren't all hunky-dory in Closet Land, for just then the couple heard footsteps coming down the hall. Heavy steps. Men's steps.

Governor's steps, Henry thought.

The door to the study whisked open. Men entered. Lights flicked on. The door to the study slammed closed.

"Now then..." the voice of the governor said, as Henry reached for the shuttered closet doors. They didn't close all the way; anyhow they didn't *stay* closed. They kept refolding back, leaving a half-inch space between the collapsible doors even at the fullest extent of their hinges. *The better to see you with, Mr. Governor.*

And see Henry did, even if through only one eye.

The governor's study served also as a showroom and office. Bookcases lined the walls, but only a few: this wasn't the library. Flush against those walls leaned any number of display cases which housed the governor's venerable collections. Vases, old parchments, and other curios reposed under glass. A desk, a lounge chair, and a pair of sofas held sway at the center of the room. On the walls hung works of fine art and war paraphernalia.

Sipping at something with an olive in it, the governor sat down on his patent leather sofa. His guest stood in a gaudy, yellow-and-black-checkered suit with his hands at his sides: the governor had yet to offer him a seat.

Henry knew this other man. His name was Aldo Ruocco. Aldo frequented the mansion, although much less frequently of late. In times past, Aldo would be in and out of the mansion with ever the smile. A few times he'd even pinched Henry's cheek. Now, smiles met Henry on the way in, scowls and curses on the way out. The governor had refused to see Aldo over the previous two weeks.

"What's the story out there?" Margaret whispered.

Henry bid her stay back. "They're having a meeting," he whispered. "The other guy is a business associate. Shhh." Henry dared not to tell Margaret about the few—maybe more than a few—shady characters who frequented the premises. A business associate, yes, and yet Henry's every instinct said Aldo was much more than that. Once he had tried to slip Henry a five spot when the governor refused to see him, but Henry just looked away. Aldo Ruocco seemed different to Henry, and not in a good way.

"Mr. Ruocco," the governor said, sipping his drink as he leaned forward on his sofa. "I thought I told you never to come here again. My business with the Ruocco family is quite through. I've agreed to meet with you today only out of the respect I have for Don Carlo."

Aldo flashed a toothy grin. "Business with the Ruocco family is never finished until Don Carlo says it's finished. This jacket here— you see this?—is Don Carlo's reminder to you the Ruocco Family can still *sting like a bee* ever the need should arise."

Mafia, Henry thought. He knew it.

The governor set his drink aside and stood. "Are you trying to intimidate me? Listen, you're small potatoes coming in with lines like that, dressed up like that, and small potatoes otherwise, don or no don. The Ruocco Family is *through* in Providence." The governor settled back into his chair and sipped his olive drink. "Anyway, what is it you wished to tell me that's so important I had to give up playing Pin the Tail on the Donkey with my son out in the gardens? You have five minutes."

Aldo straightened his tie. "I will once again repeat Don Carlo's offer. Twenty percent, Governor Barr, goes straight to you, filtered through the usual sources, if the status quo is maintained. The Family's interests in the textile and jewelry unions grants us considerable vantages in these sectors. Obviously, we should like to keep them. Needless to say, we *will not* keep them if this proposed bill of yours passes."

The governor rolled his eyes. "This again? I thought we went over all of this already."

"Without labor strikes how is the Family supposed to make any profit, Governor?" Aldo flicked a speck of lint off of his loud suit. "The companies pay us to end those strikes and the unions pay us to begin them. Our gain is made from—"

"Find another way to make money," the governor studied his drink, "besides pulling the strings on these lucrative *peace* deals of yours."

"Modest wages," Aldo went on, "long hours, unsafe working conditions...these have been the standard for those mill and factory workers and are the Family's whole grounds for profit. Yours, too, as far as our collaboration is concerned."

The governor rose. "Times have changed, Mr. Ruocco." The governor walked slowly over to his desk. "I plan to sign the bill as early as Wednesday. As the very keystone to my groundbreaking new initiative, it must not fail."

"If a certain beloved something of yours out in the gardens even makes it until Wednesday," Aldo said with a smile.

The governor lost whatever hint of smile he had. He eyed Aldo for a moment then made briskly for the door. He opened it, then whistled in the direction of the billiards room.

"Who are you calling for," Aldo asked, craning his neck.

"An individual who might interest you." The governor returned to his desk. "The consiglieri of the Caniglio family out of Boston, Luca Caniglio." The governor folded his hands. "Yes, that's right, Aldo. Don't look so surprised. The Caniglios are looking to expand their territory. Providence is the next logical step. Their interest in this city is mostly in various black market activities. The progressives will have their way, mark my words: prohibition is coming. Also, the Caniglios have agreed to a most gracious 30% cut." The governor sipped his drink. "A few ducks float in their pond already: theater owners, cops, one or two lawyers, a handful over at the prison…"

"You're bluffing," Aldo said.

Moments later, another mafioso type walked through the door.

"Luca!" the governor called out to him. "Ah, so good to see you. *Buongiorno, buongiorno!* Please, come in, do sit down."

Luca walked a few steps and stopped. "And who is *this,*" he growled, pointing at the man in the chair. "The Pope?"

"That—" the governor looked at Aldo, "is someone who was just about to leave."

Luca declined the governor's offer of a leather seat cushion. "No, I will not sit down," he declared. "Not until this *bimbo* in the banana suit leaves. Do you know who this is, Governor?"

The governor nodded.

Luca narrowed an eye. "It was our understanding, Governor, you had washed your hands clean of the Ruoccos. That you had cut off dealings with them. Cut. Off."

"They are cut off, as of right now. That's what this meeting here was about."

"Cut off?" Luca's eyes bulged. "One of them is about to enjoy a seat, at this very moment, in your home. What does that say about our proposed partnership? Where's the respect?"

Grinning, Aldo settled into one of the Sheraton-style chairs opposite the governor's desk. He lit a cigarette. "Governor Barr will continue to remain on board with the Ruocco Family because he is a reasonable man. Thirty percent, Governor." Puffing away, Aldo crossed his legs. "Thirty percent if you drop that legislation and keep the status quo."

"Either I'm out that door, or he is," Luca warned.

"OUT, Aldo," the governor said, pointing at the door.

Aldo raised a finger. "But first, Governor Barr must give Don Carlo a straight answer. He has yet to do so. He says yes, he says no, he says maybe, he says give me until tomorrow to think about it…"

Tempting steps toward the door, Luca stopped, and turned. "If this man refuses to leave," he said, calmer, "what token, Governor, may you give the Caniglio Family as a sign that you are a man of your word and that your dealings with the Ruocco Family are indeed, as you say, cut off?"

The governor wet his lips as he thought it over. "I will give you a token." He reached up for one of the sword handles protruding from a pair of scabbards affixed in crisscross fashion on the wall directly behind his desk.

"What was that sound?" Margaret whispered. "Like metal against metal."

Henry's heart pounded. "The sound of all hell about to break loose," he answered.

The governor proceeded to deliver an address, as governors so often do. Only this address sounded to Henry more like a poem. While reciting his rhyming lines, he padded a slow course around the room with little lobs of his Samurai sword from one hand to the other, until at last he positioned his feet directly behind Aldo's chair.

Aldo stole nervous glances over one shoulder then the other. Still, he stayed in his seat.

"Quoth the raven, nevermore," the governor said—then, a *woosh* sound, which gave way to a sickening *thwack*.

Henry clamped his eyes shut and groaned inwardly.

"*There's* your token, Luca," the governor said. "You can wrap it up in this towel here." He reached behind his desk. "I use it to mop my brow on these warmer days, but it's dual purpose. There's a leather handbag in that closet over there, too. Let me go get it for you."

"What happened?" Margaret whispered. "What…"

"My gift to Don Caniglio," the governor said, halting in his bloodied tracks on his way to the closet to admire his handiwork. "A not-so-happy ending for the Ruoccos, a brave new beginning for the Caniglio Family."

"Thank you, Governor," Luca said, claiming the towel and making steps in the direction of the severed head.

With a soft thump, Henry fell back against the wall of the closet. He felt sick. He felt like vomiting. The governor was coming. His wife must have noticed the bulging eyes of his distress, because immediately she moved to assume Henry's spot at the crack in the door. Henry stretched his hand out to warn her, but it was too late, she was already looking out.

Margaret's face twisted into a mask of agony; and then, she screamed.

Why in the world would she have screamed? Henry wondered, and would forever wonder. Margaret was no screamer. Even in the face of those big rats in the kitchen that one time she hadn't screamed. Even in the sack in the privacy of their very own home she hardly made noise.

"Who's there?" the governor hollered.

The butler and his wife, of course.

The governor beckoned them out of the closet with an order to "reach for the skies," even though there had been no firearm involved.

Moments later, a scramble of men appeared in the doorway— men who had rushed over from the billiards room, no doubt, at the siren call of a woman's scream.

The governor bid these men enter.

The governor rubbed his chin as he studied the pool of blood and the sword all but swimming in it. "You men saw what happened here, of course," he said to them. "This man—" he said, pointing at

Henry, "is an individual in my very employ, I'm ashamed to say. Henry Ronsellier, is his name. Recently drafted, and graced with the high calling of a soldier, he abandoned that calling when in a fit of rage, rebellion, madness, he violated the sacred grounds of this office by bursting in here, whereupon he proceeded to blame me—me!— for his draft notice. Then, after I brazenly defended President Wilson's Selective Service Act which mandates the drafting of its citizens, in a frenzy, he rushed over and drew this sword out of its scabbard here..."

The governor pointed up at the wall at the emptied scabbard. "He rushed at me with it, yelling 'Death to big government!' and 'Stop the War in Europe!' He swung wildly at me, as indeed I was his target. Suffice to say I happen to know a thing or two about swordplay from my time in the Spanish American War, and was able to evade his blows." The governor shook his head at the mess on the floor. "Poor Mr. Ruocco here, however, wasn't so lucky."

The men blinked at the governor after he had finished speaking. These men numbered one and all as close friends and staunch political backers, Henry noticed. As if in unison, they peered over at the olive-skinned stranger with his arms folded whose brooding dark eyes awaited their response. Even if these men did not know the name *Luca Caniglio*, it was clear from their shrinking glances they could well have guessed as to the *type* of man he was.

The one in the starched high collars stepped forward first. "That was exactly what I saw, too, Governor," he stated. "That boy rushed at you, wielding that saber for all he was worth, but you sidestepped him time and again." He pointed at the headless torso. "However, that gentleman in yellow who tried to shield himself behind your noble, manly person, never saw it coming that one time you ducked. His head hit the floor, and the rest of him fell back onto that chair."

The man in the brown felt derby stepped forward next. "We all heard the sound of a woman scream—this woman here, his wife, I guess she is. She kept screaming 'Stop, stop!' The boys and I hurried over as quickly as our feet would carry us. We did see this crazy young fool take that sword off of the wall, and we did see him go at you with it. We were tempted to step in and assist. However, we knew, Mr. Governor, that you, of all people, would have the situation well under control. Boy, did you ever!"

The red-bearded one scowled menacingly at Henry as he, lastly, stepped forward. "As soon as this *boy* saw he'd killed a man, he dropped the sword—like a COWARD—and ran to his wife." Clasping his hands together then raising them over his shoulder in the guise of an Olympic champion, the bearded one declared, "Oh, how heroic, how magnificent, Mr. Barr, was the dexterous manner in which you avoided the sword swipes of this *villain*. Bravo!"

The governor nodded. He pointed at the three men standing in the rear. "How about you guys?"

These men appeared recognizably more reticent—and nervous —than the first three. They stepped forward.

"Er, yeah, Governor, that's what...I saw, too, I guess," the first one muttered.

"Draft dodger, geez," said the second, shaking his head.

The third man looked as white as a sheet. He just nodded emphatically.

After a quick look down at his hands, Henry paled, too. Exhibit A, Your Honor: Mr. Ronsellier's requisite butler gloves. Why should it matter that his fingerprints are not on the sword?

Another man, who had quietly slipped off during these rounds of witness selection, would later get tracked down, and he, too, would testify against Henry at the trial.

The governor slapped his palms together in the manner of dusting them off and so much as to say that the matter was concluded. "Would someone please call the police," he said, calmly.

"Oh, my God!" Margaret said, with tears in her eyes.

Captain Harris was so far three for three with his Pepsi. He drained the last of his third then set the can down on the table. "That's a good story." He belched. "Unfortunately, even if every last word of it's true, there's really nothing that can be done for you at this point. You'll be heading back to your cell in a few hours, Mr. Henry. You'll be allowed to have books, see and speak with onboard C.O.'s, get some real food into you—"

"And get a lavatory like they had at that fancy mansion place!" Day put in.

"You see..." Harris said, smiling at the Forever Young Prisoner, "even though it was a bit slow going at first, you were able to get the whole of your story out just fine."

Henry said every day for seventy years he had spoken words aloud in his cell.

"Just talking to yourself kinda like?" Harris asked.

Henry shook his head. He clarified that it was the "last words" he spoke at his sentencing he recited every day. Reiterating those words kept his voice alive, "as well as my heart," Henry added. Over the first few years of his imprisonment he had recited the whole of his speech every day. Then, he truncated it to the last few sentences. Then, only the last sentence. Then, only the last half of the last sentence.

"Because it got bothersome having to say the same long thing over and over?" Harris asked.

Henry nodded vigorously. "But, you see," Henry clarified, "in saying that last part I was... still...still for the most part...still, *basically*, I mean...saying that whole long thing even so."

Harris nodded. "I understand. The heart and soul of the message were there even if all the words weren't."

Henry nodded, pointed at Harris, gave a thumbs up sign.

"I like that part in the story where that fancy ol' gal offered to give you her coin back," Day said. "Did you ever get the coin?"

Henry's face saddened as he shook his head.

"No?" Harris said. "Never got it? Well, we've decided you'll get to keep this one." He slapped his hand down on the table. Sliding it back revealed a penny. Henry's penny. The *imaginary banker's* penny. "The boys found it on the sink. Yours?"

Henry sat staring at the coin.

Patting Day's hand, Harris said, "I like that part in the story where you, Kearney, and Sergeant Smith, set out to try to convince Monty Jenkins to come to his senses and forget he ever saw anything here. And were successful in your mission."

PART THREE
OUTER SPACE

CHAPTER TWENTY-FOUR

"The new Tommy McConnell character has been unlocked!" Danny kept saying.

My new yellow scrubs were for very realz kinda the mac. Granted, they tended to attract attention I didn't always want: fools doing double-takes at the chow hall, feezys wondering if I "like liked" other pastels like pink or purple, and even a few dared asked when my parole hearing was scheduled to go down. It was all good, though. Yellow meant Out.

On the road to "Out" lay the work crew. There, I classed as just another member of Team Yellow. Billy in his yellows, Hector in his yellows, Crusher T in his yellows, working alongside Tommy Mac in his yellows at the graveyard or on Route 1, proved about as welcome a change in scenery from the humdrum of a cell as I could've ever asked for. The only non-yellow one on the crew was Sargent Sausage, so dubbed by the regulars because of that badass bulge in Sarge's pants. Frankly, the million-and-one pussy tales and dick jokes had long since run their course for me. I just pulled weeds and scrounged for trash in silence. All the while I thought about Lilya, and Henry.

Until, finally, the big news arrived. Lilya's letter. She wrote to ask that I call her. After work, officially completing my third week on the outside work crew, I made the call.

"I'll tell you later," Lilya said, after I had asked for updates on her new job at Walmart. "I like it. It's tight. I got promoted to cashier. Listen…"

Lilya gave me the lowdown on our FOIA records request into that would-be name "Henry Ronsellier." She explained she'd decided to "play it right" and hire a lawyer, and a private investigator.

"To make a FOIA request?" I exclaimed. "Walmart doesn't pay *that* well, does it, Lil?"

"Your mother paid for it. Remember, you gave me her number? Listen…"

"My mother?"

"I called her and explained the situation. She said she wanted to help. The least she could do, she said, after all those years of just standing by."

I snorted at this laughable mention of a "gift" from someone, arguably my first since that yellow-and-blue bike for Christmas that one year. "That's boss." I smiled into the phone. "Go Mom."

"Yeah. And go lawyer guy, too. Oh, that reminds me, he's coming—"

I waited for what must have been five seconds for Lilya to finish her sentence, but nothing, absolutely nothing, sounded from the other end. "Who's coming?" I said. "Hello?"

Our connection flatlined. Nothing. Dead.

I slammed the phone down. "Fuckers." But then I remembered Mom's advice about "unnecessary profanity." "*Bastards,*" I said. The boys in blue needed to stop playing games and leave well enough the *fuck* alone. I tried to call Lilya back, but the call-forwarding system rejected my four-digit password. I slammed the phone down. "Big stupid *bastards.*" I stomped back to the cell.

I sat at my desk with my hands folded.

Sorting his laundry, Danny said, "What are you doin' just staring at the wall there, homie? Shouldn't we be out celebrating with this kickass news from Lilya? I've been thinking we should invite the homies over and make burritos!"

I replied, while alternating glances at the wall and my folded hands, "I don't know what I'm doing. Waiting, I guess."

"Waiting for what? Burritos?"

I stood, rotated my chair to face Danny, and sat back down. "Say, Dan, have you ever experienced that phenomenon of, like, multiple striking coincidences?"

Danny set his laundry bag aside. "Yeah." He walked over. "Let me think. So, okay, you're chillin' in your crib straight-up *jonesin'* for some dope when all of a sudden your dealer shoots you a text: he's got some, are you looking? Sure, it's happened."

"I had a dream last night. Some lady. She said 'He's coming...'"

Danny straightened. "Who's coming? Old Morgan? You know, you've been slacking ever since that visit with your mom. Not sure what else your hand has been grippin' over these past few months, but it hasn't been that penny."

"I don't know who's coming," I said, sullenly.

"Who was the lady?"

"I dunno. She had dark hair." Maybe Margaret Ronsellier, I wanted to say, but didn't dare say that.

While Danny mulled over dark-haired ladies—or just ladies in general—and returned to the pile of laundry on his rack, I returned to my previous pose of folded hands, desk, wall.

Minutes later, Danny said, "You're waiting for whomever to come, right?"

I said over my shoulder, "I guess." I wheezed out a sigh. "I don't know. I don't flippin' know anything anymore."

"Say no more," Danny said, and stepped over to my duffle bag. He shuffled through it then drew out of it the EVP recorder. "You're waiting for...whomever, maybe Old Morgan. You're watching for him, but you're not *listening*. Maybe now's the time we need to record. Maybe that old ghost has a message for us after all."

CHAPTER TWENTY-FOUR

"Maybe," I replied. "Hell, let's do it."

Danny placed the EVP recorder atop my desk then pressed the record button. We waited in silence.

And continued to wait until Danny said, "Someone's coming."

I heard it too. Footsteps out on the gangway. Cop boots, cop steps —and close. The recorder showcased in open display atop my desk. If I had attempted to rush over to hide the thing in my duffle bag it would have run me the risk of getting caught with my hand in the cookie jar. I stuffed the recorder into my front pants pocket.

It was Gaetske, alongside none other than Officer Rooney.

Gaetske said, "The warden wants to see you, McConnell. Not later today, not tomorrow, not after you finish reading a chapter in your book."

I laid a heavy stare Rooney's way.

Who, smirking, put in, "Only this time you'll have an escort. We don't want anyone getting lost."

The silence on the walk over to the warden's office felt only slightly less awkward than when just yesterday I had asked Danny what he imagined Lilya's thoughts might be about dating a piece-of-shit ex-con named Tommy Someone-or-other. Though, what made the trek alongside my old nemesis even more unnerving was the visible bulge in my front pocket. I jostled my hip around in an attempt to try to get the bulge more on the inside of the pocket than the outside of it. With any luck, I would be mistaken for another Sergeant Sausage and not an offender with a recording device in his pants. Ascending the steps of the Barr Building, I wiped the recorder clear out of my mind fearing it might show on my face. Cops notice stuff like that.

Entering his excellency's chambers, I found the place to be equally as spacious and arresting as had been my first impression of it. The warden himself, though, looked somehow thinner, paler this time around. He asked me to sit down. Rooney stood guard at the door.

"Well, Mr. McConnell," the warden said, glued to his seat this time, "so nice to see you again." He folded his hands atop his desk. "And how's prison life been treating you these days?"

I shrugged. "Prison's prison."

The warden motioned for Rooney to close the door. Rooney did so. "Good, good," the warden said. "Now, let's get down to brass tacks, shall we?"

Better brass tacks than brass knuckles, I almost replied.

I said that would be fine. I was down with that. Might as well. I was here, and it wasn't like I had a whole lot else going on.

"That's funny," the warden said, raising the corner of his mouth a millimeter in an attempt at a smile. "You are a humorous young man. Humor is medicine for the soul. Or as my grandmother used to say, 'laughter brightens the eyes and lifts the spirits...'"

I resisted the urge to recommend the warden might do well to try Grandma's medicine himself. With that mess of anger lines wrinkling the holy hell out of that face of his—with its piercing black eyes and fixed scowl—the warden looked to me just then, as he had at first, like the most unfunny man I had ever met. But then I remembered Mom's advice about "wise remarks" and just shut it.

"Speaking of way back in the day," the warden said. "You were on the low side, way back in the day, were you not?"

"True that, boss." I swallowed. "I mean, yes, Warden, absolutely I was on the low side."

"And wasn't it *there* where a great many other offenders used to call you this...this, oh, what was that name they used to call you over there?"

"Sherlock," Rooney put in.

"Yes, yes, *Sher-lock*," the warden said with his hand over his lip. "Sherlock, on the low side. Wasn't that so, Mr. McConnell?"

I nodded. Then nodded again, just for the heck of it. And again. And again.

The warden leaned in. "And so why, exactly, do you think they called you by this most *unusual* of names?"

I looked over my shoulder at Rooney who grinned at me with

teeth that no doubt arranged as crookedly and falsely as the rest of him. I said to the warden, "Why? Because of my investigation into the mystery of the Forever Young Prisoner, of course."

The warden leaned back in his chair. "Investigation?" He steepled his fingers. "Ah." He raised a compass in Rooney's direction. "This is an honest young man we've got here, wouldn't you say, Officer Rooney?"

Rooney smiled. "Yes, honest."

"In fact, I have a feeling," the warden said, with his eyes still deadlocked on the officer's, "don't you, too, Officer Rooney, have a feeling, what with how well-behaved, compliant, and *forthright* Mr. McConnell has been with us thus far..."

Rooney nodded

"...a feeling," the warden went on, "that Mr. McConnell's parole hearing which is *right* around the corner, will end up going well for him." The warden cracked his minuscule smile again. "Just a hunch. Just a hunch. Now, as for this *mystery* of your Forever Young Prisoner..." Raising an eyebrow, the warden leaned in. "Mystery, you say?" He leaned in all the more. "Not a mystery. You were misinformed."

"Misinformed," Rooney echoed from his spot by the door.

The warden stood. "We hear you and yours have hired an *attorney* for Mr. Ronsellier. Very well. Perfectly well indeed. That's Mr. Ronsellier's legal right, his right to counsel." The warden stepped over to press his hip up against the front ledge of the desk. He folded his hands. "McConnell, the only *mystery* with regards to Henry Ronsellier is that his case file was a very long time ago somehow *passed over* when the initial transfer was made from paper to digital record-keeping. We've since taken care of this little oversight. Mr. Ronsellier is now in the system. All thanks to you, and this lawyer friend of yours."

"He's in the system now?" I said, trying to keep a straight face. "But wait, I don't get it."

"Yes, that *sword murderer* is in the system," the warden affirmed.

"Sword...murderer?"

Rooney clarified, "Your Forever Young Prisoner *friend* chopped off a man's head with a Samurai sword."

My eyes bulged as I turned to Rooney. "Day-um."

The warden returned to his desk, "Your Forever Young Prisoner is a prisoner not unlike any other, Mr. McConnell. He's fed, clothed, and provided with reading materials. His cell is just like any other in Supermax, even though his cell is not exactly *in* Supermax."

I cleared my throat. "What about all of those rumors—"

"What?" The warden's eyes bulged. "That he was locked away in some...some *dungeon* for seventy-plus years, given bread and water only, no toilet, no place to wash or change his clothes, roaches and rats, no lights, no outside access, wasn't spoken to or allowed to speak to anyone..." The warden pointed at me. "*That* was the work of past administrators. I had nothing to do with any of that. Not this group of soldiers here. Not on my watch." The warden sat back down. "Once those," he made a flailing motion with a limp wrist as he wrested for the word, "*Caniglio* peoples, once their influence waned, it was pretty much life back to normal for Henry Ronsellier." The warden looked at me from across his desk. "Any questions?"

"Well, *yeah*," I said. "Like, a million of them." I ran my hand through my hair as I thought about it. I cleared my throat. "No questions." Best not to ask dumb questions of the wrong people until I knew more and could cover myself.

"Good," the warden said. "No need to investigate any further into some *mystery* which isn't one, never was one. You can put this whole ordeal behind you and move on to do actual, meaningful things with your life now. Good luck with your parole review, McConnell. Now, get outta here, before I call the cops."

I actually laughed at that one. Maybe the warden did have a sense of humor. And maybe, too, the *mystery* of the Forever Young Prisoner really did all add up to nothing more than a simple paperwork error. Yeah, and pigs fly, the Pope is Jewish, and heroin's a one-hit-wonder. We still had work to do, it sounded like.

CHAPTER TWENTY-FIVE

The word "work" spelled differently for me now, no longer with four-letters. Okay, maybe with four letters, but no longer a four-letter word. I liked Team Yellow. I liked the feel of sweat dripping down the sides of my nose and calluses on my hands. I enjoyed traveling out to the various work sites with the guys. Dirt, dust, and power tools really got me going, too. I enjoyed getting up at the crack of dawn each day—psyche, yeah right. No complaints about free coffee! And, although it may sound lame, what I enjoyed most of all was the sense of accomplishment I'd have on the ride home in the van each day.

Digging post holes had to be the most physically challenging of all of our tasks, and so maybe that was why I enjoyed it the most. The construction of barbed-wire fence alongside some of the most out-there roads in all of Rhode Island necessitated the erection of fence posts, which necessitated the digging of post holes. So, I dug those holes. We dug. We all dug. Two men per hole.

Rook, my hole homie, and the only other Gen Zer on the crew, eyed my left calf I kept scratching. "You got an itch?" he asked.

The square of duct tape donated by one of Slider's friends on the first floor kept snagging my leg hairs whenever I did anything but stand motionless. That tape secured an audio recorder to my calf. A recorder in my cell with the warden's voice on it posed major concerns. I had to get rid of it ASAP.

One very convenient thing about my scheme to make good on this intention was that strip searches on the work crew happened only on the way in, not the way out. That we dug post holes on this raw, but still sunny afternoon in mid-January listed as yet another great convenience.

Of course, a hole already dug meant burying something in it simply became a matter of tossing it in. And so that's what I did.

"What's that?" Rook said, funneling his sights down at the fruit of our labors.

"Something you didn't just see," I said, shoveling dirt over the recorder wrapped in its chow-hall napkin. The fence post lay mostly buried and secure in the hole by this point. We were simply filling in around the sides to better secure it. My treasure lay no more than an inch from the surface, nudged up against the post.

"Done," I said, smiling at Rook.

Rook didn't care, he was just a rook. "When's your parole review, Tommy?" he asked on our walk over to the next patch of earth to be dug.

"I dunno." I scoured again for Sergeant Sausage, whom, I noticed, remained seated in the van sipping hot chocolate and listening to True Crime.

While at the library a few days later, the call came. Mr. Librarian stepped over to interrupt my reading of *From Felon to Freedom: Career Paths for the 21ˢᵗ Century Convict* to say I was wanted back at the pod. Back at the pod, Gaetske informed me I had a lawyer visit, then wrote me a pass.

The "Lawyer Meet Room" situated along its own separate hallway. Its turnoff came just before the Visits Room. I hadn't seen or spoken to my lawyer since way back at my sentencing hearing. Was he even my lawyer still? I didn't know. No matter. In prison, every visit more than pays for itself in the diamond currency of scenery change. I knew that now.

I knew Steve Vitelli, too, sure enough. His fluffy black hair and striped lawyer-suit were about as telltale as a red birthmark on a Forever Young Prisoner. Steve was my public defender—*was*. He rose as I entered. He walked past the table at the center of the room where his briefcase reposed and shook my hand, firmly. "Good to see you again, Tommy. It's been a while. Have a seat."

The place looked janky-ass bare and the soft yellow lighting offered the promise of a headache. I sat down at the table opposite Steve. Ours, along with five or six other tables, fairly filled out the premises. A few tables, a rug, walls, and a vending machine—comprised the whole of it. No one was there but us.

"Am I in trouble?" I asked.

"Trouble?" Steve chuckled. "Why is that *always* the first thing that pops into my clients' minds? No, you are not in trouble. How is prison going?"

"Prison's prison," I said.

Steve clicked his pen. "I hear your review is coming up. I wish you the very best of luck with that."

I shrugged in response to Steve's pleasantry. Possibly, it was my shoulders' way of saying they needed to get some exercise—I hadn't hit the weight pile in months—but more likely it signaled my concern over the prospect of having to face the real world all over again. Prison stood as a refuge against hell with a lot of false advertising: the outs. Temptations, challenges, and responsibilities, all roamed like vampires out there.

"Don't get your hopes up, though," Steve said. "With charges like yours the board usually won't budge on the first try." Steve put his chin in his hand. "You know, if we'd taken your case to trial we just might've done it. You could've argued self defense. The victim had a record, you know, and at least three witnesses said he'd provoked you. If only we had delved a little further and obtained proof of some kind of," Steve squinted as he pondered, "stirring, or *little motion* that made you *think* he was readying to move on you, then we could've—"

"No." I shook my head. "I did it. I own that shit. He was talking smack, my Angry Tommy side got the better of me and I just went off on that fool."

"And kept going off on him even after he was down. Hence the prison sentence. Still, there's angles we might've worked instead of you just accepting a three-year prison term."

I looked at Steve. "Maybe when I get out I'll find that guy and apologize to him."

Steve clicked his pen. "Forgiveness is not a word in everyone's vocabulary, Tommy. People hold grudges. They tend to take things personally. It could worsen matters." Steve opened the folder in front of him. "But that's not what I'm here to talk to you about today. I'm here to talk to you about—"

"Let me guess. Something to do with my mom, my sister, my dad? With Lilya? Something to do with Danny? Whatever it is, I didn't—"

"Henry Ronsellier," Steve said softly.

I guffawed. "*You're* the lawyer Lilya's been telling me all about? But you're a public defender. Public defenders don't, they can't—"

"I'm in private practice now. I don't work for the State anymore. I'm officially an associate at Teague & Teague. I do criminal law and post-conviction work. Which brings us to your friend."

"I'd *like* to say Henry Ronsellier's my friend," I snorted.

"Oh, I think he's your friend," Steve said. "You're *his* friend anyway. Did you know...did you *know*, Tommy... that Henry asked me to relay a message to you?"

"Message?" The weight of Steve's words literally brought me to my feet. But then standing started to feel a little wack, so I sat back down. "Message?" I said, calmer. "You mean you've talked to him?"

"Talked? Why, we met here in this very room, just like I'm meeting with you now. I'm his lawyer. Henry and I have not only the legal right, but the legal obligation, to meet as lawyer and client."

Having no idea what to say to all of that, I just sat and listened to my heart thump.

Steve drew a sheet of paper out of his folder. "When we met, Henry signed this affidavit which gives you power of attorney. It gives me permission to speak with you about his case." Steve laid the paper down in front of me. "I shared with him all about you. All that your friend, Lilya, shared with me up until now about what you've done for him while here in prison. About your meeting with Monty, the library, Sherlock, all of that."

"No fucking way. I mean, no way." I studied the form. "What did he say? His message to me, I mean?"

Steve curved a smile. "Henry's message to you was…Thank you, Tommy. I knew you would come."

"Thank you, Tommy. I knew you would come," I muttered. I bit my lip and tore my sights away, struggling in vain to fight back the tears.

"Want a tissue? I always bring them for my clients and their families just in case."

I nodded. "What was he like?" I asked, sniffling.

"Very quiet. He seemed utterly content to just sit and observe. I don't know what fascinated him more: me, or this room here. His eyes were all over it. At one point, Henry asked if I had ever met Ronald Reagan or Michael Jackson. He seemed to know somewhat about the modern world but only in terms of historical events, big-name personalities and the like, as if he'd learned from a course or from reading books."

I listened with rapt attention, blowing my nose occasionally, as Steve went on, "To say that man's an enigma would be quite the understatement. His voice sounded like wind down a tunnel, but I think that was more from nerves than anything else. He said he was 'quite beside himself' at having a lawyer. His slow, awkward movements made him seem very old."

"But he didn't *look* old?" I asked, with no small emphasis on the word.

Steve's eyes bulged. "Noooo." Steve swallowed. "He looked to be about your age, maybe younger." Steve sighed. "Oh, if only I could rack that brain for even a half-hour....but I'm just his lawyer." He checked his wristwatch. "Look, I have a hearing downtown soon and so I'll be brief. I need your help."

"My help?" I wiped my nose, then stopped. "Wait, so, they let you meet with him...which means...he's in the system now, which means..."

Steve inched a smile as he sifted through the file in front of him

"...which means you have his case file." I leaned forward to try to get a better look at it. "How, though? I thought it was in some secret filing cabinet."

"That's right," Steve said, tucking the file back into his briefcase. "Your help." He checked his watch again. "Here's the bottom line. My intention is to file a Rule 35(a) motion on Henry's behalf. It's sort of like a habeas corpus filing only it would be with the county court. The Rhode Island rule is vague, unfortunately. The equivalent federal rule, Rule 35(c), is much more concise, and would work a whole lot better for us."

I absolutely hated it when lawyers ignored direct questions. They probably took whole classes on that in law school. "Why can't you file that, then?" I asked.

Steve shook his head. "No jurisdiction in federal. Henry's dealings must be with the county." He exhaled. "Another problem with the Rhode Island rule is there's a time limit to filing which has long since expired in Henry's instance. However, his is a Class I felony and there's usually no time limit with those. Also, if we can prove he didn't have access to a lawyer up until now I'm fairly sure we can get an exception."

"A rare exception," I muttered.

Steve folded his hands. "Henry's sentence is life without parole, Tommy. Do you know what that means?"

I blew my nose. "It means he can't get out, ever. He's in for life."

Steve nodded. "For his entire lifetime, right? But what's a lifetime

—is the question I plan to propose to the court. Is it eighty years, ninety? Henry has spent over *one hundred years* in prison, and seventy of those years were spent in the most horrid conditions imaginable: no lights, no bathroom, no access to his lawyer or visitors, roaches, rats... Any reasonable person would say Henry Ronsellier has served his life sentence already."

"I'd say that," I offered.

"However, there's one problem. The release of a prisoner who was sentenced to life without parole has never been done before, and I'm fairly sure it's never been argued before. We'd be writing new law." Steve reached into his briefcase. "I researched, and found not a single case on the subject. Nothing. Without case law support, we'd be forced to use only the bare-bones argument of reasonableness."

"Oh," I frowned.

"Until..." Steve smiled, "at our meeting two days ago, and after I had explained all of this to him, Henry wrote down for me..." Steve drew out of his folder a yellow sticky note, "*this*." The words scribbled in cursive on the note read:

Heck v. Harris, 1985.

"A rare exception?"

"So to speak. It's an older court case in some ways similar to the instant case, only in *Heck* the sentence of the movant, one Cheryl Heck, hadn't been a life sentence. Anyhow, she won, and not for arguing the unconstitutionality of her *sentence* but the unconstitutionality of her *prison conditions*. The ruling never got appealed so it's not much of a precedent. Worse, it's an out-of-state case, New Hampshire. But it's something. Somehow, I don't know how, Henry knew about this case. It's no slam-dunk, but I think it'll work."

"You think?"

Steve folded his hands. "The State, on its own, is never going to release Henry, Tommy. Nothing will ever happen unless an argument is presented before the Court on his behalf. We have to present *something*. We have to try." Steve leaned back. "One other problem."

My shoulder's slumped.

"We have no way of proving those bad conditions suffered by Henry over the first seventy years of his sentence really were bad. There's no proof."

I snorted in disbelief. "Henry's own words?"

"Which helps," Steve agreed. "But at the end of the day it's just hearsay. The state will come in with their own witnesses—say, the warden, or an ex-warden—who will testify Henry never at all experienced unconstitutional conditions. No, what Henry needs is hard evidence, or another witness."

I squelched a smile. "What if the warden *did* decide to testify about those bad conditions, though?"

Steve shook his head. "Never in a million years. It would set into motion all sorts of liability for prison officials, and maybe even for the warden himself. He'd never do it."

"Yeah, but what if he did?"

Steve looked at me long, hard, and suspiciously.

I darted glances around even though the Lawyer Meet Room was legally off-limits to any form of monitoring. Lowering my voice, I said, smiling, "An audio recorder, with the warden's testimony on it. Would that work?"

"Is...the recorder yours?" Steve asked, weakly. "You did the recording yourself?"

I nodded, slowly, and nodded again, and again.

"I don't wanna know any more." Steve latched his briefcase and stood. "You just get me that recorder."

"I can't," I said. "But maybe Lilya can, if you'd be willing to part ways with one of those sticky notes so I can write down directions to where that bad boy's buried."

Found by Steven Vitelli, esquire, inside of Henry Ronsellier's inmate case file:

CHAPTER TWENTY-FIVE

Dear Dr. Timothy Hansen,
cc: Rhonda Levine, MD, John Knowles, DO

Thank you, Dr. Hanson, and your associates at the Rhode Island Department of Health and Human Services, for again entrusting your patient to our team. We celebrate forty years of service to the state of Rhode Island and its criminal justice affiliates. Our conclusions state similar to our previous analyses, and are outlined at the conclusion of this report.

Overview: Telomeres are repetitive, layered segments of DNA found at the end of chromosomes. These segments act as protective caps and shed layers every time the cell divides. A cell divides 50 to 70 times at which point the Hayflick Limit is reached, where the cell can no longer divide and cellular death ensues. This process of telomere attrition, also known as mitosis, corresponds to a normal human lifespan of 80-90 years. The end-of-the-line Hayflick Limit approximates to a reading of 4.0 base pairs (bp.) A healthy 18 year old might have a telomere length reading of 8.0 bp. The test administered at our state-of-the-art laboratory in North Providence compared the subject's average telomere length to reference ranges of age-matched populations.

Procedure: A Telomere Length test was administered for the patient, Henry Ronsellier, per your instruction. Our lab technicians performed the test on the 10 ml blood sample provided by the Department of Corrections. White blood cells were targeted for telomere length determination.

Findings: Mr. Ronsellier's average telomere length was 8.62 bp. Telomere attrition is not advanced. The Hayflick Limit, and cellular death, are not within range.

Mr. Ronsellier's average telomere length reading presents a true cellular age of 23 years, 10 months, 5 days. This is Mr. Ronsellier's true biological age.

Previous tests on this subject produced similar findings:

June 14, 1984: 8.11 bp
June 19, 1988: 8.11 bp
June 6, 1992: 8.10 bp
May 4, 1996: 8.13 bp
May 29, 2003: 8.11 bp
June 14, 2010: 8.12 bp
July 11, 2015: 8.11 bp

<u>Conclusion</u>: Cells cannot infinitely replicate, but Mr. Ronsellier's appear to be doing just that. Mr. Ronsellier's telomere length readings have remained constant at approximately 8.1 bp over a lengthy period of time. This is inapposite to the commonly held logic of telomere attrition. His chromosomes are either not dividing, or no genetic material is lost on the divides. Either way, the subject is not aging.

Please let me know if you have any further questions or concerns.

Yours,
Dr. William Doyle, MD,
Cellular Laboratories Group, North Providence, RI
June 4, 2018

CHAPTER TWENTY-SIX

Danny, Chopper, Mike, and Slider, all sat chilling in the cell either playing cards, or pretending to play cards, upon my return from my parole review hearing.

"How'd it go?" Chopper asked, laying his cards down on the floor face up.

I told Mike to move it or lose it, the desk chair belonged to someone else. "How'd what go?" I asked, sitting down after Mike had bailed. Parole was personal. The prevailing wisdom advised to never share your review or Out dates with anyone. It could come back to bite. Others might seek to settle scores. I had made the mistake of telling not only Danny, but Chopper. Now, Mike and Slider knew, too. However, I guess it didn't matter so much if only the guys knew, and I had no enemies. Well, the mohawk boys, but they'd hit the road. Although, maybe they had friends. I would have to keep my eyes peeled.

"I'll know in a few days," I told them. "The board doesn't make decisions right on the spot."

"Yeah, but how did it *go*?" Danny asked, ditching his cards with a quick flick of the wrist as he sat up on his rack.

I shrugged. "Good, I think. They liked my parole plan. I'll parole out to my mom's crib in Coventry. No job, but it's hard to get one while you're locked up, and I'm pretty sure they understand that." I cocked my head. "I think when I get out I'll either mow lawns or butler."

"For what it's worth," Slider said, "they do want you outta this prison, Mac."

"Yeah they do," Chopper agreed. "I can tell by the way the popo —all except Gaetske—have been throwing shade your way of late. Did you just say you wanna be a butler?"

"Hey, Slider," I leaned forward in my chair, "Henry's lawyer— that guy I was telling you about, Steve—told me he plans to file a 35(a) motion on Henry's behalf soon. What happens after that?"

Danny rolled his eyes. "Tommy's more about *Henry Heck* getting out than he is about himself getting out."

"Not *Heck*," I corrected Danny. "His name's Henry *Ronsellier*."

Slider answered, "After your lawyer files the motion, the State will respond. They'll write their rebuttal and say why Henry shouldn't be released. Occasionally, the judge will rule on the briefs alone. But usually the judge will schedule a hearing. The whole process could take a couple of months. You'll be called as a witness to testify that the recorder was yours and you recorded it."

"I'm actually looking forward to that," I said.

"You should be looking forward to getting out," Danny quipped.

I ignored Danny, even though he was right. I announced, "Henry was a sword murderer, you fools know that?"

"You told us already," Mike said.

I turned to Slider. "Henry will be there, too, won't he? At the hearing?"

Slider nodded. "It's required."

I shook my head. "I wish I knew more. I'd ask Lilya or Steve but the phone's not processing any of my calls right now."

"So," Danny interjected, "and not to change the subject, but when's your best homie finally gonna get to meet the forever elusive, mysterious, and delirious Miss Penny Red Hair?"

I reached into my duffle bag and withdrew my penny from the warden. I flipped it Danny's way. He caught it. "There," I said. "You've met."

The very next day, Gaetske stopped over and said....that I had gotten parole.

I supposed this news should have excited me more. Granted, it didn't come as much of a surprise. The four of us celebrated with burritos and Danny's Chocolate Honey Bun Surprise which Danny, talking out of his ass, claimed was an Italian thing.

Chopper's ass had its say once or twice, too. We all laughed. Chopper said it meant his burrito really hit the spot. He asked why I no longer wrote.

"Yeah, I hear you're a really good writer," Slider said. "For what it's worth, how come you never shared with me any of your stories?"

"Because my stuff's wack. I'm retired now."

"Write something different," Slider suggested. "Try something new."

"Different?" I said. "Like what?"

"We'll call it..." Danny offered, with frosting all over his lips, "The True Story of the Forever Young Prisoner. It'll be a novel. Reads like fiction, but is a true story."

I blinked at Danny. Why the hell hadn't I thought of that? No, wait, I had. That one day in the chow hall those millions of years ago. "Well, if Henry doesn't win at his hearing there won't be any story to tell." Maybe putting first things first stood as the reason for my forgetfulness. I suddenly felt awfully proud of my bad memory.

"And even if he does win, the State will appeal," Slider noted.

About a minute later, after the guys decided to play an actual card game and I stared at the wall the whole while with my thoughts ping-ponging, I said, "I've even got a cover in mind."

Slider lowered his cards. "You mean for your book, Mac?"

I nodded. Turning to Danny, I said, "Hey, do you remember Watson, low-side, resident pencil portrait artist, played b-ball?"

"Sure, I do. Absolutely. But Tommy, there are plenty of good artists here on the high-side. Better than Watson, even. Hey, let me introduce you—"

"No. I want Watson. He drew a donkey once. Maybe he's got it in him for one more."

Danny cocked his head. "One more what?"

"Donkey," I said. "His shit's powerful, you better believe it."

Danny eyed me warily. "I thought you didn't like donkeys."

I pondered. Dreamily, I replied, "Sometimes prison's worst turn out to be prison's best. Time heals. Time destroys. Time is a thing of wonder."

Later that evening, I borrowed Danny's phone code to call Lilya. I figured if they pressed Danny about the code I'd cover and tell them I stole it. Which was kinda how it all went down anyway.

Lilya congratulated me on my parole and said she couldn't wait to see me. Also, she said Steve had met with one of the editors at *The Providence Times* earlier in the day, who, according to Steve, sounded "super interested" in hearing Henry's story.

All in all, things looked to be headed somewheres.

My last day at the office proved bittersweet, mostly sleepless, and sappier than I would have preferred. At least I didn't get ambushed on my way out for whistling too loudly in the shower or for whatever other reason—or for no reason at all. I said goodbye to the homies. Danny gave me a hug. I told him "Don't leave the light on for me." He would be out soon enough himself. Chopper, Mike, and Slider gave me a fist bump, and then a hug.

Packing up didn't present much of a challenge with my wares numbering little to none. I debated whether I should keep that bible from Brother Reverend So-and-so. "Need all the karma I can get," I said, deciding to pack it finally.

"Karma?" Danny said. "You got that shit comin' outta your ears. You need to share some with the rest of us!"

My cell door clanked open at three a.m. on the morning of the 25th of January. My escort stood on the threshold of the cell tapping his cop toe while I got in one final fist bump with Dan. The escort was none other than Perry, Captain Baldy himself. But like I cared at that point.

Passing the community showers along our way, I said, "I won't miss those." We marched on. "That, either," I pointed to the main pod door with its god-awful click-lock sounds. "Or that," I flicked a nod at the yard. "Or your sorry ass," I said to Captain Baldy, who with a frown looked straight on. "You, neither," I informed the weirdo in the vest, who extended his fist in request for a bump but who stood on Perry's side of our paired march, wholly outside of my reach.

We continued our trek along the black-and-white tiles of what-ever hallway it was in Drac's Castle, when suddenly I stopped, and turned, slowly. I looked. No one there.

"Having second thought?" Perry narrowed his eyes. "I don't blame you. Your shoes are the last ones I'd wanna be in right now."

Captain Baldy scraped his own shoes a few steps forward then pivoted to face me. Mohawk Boy suddenly emerged out of the shadows of an adjacent hallway and stepped over to flank the captain. The two men stood with their hands on their hips, scowling.

"We've played nice so far, but no more," Perry declared. "The warden's not exactly thrilled you recorded him. His admissions were made to you in good faith, off the record. Talk to the press about that recorder and it's over for you, McConnell."

"We have homies on the outs," Mohawk Boy warned, smacking his fist. "We'll track you down. Your little girlfriend, too. We know where she lives."

"Girlfriend?" I furrowed my brow. "Oh, you must mean Shayna, Jewish Princess. Of course that's who you mean. She lives in Fall River now, I think. Or Springfield. Good luck trying to find her and she knows Kung Fu....or anyhow her tongue does." I cleared my throat. "Hey, er, and not to change the subject, but did you guys just see that weirdo standing over by the door back there: mustache, sideburns, white dress-shirt, black vest, hair parted down the middle like one of those..."

Old west bankers?

With a shake in my voice, I continued, "He, er, offered me a fist bump but he was too far away to..."

Gripping a penny.

Mohawk Boy snickered. "Get outta town. Over by the Pod 1 door?" Stretching a toothless grin, he turned to Perry. "Fool wants us to think he's seen Old Morgan."

"I am getting out of town," I said, pointing to my In-and-out bag.

"Don't bother trying to frighten us with your pennies or ghost stories," Perry warned. "They won't save you. Nothing will at this point, son."

Mohawk Boy bailed after a few additional choice words then Perry, with measured, wordless paces, escorted me to Depart. There I exchanged my yellows for the standard dress-out gear: beige slacks, navy dress-shirt, white socks, and black shoes. Perry got one last leer in, then the Depart officer led me out to the gate.

I would like to have said the falling snowflakes reminded me of cotton, or dandruff, but that wasn't it at all. Already two seconds out of the door, and temptation had staked a claim.

Mom's car sat idling alongside the curb in the parking lot. With the exception of the windows, the whole car lay covered over in sticky, wet New England snow. Mom and Penny waved excitedly out their windows at me. I waved back. Turning, I indulged one last look at Drac's Castle.

"I'll miss you," I said to it. The *magic and mystery* of Drac's Castle was what I was going to miss, not the architectural monstrosity itself.

Out on my own, with nothing more to investigate, and no more to do for Henry except wait and hope, magic and mystery would have to come all on their own. Magic and mystery were difficult to come by in The Ocean State, if experience had anything to say for it. I thought of Harry Potter just then, my old homie from the low side. Now that I was out I could write him a letter. Something very important I wanted to ask him.

I bear-hugged Mom and Penny then clambered into the Mom Mobile. Instead of sharing with them about all my ghostly encounters or my joys at the thrill of freedom, I said, "What happened? Henry's case file? How did you guys get it?"

Penny coughed and flicked a nod.

I hadn't even noticed the black gal in the pea coat seated alongside me in the backseat. "Oh. Hi, Lil."

"I'll let your little friend explain," Mom offered.

Smiling, I shook my head. "Why does everyone keep saying that? She's not so very *little*, is she?"

CHAPTER TWENTY-SEVEN

That Monday had started off with the breakfast of champions, cigs and coffee. Part of getting right was eating right, someone had told her recently. But all Lilya could do was stare at the box of Wheaties on her counter, think luckless thoughts, and puff away.

Later, sitting hunched over in the Walmart break room, she painted her nails Sparkly Winter Blue and stressed over things she couldn't quite place a blue fingernail on. Storm clouds brewing, it felt like. But felt only. On the surface, the skies looked clear. Tommy had made parole, clean sure felt good, and she didn't hate her job. She encouraged herself with sunny reminders about Tommy's release and the good times they'd have once he got out, but one look at her fingernails and the blues rained down all over again. Everything hinged on some Forever Young Prisoner guy. What bothered Lilya the most was there was nothing she—or anyone—could really do for him. That she stood willing to risk anything at all for some holed-up stranger from yesteryear proved testimony enough to her feelings for Tommy. In between sighs, she stole glances at her untouched cheesesteak sub.

Sasha from Electronics kept stealing glances at it, too. "You gonna eat that?" she asked.

Just then, the call came. Lilya eyed her cell phone. Tommy's mom. She answered, "Don't tell me it's on *right now*."

"It's on *right now*," Andrea Weiss replied. "That private dick Steve hired just called. The main records lady just made good on her scheduled half-day off to go to the dentist. Her car just left the parking lot. This is it. Go time."

Lilya eyed the clock on the wall. Only five minutes of break left and she hated to have to ask for time off, especially on such short notice. Technically, Steve and Andrea didn't exactly need her. However, she wanted to tag along for Tommy and Henry's sake. Too, for her own. It wasn't every day a girl from the streets got the chance to write history even if that chance looked to be as good as a cheesesteak sub surviving on a breakroom table all by its lonesome after its owner had bailed. Lily stood. "All right, I'll catch up with you guys over at the prison in twenty." She hung up.

"Amanda..." Lilya said, trailing her boss all the way to the Customer Service desk. "I was wondering if I could cut out a little early today. Remember, er, that lawyer guy you overheard Sasha and I chatting about the other day?"

"Overheard? Don't be silly."

"Yeah you did. So—"

"Is this a medical or family emergency, Miss *I Wanna Go Home Early*?" Amanda placed her hands on her broad hips and peered in.

Lilya swallowed. "Well, er, not really. Sort of, I guess. Not my family, though. That lawyer guy, Tommy's mom, and I, plan to join forces and go bust into that records room, no holds barred, and—"

"Blow everyone away to high hell and steal the secret file?"

Lilya swallowed. "—and see if our chances are better at getting the backup worker to give us the file than the main records-lady giving it to us."

Amanda creaked a smile. "Well, that doesn't sound like much of a grounds for a bestseller, now, does it?" She clapped Lilya on the shoulder. "I'd expect a little more *grit* and *initiative* from a real go-getter like Lilya Jenkins." She lost her smile. "You're not back in an hour, you're fired, do you hear me?"

Lilya's eyes bulged.

Amanda touched her arm. "That was a joke, sweetie. You're one of my best workers, Lilya. You've clocked perfect attendance since your start date. Of course you can take the afternoon off to go rescue the Ageless Prisoner and save the world or what have you."

"*Forever Young* Prisoner," Lilya corrected.

Afterward, Amanda stepped over just as Lilya stretched her lanyard and card to punch out. "You know, you could've just told me you weren't feeling well. That's the going excuse. You do have sick time."

Lilya stood blinking. "But, that would be lying." She bolted so hurriedly for the exit she nearly barreled over the greeter.

The backup records clerk came with few surprises, at least in terms of form. A middle-aged man with narrow shoulders, tight lips, and a decidedly uptight sense about him, he reminded Lilya of one of those stereotypical old-school clerks. The sour, grimacy expression on his face suggested a lemon hidden somewhere. *Dour* was the word she was looking for, definitely that. Lilya bet he collected coins and hadn't had a good lay in ages—if he even gave half-a-lay about stuff like that. Lilya didn't give half-a-lay if he did or not.

Steve told the clerk he wanted a copy of the case file of inmate Henry Heck.

The dour clerk twisted a wry smile. He punched some keys on his keyboard and said there was no Henry Heck in the system.

"Henry Ronsellier, then," Steve said. He spelled out the name.

The clerk sat blinking. He typed, then announced there was no one with that name in the registry.

"Sir," Steve said, with frustration in his voice, "we are here to make an official FOIA request for inmate Henry Ronsellier. I realize he's not in the computer, but we have it on reliable information that his paper records are in this records room here." He pointed. "They are stored in a locked cabinet with the label Non-Sequiturs on one of its drawers."

The clerk leaned back in his chair and smiled. Shrugging, he replied, "No idea what you're talking about, *sir*."

"There's a key in the office that opens the secret—" inwardly, Lilya swore at herself "—I mean, the *not-secret-at-all* filing cabinet." Maybe she shouldn't have come.

The clerk steepled his fingers. "I think what you folks need to do is come back when the regular clerk is here. Her name is Ms. Ward. She can assist you in this matter. I'm just a fill-in."

Andrea stepped forward to the counter. "I would like to show you something, Mr…"

The clerk groaned. "Blake."

"Mr. Blake, this is a genealogy record. I had it done online. It's official. See this emblem and certification here?" Andrea pointed to the documents in her hand. "This is a name tree. This entry here going way back says *Henry Ronsellier*. Henry is my great-great grand-father, Mr. Blake. His daughter, my great-grandmother, was a very dear and precious woman. Her name was Mildred, but we all called her Old Miss Ronsellier. She lived on Milldale Street. That's in Greenville. She lived alone. For years people thought she was crazy because she kept experiencing dreams and visions of a man." Andrea pointed to a name on the tree. "This man, Henry Ronsellier, her father. The father she never knew because *you people* locked him away for her entire lifetime. Henry Ronsellier is family, Mr. Blake."

The clerk studied the genealogical chart. He wet his lips. "A relation?"

Andrea nodded.

The clerk moved his tongue around his mouth as he glared nervously at the record.

"My son is an inmate here, too," Andrea added. "His name's Tommy McConnell. Tommy's been catching hell from you people for trying to seek out his great-great-great grandfather. All he wants is to be reunited with his ancestor. Family members should be allowed visits."

The clerk looked up. "*McConnell* is related to Henry?" He eyed Andrea's printout. "Yes, here he is. Thomas McConnell." He sided a glance at the lawyer then said to Andrea, "I never did like violence. I hate when it comes to that. Your boy is in danger, ma'am."

Before Steve could get a word in edgewise to ask what that meant, the clerk took off for the back room.

He returned five minutes later with Henry Ronsellier's full case file. "Take this," he said. "Peace for the dead is knowing their ancestors are taken care of and getting along. I had a dream last night, too. My deceased grandfather. Never mind what he said. Now go."

Andrea, Steve, and Lilya sorted through the information afterward: Henry had signed for *their* power of attorneys, too.

Name: Henry Ronsellier.

Born: 1893. "He's 130 years old," Lilya exclaimed.

Charge: Murder in the first degree.

Sentence: Life without parole.

Location: Supermax, Pod 7.

CHAPTER TWENTY-EIGHT

Getting out is like being born. There's really no better way to describe it. The backseat of Mom's Honda felt like the Space Shuttle, the two-lane highway like the Yellow Brick Road, the dumpy cashier at the Cumbie station might well have been Wonder Woman, and the store itself outer friggin' space. Coffee costs money—tight! Coins weren't nickel or copper, but gold and silver. "The emperor's new clothes," I told Penny, after she'd asked about my new threads even though I didn't quite know what that expression meant. I felt like an emperor, anyway. Everything seemed so foreign, larger-than-life, and otherworldly. The world was so damned *big*.

Touchdown in my new world happened at a cobalt-blue colonial in the small town of Coventry, Rhode Island. Mom called the environs "the suburbs," while I called it "the ass-end of outer space." Mom and Penny proved themselves to be worthy hostesses. Once I got over my culture shock, I planned to let each of them know how much I appreciated the free ginseng tea, ten packs of underwear, case of vitamin D tablets, batman t-shirt, and a book titled *How to*

Get Your Life Back Together Again. I told Mom, "I never had it together in the first place!"

The Batman t-shirt was cartoon style with the word "Kapow!" on it, with Batman knocking out some villain—like the kind a ten-year-old might wear. I wore it proudly, and regularly, at least around the house. Mom liked that I wore it. I think she was secretly proud of having a badass for a son.

A sugar mamma she was not, however, apparently, damn it. She ran the place like it was a regular halfway house. Up at six, in bed by ten, wash those dishes *now* not next week. A parole requirement, she wanted me working ASAP. Go Mom.

I had no plans to work as a butler or mow lawns, be it known. It's called sarcasm. Over the following weeks, I put in applications at a warehouse and some big manufacturing plant. Doubtful they would hire me because of my felon status, but I applied anyway. Also, I applied at the gas station down the street from Mom's house. They hired me...maybe, or maybe not, because Penny knew the manager, or rather he knew her.

Penny's "wicked awesome to have a brother" line repeated about ten times daily, but I could tell she meant every word of it every time. She dropped questions endlessly. A little redheaded cutie, she got plenty of looks from gas station managers and the like. Too many looks, as far as big brother was concerned. We chilled, went for walks, and played video games. A couple of times I ended up saving the two of us some fuss when I turned the tables on her questions. One time she asked what I used to do on Friday nights when I was her age. I answered —the usual, how about you? She didn't need to know all about her former drug-addict brother. *That was Then, This is Now*, to quote the title of the newest book on my shelf. I had my own bookcase now.

Penny toured me around the campus at the University of Rhode Island. I met some of her friends whom she partied and skied with. Granted, the kind of fools I usually chilled with didn't snack on chips and watch ESPN for "funsies." Normies, normies everywhere. I thought I had died and gone to normie heaven. I hadn't decided yet if this was a good thing.

"If normies aren't your thing," Mom said at one point, "then why not pay a visit to your old neighborhood, say hello to Frank and Trixie while you're over there."

"Sure." I shrugged. "Why not?"

So I did. Frank answered the door. I said, hi, I'm here, I'm back, long time no see, I'm with my real mom now. Frank actually had a hard time opening the door at first. He kept knocking his wheelchair into it. That stroke he always feared must've for realz have happened. He told me through his oxygen mask that Trixie was in the psych ward again. I said, "So nothing's really changed, then."

"Hearing voices now, too, though," Frank clarified. "And talking back to them bitches. Kept crying out to you, too, even, though you was a million miles away. All that crazy shit she kept rambling on about you and some *mission*. She'd break down crying or laughing..." Frank gripped the wheels of his ride until his knuckles whitened. "She's in a better place now except for them fuckin', damned, son-of-a-bitch bills the State refuses to cover."

I adjusted my sunglasses, and finding no comfortable response to all of that just stated my peace: that I was sorry for running away, thanks for the memories, good luck, and gave Frank a handshake. Yes, I shook his damned hand. I actually felt sorry for Wheelchair Frank. The old neighborhood hadn't changed much, either.

Just about to slam the door in my face, Frank said, "Oh, I forgot. You had visitors."

"Visitors?"

Frank nodded. "Devil Coyotes. Some of 'em had mohawk hair. You running with that local gang now? Wouldn't surprise me, a shit-head like you. They were looking for you, wanted to know where you was at."

"Nowhere," I said. "Next time, tell 'em I'm *nowhere*. Tell 'em I launched off and landed somewhere in *outer space*." I let out a breath. "Where I'm still trying to find my way..."

Mom's house way out in the sticks technically didn't classify as outer space; however, it was far enough outside of Devil Coyote's territory to arguably relieve a fool of overmuch worry. I worried anyway. Stressing out, and in a moment of weakness, I checked in with my old dealer on my way home. Yeah, I bought some stuff.

When I was off from work, I hung with the fam. Otherwise, I chilled with Lilya or paid a visit to my parole officer.

One fine occasion, Lilya decided to join me. I didn't have a car, but Lilya did, sort of, if you want to call a rusty old Sonata with one headlight and a saggy front bumper a car. She picked me up and gave me a lift downtown to see my P.O., Miss Blansett.

Miss Blansett sat in her office with another client when we arrived, and so Lilya and I chilled with our phones in the waiting room. I asked Lilya to tell me on a scale of one to ten how bored she would be if I were to tell her all about my new life out in the boonies.

"Did you say *wife*?" Lilya asked.

"Life," I said.

"Oh, you got me nervous there for a sec. I thought you'd found someone else."

Lilya and I looked at one another.

"I don't know where my life's going just yet," Lilya said, studying her pink fingernails after I'd finished sharing my piece. "I'm just a funny, awkward character for the time being."

I leaned over, squinting to focus, then reached for Lilya's hand. I, likewise, studied her nails. "What's this?" I asked. "Along the edges here? It looks like—"

Lilya pulled her hand away. "Probably just a previous coat color that didn't fully get covered over," she said, looking far off. "I'm fine."

I thought about that, nodded, exhaled, leaned back, and checked my own nails. "I had that happen to me once. Bleeding along the edges. I think it's because of some kind of vitamin deficiency. Mom's the Vitamin Queen, though, Lil. She can hook you up." I rotated in my seat to face her. "Funny, awkward character, huh? Well, would you like to be a character in a book?"

Lilya brightened. "You're writing a book, and you wanna base a character off of me, is that what you're saying? Who's the character?"

"Her name's Lilya Jenkins," I smiled. "She's a minor character, but super important in the plot-line of *The True Story of the Forever Young Prisoner.*"

"Tight! Have you started writing it yet?"

"No. The storyline's still a work in progress. By the way, did you see yesterday's headline?"

"Yeah, I saw it. I was at the 7-11. 'The Forever Young Prisoner's Ticket to Freedom.' The article talked about Steve's filing and some of the background of Henry's case way back in the day. A very nice headline and article, Tommy. Nice for Henry."

"Yeah it was. Steve thinks the press will be key, and my recorder the big key. Thanks for digging that up, by the way. The State's tripping, he says. They don't want that recorder to be played in court."

"Maybe they won't reply to Steve's motion, then," Lilya said.

"They have to. It's what their lawyers get paid to do."

"Let's hope they don't," Lilya said.

Not long afterward, while in the middle of catching up on my Facebook posts, Miss Blansett opened the door of her office and walked out alongside her client.

With a smile stretched as wide as the Rio Grande, I leaned over and whispered at Lilya's dangly left earring, "A mystical, magical, Guatemalan-Mex lad who I knew back in the joint." Lilya smelled like flowers, honey, or something nice like that.

"Whassup Harry Potter?" I said.

Niño looked over and smiled.

I walked right up to him. "Tell me, Niño, have you ever experienced that unique phenomenon of multiple striking coincidences?"

Niño smiled wryly at my odd greeting. "Hello, Tommy. Hello, Tommy's friend," he said to Lilya. Lilya, giggling, said hey. "All the time. Why is it you ask this thing?"

"Well, I actually planned on writing to ask you something, but here you are. How long have you been out?"

"Is this the thing that you were wanting to ask me? How long I have been out? One month."

"It's tight, isn't it?"

"*Si*," he said. "Being out is tight, *si*."

I cleared my throat. "You told me once that some curses, blessings, and whatever else…work, and some don't? Why is that? Why do some work, and some don't?"

Niño smiled. "You know who the judge is?"

"Do I know what a judge is? Sure."

"He makes a decision. Why is it that he makes a decision for you for yes?"

Lilya put in, "Because your argument is strong, your case is good, your cause is righteous."

"*That*," Niño said, pointing at her. "Good luck to you, Tommy," he said, after we exchanged a fist bump and phone numbers. "Perhaps we see each other again some time." He waved goodbye as he headed for the door. With his hand on the knob he stopped, and looked at me. He walked back.

"You have the distress. The worry. I can tell this thing," Niño said.

Lilya offered, "He just got out. The whole Henry Heck situation, too."

Niño said to me, "I have a dream last night. You and a boy with a funny hair stripe. What is it you call this hair?"

I groaned. "A mohawk?"

Lilya's eyelids fluttered as she cut a glance over at me.

Niño nodded. "The mohawk man. He chop you with an ax."

I gulped. Anyone else with a dream about me, a mohawk man, and an ax, and I would simply brush it off. Niño having a dream about all that, and it was time to start stressing the fuck out. I felt something inside of me sink. "Harry Potter," I said, weakly. "Give me a blessing. Of protection, so the mohawk men don't get me."

Niño asked why, explain. I did. I told him everything. Ms. Blansett tapped her foot impatiently while she stood outside of her office but she was going to have to wait.

Niño said, "Okay. Blessing. *Si*. Come, I say words for you." He wrapped his arms around me and squeezed. At the top of his lungs he blasted out some *español* over a span of ten seconds. "Now, you good."

"Just like that?" Lilya said. "And he's good?" She peered in at Harry Potter. "Are you sure?"

"Good," I said. "That's what I'm gonna be from now on. I promise. No more getting high when no one's looking. Then, Lil, we'll both be 24 carat. Love that homie," I said to her as I padded off to meet with my P.O.. "If everyone was like that Potter fool, the world wouldn't need prisons." Okay, maybe that was a slight overstatement.

"You *love* him? What do *you* know about love?" I heard Lilya say from the other side of Ms. Blansett's door.

We went out for ice cream afterward at one of Penny's choice spots in Kingston. Lilya didn't seem at all herself on the drive over and as she spooned her turtle sundae. "What's wrong?" I asked. Reaching for her trembling hand, I told her that I, too, was nervous, and felt the same way she did. That was when, and where, with whipped cream and jimmies all over my chin, I finally worked up the nerve to ask Lilya if she might be interested in a boyfriend.

"Steve called," Mom said, right as I had walked in the house after wrapping up another long hard day of manning the register at the gas mart. A month of perfect attendance, and only one customer complaint so far.

I called Steve back.

Steve let me know the State had filed their response to Henry's motion. The gist of the State's argument, Steve said, ran along the lines of 'a life sentence is a life sentence, period'. Case law support was "minimal," he added, and their argument, overall, offered few surprises. The State did include a Motion to Strike in their rebuttal.

"What's that?" I asked.

Steve explained, "The State has asked the court to strike evidence from the record—your recorder. The State argues this evidence was gained illicitly in violation of prison rules, and as such should be stricken from the record. Really, it's no surprise. That recording spoke in regards to conspiracies, mafia influences, illegal behaviors on the part of former wardens, all kinds of malfeasance."

"Will that happen?" I asked, sipping the Chai tea Mom had poured for me. "Will it be stricken?" I swallowed the potassium supplements she'd given me, too. One of them I had to chew because it wouldn't go down. "Horse pills" she called them.

"I don't know, Tommy. We'll have to wait and see."

"Steve called," Mom said, right after I had walked in the house after wrapping up another long hard day at the office. Two-months-and-three days of near-perfect attendance, and only two customers had thrown coffee at me so far.

"Tommy," Steve said, "come to my office as soon as possible. We have a problem. I'm here until six."

I asked Steve why.

He said, "Just come," and hung up.

An hour later, Lilya and I stood waiting with our hands in our pockets in the lobby just outside of Steve's office. The view was straight fire. Twenty floors up meant the whole of downtown lay sprawled out beneath us. We could literally see the ocean. I had to tear my sights away when Steve opened his door and waved us in.

"What kind of problem?" I asked, sitting down.

"A big one," Steve said from the other side of his desk. He let out a deep breath. "There will be a media event, okay? Q & A. Wednesday, on the steps just outside the courthouse. Henry will answer the media's questions. He's talking more now. Clearer. Longer sentences. He can talk. It's his confidence level that's the issue. I'll be there, too.

We're expecting a big turnout." Steve leaned back in his chair. "Now, the problem is that Henry has no place to go afterward. Sure, he could just mosey on down to that shelter on Fulton Street—"

"The Outreach, on Fulton?" Lilya said, furrowing her brow. "Y-uck. Not there."

"Wait, wait, wait," I said. "Hold on." I looked at Steve. "Are you telling us—are you *telling* us—that Henry's going to be released?"

Steve smiled. "That's what I'm telling you."

I shook my head and laughed because I didn't believe it. "Why? How? Speak up, my good man."

Steve explained, first off, the State's Motion to Strike had been denied. The court held that although recording the warden might have overstepped prison rules, it didn't violate state law. The recorder qualified as "valid, exculpatory evidence."

Lilya pumped a fist. "Psyche!"

"As for our primary argument..." Steve said. "The court agreed with the New Hampshire court in *Heck v. Harris*." Steve read from the papers in his hand, "*The Eighth Amendment is all too often construed as apples for oranges. A prison sentence should be measured in mileage, not calendar years.* Henry's motion was granted, guys. Henry has officially served his life sentence. He will be released this Wednesday."

"Wednesday?" I said, all matter-of-fact like that. I guess I still couldn't believe it. Where was the catch? There had to be one. Steve didn't look like he was joking, though. I should've asked Lilya to pinch me just then, just like she'd pinched me on the drive over, and the evening before.

"No hearing? No hearing?" Lilya said, excitedly.

Steve shook his head. "Officially, because the court ruled that one hundred years constitutes a life sentence, period. Unofficially, because of all the social and political backlash over this case. *The Boston Herald, The Providence Times*, even the *Hartford Courant* have all published front-page pieces. Did you know the governor chimed in? He wants Henry out."

Lilya said, excitedly, "Have you seen those bumper stickers they're selling now?"

"*Free Henry*," Steve said, shaking his head.

I hadn't seen any of those, even though Lilya kept telling me about them. I lived too sheltered a life out in the country.

Steve curved a smile. "If you've been *Henrified* that means you got screwed over."

I hadn't heard that one, either. What was wrong with this picture? Wasn't I, Tommy fucking McConnell, the one who had rescued that fool? I thought about it. And, honestly, I really hadn't rescued him at all. Pure luck, in many instances. Being in the right place at the right time. *The right words at the right time.* Time and chance haled as the real heroes of the day. "Will they appeal?"

Steve nodded. "Probably, but who cares? The governor keeps hinting he'll pardon Henry." Steve folded his hands as he looked at me. "So, you think you can help Henry out, Tommy? He says he trusts you because you're the one who *came* for him. Even if you could do something like just...walk him over to the Outreach Center..."

I exhaled. "When's this media session?"

"3 p.m.," Steve replied.

I said, "I'll have to rap with my mom first, but I think she'll go for it. I mean, he's literally fam." I sat racking my brain for a moment. "Okay, Burnside Park. There's a bench on the street side of the park —big tree right next to it. Tell him I'll be there on Wednesday. Tell Henry," I paused just to get a grip, and keep my voice from cracking and eyes from watering, "that I can't wait to see him."

CHAPTER TWENTY-NINE

My boss let me bail two hours before my shift ended. "You've been getting along well," Stacy said. "Don't mess it up now. No drugs."

"I'm not leaving to do *drugs*," I said, reaching for the magazine rack to rustle up the day's edition of USA Today. The headline read "Freedom Day for Henry." I folded the magazine under my arm and pushed open the door of the gas mart. "Think I'm gonna go hang with that Forever Young Prisoner guy for a hot minute."

Stacy guffawed. "Downtown? Have fun rubbing elbows with those ten thousand others who wanna get a look at the Eighth Wonder of the World."

"Ten thousand?"

The crowd numbered around six thousand, tops, so they claimed. Downtown simply could not accommodate any more than that, so thousands of others were told to hit the road with reminders to stop by for next month's Clam Bake Festival. Not a few of the attendees had set up tents in the early morning hours on the court steps and along street corners. Vendors sold FYP t-shirts, buttons, and stickers. The stans held signs. Food booths populated the sidewalks along Snow Street. Lobster rolls sold for $40 a pop. The popo sectioned off most of downtown.

That Steve had filed an appeal for Henry's release begged notice, locally. That the Court had granted it carried the glad tidings nation-wide. Henry was now officially *a thing*.

Meanwhile, Steve had since relayed precious little to the public about my behind-the-walls investigation, and the information he did share mentioned no names. Steve thought it was best that I focus on my parole. I was all about that, too. I had three months left and the last thing I needed was major distraction, epic fail, and end up back in the can. I kept low pro. Call me shy, but don't call me stupid —or a shithead, or a mistake.

Actually, Mom came out and said that I was the "best mistake she had ever made."

I decided I could live with that.

Lilya and I knew arriving at the 3 p.m. start time wasn't going to get us front row seats, or even back row ones. We settled for a park bench in Burnside Park instead. We sat for a whole hour, waiting. We watched the world go by, played with our phones, and with each other's feet. Lilya was killer at footsies. Strong, randy, energetic toes. I liked that in a woman.

Besides the obvious, maybe another reason we kept playing foot-sies, and fidgeting, was plain and simple nerves. Lilya seemed anxious, too, surprise surprise. Mom recommended chamomile, but Lilya said herbs weren't going to solve her little problem.

Someone was coming. Nope, a small band of people. Nope, a small crowd of people. Nope, a large crowd of people. A literal parade marched down Washington Street headed in our direction.

A man with a curly mustache led the charge. This ringleader twirled no baton, nor wore any woolly, oversized headpiece. He veered his neck occasionally to blurt out responses at the swarm of reporters surrounding and haranguing him as he footed a path straight towards us.

"Your twin," Lilya said, with a nod at my dress-out ensemble.

"My great-great-great-grandfather," I corrected.

I stood, so he could see me in my dress-out ensemble.

Lilya stood.

Seemingly everywhere, the popo worked to divert traffic and cordon off Dorrance Street in advance of the herd of humanity headed east along Washington. Clearly this excursion had not been in the city's plans.

The herd numbered in the low hundreds, if I had to guess. A younger crowd, these were the diehards. They waved "Free Henry" signs, cheered, and chanted. But these I saw only at a glance. My sights remained fixed on the ringleader. Awkward, wobbly, all knees, his slight lean forward appeared to pulley the rest of him along. His twirly blond mustache stretched wide under his nose and made him look like a friggin' relic. His wide eyes cut glances at the tall buildings all along the way. No birthmark, at least that I could see. Nor glasses.

He looked young. Twenty-something.

Traipsing his thin, gangling frame closer still to Burnside Park, he noticed me finally. We locked gazes. He smiled.

He coursed the sidewalk then breached the edge of the park's grass. The throng engulfing him grew quiet.

"Golly!" he declared, reaching for my hand, "I'd say we were the toast of the town." He shook my hand. "Are you the fellow they call Tommy McConnell?"

I nodded. "Yes...yes, I am."

"Are you the fellow they call the Forever Young Prisoner?" Lilya asked with a smile.

"So they say," Henry said. "But you may call me Henry." He stretched his arms wide and high as if he meant to swallow up the whole of downtown in his embrace. "Providence. Beloved city. Home!"

I swallowed. "Those, er, are skyscrapers over there," I said, finding my voice finally, and pointing. "And traffic lights..." I watched as Henry eyed the cars, in particular, with their aerodynamic exteriors, vivid colors, and glistening, metallic frames. They must have looked to this Edwardian gentleman like so many saucers from outer space.

Outer space. No shit, Sherlock. *Same.*

Henry stood marveling. "Not a horse, hat, carriage, or dress in sight!"

I shook my head. "Nope. All banned. No need for that sh…" *watch your tongue,* I heard Mom say "…nonsense anymore," I finished my sentence. "This is the future. Things are different now."

"You're telling me, old boy," Henry said, siding a glance at Lilya.

"Old boy," Lilya snickered into my ear.

Henry held my gaze as his smile slackened a bit. "Thank you, Tommy McConnell. For coming for me."

"Who is this person?" one of the reporters said in a loud voice. "Someone Henry knew in prison?"

"Who are you?" another reporter asked.

Henry cleared his throat. "This…is the gentleman who saved my life."

"Saved your life?" voices everywhere said all at once.

Cell phones raised all over the place, pointing at us. Lights flashed. Photos snapped. Stirrings. Commotion. People pushing, shoving. Dozens of voices all at the same time asked questions.

Someone cried out, "Was it you who recorded the warden?"

"Your name's Tommy McDonald?" another yelled.

"Henry," I said, over the sounds of downtown on steroids, "come stay with me and my fam—*your* fam—at my mom's house in Coventry. You can stay as long as you like. You got nowhere to crash, right?"

Henry nodded. "I accept. It would be an honor."

Then, things started to get a little out of hand. A few of the stans broke through the small ring of reporters to try to touch their hero, the anomaly.

"Let's blow," I said to Lilya and Henry and started walking. Lilya started walking. Smiling, Henry shooed away one of the stans, and started walking. We quickened our pace. Finally, I stopped. Something felt horribly wrong and it wasn't just Lilya's finger tapping on my shoulder every step of the way. It was what she said while she tapped, and she was right. We couldn't just ditch these Henry supporters, many of whom had sacrificed greatly on Henry's behalf, not just by coming out on this landmark day, but in a load of other ways, too. A few words were in order.

I turned to address the crowd. "Thank you all for coming out today and supporting Henry. We're sorry we couldn't answer all of your questions, but we do plan to write a book. You won't be disappointed."

"A book?" one of the reporters cried. "About how you saved the Forever Young Prisoner's life?"

I nodded. "About how I helped set Henry free."

Voices cheered, fists pumped, and signs waved when I said this word "free."

I slumped my shoulders and sighed, feeling kinda crappy for taking all of the credit. "Actually, that's not exactly true," I announced, lowering my head as the crowd quieted. "See, I'm just a former drug addict is all." I looked down at my shoes and the toes twitching inside of them. Nerves. "I made a goal, showed up every day, and asked a lot of dumb questions." I looked up. "You don't have to be a superhero to do great things. Sometimes, you just gotta wanna something then go do it...and for me, doing it meant showing up every day, being there, and taking nothing for granted. I'm glad I was able to be there for Henry."

The crowd cheered, but not too loudly. Probably they wanted a superhero not a nobody from the wrong side of the tracks with a few lame lines about goal-making. It didn't matter. Henry had made it, and I'd done my part. I cleared my throat. "I haven't started writing the book yet. I wanna focus on my parole, not getting fired by Stacy, and taking my vitamins. C'mon, let's go," I said to Henry and Lilya.

"Mr. Ronsellier, I'm from National Geographic magazine and we'd like an interview—"

"I'm from the New York Times and we'd like to run an exclusive—"

"Sir, sir, I'm from the pathobiology research unit at Johns Hopkins University—"

Henry waved at the crowd. "May one and all, young and old, have a gay old day. And thank you. It's good to be back. Thank you kindly. Thank you."

We were all thankful the stans didn't follow us into the parking garage. Actually, some did. While Lilya fumbled through her crocodile purse in search of her keys, and Henry and I waited, two young girls approached. The younger one held out a large photo to Henry. I leaned in to get a closer look. Henry's mugshot.

"Can we have your autograph?" the older girl asked.

Henry stood with wide eyes looking at the girls, the photo, the girls. "Why, that's me," he exclaimed. He studied at length the photo and the purple pen provided by the girls. He stood pondering. Finally, he signed the photo. "Thank you," he said.

They girls said thanks, too, and scurried off giggling.

"No need to thank them," I said, opening the passenger's side door for myself and unlocking the back door for Henry. "That's what they're supposed to say to you, not the other way around."

Henry smiled awkwardly. "Of course, I'd forgotten, thank you. Too, I'd forgotten how to make my signature. But then I remembered. Oh, and speaking of forgetfulness...those young ladies forgot their pen."

"Keep it," I said. "You're gonna be writing soon."

Lilya gunned the ignition.

I turned to check in on Henry, who looked puzzled.

"It's a safety belt," I explained. "It fastens you in. Like chains. Prison all over again. You don't gotta wear it." The car bucked as Lilya accidentally put the stick into drive instead of reverse. "Actually, better wear it, bro. Lil's driving."

"Maybe one day I'll take a driver's ed course and get my license," Lilya said, wheeling the turn out of the garage and leaving a set of skid marks in her wake.

"Classes cost money," I pointed out, lighting one of her cigs. "Want one?" I extended the pack to Henry.

He reached for a cig and tucked it under his lip. I lit that bad boy up for him.

He coughed for about a minute straight.

"Good, huh? That means it's working. Hey, Henry," I said, "we're gonna help you out, 'k, bro? Make a real modern man-ster out of you."

Henry coughed. "I would like to fit in."

"Yeah you would. Now," I cleared my throat and turned to face him, "first off, no mustaches. They were banned a few years after hats. Second, you can't be acting all Bob Hope style and shit sayin' stuff like *golly*."

"Let him be, Tommy," Lilya said. "Just let him be himself."

"I can't be taking him out to the clubs he keeps talking like that."

"When was the last time you went to the clubs?"

"That's not the point." I reached back to pat Henry's leg. "Henry, we're gonna get you all fixed up, 'k?"

"All fixed up," he smiled, as he watched the cars fly by.

Meanwhile, Lilya eyed her rear-view mirror. "We're being followed," she said, adjusting it. "These mohawk guys in back of us...they friends of yours?"

My pulse quickened. "Really? Don't let them follow us home. Think you can lose them?"

"In this thing?" Lilya looked at me. "I thought *Harry Potter* said you were going to be protected from now on." She leveled her sights on the road. "Now, me, they'll think twice about harassing after that one dude got a taste of some *Hot Pink Surprise* in his eyes, or whatever was left of them after their little scratching session."

I sat up. "Really, Lil? They've been harassing—?"

"Go-getters aren't born, they're made, sweetheart. Sista' can handle..." she flipped back the hem of her pea coat and showcased the belt with holster.

"Holy hell, Lil. You're packing iron?"

"Concealed carry in the state of Rhode Island requires a permit," Henry expounded from the backseat.

"He used to read a lot," I clarified for Lilya.

"It's Clownaround's. He said I could borrow it."

I patted Lilya's arm. "We'll schedule you in with Harry Potter. Get some *words* on you, okay? You, too, Henry," I said to him.

Once we hit the freeway, our cat-and-mouse tailgate leveled up to a for realz car chase. Lilya weaved through traffic at probably double the speed limit while I sat watching the multiple collisions we nearly had with Hyundai and Ford bumpers as Henry took in the sights.

He pointed. "That sign we just passed...said Coca-Cola. I should like to try some. Oh, I do so remember those soda fountains with their—"

"Not now, Henry," I said, looking over my shoulder at the red Jetta only a few cars back and gaining fast.

"We're speeding, I think," Henry said, watching a 55 MPH sign whiz by.

"The cops are all downtown cleaning up that big mess you just left," I assured him.

Lilya sped up even more in an attempt to pass a semi. Flooring it, she barely slid us through a ten-foot gap separating it from another eighteen-wheeler.

"It's not that she's a bad driver," I clarified for Henry, "but that she just doesn't care."

"I care," Lilya grinned. "Just not while I'm at the wheel *of two tons of hot steel*. Like that one? I made it up myself just now. Remember to include it in your book. Whew, Harry Potter sure helped us pull through that one!"

"But," I added, "we'll just have to let her be herself, I guess."

Seconds later, Lilya hooked the turnoff onto the exit. Hairpin turns at 40 mph was kinda her thing, chase or no chase. Although, she wheeled a tad faster this go-round. Only the luck of the Irish,

Harry Potter, or the damned universe itself, prevented us from flipping and dying.

"This is *quite* the motor car," Henry said, leaning into the turn while clutching his seat belt.

The red Jetta didn't flip, either. Matching Lilya's speed, but probably not anticipating so sharp of a turn while cruising at Mach 5, it failed to compromise the bend and rammed headfirst into the roadside steel barrier. I watched the whole thing over my shoulder.

"*C'est la vie*, as the French would say," Henry quipped, returning to his window.

I looked at him as if in amazement.

Henry's eyes widened. "What I mean to say is *good*. Those were the bad guys, correct?" He folded his hands and resumed taking in the sights.

"Good times, good times," I said, gulping.

Smiling, Lilya cracked her knuckles and motored on.

We drove in silence along Route 117 until finally I decided to pop the big question. "So," I said, all casual like, "what was it like down there? In the Pit of Heck? Those many years?"

Henry creased his brow as he pondered. Finally, he snagged the book lying beside him on the backseat and showcased the cover.

That was Then, This is Now.

"Nice. To hell with the past. Focus on the future." I nodded. "Same."

"Same," Lilya said.

"I have a question," Henry said, eyeing with bemusement either the turkey strutting around the parking lot of the Coventry Dunkin' Donuts or the woman in yoga pants on the sidewalk with her eyes, too, on the turkey. "What is this thing called DNA? And why does everyone and their neighbor want mine?"

"Fuck it," I said, and told Lilya to hook a turn into the Dunkin' parking lot. Somewhat reluctantly, she did so. While she yanked the parking break, and Henry craned his neck to gaze in wonder at his new feathered friend, I folded my arms.

"Why didn't you tell me?" I asked.

Lilya swallowed, closed her eyes, and let out a deep breath. "I didn't want to worry you. You have a lot going on right now, and enough to worry about as it is. I'm sorry. That's just the kind of person I am."

I narrowed my eyes. "The kind of person you are? What's the hell is that s'pose to mean? You've got a screw or two loose, is what I think it means."

"It means she cares," Henry noted from the backseat.

"I'll try not to be so nice," Lilya said, with her eyes on the windshield as she gunned the ignition.

"Try not to be so nice," I agreed.

We rode in silence.

Sighing, I leaned back in my seat. "Not that don't at all appreciate everything you've done for us, Lil, or that Hallmark card with the five thousand hearts you drew on it. Thanks, again, for everything."

"Thank you, miss," Henry said, tipping an imaginary hat.

CHAPTER THIRTY

By the end of a month's time, Henry boasted a job, a driver's license, a mountain bike, a "jolly wardrobe," almost a thousand dollars saved up, a pseudo mom and dad even though he was like five times their age, a "sister" who idolized him even more than she did her real brother, and a work ethic like you would not friggin' believe. For fun he messed with puzzles. Jigsaw. Crossword. Anything puzzle related. He spoke often of wanting to own a horse.

On one occasion, Mom showed her true colors when she said, "Why can't you be more like your big brother?"

"Big brother?" I said, puzzled.

Of course, all of this made me feel like a complete POS, until finally I decided to do something about it. I signed up for driver's ed classes, bought a Dodge Viper in lieu of Blaze the Bronco, and worked OT at the gas mart. I trimmed a rose bush despite getting prickered like five-million times. I allowed my kid sister to borrow Henry's purple pen to do her homework and even called her "Penny Morgan" for once instead of "Penny" or "Carrot Head." Money mattered less now. Penguin publishing house had called and offered me a $100,000 advance on my Forever Young Prisoner story. I'd jumped on that shit.

Dad flew out a week later. Ken worked out. Ken was the man. Ken slept at a hotel because Mom banned him from sleepovers. Ken said I should have haggled. Dad explained that Henry Ronsellier was the shit even out on the left coast, and that I could've signed a deal for five times that hundred-k I'd signed for. I told Dad it didn't matter and that one must live in the moment because next thing you knew you're old and bald like Favorite Son Henry.

Henry's hairline apparently wanted no part in all of the good times. The brim of his forehead lay bare. "Predisposed to hair loss," Mom said. "Male pattern baldness runs in the family," she explained. All of the Ronsellier men lost hair in their mid-twenties.

"Why's it falling out, old boy?" Henry ran his hand over his brow. "Am I aging?"

"Prolly, old boy," I told him. "Maybe it's 'cause you're a ghost."

"A ghost?" Henry dropped his multivitamin into his green tea. "Holy cats!"

"Nah," I said. "But you've definitely got the flavor. Ghosts stop haunting places once the mystery of their whatever is solved. They leave. They die. They move on. Your mystery's been solved. Now, you're moving on. Next stop: middle age. Think of it this way—you'll get to see how the other half lives." I flicked a nod at my new wheels in the driveway. "C'mon, let's go for a spin. Let's go see Margaret."

Henry lowered his tea. "Margaret?"

Forest Hill Cemetery lay unchanged. The graves, the trees, the cool breeze coming in from the ocean a few miles away. No Cali or Sergeant Brunansky, though, thank the gods.

However, Margaret's grave sure looked different. Instead of a pile of dirt and rocks towering beside it, now a widowed husband did. Henry stood immovable with his sights transfixed as he looked down at the grave. "My dear..." he kept saying. "My dearest dear..."

Lilya reached for my hand.

"Wanna go for a walk?" I asked.

"Yeah," she said. "Let's give him some alone time."

We toured the grounds. Strolling around a graveyard with a for realz girlfriend sure had a different vibe to it than the usual meets and greets at the clubs. Lilya told me all about her job at Walmart. She said her boss, Amanda, put in a word with the higher-ups to promote her to shift manager, but since she'd started taking courses in cosmetology she probably wouldn't be able to juggle the longer hours.

"Cosmetology?" I asked.

"Hair, nails, stuff like that. Hey, smile pretty," Lilya said, flicking a nod.

I squinted into the sun. "Looks like we gots company."

Lilya giggled. "The paparazzi."

The lone photographer who slunk around as if in stealth mode with his camera and zoom lens—that he kept adjusting in-between shots—clearly had us in mind. He held his camera horizontal, vertical. He stood, he crouched. He hid behind the line of trees at the edge of the graveyard hoping we wouldn't see him.

"Maybe he's just taking pictures of that deer there." Lilya pointed.

Not three feet away from where Henry stooped to pay his respects, a beautiful, spotted brown doe stood eyeing us.

"Look, Tommy. What lovely black eyes she has."

Not only eyeing us, but with an almost knowing look in those eyes. *A deer's a deer*, I assured myself. I swallowed. Except for when it's not, maybe. I didn't know what surprised me more...that Henry didn't notice a deer chillaxing right beside him, or that a deer didn't mind getting that close. With his back turned, maybe he just didn't see her.

Lilya tugged at my Batman t-shirt. "Hey, get your eyes off that deer and look."

The photographer waved at us then winged shut the door of his Lexus.

"You gonna go over there and smash his camera?" Lilya asked,

"Like the movie stars do?" A gleam shone in her eye. "Or should I go do it? That wouldn't be very *nice* of me, now would it?"

I snorted. "There are other, more meaningful ways for Betty White to show she means business, Lil." Exhaling, I watched the Lexus pull out of the parking lot. "We've been snubbing the press long enough. I've discussed it with Henry, and I think I'm gonna call those people back at the Tonight Show and tell them we'll do it. Dad keeps telling Henry he needs to quit playing Lone Ranger, get out of his comfort zone, and go meet the press. Same."

"Same," Lilya said. "I wanna go to NYC. Times Square, Central Park, all those wicked cool stores and shops..."

"You're gonna walk the heart of it," I said. "That, or Henry will tour us around on horseback while I catch up on sleep and you hold the rear and pick off bad guys, who knows." I called to Henry, "You ready to go, homes? We still gotta go downtown to scope out apartments."

~

From the June 9, 2023 Sunday edition of *The Providence Times*. Sage Springer reporting:

When it rains it pours, a wise man once said.

Some have called Henry Ronsellier, the Forever Young Prisoner, a wise man, for his stated intentions to adapt to his new world before venturing out into it with its billion-and-one fans, curiosity seekers, and haters.

There is no doubt Henry is a rainmaker. It is rumored he and his claimed rescuer, Thomas McConnell, recently signed a six-figure deal with Penguin Random House for the rights to their story. Society as a whole stands to benefit immensely from the telling of this man's tale. This cannot come soon enough.

Still others call Henry Ronsellier a fraud. In a recent interview with Channel 6 News, Henry displayed some rather obvious signs of hair loss—proof of aging if ever there was.

Whatever your label for Henry Ronsellier might be, all may agree that the magical story of his release and longevity have taken Southern New England by storm. The streets of downtown Providence remain flooded with FYP stickers, t-shirts, and an overall celebratory vibe.

When it rains it pours.

And flooding social media, too. A new photograph surfacing on YouTube has already attracted over 5 million views. Professional photographer Edward Jones authored the video.

Jones's photograph shows Henry at Forest Hill Cemetery in Cowesett, crouched beside the grave of his long-departed wife, Margaret Ronsellier, who was reportedly a victim of poisoning. Next to Henry stands a mystery woman. Mr. Jones said there was no such woman at the graveyard at the time the photo was taken, only a deer. The woman wears a long white dress. Translucent, with long black hair, some have called her a ghost. Unfortunately, no original photo of Margaret Ronsellier exists. However, Ms. Ronsellier's great-great granddaughter, Andrea Weiss of Coventry, says the photo "does match Margaret's description." Henry himself could not be reached for comment.

The photograph has been scrutinized by experts and no proof of tampering has been determined.

Says Gracie Woodson of the Ocean State Spectral Society, "If this photo is legit, it is one of the most profound examples of the supernatural on record."

When it rains it pours.

Smiling, taking a deep breath, I put the newspaper down and picked up my cell phone. I tapped his number on the screen.

"Yeah?" Danny answered.

Smiling, I said, "I just called to say I love you."

Danny paused for a moment, maybe to allow his mind to clear

off the muddling effects of whatever narcotic it was on and process my greeting. He laughed out loud.

"How's it going?" I asked. "You guys like your new place?"

I listened, and listened, as Danny rambled on about life on the outs.

"Yeah, Lilya's with her grandfather right now," I replied. "Actually, I think they went out for cheesesteaks then afterward planned to go bowling. I hope she doesn't take my advice and actually pour nail polish into the holes of Monty's bowling ball. That wouldn't be very *nice*. Who would've guessed, right? Hey, the two of you ever gonna get clean and sober enough so you can stop by?" I rifled through the short stack of papers on my lap. "Tell Chopper I have three-hundred-and-fourteen page list of cockroach names here if he's interested..."

"Hi, Jeff?" I spoke into the phone. "Tommy Mac here. You. Me. The Providence Public Library. Let's talk books."

I placed the phone down, thought for a moment, picked it up again, and punched in her number. "Er, hi. Ms. Flounders...I mean, Ms. Flanders? This is Tommy McConnell. You were my pretrial therapist..."

CHAPTER THIRTY-ONE

That summer, Henry and I rented a high-rise apartment on the east side. It wasn't at all like Mom's house out in the country. For one thing, our apartment complex, called the Atlantic Towers, had developed in the months afterward kind of a bad rep. Over that time, two men with mohawk hairdos had entered the building—and neither came out alive. The first was found trapped in the elevator. Cause of death: heart attack. The other slipped and fell in the stairwell and broke his neck or something awful like that. A detective from the local precinct went on record to say, "It appears the young men were confronted by someone, or something, and died of fright."

I called and told Niño.

"This thing you tell me makes me sad," he said. "But sometimes it happens when the bad ones continue with their badness." Niño added he saw me on TV and was *"muy contento"* I hadn't been afraid to talk about the recorder.

Another big difference from Mom's crib involved the paying of bills, taking out of trashes without multiple mom reminders, and making one's own meals—which usually meant Hot Pockets and

Fritos, unless it was Henry's turn to cook in which case it would be something more Canadian like open-faced hot turkey sandwiches with mayo and peas.

Another big difference? The crowds Henry and I always seemed to attract whenever we stepped out the damned front door. This was downtown, in case we didn't know.

Not everyone recognized the Forever Young Prisoner, but many did. Henry was an autograph-signing machine with his purple pen. Finally, I recommended Henry go incognito. Reluctantly, he agreed. Without too much fuss, he would wear his tank top, Sox cap, and shorts, but the one thing Henry refused to do was ditch the stash. At long length, I came up with an idea.

Taking a break from our Scrabble game to check his look in the mirror one day, Henry said, "Ah, so good of you, Tommy, old boy, to have enlightened me on the adverse effects your cellphone technologies have on handlebar mustaches. Now I know why no one sports them." He brushed his finger across his clean upper lip.

"Attack of the killer mustaches," had been my advisement. The right amount of radiation and those bad boys will twirl up your nose and right on into your brain. Technology, love it or leave it. It's called *looking out for one's friends*. It was because I cared.

Still, people recognized him.

"Henry," I advised, "wear sunglasses when you go out."

Henry blinked as if not understanding what that meant. "Indeed, I am a mite farsighted," he pointed out, perhaps thinking I had meant regular glasses. He explained that back in the day he hadn't been able to afford "spectacles" after his original pair had gotten sat on and smashed on the carriage-ride over to Providence.

I couldn't help but twist a smile when he said that. "Lenscrafters," I said, beaming. "Get your butt in the car and let's go get you some spectacles."

Henry picked out a pair of old-school circular frames. Prescription sunglasses, to boot. We could afford that shit now. Henry said the glasses helped him write better.

Little by little, we chipped away at our creative non-fiction piece. Henry's purple pen was gangbusters as he outlined and scratched notes on the few chapters I had assigned to him. "You're slaying it," I told him. Still, Henry didn't think of himself as much of a writer...which is maybe why he insisted his sections be written in the third person. Or maybe not. Every time the subject came up, he would raise and showcase *That was Then, This is Now*. Like soldiers after a war, maybe some memories are just too painful. Or maybe he just wanted to move on. "I'll write the opening lines but not a word more," he instructed. Old people, go figure. Young-old ones, too.

"Not much of a writer? That's why I'm gonna ghost write for you," I said.

"Ghost...write?" Ghosts were actually a touchy subject for Henry. Whether at the mall, a restaurant, or during the course of his daily afternoon walks in the park, fools would stare at stealth-mode Henry for minutes on end then stop by to tell him he exuded an "aura."

"I'm no ghost, thanks," Henry would reply as he finished smashing his Big Mac or sipping his Orange Julius.

"Forgot to wear his deodorant," I'd tell them, shaking my head, and having his back. "There's your damned aura."

Not that Henry didn't believe in ghosts.

In fact, he so much as encouraged me to help him unlock one.

"You spoke in your sleep again," he told me one morning, after snatching his cap then pausing with his hand on the door.

"What did I say this time?" I heard myself say for, like, the millionth time.

Henry cleared his throat as he looked at me. "*Loose board under basement vault lonely at The Old Page* is what you said."

"Old Page? Vault? Something on Page Street, maybe?" I thought about that. "The only thing on Page Street that's old, though, is the Loan and Trust." Why did that bank sound familiar?" My shoulder's slumped. "Where Sal said Old Morgan used to work before he was framed," I unthinkingly verbalized my thought.

Henry's eyes bulged. "Evidence, maybe, hidden under those

floorboards to support Morgan's innocence?" He hopped up like a regular young squirt to go research on the computer all about the Loan and Trust, which, indeed, as things would turn out, was referred to colloquially between the 1920s and '60s as *The Page Bank*.

I rolled my eyes. "No more adventures, please."

"Our readers will want an encore," Henry said, typing. He smiled over his shoulder. "More *pages* to read, please, they'll say. We must not disappoint them."

"Whatever happened to the Lone Ranger?" I settled on the sofa with a bag of Fritos. "That guy who wanted no more from life than to fiddle with crosswords and dream about horses?"

Henry reached for the slim volume beside him on my desk. He raised it.

That was Then, This is Now.

Our little Henry was growing up before our very eyes. It was only a matter of time before he asked me to take him skydiving.

Also, with reference to ghosts, was the newspaper's "deer" photo that Henry pinned to our little bulletin board in the living room. It sat at the very top of his list of prized possessions.

His penny sat pretty high on that list, as well. The one he referred to as his "gold coin," and I called his "lucky penny." The one he claimed the *ghost* of Old Morgan had given to him back in '47 or whenever the hell it was. He said he kept it to remind himself the whole of his ordeal wasn't just a dream, and that miracles do happen. Yeah, as if the reflection he saw every day in our bathroom mirror wasn't miracle enough.

"It might help with our investigation, too," he noted.

"Ain't gonna be no damned investigation," I snapped, even though I knew that wasn't true. Like cell phones and twirly mustaches, certain things in life are just inevitable.

I kept telling Henry his lucky penny should be displayed in a museum, alongside himself—then everyone could be reminded of miracles and stuff. He knew it. Next on our itinerary was an appearance on The View. Lilya was invited but not driving; ditto for the penny. Whoopi and the crew would grill Henry about his agelessness, and he would go on about Margaret, his cockroach friends, Old Morgan, and the penny. Guaranteed. Oh, and Henry's purple pen. Go ahead and try to snatch that thing away from him like Jimmy Kimmel did that one time, I dare you. So often I tended to *forget* my pens—or leave them behind in places like graffitied cells in solitary. Waving his pen in the air, Henry declared to audiences everywhere, "Hold on to your pens!" Whatever that meant.

I had a prized possession, too. See, I had made "staying clean" my new goal. This goal I needed to say out loud and stick to, just like Henry had done while in The Pit. Superheroes evolve in line with the efficacy of their words. Every day I showed up to recite my goal. The words had become life for me—so far.

It was an excerpt from the transcript of Henry's trial. Henry's last words, that his lawyer had "ghost written" for him. The newspapers had featured it. I laminated then tacked it up alongside Henry's deer photo. Every day for one hundred years Henry had recited these words, and thank the gods he didn't have to any longer, because finally his goal had become life for him—so far:

Worthy sirs. Your Honor. Gentlemen of the press. Ladies and gentlemen...I stand before you as a man convicted of the heinous crime of murder. Although I bear this label of "murderer," I am not the man you think I am. I am the same man who with ten dollars in his pocket came to Providence with the American Dream of making a better life for himself in the city. I am the same man who grew up in Smithfield, toiling the fields from sunup to sundown to earn an honest wage. I am the same man who contributed regularly to the Salvation Army and the War Relief Fund. On that fateful afternoon of August 24, 1917, I was no less this same man.

The interests of justice have been perverted in these proceedings. My lone witness, my dear wife, was taken from me a day before the trial. At least two of the jurors were reportedly bribed. Witnesses have spoken untruths and withheld the truth.

There is no greater betrayal than those perpetrated by our institutions of law and order.

So often it happens men so betrayed will become the most bitter and vengeful of all peoples. The conditions of their incarceration will only exacerbate this ill...until they become equally the agents of cruelty and injustice as their accusers.

My purpose is to be the same man as ever I was. Through isolation and loneliness, I am purposed to be the same man. Through steel bars, chains, and prison walls, I am purposed to be the same man. Whether it be days, weeks, months, decades, or centuries from now, may Providence return me to Providence the very same man I was, the same man who stands before you this day. Thank you. And this, is all I have to say in my defense this day.

THE END

AUTHOR'S EPILOGUE

When I heard that knock on the door of my Tulsa, Oklahoma apartment in January, 2014, I never would have imagined that on the other side of it stood four officers there to arrest me. My charge? The untimely mailing of two appeals against my standing protection order. Statute dictated I was supposed to have waited four years to file those appeals; however, because mine was a post-conviction challenge for a short list of constitutional violations perpetrated at my original protection order hearing, it was my understanding that time didn't matter.

Time matters.

"Time is a thing of wonder," as Tommy would say.

My filings were ruled "untimely," denied without a review on the merits, and I was charged with two protection order violations for the otherwise required service of those legal documents upon the victim. That no citizen in the history of American jurisprudence has been recognizably convicted for the untimely filing of a legal document, was a fact that seemed to deter my captors not in the slightest. Moreover, because mine were consecutive filings, I was cited for Class 4 Felony Stalking. A serious charge.

The DA in my case lobbied for a max 8 year prison sentence. The judge handed me a 4 piece.

Ironically, my years spent in the Colorado prison system turned out to be some of the most well spent and educational of my life. No less significantly, I got a book out of it.

Gripping one of those prison pens that runs dry after ten days, I began writing *The Forever Young Prisoner* about a month into my tenure at Trinidad Correctional Facility in Trinidad, Colorado. Six months later, I had completed an 18,000 word novella. It was fairly horrible. Not just the story, but the writing itself.

Outside of my apparent inability to construct a good sentence, and the seeming days it would take for me to pen a halfway decent one, I simply could not figure a way to make Henry's agelessness make sense. Sure, I had some ideas, but none of them made sense.

After my parole ended in 2019, I moved back East to the state where I grew up, Connecticut. Settling into old apartments, I experienced my fair share of unexplained phenomena. Finally, the strange occurrences died down, but all of that sure got me thinking.

Finally, in April, 2022, I had an idea which helped me piece together some feasibility into the question of Henry's agelessness. The experience was like shaking up then snapping open one of Harris's cans of Pepsi. A month later, I took a hiatus from my factory job and set out to finish *The Forever Young Prisoner.* Junking my previous foray entirely except for a few lines extracted from my Chapter 2 chow-hall scene, I wrote pretty much wrote the entirety of the novel over the span of the next three months. Story, details, characters, all stopped by to say hello and then decided to stay awhile. Forever, actually. Along with my one-hundred-page manuscript came only two pages of scrap. After years of not writing at all, I found to my surprise my writing style had blossomed.

Much of the inspiration I had for setting in the story derived from my time spent in Colorado prisons. The low side was based on a combination on Trinidad Correctional Facility and Delta Correctional Center. The high side was based, in part—with its checkered floors and Gothic overtures—on Territorial Correctional Facility, which I believe is the oldest prison in Colorado. My few months spent in the Tulsa and Boulder County Jails didn't figure much into the story.

Yes, keys fastened to our belts on the low side and deer roamed the yard freely. Too, most everyone seemed to talk the way Tommy, Danny, and those other fools in the story did.

Although, presently, I live less than five miles from the Rhode Island border, I can't say I know any more about the *Rhode Island* prison system than any of my readers. Nor am I particularly keen on knowing. The "True Story" of Tommy and Henry takes places in a fictional Rhode Island. Theirs is the stuff of dreams.

"It's good to have dreams," as Tommy would say.

Thank you for reading. May the universe grant us an opportunity to meet again like this in some future project.

Marcus Lessard
March, 2023
Putnam, Connecticut

BIOGRAPHY

Marcus lives in Connecticut with his cat, Kit Kat, and memories of his prison years which swirl in his head from time to time.

In 2015, Marcus was sentenced to four years in prison for the untimely mailing of legal documents in violation of a standing protection order. Dreams that his ex was in a suicide situation, and his lively emails to try to get her attention, featured as evidence in support of that protection order. He received ghostly messages in dreams and a ghost appeared to his mother as lead-up. While in prison, Marcus began writing The Forever Young Prisoner.

Website: Marcuslessard.com

Facebook: facebook.com/marcus.lessard.author

Amazon.com: https://www.amazon.com/dp/B0BZFGFN45

Goodreads: https://www.goodreads.com/book/show/123945486-the-forever-young-prisoner?

IngramSpark.com

Kobo: www.kobo.com/us/en/ebook/the-forever-young-prisoner

Contact: fyplessard@gmail.com

www.ingramcontent.com/pod-product-compliance
Lightning Source LLC
Chambersburg PA
CBHW021344310726
48971CB00001B/278